Prai~

"Adib Khorram is one of my favorite authors of today."
—Kacen Callender, *New York Times* bestselling author of *Stars in Your Eyes*

"Adib Khorram couldn't write a book I wouldn't love."
—Leah Johnson, Stonewall Honor–winning author of *You Should See Me in a Crown*

I'll Have What He's Having

Kirkus **Best Romance of 2024**
Library Journal **Best Romance of 2024**
New York Public Library Best New Romance of 2024
Libby Best Romance of 2024 Finalist
Indie Next Pick

"This warm, spicy romance is a love letter to Persian food, good wine, and queer community...A sensuous and immensely satisfying queer love story." —*Kirkus*, starred review

"With an eminently likable group of characters, a generous helping of wine and foodie culture, and an extra steamy and tender love story, YA author Khorram's first foray into adult fiction will warm readers' hearts." —*Library Journal*, starred review

"[A] swoony, fresh romance." —*Entertainment Weekly*

"[A] thoroughly satisfying adult debut...This is mouthwatering." —*Publishers Weekly*

"Gorgeously sensual and gorgeously real, Adib Khorram writes the perfect romance…An absolutely unmissable read for anyone who loves spicy stories, happily-ever-afters, and swoons that will make your toes curl with delight. Five stars!"

—Julie Murphy and Sierra Simone, bestselling
coauthors of *A Jingle Bell Mingle*

"This book has all the ingredients I love in a romance: big feelings, delicious tension, and characters that stay with you long after the last page… [It's] the whole romantic package, and, like the decadent food in the book, it left me craving another bite!"

—Adriana Herrera, *USA Today* bestselling
author of *A Tropical Rebel Gets the Duke*

"From first sip to last drop, *I'll Have What He's Having* is a richly characterized, sensual romance that celebrates gay men who, like the finest wines, only get better with age."

—Timothy Janovsky, *USA Today* bestselling
author of *You Had Me at Happy Hour*

"Adib Khorram brings all the heart and cultural specificity he's rightly celebrated for and adds just the right amount of romantic heat to his literary recipe. David and Farzan will warm your heart, make you laugh, and leave you hungry for more."

—Abdi Nazemian, Stonewall Award–winning
author of *Like a Love Story*

"Clever, sexy, and charming, *I'll Have What He's Having* is the refreshingly relatable queer romance of my dreams…Be prepared to fall hard for this one."

—Julian Winters, bestselling author of *I Think They Love You*

It Had to Be Him

Also by Adib Khorram

I'll Have What He's Having

It Had to Be Him

ADIB KHORRAM

FOREVER

New York   Boston

Copyright © 2025 by Adib Khorram
Reading group guide copyright © 2025 by Adib Khorram and Hachette Book Group, Inc.

Cover illustration by Forouzan Safari. Cover design by Daniela Medina.
Cover copyright © 2025 by Hachette Book Group, Inc.

Hachette Book Group supports the right to free expression and the value of copyright. The purpose of copyright is to encourage writers and artists to produce the creative works that enrich our culture.

The scanning, uploading, and distribution of this book without permission is a theft of the author's intellectual property. If you would like permission to use material from the book (other than for review purposes), please contact permissions@hbgusa.com. Thank you for your support of the author's rights.

Forever
Hachette Book Group
1290 Avenue of the Americas, New York, NY 10104
read-forever.com
@readforeverpub

First Edition: September 2025

Forever is an imprint of Grand Central Publishing. The Forever name and logo are registered trademarks of Hachette Book Group, Inc.

The publisher is not responsible for websites (or their content) that are not owned by the publisher.

Forever books may be purchased in bulk for business, educational, or promotional use. For information, please contact your local bookseller or the Hachette Book Group Special Markets Department at special.markets@hbgusa.com.

Print book interior design by Taylor Navis

Kansas City skyline: Paulrommer SL/Shutterstock.com; Milan skyline: Greens87/Shutterstock.com

Library of Congress Cataloging-in-Publication Data

Names: Khorram, Adib, author.
Title: It had to be him / Adib Khorram.
Description: First edition. | New York : Forever, 2025.
Identifiers: LCCN 2025017340 | ISBN 9781538739556 (trade paperback) | ISBN 9781538739563 (library hardcover) | ISBN 9781538739587 (ebook)
Subjects: LCGFT: Romance fiction. | Queer fiction. | Novels.
Classification: LCC PS3611.H667 I85 2025 | DDC 813/.6—dc23/eng/20250414
LC record available at https://lccn.loc.gov/2025017340

ISBNs: 9781538739556 (trade paperback), 9781538739563 (library hardcover), 9781538739587 (ebook)

Printed in the United States of America

LSC-H

Printing 1, 2025

For Candida Bing
(I'm still open to being adopted.)

Content Guidance

Content guidance is available on Read-Forever.com.

Wine exhilarates the soul,
Makes the eye with pleasure roll;
Lightens up the darkest mien,
Fills with joy the dullest scene;
Hence it is I meet thee now
With a smile upon my brow.

—Abolqasem Ferdowsi, *Shahnameh*

one

Ramin

Ramin was sweating.

He'd picked the Brazilian steakhouse for their two-year anniversary dinner because it was Todd's favorite place on the Plaza. Todd had been trying to increase his protein intake the last few months. And hitting the gym harder. It showed in the way Todd's dress shirt hugged his shoulders.

Granted, Ramin loved Todd's shoulders—since Todd had moved in eight months ago, Ramin drifted off to sleep with his head against their solid warmth every night (not to mention he enjoyed holding on to them as Todd fucked him)—but he'd loved them before, too, back when Todd wasn't so worried about their definition or the occasional stretch mark. Honestly, Ramin had enough body dysmorphia for the both of them.

That was for Ramin to work out with his therapist, though.

Tonight had to be special. So he'd picked Todd's favorite place for dinner. Even though every time he came here, he got the meat sweats. The sticky feeling on his forehead made him feel like a teenager again, fighting off acne; the dampness under his armpits was worse. Was it showing through his shirt?

Bad enough he was sweating with anxiety about asking Todd such a life-changing question, but meat sweats, too? He really should've planned this better.

"What're you thinking?" Todd asked, a smile lighting his features.

Ramin must've been staring. But he couldn't help it!

Todd was handsome, his well-kept beard sharpening his jawline, his brown eyes perpetually cheery. He'd gotten golden highlights in his coiffed brown hair about a month ago, which gave Ramin flashbacks to high school, but like Ramin, Todd hadn't been out as a teenager, and everyone deserved a second adolescence. The highlights made Todd happy, so they made Ramin happy.

Todd even had the kind of cute button nose that only white guys ever seemed to get. Ramin's own nose was large, like most Iranians. He had horrid visions of a bead of sweat dripping down the length of it but stuffed them down as he gave Todd a smile of his own.

"Just thinking about how handsome you are."

"Aw, babe." Todd's smile deepened, but then he shifted in his seat. "Sorry. I'll be right back."

He set his napkin next to his plate and stood. Todd's wineglass was mostly untouched—he'd cut back as part of his diet, so much that he rarely even had a glass with dinner anymore—but he'd downed four glasses of ice water and put away a lot of steak.

"I'll be here," Ramin said, reaching for his own wine, a nice if uninspired Malbec. He assumed. His taste buds weren't working tonight because of the nerves. He wouldn't have been able to tell the difference between a bottle of Screaming Eagle—a California cab that went for $2,500 a bottle—and some Boone's Farm at this point.

(Not that he'd ever had Boone's Farm. He had been solidly Team Franzia in college, a secret shame even his best friends didn't know about.)

Nevertheless, Ramin finished his glass. They called it liquid courage for a reason, right?

He flagged down their server.

"Could I get the champagne now, please?"

Their server—a young, russet-skinned woman with her hair tied back in a ponytail—nodded and disappeared toward the bar.

Ramin checked his pocket for the eight hundredth time. When he'd started planning this night months ago, he'd envisioned sticking the ring in the top of Todd's favorite dessert, a crème brûlée, but Todd wasn't eating dessert these days. And the thought of dropping the ring into the bottom of a champagne glass alarmed him, because what if Todd didn't notice and choked on it?

So he'd just have to hold the ring out and ask.

He could do this. He wasn't really worried that Todd would say no, after all. They were in love. They'd been together for two years. They'd moved in together and everything was going well.

They were happy and perfect.

So why did his heart keep fluttering?

(Well, he did know—those same old insecurities, creeping up again. But also: therapy.)

Todd returned, scooting in so their knees brushed. Ramin grazed his foot along Todd's ankles and smiled, and he tried not to be annoyed when Todd shifted in his seat and moved his foot away.

Todd could be weird about PDA sometimes, but what gay man didn't have the occasional worry on that front?

"Hey," he said softly.

"Hey." Todd cocked his head to the side. "What're you smiling about?"

Here we go.

"I wanted to ask you something, actually…" Ramin swallowed and looked into Todd's eyes. They were crinkled up a bit, giving him that little divot between his eyebrows that he kept wanting to Botox away. But Ramin loved that little divot. He loved those crinkles. "I've been thinking a lot about us lately, and our future, and…well…"

His hand shook as he pulled out the box and opened it. The noise of the restaurant seemed to die away around him, until they were in a perfect little bubble.

"I was wondering if...you'd want to get married?"

Okay, that came out super weird. Todd's divot turned into a full-on furrow.

Ramin cleared his throat, fought the flush rising up his neck, and pulled his foot out of his mouth to do this properly.

"What I meant is: Will you marry me, Todd?"

Todd stared at the ring in the box, a plain gold band, because gold always looked good against Todd's skin. It wasn't so favorable against Ramin's, but he had a matching one tucked away anyway. That way everyone would know they were a pair.

Ramin studied Todd's face. He wanted to remember this moment forever. Except...

Todd's eyebrows were still furrowed. Ramin waited for them to rise, for Todd's face to break into a beaming smile, for him to laugh and lean closer and tell Ramin *yes*.

Instead, that furrow softened into something more like...

Oh God.

Pity.

"I...I'm sorry, Ramin. But no."

No?

Ramin's brain did a hard reset.

"All right, gents, let me just open this for you..." The pop of the cork sounded like a cannonball, shattering all his dreams for the future. Ramin started in his chair. He hadn't even noticed their server returning.

Todd gave a tight-lipped White People Smile as their server poured the champagne. Ramin couldn't even muster that. His eyes were burning, and he told himself it was the smoke from the grill and not the urge to cry.

All at once he remembered the part in *Legally Blonde* where Warner dumped Elle instead of proposing, also in the middle of a restaurant, and for a second he wanted to laugh, because he loved that movie, but he'd never thought of himself as an Elle.

Their server finally retreated. Ramin didn't touch his champagne; neither did Todd.

"No?" The word felt like sand in Ramin's throat.

Todd shook his head. "Look. I've been feeling this for a while, but…"

He pursed his lips. "Things have become stale between us. Don't you think this has kind of…run its course?"

"Run its course?" Ramin croaked. Shit, now there were tears, and Ramin's nose always ran when he cried, so this was about to get ugly. "But I love you."

Todd sighed. "I love you too, Ramin, but…"

Todd bit his lower lip. Ramin always liked to nibble on it when they kissed. Liked how he could feel it curl into a smile, because that meant Todd liked it, too.

"I want more out of life than just…moving in together and getting married, date nights every Tuesday, dinner with your friends every Thursday. Lately things have just been so…"

Ramin loved date night. He loved dinner with his friends.

He loved his life with Todd. And now Todd was throwing it all away?

"So what?" Ramin asked around a sniffle. He reached for his napkin—a black fabric one. It was going to be super gross when he was done emptying his tear ducts and sinuses into it. He'd have to make sure to leave an extra-large tip. And what was he supposed to do with all this champagne they weren't going to drink? Did they have to split the bill now?

Ramin blew his nose, wiped at his eyes.

"So what?" he asked again.

Todd sighed and looked down at his hands for a second before meeting Ramin's gaze.

"Boring."

Ramin swiped away his tears with the back of his hand before he opened the door.

"Hey," Farzan said, squeezing past the storm door.

"We come bearing wine," his boyfriend David said behind him. "And cheese."

Farzan held up a plastic Hy-Vee bag. "And peanut butter cookies."

Farzan Alavi was Ramin's best friend. They'd known each other nearly all their lives, ever since elementary school, when they'd been the only Persian kids in second grade. And then Arya, their other best friend, had come along in fifth grade, and they'd been inseparable ever since.

Farzan was handsome, with an elegant Persian nose, rich sepia skin, and warm brown eyes. He took in Ramin's sorry state—red nose, swollen eyes, untucked shirt—and pulled him into a hug.

As soon as Ramin had left the restaurant—alone, since Todd called a Lyft and went to go stay with his brother until they could figure out how to disentangle their lives—he'd texted the group chat.

It had taken his friends all of thirty minutes to rearrange their evenings. He needed them, so they were here.

David Curtis, Farzan's boyfriend of nine months, was a new addition to the group (and the chat—he'd finally been added). He was a handsome Black man with impeccable fashion, impeccable taste in wine, and—since he loved Farzan—impeccable taste in men.

Much better taste than Ramin's, it turned out.

Farzan let Ramin out of the hug and steered him toward the kitchen. "Babe, can you open the wine?" he asked David.

"On it."

Ramin's eyes burned. *Babe.* Ramin didn't have anyone to call babe anymore. Or honey. Or sweetie. Or love. Or pumpkin.

Not that he'd ever called Todd *pumpkin.*

"You like Barolo, right?" David asked, quirking a slitted eyebrow.

Ramin cleared his throat. Crying always made him hoarse. "Love it."

"Good." With practiced hands—David was a master sommelier, after all—he opened the bottle, pulled down four of Ramin's glasses, and poured four perfectly equal servings.

Farzan pressed a glass into Ramin's hand, but Ramin didn't drink.

"We have to wait for Arya. I don't want to tell this twice."

As if on cue, Ramin's doorbell rang again—only for Arya to jiggle the handle and let himself in.

"Sorry. There was traffic on the Broadway bridge. I thought the new one was supposed to make it better."

Arya was still dressed in a black power suit, his nails painted gold, his head freshly shaved (not that there was much *to* shave, since he'd gone bald at twenty-five), though he'd loosened his tie. When Ramin texted, Arya had thanked Ramin for giving him an excuse to duck out of the charity gala he was working. And then immediately apologized and promised to be there in thirty minutes.

Arya kicked his shoes off and pulled Ramin into a hug with one arm, while the other stretched toward David for a glass of Barolo. Ramin choked out half a laugh.

"Okay. Tell us everything."

They settled around the navy-blue sectional in the living room. Todd had spotted it at Nebraska Furniture Mart to replace Ramin's old, cushy—and probably boring—couches. The sectional looked stylish, but the cushions were hard as rocks. Ramin's ass was numb by the time he reached the story's end.

"And then," Ramin said with a final sniffle. "He said I was too *boring*."

"Fuck Todd," Arya interjected for the fifth time that night.

Ramin let out a shuddering sigh and sipped his Barolo. A long-ass sip. It was good wine—David always brought good wine—but wasted on him when he'd been crying so hard he could barely taste the notes of chocolate and leather and blackberry. All he wanted to do was get drunk. Get drunk and forget tonight ever happened.

Ramin wasn't a heavy drinker, but fuck it. Fuck his liver, too. Fuck his life.

And fuck this sectional. His ass had gone from numb to full of prickling stabs. He slid down onto the plush Persian carpet, the one he'd inherited from his parents. He ran a hand across the soft fibers and stared into his nearly empty Barolo.

"Am I really that boring?" he asked, because he couldn't say what was really spinning through his mind. *Too fat. Too ugly.* A thousand awful things men had said to him over the years, things he'd said to himself, things he'd spent lots of time and money on therapy to unlearn.

Hm. When you thought about it, wine was really just after-hours therapy. Ramin drained his glass.

"What? No," Farzan said. He copied Ramin, sliding to the floor, only to bang his elbow on the angular coffee table Todd had picked to go with the sectional. "Fuck."

"Sorry," Ramin hiccupped. He'd been so happy when Todd had agreed to move in with him. He thought it was a step toward their happily-ever-after. And it had been, for a while, even if Todd had questionable taste in furniture. Ramin had wanted it to be *their* house, not just *his*. He'd lived alone ever since he bought the place at twenty-five, paid for with his inheritance from his parents.

And then Todd had come along. And Ramin had thought they were going to be forever.

But he was too *boring*.

Ramin sniffed and wiped at his eyes, but not before he caught the glance Farzan shot David's way, the sad little smile David shot back.

David had a beautiful smile, bright white teeth against midnight brown skin, his dark eyes full of light. He was so smitten with Farzan that if Ramin didn't love his best friend so much, he would've been jealous.

He still *was* a tiny bit jealous.

David turned that smile on him, gesturing for Ramin's empty glass.

"You're absolutely not boring, dude," Arya said. And then he muttered again, "Fuck Todd."

Farzan nodded. "Can I be honest?"

Ramin shrugged. His heart was already in a million pieces. What did one more piece of bad news matter?

"I think Todd's going through some sort of..." Farzan pressed his lips together, ran his free hand through his hair, pushing it off his forehead. It was mostly black—though there were a few grays—wavy, and longer than Ramin's. Ramin always kept his short and neat and "professional" for work. Boring.

No one would ever call Farzan boring. In addition to being Ramin's best friend, he was a killer chef. He'd taken over his parents' Iranian restaurant, the only one in Kansas City, when they'd decided to retire. He'd even expanded its success, with Ramin and Arya as his silent partners.

Farzan had made Shiraz Bistro the beating heart of Kansas City's Iranian community.

Ramin just did marketing.

David returned with Ramin's glass and another opened bottle. Ramin took a sip (okay, a gulp) and barely tasted anything, though he nodded at David as if he had.

"It's good, thanks." He turned back to Farzan. "Some sort of what?"

"Midlife crisis?" Arya scoffed before Farzan could answer. He slid onto the carpet on Ramin's other side, bumping Ramin's shoulder and threatening a spill.

"Shit, sorry."

Ramin shook his head. He had plenty of experience getting wine stains out of the carpet. Plenty of sex stains, too. Last winter, when he and Todd had gotten snowed in, they'd pushed the horrible coffee table out of the way and fucked on the carpet. And missed the towels.

Ramin flushed at the memory. His skin was much lighter than Farzan's or Arya's—his family probably had some Russian several generations back, which would also explain the green eyes he'd shared with his dad—and he could never hide a blush.

But he pushed the thought away. Like Arya said: Fuck Todd.

"What do you mean, midlife crisis?" he asked.

"The highlights? Going to the gym all the time? The Lasik?" Arya gestured around his eyes. "He can't handle the creeping footsteps of his impending forties."

Ramin bit his lip. There may have been a bit of truth there. Todd's skincare routine had gotten intense the last few months.

"Maybe," Ramin admitted, going for another sip and finding his glass empty. Wait, was this his second or third? He'd lost count. But the bottle still seemed full. He held his glass out and David, good friend that he was, poured out another.

"Drink this first," Farzan said, pressing a glass of water into Ramin's other hand.

Ramin chugged it, annoyed that he had to double-fist. Water was boring. Like him.

He sniffed a few times, sipped his new wine. Out of the corner of his eye, he caught Farzan and Arya making eyebrows at each other, like they were telepathically arguing. When Arya finally shrugged, Ramin wasn't sure if it was because he'd won or lost. But Farzan gentled his voice. "I've got to say something."

Ramin's stomach flipped. He didn't like the sound of that.

Farzan took a drink of his own wine, swallowed, and set the glass on the coffee table. He ran a hand through his hair, blew out a breath, then straightened his spine and met Ramin's eyes.

"Look," he said. "You know I love you."

"I love you, too," Ramin said. Ramin was an only child, but Farzan and Arya might as well have been his brothers. They were ride or die.

"But I was never that crazy about Todd."

Ramin sputtered. That didn't make any sense. He'd been with Todd for two years. They had dinner with Farzan and Arya every week. David too, now.

He blinked and found his voice. "Why didn't you say something?"

"Because you were happy! And that mattered more than anything. It still does. But, Ramin…" Farzan squeezed Ramin's shoulder and gently shook him. "I don't know how anyone can look at you and call you boring. He was an asshole. And you deserve better than that."

Ramin squeezed his eyes shut.

"What if he's right, though? What if I am boring?"

"Dude." Arya grabbed his other shoulder. "You're Ramin Fucking Yazdani. You're awesome."

Ramin shook his head and drained his glass again.

On Farzan's other side, David cleared his throat. When had he slid down to the floor? He was snuggled up against Farzan, their fingers twined together on the carpet. Ramin thought of Todd's fingers. Of the ring he'd so carefully picked out and sized. It was...somewhere.

Who the fuck cared.

"Huh?" Ramin asked. David had said something.

"Not to be the bad guy, but I think we'd better cut you off."

"I'm fine," Ramin said, shaking his head, but the room took a while to catch up. "Oh. You're probably right."

"Just looking out for you," he said softly. Ramin liked David a lot, liked how perfect he was for Farzan, but he was still new to the group, and sometimes he acted a little intimidated by how close Ramin and Farzan and Arya were. Which maked sense. Made sense.

Ramin was definitely drunk.

"Thanks," Ramin said. "I like you, David. I'm glad you and Farzan love each other."

Farzan and David looked at each other then. Ramin could feel the love radiating off them like a furnace.

He used to have that with Todd. Didn't he?

He did. He knew he did. He'd loved Todd with his whole heart. And Todd had loved him, too. Once.

Not anymore, though. What hurt the most was, he'd never know exactly when he'd lost Todd's love. What the tipping point had been. Which new wrinkle or new pound or new ache or new nose hair had soured things between them.

Fuck, he didn't want to think about this anymore. He was so *tired* of thinking. So tired in general.

"I'm going to bed," Ramin announced, trying to stand but falling back against the couch. "Oops."

"I got him." Arya tucked an arm under his shoulder.

"You do," Ramin said. "I'm glad you're my friend. I'm glad all of you are my friends."

"Okay. Let's go."

Arya led Ramin upstairs—had the staircase always been this wobbly?—and maneuvered him toward the bathroom.

"At least brush your teeth," he said. "I'll—Shit, is that all Todd's?"

Arya pointed toward the eighteen bottles of skincare on the right side of the sink.

Ramin nodded.

"Please tell me we can get rid of his shit. And that awful sectional. I think I broke my coccyx."

Ramin swallowed back a sob. "We still have to work all that out."

"Fuck Todd," Arya said for the bajillionth time, though this time he just sounded resigned. "I'll get you some more water. Brush your teeth."

Ramin did, laughing when he spat and the water turned purple. He looked in the mirror. His eyes were puffy, nose red, tongue wine-stained no matter how much he scrubbed.

He was a mess. A boring mess.

Arya returned with the water. Ramin downed it, only spilling a little on himself. He handed the glass back and flopped onto his bed.

Arya sat next to him.

"You gonna sleep like that?"

Ramin tugged down his shirt where he felt a draft on his stomach.

"I'm fine."

Arya didn't move, though.

"Really. I'm okay. I don't feel sick. Just sleepy."

"Okay. Love you, dude."

"Love you, too."

Arya left the door cracked behind him. The ceiling spun a bit as Ramin stared up at it. Now that he was actually lying down, he didn't feel tired anymore; he felt hollow. Empty. Like his whole future had crumbled. And it had, hadn't it?

He squeezed his eyes shut, but he was cried out. When he opened them again, the room took a moment to settle.

Ramin didn't get drunk very often. He was thirty-eight now. Two glasses of wine was usually his limit. But the Barolo had been so good. Ramin loved Barolo. And Barbaresco. And Nebbiolo. And Chianti. And Brunello. And Amarone. And Pinot Nero. In fact, Italy was probably Ramin's favorite wine country.

He'd always wanted to visit, but the time had never been right. He kept hoping work would send him there—SNK had an office in Milan, in fact. But he'd never gotten sent there, not even for short trips.

Ramin had planned to suggest it for their honeymoon. But that was never going to happen. Not anymore. Boring people didn't get honeymoons.

Fuck Todd, Arya whispered in his ear. Not real Arya. The little Arya in a devil costume that lived over his shoulder sometimes.

Fuck Todd, the little Farzan in an angel costume agreed.

"Yeah. Fuck Todd," Ramin muttered to himself. He wasn't boring. He'd prove it to Todd. Prove it to everyone.

Prove it to himself.

He reached for his phone, but it was…well, probably downstairs somewhere. He couldn't remember. His iPad was on the nightstand, though. He punched the wrong passcode in twice, giggling at his clumsy fingers, before he finally unlocked it.

How much did flights to Italy cost, anyway?

two

Noah

Noah kept his voice even, trying to reason with his son as he pulled into his ex-wife's driveway, but Jake was in no mood to be reasonable.

"You *promised*!" Jake wailed. His face was all red and scrunched up.

"Jakey," Noah said, holding in a sigh. He hadn't *promised*. He hadn't even said *yes*. He'd said *We'll see*. But lately Jake had been treating every slightly positive answer like some sort of blood oath.

This time, it was having McDonald's for dinner.

But tonight was Angela's night, and she had already planned for dinner. Noah couldn't tell Jake that, though, without making Angela into the villain who'd said *no*. So he was stuck.

"Sometimes plans change."

Surprises happened. Things came up. Marriages fell apart.

That was life.

"Come on, your mom's waiting."

Jake huffed and got out of the car, running for the garage door to punch in the code. Noah took a deep breath and followed more slowly.

It still felt weird, sometimes—well, all the time—coming to Angela's house. It had been *their* house, before the divorce. Angela had suggested selling it and splitting the money, but Noah had insisted she keep it. She'd been the one paying the mortgage, after all. She'd been the family breadwinner, being a partner in a law firm, while it had made more sense for Noah to stay home with Jake.

Now he had his own little apartment, and he'd taken up carpentry again, but he insisted Angela keep their old house so Jake could have at least a little stability.

By the time Noah made it to the kitchen, Jake had already blazed through the house and up to his room.

"Hey, Noah," Angela said, pulling him in for a side hug without spilling her coffee.

Angela Russo—she'd kept her name when they got married for professional reasons, so she'd never had to change it back after the divorce—was a head shorter than Noah, soft and fat, with her brown hair pulled back into a tight power ponytail. She had mischievous blue eyes and a bright smile she'd passed on to Jake—when he wasn't mad about McDonald's, at least.

"Hey." He dropped the hug and looked around the kitchen. It was still more or less decorated the same, though Angela had bought a set of purple-enameled cookware after Noah moved out. A big Dutch oven was on the stove, bubbling away with something that smelled . . .

Good might've been too generous, but edible, certainly.

Noah had always been the cook in the family. He'd had to learn early on.

"Go ahead," Angela said, resigned.

"What?"

"Say it."

"I wasn't going to say anything."

Angela quirked an eyebrow. Noah shook his head and pressed his lips together.

Finally, she laughed. "I was trying a new recipe. I don't think it's a good one."

"Well, Jake *did* say he wanted McDonald's tonight."

"Is that why he was in a huff when he came in?"

"He claimed I promised him."

"Nine going on fifteen," Angela sighed. "Where's this coming from all of a sudden?"

"No idea." Noah wished he did. He'd been talking it over with his therapist, but she thought it was probably just a phase. "Well, I better go…"

"Actually," Angela said. "Are you free?"

"Why?" Noah asked. Though he was. Truthfully, the night life of a divorced thirty-eight-year-old dad wasn't particularly thrilling.

"Want to grab some Mickey D's and have dinner with us? There's something I want to talk to you about."

She said it lightly, but *there's something I want to talk to you about* was never good. It usually led to *Jake has the stomach flu* or *I ran into your mother at the grocery store* or *I accidentally pulled the car into the garage too far and hit the freezer.*

One time it was *I don't think we should be married anymore.*

But it sounded important, either way.

"Sure. I'll go grab it."

"Best. Day. Ever!" Jake pronounced before stuffing way too many fries into his mouth.

Now that he wasn't mad at the whole world (but mostly Noah), he was back to smiling and laughing.

Jake had his mom's smile—and her brains, thank goodness—but he had Noah's big brown eyes, and Noah's peachy complexion, and Noah's thick hair, though Jake's was more chestnut than black.

He also had a missing front tooth. He wedged a fry in the gap and showed it off. "I'm a narwhal!"

Noah snorted and mussed Jake's hair. When Jake wasn't raging against the unfairness of the world, he was Noah's favorite person.

Well, he was Noah's favorite person all the time, but it was certainly easier to get along with him when he wasn't being a nine-year-old misanthrope.

After dinner, Jake wanted to go play with his Lego sets, but Angela asked him to wait.

"I've got something to discuss with the both of you."

Noah's burger turned into a spiky lump in his stomach. He swallowed. "Sure."

"You know how we always talked about going to Italy? Back when we were married?"

Angela's grandparents were Italian. Though they'd raised their kids—including Angela's dad—in Kansas City, they'd moved back to Italy long before Angela and Noah had even met.

He and Angela had always talked about visiting them, with Jake, too. He was their first great-grandchild.

It never happened, though.

"Well, I think we should."

"Should what?" Noah asked. She wasn't seriously suggesting…

"I think we should go."

"To Italy?" Jake asked. "Do they have macaroni and cheese there?"

"Maybe," Noah said, then course corrected, because the last thing he needed was Jake thinking he'd promised Italians had mac and cheese. "Actually, I don't know. You'll have to find out."

He turned back to Angela. "You're taking Jake, I guess?"

"I'm taking both of you," she said. "If you'll come."

"I can't afford a trip like that!" Noah was doing okay financially, but an international trip wasn't exactly in his budget.

"I'll cover you," Angela insisted. "Noah. You wouldn't split the house, you wouldn't take alimony, you wouldn't take anything. Take the trip at least."

Noah shook his head. Angela's grandparents weren't even his family anymore. One of the hardest parts of the divorce had been losing Angela's big extended family. Noah's own was…

Well, *complicated* didn't even begin to cover it.

Angela sighed. "You know what sweat equity is, right? It's when the work you do counts for something, too. You paid into our marriage just as much as I did. Let me pay for the damned trip."

Jake gasped.

Noah jokingly put his hands over Jake's ears—he'd heard his mom swear before, plenty of times, even if Noah didn't swear much himself. Jake shook Noah's hands off with a laugh.

"Fine." If money wasn't a good enough excuse, at least his job was. "If I can get the time off work."

"I already talked to Rick. He said you're good as long as you bring him back a souvenir."

"You what?" Noah blinked. Rick was the union's business agent, the one who matched carpenters to jobs. He wasn't Noah's boss, per se, but he *did* keep Noah's schedule. Angela couldn't just talk to him. "I—"

"There's another thing."

Noah's stomach dropped. There was something in Angela's voice, some little shake. Like the day she'd said she wanted a divorce.

"Nonno and Nonna are thinking seriously about retirement. You remember they have that little wine store?"

Noah nodded. It was somewhere on a lake in Northern Italy. He'd seen it on a map, but he couldn't remember the name.

"They asked if anyone in the family wanted to take it over, and I told them . . ." Angela swallowed. Her cheeks were turning pink. "I told them I would."

Noah's brain ground to a halt.

Angela? Wanted to move to Italy?

It made no sense. Angela had worked so hard to become a partner at her firm. She had family here; she had friends. She had Jake.

"We're moving to Italy?" Jake asked, his voice quiet and nervous.

"I am," she said. "And we're going to go look at it and see if you want that, too. Okay?"

"What about my friends? What about my soccer team? What about—"

"Hey." Noah kept his voice gentle, even though it felt like an elbow to the heart that Jake had skipped over *What about my dad?* "We're not doing *anything* without taking your feelings into account. Okay, buddy?"

It felt like he had sand in his throat, but he couldn't worry about his own feelings right now, not right in front of Jake. He wished Angela had talked to him about this first, given him time to process it on his own before dragging Jake in, but he swallowed that back.

He'd deal with that later, too.

"You get to decide if you want to move with your mom or stay here with me."

"Exactly," Angela said. "That's why I want us to go together. So we can all see it and make an informed choice. All right?"

"You're staying here?" Jake asked, voice small.

"I am," Noah said. "But no matter what, we both love you. Okay?"

"Okay."

Noah looked back to Angela, who at least looked a little guilty, her bottom lip tucked under her teeth.

"Sorry," she said. "I didn't mean to spring it on you like that. I just wanted to get it all in the open."

"It's fine." Noah bit back a sigh. It *would* be fine. "When were you thinking of going?"

three

Ramin

Lost?" Ramin asked. He nearly had to shout to be heard over the bustle of hundreds of people grabbing their luggage at Milan Malpensa's baggage claim.

"Yes," the luggage attendant—a youngish woman with her blond hair in a bun—confirmed. "I'm sorry, Mr. Yazdani. It looks like it got sent to Amsterdam."

"Amsterdam?" Ramin worked to keep his voice light. He'd done enough customer service calls himself over the years; he knew how thankless it could be, how a rude person could ruin your day. He wasn't going to ruin this woman's day just for trying to help him.

"Sì. I'm sorry, Mr. Yazdani. We'll get it here for you as soon as we can."

Amsterdam.

What the fuck was Ramin supposed to do without his luggage? All he had was his backpack. That wasn't enough to last him eight weeks.

The morning after his disastrous proposal, he'd walked downstairs and announced to Arya, who'd crashed on his couch, and Farzan and David, who'd crashed in his guest room, that he'd booked himself a trip to Italy. Spur of the moment. Spontaneous.

Interesting.

"Will you be staying in Milan?" the attendant asked him.

Ramin nodded. He'd found an apartment he could book for eight weeks. Actually, it was fifty percent off if you booked more than four weeks, which was his original plan. But he'd been drunk off Barolo, and eight weeks for the price of four had seemed like a great deal at the time.

"If you can give us your contact information here, we can let you know as soon as we find it. Thank you for your patience, Mr. Yazdani."

Ramin nodded and filled out the little form, fiddling with the new studs in his ears as he did. *Brand* new. Interesting New Ramin did things like get his ears pierced on the way to the airport.

Not the smartest choice he'd ever made, but at least his wound wash was in his backpack. Along with his laptop and phone chargers and passport and PrEP.

Not his condoms and lubes, though. Those had gone into his smaller carry-on suitcase. But when the gate agent back at his connection in Atlanta had begged for people to check their carry-ons because there were too many bags and too little bin space, Ramin had done it.

Boring Old Ramin behavior at its finest.

But maybe this was a blessing in disguise. He'd come to Italy to reinvent himself. Why not start with his wardrobe?

Ramin thanked the attendant for her help, noting her name tag— Silvia—to mark in his phone. He hoisted his backpack higher and headed for customs empty-handed.

If this wasn't a metaphor for Ramin needing to let go of all his old baggage, he didn't know what was.

As the taxi sped toward the heart of Milan, Ramin found his second wind. Colorful stucco buildings alternated with white marble churches. Piazzas and fountains interrupted the journey every few minutes, but that certainly didn't slow his driver down. Or any of the other cars, for that matter.

"Is this your first time in Italy?" his driver asked. His name was Davide, and he was in his sixties, with a shock of white hair beneath his pageboy cap, and a huge pair of black plastic glasses taking up half his face.

"Sì," Ramin said, because he'd spent the last three weeks feverishly studying what Italian he could. "Mia prima volta."

"Ah, you speak Italian?" Davide asked brightly.

"Not very well," Ramin confessed.

"Not too bad," Davide rumbled. His voice was nearly as low as the car's engine. "Where are you from?"

"The US. Kansas City. But my parents were from Iran."

"Iran! Mosaddegh!" Davide grinned in the mirror. "Viva Mosaddegh!"

Ramin nodded, bewildered that Davide even knew who Mosaddegh was. Ramin himself hadn't known much until he got to college. His parents had been kids when the coup happened, and surely Davide hadn't even been born.

He didn't dwell on it, though, as Davide moved from dead Iranian politicians to telling Ramin about the sights to see in Milan. The Duomo, the Castello Sforzesco, Davide's favorite piazzas, the best spot for an aperitivo. Ramin nodded and tried to remember them all, but he was eager to explore and discover things on his own. Get to know the city. Live like an Italian.

Be interesting.

At last they pulled up at his apartment building: a tall edifice painted saffron yellow with white trim around the windows and balconies, nestled between similar buildings in pink and sienna and white.

Davide shook his hand, shouted another "Viva Mosaddegh!" with a raised fist, and sped off without even using his blinker. Ramin took a deep breath, twisted his studs, fixed the hem of his shirt, and finally rang the buzzer his email instructed.

"Dimmi," a deep feminine voice said.

"Uh. Ciao? I'm Ramin? I'm renting—"

"Ah! Ramin! Be down shortly."

It wasn't long before the metal gate swung open and his hosts stepped out.

"Ciao, Ramin! I'm Paola, and this is Francesca." Paola was stunning, her red hair long and flowing down the back of her sleek, rose-red dress. Francesca, on the other hand, had a short black pompadour, and she wore jeans, a sport coat, and a bolo tie.

Ramin didn't like to make assumptions, but he had the feeling he'd rented from a pair of fabulous Italian lesbians.

Being Interesting New Ramin was off to a great start.

"Ciao. Piacere," Ramin said, shaking both their hands. He didn't see any wedding rings—though same-sex marriage still wasn't legal in Italy, a fact he'd forgotten to look up while drunkenly making plans—but they wore a matched set of gold pendants that looked like they'd join together to form a heart. "Thank you for hosting me."

"Please! We're excited! Come, come. Where's your luggage?" Francesca asked, holding the door for Ramin.

"Amsterdam," he said with a shrug.

Paola laughed, a musical thing that set her very white teeth against her very red lipstick, but then she realized Ramin wasn't joking. "Truly?"

"Yeah. I'll be okay, though."

"What a disaster, having to shop for clothes in Milan," Francesca said drily as the three of them piled into an elevator that looked suspiciously like it was only rated for one person. Ramin sucked in his stomach but still got jabbed by an elbow as Paola hit the button for the seventh floor, which was also the eighth floor, because in Italy, the ground floor counted as zero and not one.

Ramin was trying to be Interesting and New, but he hadn't been able to help occasionally googling "things to know about visiting Italy" when he couldn't fall asleep. It was either that or think about Todd.

"Here we are!" Francesca said when they spilled out of the elevator. The seventh (eighth) floor landing was wide and open. Sunlight poured in through the skylight above.

She and Paola led Ramin down the hall, past identical gray doors, to his apartment—8D.

It's an omen! little devil Arya whispered into his ear.

Ramin hoped so.

Francesca pulled out a heavy keychain and let Ramin in—first through the outer gray door, which had a dead bolt and a lock in the knob, and then through the heavy red *inner* door, which had a latch and what looked to be the lock off a bank vault. You had to stick the key—a weird-looking thing without teeth—in and crank it hard, three times, before the door finally opened into Ramin's apartment.

Ramin stepped inside and took in the space. The afternoon sun streamed in through the windows over the long, narrow kitchen. It had a kitschy-looking yellow refrigerator and a lurid green IKEA dining table. Beyond that, through a set of sliding doors, was the living room, with a bright red couch and a TV and more windows; to the right, a short hallway led off to the bathroom and bedroom.

"It's perfect," Ramin said once Paola finished a quick tour. "Thank you."

"If you need anything, we're right next door," Paola said. She made to leave, her heels clicking against the floors, but Francesca stopped her and said something in Italian way too complicated for Ramin to understand.

"Ah, you're right!" Paola swooped back into the kitchen to pull out a black binder from the small bookshelf in the corner. "This is full of recommendations: restaurants, bars, cafés, places for aperitivo—do you know about aperitivo?—theaters, shops, clubs, whatever you need."

Ramin thumbed through thirty or so pages of recommendations. It was incredibly thorough, but . . .

"What about, uh, the gay scene?"

He felt his cheeks heating. He really hoped he hadn't read the two women wrong.

Usually his gaydar was pretty accurate, but that was back home in America. Did Italian gaydar work the same?

Thankfully, Paola's eyes lit up. She looked at Francesca and had the kind of silent conversation that Ramin used to be able to have with Todd.

"Sì sì sì, we'll get you a list. You have to have a card. We'll get you one."

"Card?"

"All the gay clubs take a membership card. It's not like that at home?"

Ramin shook his head, flabbergasted. In all his googling, he'd never heard that about Milan's clubs. The few spots he'd been to in Kansas City certainly hadn't needed a membership card, just a cover charge and a good body . . .

No. That was his dysmorphia talking. His body was a good body. A healthy body. A strong body.

Maybe it was boring, but even if it was, fuck Todd for saying so.

"Crazy Americans!" Francesca said fondly. "Allora, we'll let you get settled, and we'll get you a card. Okay, Ramin?"

"Okay. Thank you. Grazie."

"Grazie te, Ramin," Paola said, pulling Ramin in for air kisses on the cheek. "Ciao!"

Ramin closed the door behind them—cranking the dead bolt three times, just like they'd instructed—and then he was alone.

"Well," he said to the empty apartment. "I guess this is home for a while."

The afternoon heat smacked Ramin in the face as he emerged from a boutique minus several hundred euros and plus four big bags of clothes. He wore a just-purchased azure polo and white linen shorts, relieved to finally be out of his plane clothes.

Relieved to be free of the swampass, too. His jeans were not meant for the late Italian summer.

Now he just needed food.

Boring Old Ramin would've found a salad bar. Or a grocery store.

Interesting New Ramin, on the other hand, spotted a gelateria across the cobbled street and thought *fuck it*. He was allowed to eat gelato for lunch.

The tiny (and blessedly air-conditioned) gelateria had a service counter at the front and two narrow bar tops along the walls, each with three tall plastic stools. Ramin listened in as the people in front of him ordered. He understood a bit—lemon, vanilla, peach—but the rest of the conversation went over his head.

He had a decent knack for language, decent enough at least to ace his honors French in high school. Not that he ever used French in real life. And a decent knack didn't do much when you only had three weeks of practice under your belt. Ramin cleared his throat as he approached the counter.

"Buongiorno," he said.

"Buongiorno," the vendor, a curly-haired masc person in their twenties, replied. Ramin smiled, remembering how curly his own hair had been at that age. He kept it much shorter now, easier to care for, with a sharp part down the left side. He'd adopted the style when he first started at SNK, Stark-Norris-Kauffmann, the marketing firm that hired him right out of college. The style was casual enough to be approachable, yet professional enough to lead a meeting or talk a highly stressed client off an imaginary ledge.

He was about to order a lemon sorbetto—literally, was there anything finer?—but once he actually saw the spread of flavors at the counter, something else caught his eye.

Ramin cleared his throat again. "Per me, un Persiano, per favore?"

The vendor nodded and asked something way too quick for Ramin to catch.

"Uh..." Ramin said.

"Cup or cone?"

"Ah! Una coppetta, per favore."

Ramin paid, took his cup, and found a stool in the corner, facing out the windows to people watch. He tucked his bags beneath his stool and dug in with the little plastic spade. The gelato was smooth and creamy, a perfect balance of rosewater and cardamom, with just a bit of crunch from the ground pistachios on top.

He never expected to find bastani in a gelateria in Milan. Italy really *was* magical.

As Ramin savored another bite, the door chimed, letting in two new guests. One was a man about Ramin's age, resting a gentle hand on the head of a boy who looked so similar they had to be family. Ramin did a double-take, seeing a blue Kansas City Royals T-shirt on the father, but then shook his head. He'd only walked a few blocks today, and he'd already seen a ton of folks wearing US team apparel, though mostly basketball now that he thought about it. He'd thought they were tourists, but most had been speaking Italian.

He wondered if these were Italians, too, until the son started talking in English.

"I want one scoop. No, two! In a cone."

The dad laughed and played with the kid's messy chestnut hair.

Ramin's heart clenched at the sight.

Adopting kids had been part of his plan, once he and Todd were married. Ramin hadn't given much thought to having them when he was newly out and in his twenties, but as he'd gotten older, he realized that he kind of wanted children. He thought he'd be a good dad. And he liked the idea of having a family.

But that was probably boring, too.

"Do you think they have bubblegum?"

"Hah, I don't think so, buddy, but let's look," the dad answered.

Ramin's heart skipped a beat. The man's voice was deep, mellow, the tiniest bit grainy, and weirdly familiar.

Ramin tried to eye him without being super obvious. He had messy (but not *too* messy) black hair and a sharp jaw. He looked strong, with broad shoulders, a defined chest, and arms that filled the holes of his shirt. He wore a pair of light blue jeans, and his thighs filled those out, too. He looked like he spent time in the gym, but not *too much* time; he seemed built for practical strength rather than for vanity.

The man turned, staring at one of the signs on the wall, and Ramin glimpsed warm brown eyes, a day's scruff on his cheeks, and a cleft chin. Ramin nearly dropped his cup. He gripped it tighter and hoped the guy hadn't noticed him staring.

Holy shit. It was impossible. Wasn't it? His heart skipped another couple beats. Could the whole gelateria hear it?

But no. The probability was basically zero.

"Okay, buddy. You know what you want?" the man asked, and fuck it, Ramin could swear he knew that voice, even twenty years later.

Noah Bartlett. His old classmate. It couldn't be, could it? No. But what if it was? Fuck, the guy even looked like Noah. Noah, if he'd aged like fine wine.

Ramin had never thought that about a person before—that they had aged like fine wine—but damn. He risked another glance. There were laugh lines around the guy's sparkling eyes, and way more hair on his forearms. He looked like a man, not a teenager. But he knew that face. That voice.

Impossible. Right?

"Mmmmmm, pistachio!" the boy said.

"Two scoops of pistachio in a cone, per favore," probably-definitely-not-Noah said. "And one scoop of lemon for me. Grazie."

"What about Mom?" the boy asked.

"We'll let her pick when she comes."

Okay. Ramin had—very occasionally, and only when he couldn't sleep—looked Noah up over the years. Well, tried to look him up, because Noah didn't seem to have a profile on *any* social media, at least not one that Ramin could find. Even combing through his exceedingly neglected Facebook account (because seriously, fuck Mark Zuckerberg) to see if he could find mutual friends had yielded nothing. As far as the internet was concerned, Noah Bartlett didn't exist.

So this couldn't be him. It couldn't be Ramin's first crush. Not that he'd understood it was a crush. He'd been seventeen and growing up in suburban Kansas City and *closeted* didn't come close to describing it.

He hadn't been able to put words to the strange draw he'd felt toward Noah. He told himself it was jealousy—that Noah was handsome and fit, while Ramin had felt fat and ugly, his nose too big for his face, his stomach too big for his shirts. He told himself it was friendship, that Noah had everything going for him, that by all rights he should've been awful to Ramin like all the other popular white boys, but he never was. He told himself it was admiration, that he wanted to be like Noah, who had half the girls in their class crushing on him, or dating him, or whispering about him and giggling every time he walked by...

Ramin shook himself.

First, it probably wasn't Noah. Kansas City was half a world away. Well, a third of a world at least.

Second, even if it *was* Noah Bartlett, it didn't matter, because there was no way Noah would remember him.

Third, and most important: He was Interesting New Ramin. He was here to drown himself in foreskins, not dwell on a teenage crush.

Ramin squeezed his eyes shut as brain freeze shoved a dagger into his forehead. He pressed his tongue against the roof of his mouth. That was supposed to help, right? When it finally went away, he opened his eyes to find probably-not-Noah gone.

Relief and disappointment warred in his chest for a second before relief won out. And if he heard a small, sad whisper of *what if* in the back of his mind, well, he ignored it.

He finished his gelato, wiped his mouth on the scratchy napkin, and was about to scoot off his stool when a voice spoke behind him.

"Scusi. Are you American? Sei Americano?"

Ramin froze. Turned and faced the voice.

It was the guy. Probably-Not-But-Maybe-Noah.

Who hadn't left but was instead standing *right behind him.*

Up close, he was even more handsome. His cheekbones were strong, his jawline defined. His upper lip was heavily bowed, his bottom lip thick and round, turning his mouth into a heart. The light streaming into the shop caught in his eyes, made the honey in them shine.

One hand still rested on his son's head; the other held up a cone of lemon sorbetto, showing off a bicep that was testing the tensile strength of his sleeve. A little vein squiggled toward the crease of his elbow.

Ramin reminded himself to breathe.

"Sì. I mean, yeah. Yes."

A grin blossomed across the man's face, just a tiny bit crooked, and those eyes sparkled even more. That smile could boil lakes.

Ramin worried he'd pass out. Slip off his stool, concuss himself on the counter, spend the rest of his time in Italy as Awkward Comatose Ramin.

He made himself unclench his ass and hoped it didn't show in his face.

"This might sound weird, but you're not from Kansas City, are you? Did you go to Northland High? Class of '05?"

On second thought, ass clenching was good and healthy and normal.

Because holy. Shit.

four

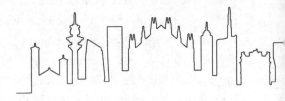

Noah

Twenty Years Ago

H ey. Hey," Noah whispered. "Ramin."

To his left, Ramin shook himself and looked around, like he didn't know where the sound had come from.

"Ramin?"

Ramin finally looked at Noah. Then he blinked, slowly, like he was confused. Ramin was a chubby guy, pretty quiet, but smart. Black hair, ruddy beige skin, a little bit of acne, but who didn't have that? Noah had popped a gnarly pimple on his chin that morning.

"Did you do the extra credit question?"

Noah didn't usually obsess about quizzes, but he'd actually been managing a solid B all semester (for once) and didn't want his grade to slip.

"Uh." Ramin's voice was clear and bright, though he spoke softly. "Yeah?"

"What'd you get?"

Ramin blinked again. "Zero?"

Noah sighed with relief. "Okay. Me too." He tried to play it cool, but he really wanted that B. A guy like Ramin who got A's in everything could never understand that. "Thanks."

"Sure." Ramin hunched in on himself again. It made Noah feel weird. No, not weird. Bad? Sad? Definitely something unhappy. He didn't want Ramin to hunch in on himself, though he couldn't say why. Ramin just seemed like the kind of guy that shouldn't have to hide.

The bell rang, and the rest of the class started shuffling out. One guy cuffed Ramin's shoulder with his backpack. Another muttered something that sounded alarmingly like "Osama Bin Ramen" under his breath.

Okay, maybe Ramin had a good reason for hiding. Noah couldn't imagine what it was like, being…Persian? Now that Noah thought about it, he wasn't a hundred percent sure he knew. Regardless, ever since 9/11, people had been saying things about Ramin, or some of the other Middle Eastern students. Like they had anything to do with it. As if they weren't just trying to get through high school like everyone else.

Something angry and fierce and protective (and maybe a little bit scary) bloomed in Noah's chest and he stood, nearly knocking his desk over.

"What did you just say?"

Ramin hunched inward even more, which just made Noah madder. Ramin hadn't done anything wrong. He didn't deserve that.

"Nothing," the guy said. Aaron something, that was his name. Noah didn't like him much. He tried not to hate anyone, but…

"What's your problem?" Aaron the jerk asked, but he brushed past Noah and out the door before Noah could articulate exactly what his problem was. Namely, the offensive nickname.

As the room emptied, Ramin relaxed a bit. "You didn't have to do that," he said softly.

"Sure I did."

"Why?"

Noah shrugged. Why did he? Because it was right. Because Ramin didn't deserve it. He didn't know how to explain that, though, so he said, "Because I don't like bullies."

In the hall, a trio of his girlfriend Stacy's friends walked by the open classroom door. They made brief eye contact with him, giggled, and started whispering to each other. Noah's ears burned.

He didn't like bullies, and he didn't like gossip, either.

Ramin didn't seem to care about that kind of stuff, though. Ramin might've been the only person in the whole school who hadn't heard the rumors. And Noah liked that about him.

"Well," Ramin said. "Thanks."

Ramin smiled at him then, a real smile, one Noah didn't think he'd ever seen before. He definitely would've noticed his dimples if he had. Not a lot of guys had dimples in their cheeks, just in their chins, like Noah did.

And not many people, period, had eyes as green as Ramin's, like jade catching the light. Stacy had green eyes—she was kind of conceited about them—but they were like, gray-green, not true green like Ramin's. The color of spring. Stacy's weren't nearly as striking. Noah could never tell her that, though.

Ramin was still smiling at Noah, though it had started to fade a bit. Noah smiled back, though.

"Any time, dude. See you tomorrow."

Now

Noah couldn't believe his eyes. He nearly took his hand off Jake's head to rub at them.

If you had asked Noah before today whether he remembered anyone from high school, he would've said no. Which would have been half the truth: He certainly didn't *think* about anyone. But remember?

Turns out he did. One guy, at least.

He hadn't seen Ramin Yazdani since graduation, but he knew those eyes. Jewel green, framed with long lashes, beneath heavy brows. A hint of dimples in his cheeks. Noah remembered those dimples. Ramin hadn't smiled often, but when he had, those dimples really popped.

Noah and Ramin had only really become friends senior year, when Ramin's mom got sick. Noah hadn't seen that smile very often, so every time he managed to coax one out of Ramin had felt like a victory.

How on earth was Ramin here in Milan? Did he live here? He was dressed like a local, in a crisp blue polo and linen shorts. His small stud earrings caught the daylight. He was skinnier than he'd been in high school, and he sat up straighter now. He'd used to hunch over himself, like he was waiting for the world to punch him. (Granted, it kind of had.)

Ramin—it *had* to be him, it *had* to be—took another bite of gelato, sucking the spoon clean, and his dimples deepened.

Something soft and nostalgic hooked itself behind Noah's belly button. He should say hello. Right?

But what if Ramin didn't remember him? Noah hadn't actually talked to Ramin since graduation. But they'd been friends, hadn't they? Or had Noah put more stock in their friendship than Ramin had?

Noah hadn't meant to stop talking to...well, everyone from high school, but he'd moved out of his parents' place right after graduation and spent the next few years working his butt off. Not that Ramin would've had any way of knowing that. Did he think Noah hated him?

Did he think about Noah at all?

It might've been moot, anyway, because what if this was just some random Italian that happened to look *exactly* like his old friend, if his old friend had aged well?

He looked down at Jake, happily going to town on his bright green pistachio gelato. Noah's own lemon cone was beginning to drip in a few spots, a trail of yellow trickling toward his index finger. He licked it off, the tartness bringing his senses alive.

He had to know, even if he embarrassed himself. Noah didn't have many friends—*real* friends, at least—back in high school, and he had even fewer now. Somewhere along the way, his whole world had become about Jake (and Angela, back when they'd been married). But Angela was moving to Italy and maybe taking Jake with her.

And if this really *was* his old friend, then what did he stand to lose, trying to reconnect?

He swallowed away the sand in his throat.

"Scusi. Are you American? Sei Americano?"

The guy nearly jumped off his stool. Noah hadn't meant to startle him. He was about to apologize when the man finally turned, and the light caught his eyes, and Noah forgot how to breathe.

"Sì. I mean, yeah. Yes."

That voice…soft and gentle, high and clear. But happier now. More confident. It had to be Ramin.

Nerves clawed at Noah's throat. He'd be mortified if Ramin didn't remember him. He hedged and asked, "This might sound weird, but you're not from Kansas City, are you? Did you go to Northland High? Class of '05?"

Ramin slowly nodded.

It really was him.

"Ramin, right? It's Noah. Noah Bartlett."

Please let Ramin remember him. Please don't let this moment be awkward.

"Yup. I mean, yeah. Hey!" Ramin hopped off the stool, but he stuck his foot right into one of the shopping bags on the floor and pitched forward, right against Noah's chest.

Noah nearly dropped his sorbetto, but he managed to swing it out of the way in time.

He also managed to get a whiff of Ramin's cologne, citrus and spice, and feel Ramin's warm weight against him as he took his free hand off Jake's head to steady him. Ramin blinked, so close his eyelashes nearly brushed against Noah's face.

And then he righted himself and backed away, holding up his hands like they'd been stained or something. "I'm so sorry. My bag—"

"It's fine," Noah chuckled. Ramin looked so funny when he was flustered, his cheeks turning pink. The years really had been good to Ramin—he'd gotten more handsome. "Wow. Ramin Yazdani. I can't believe it. What're you doing here?"

Ramin bit his lip for a second. "I guess part vacation, part remote work? But wait, who's this?" Ramin dropped to a crouch so he was eye level with Jake.

Embarrassment (and a tiny bit of shame) flashed through Noah. He couldn't believe he'd forgotten to introduce Jake. But Ramin had noticed Jake standing there, patiently waiting. He'd even gotten down to Jake's eye level. Like he saw Jake as a full person who didn't deserve to be talked down to. Noah's embarrassment swiftly gave way to warmth.

The Ramin he remembered had always been a good guy.

"Hey. I'm Ramin," Ramin said to Jake. "I went to school with your dad. Wait. He is your dad, right? If he's not, blink three times."

Jake giggled. "He is my dad!"

"Okay, then. What's your name, Noah's kid?"

"I'm Jake."

"Nice to meet you. What are your thoughts on fist bumps?"

Jake held up his little fist, and Ramin bumped it.

"Nice."

Noah didn't think he could smile any wider as Ramin stood back up. "What?"

"Nothing." It wasn't nothing. But Noah didn't know how to say *Thank you for being respectful of Jake's boundaries and ability to consent to physical contact, because his grandparents never were, and even though Jake doesn't see them anymore since I went no-contact, he still worries* in a way that wouldn't make him look like a weirdo in the gelateria. "You said you're working remotely?"

Ramin shrugged. "Yeah, kind of. We have an office here, too, so I'll probably go in some, but mostly I just wanted to…get away, I guess. What about you?"

Noah wanted to know more about that, not talk about himself, but he answered, "Jake's mom has family here, so we came to visit."

And Jake might move here with his mom felt too heavy to share.

Another trickle of melting gelato made its way to Noah's hand. He licked it off, and then along where the cone met the scoop. As he did, he could've sworn Ramin's cheeks flushed, a deep pink that set off his dimples.

Noah's own cheeks began to burn in response, but before he could say anything else, the doorbell dinged and Angela swept in. She'd changed out of her travel clothes into a mint green sundress that showed off her hips and boobs. They were just friends now (thanks to a lot of therapy), but she was still the most beautiful woman Noah had ever seen. "Oh. Angela, you'll never believe this. Ramin, meet Angela, Jake's mom. Angela, this is Ramin. We went to high school together."

"Nice to meet you." Ramin offered Angela a fist bump, and Noah realized he had a tattoo over his pulse point. It was black script, which Noah figured had to be Persian. He wondered what it said, and if Ramin had any more tattoos for that matter. "Noah said you had family here?"

Angela nodded. "My grandparents. This'll be Jake's first time meeting them."

"Cool. You excited, Jake?"

Jake shrugged, and Ramin's eyes crinkled up with a wry smile. "A ringing endorsement if I've ever heard one."

Noah laughed. "Well, *I'm* excited to try Nonna's cooking."

There had to be *some* good bits to this trip, after all.

At that, Jake perked up. "Do you think she can make macaroni and cheese?"

Noah shook his head and caught Ramin's eyes. They were practically sparkling with laughter. But then he looked at Angela, and it was like shutters had closed. What was that about?

Ramin seemed to notice, too. He cleared his throat. "Sorry. I'm right in your way, aren't I?" He stepped back against the bar top, smashing one of his bags with his foot.

"You're fine," she said, squeezing past to order, and Jake followed.

"Can I have seconds?"

Ramin barely suppressed a laugh. "He's a good kid."

"He is." Noah watched his son for a moment. A lot of things had gone sideways in his life, but having a son wasn't one of them. He turned back to Ramin, who was subtly trying to kick his bags out of the way. "Doing some shopping, huh?"

Ramin sighed. "My luggage got sent to Amsterdam."

Noah winced in sympathy. "That sounds like a nightmare."

"Yeah. But, hey, new wardrobe, new me, I guess." He tugged at the hem of his polo shirt. "So what have you been up to? You still in Kansas City?"

"Yeah, up in Gladstone. I took some time off when Jake was born, but I'm a carpenter."

"Oh cool," Ramin said, and he sounded like he thought it really *was* cool.

Some people could be kind of judgmental about blue-collar work. But Ramin had never been the judgmental type, and Noah was glad to see that hadn't changed.

"I'm a disaster at building things," Ramin said. "Except PowerPoint decks."

"I bet you're not so bad."

"One time I put an IKEA shelf together backwards. Despite the pictures. And I'm still not sure where some of the parts were supposed to go."

Noah chuckled. "Well, those Swedish pictures are hard to understand."

Ramin gave a soft smile. Noah caught him rubbing at his tattoo again. He really wondered what it meant. "What—"

"All set," Angela said.

Ramin jumped, like someone had just zapped him with static. Noah might've been a little shocked himself. Talking with Ramin felt like going back in time. Like he was in a different world, until Angela's voice dragged him back to the real one.

"Oh. What'd you pick?"

"Chocolate." She held up her cone. "We'd better go."

She glanced toward Jake, who it seemed had *not* gotten seconds, and whose face was turning red.

Uh-oh.

Noah had expected the jet lag to hit Jake sooner or later, and probably even make him into a little monster for a while, but it looked like the meltdown was imminent, and Angela knew it.

"Nice to meet you," she said to Ramin. "Say bye, Jake."

Jake muttered, but Ramin knelt down and offered another fist bump.

Noah's heart wanted to melt. Did Ramin have any kids of his own? He was so effortless with Jake.

"I'm glad I met you, Jake. Have fun in Italy."

To Noah's surprise, Jake cooled off enough to bump his little fist against Ramin's. "You too."

And then Angela was pulling Jake toward the door.

Ramin stood. Noah was frozen. He didn't want to go. Didn't want to say goodbye. Didn't want to leave this perfect, random, magical moment.

But his gelato had turned to mush. And his son was waiting.

"I'd better go," he made himself say.

"Yeah. See you." Ramin's eyebrows curved down, ever so slightly, like he knew it was a lie.

They'd gone twenty years never seeing each other in Kansas City. What were the chances they'd ever meet again?

But Noah's son was waiting, so he lied as well.

"See you."

five

Ramin

Ramin staggered back to his apartment in a daze. He only tripped on the cobbled stones twice.

Noah Bartlett, all grown up.

Noah had been handsome when they were teenagers. *Really* handsome. The kind of handsome that meant he had one girlfriend or another basically all through high school. All that had only been a preview, though. All the pieces of his face didn't quite fit together when they were teenagers.

Now they did.

Noah wasn't just handsome, he was *beautiful*. Striking, and fit, with that wide smile and those warm, shining eyes, and that deep voice that made Ramin's knees go wobbly. Ramin thought he'd left crushing on straight guys behind, along with acne (thanks, salicylic acid!) and wet dreams (thanks, right hand!). Speaking of wet dreams, Ramin still remembered that really vivid one he'd had, the one with Noah in it, the one burned into his mind . . .

God, Ramin did *not* miss being a teenager.

Not only had Noah been handsome, but he'd also been a good friend. Not good as in close—Arya and Farzan had been Ramin's only close friends—but good as in *kind*. Noah Bartlett had every reason to treat Ramin like shit, just like all the other straight white jocks at Northland High, but he never had.

It was no surprise he'd grown into an even kinder man.

God. Noah Bartlett. *Here.*

Here with a son. An adorable son, who had Noah's eyes, Noah's friendly spirit, Noah's kindness. Because Jake hadn't pulled away when Ramin said hello; he'd gone in for a fist bump.

And Jake's mother, too. Not Noah's wife, but Jake's mother. No ring that Ramin had noticed, either. What did it all mean? Were they married but didn't use rings? Together but not married? Just friendly co-parents? Were they divorced? Did divorced couples take family vacations together?

For a second Ramin imagined traveling with Todd post-breakup. A small, pathetic part of him kind of wished Todd *was* here. Someone to share the adventure with.

But he was Interesting New Ramin. He didn't need anyone to share adventures with. Life was his adventure!

That didn't stop the hollow ache in his chest, though. His grand Italian adventure was supposed to be a honeymoon. A romantic tour of Rome. Or maybe a stay on the Amalfi Coast. Todd loved the beach.

Ramin loved the sea itself, if not the beach. The endless crash of waves, water stretching to the horizon, clouds marching by. He would've been content to sit on a hotel balcony, sipping a glass of wine, taking in all that blue. But Todd would've wanted to be in the sand, shirtless to show off all the time he'd been putting in at the gym, short shorts (or a Speedo) to let everyone know he was gay, drinking in the attention even though he wasn't available.

Ramin shook his head as he fought with the front gate to his apartment building. Had Todd always been that way, and Ramin just hadn't noticed? Or had Todd changed as he felt the footsteps of his forties marching steadily closer? Ramin had never minded getting older. Another year of life meant another year of honoring his parents. Doing things they never got to do. Honoring his queer elders, too, the ones who fought for him and the ones who hadn't survived the fight.

He was living for the hopes and dreams of so many people.

Including his own. So fuck Todd.

And fuck himself, because seven flights of stairs was more than he'd realized, and his glutes were burning.

Once Ramin was certain he wasn't going to have a heart attack, he put his new clothes in the washer, made himself a cup of tea—in the apartment's smallest saucepan, since apparently neither Francesca nor Paola saw the need for a kettle—and pulled out his phone. Kansas City was seven hours behind, so it was just past eight in the morning there. His friends were *probably* awake by now.

Even if they weren't, they were used to Ramin texting early. He was the only morning person among them.

He opened the group chat.

Ramin
Made it to Milano!
But my bags went to
Amsterdam.

Arya
Your bags are getting 420

Farzan
Duck!!
Fuck*
Glad you made it safely!!

David

Make sure to drink all the wine for me!

Ramin

I can't drink all the wine, I would die!
I will drink a lot of it though.

Farzan

Don't die
Everything good otherwise?

Ramin sipped his tea. It was weak. The bags were probably expired. He needed to get some at the grocery store.

Everything *was* good otherwise. Right? Except for the existential crisis of running into his old crush at a gelateria in a one-in-a-billion (or maybe even trillion) coincidence. Part of him wanted to tell his friends about seeing Noah. They probably remembered him, at least a little bit, even if they hadn't been friends with him. But what was there to say? It wasn't like he'd ever see Noah again anyway.

Ramin

Everything is good

Arya

Have you found any dick yet?

Ramin snorted. Trust Arya to ask the important questions. But he couldn't get any dick until his suitcase arrived. In addition to condoms and lube, it also had his enema bulb for prepping. And besides, he wanted to get used to Italy before he ventured out in search of dick.

An image of Noah popped into his mind, more specifically the front of Noah's jeans, but Ramin shoved that away. No, nope, not going there. He was here to reinvent himself. Get under as many men as he could.

Not rekindle a twenty-year-old crush that had never gone anywhere back then and was certainly not going to go anywhere now.

> **Ramin**
> Not yet. Will report back.

One thing Ramin had learned about Italy in his research: Italians liked to eat dinner late. Really late. Like, seven o'clock was *early* to them. Any restaurant that was open before then was one for tourists, not locals, and Ramin wanted to live like a local.

He made it to six forty-five before his growling stomach got the best of him.

The late afternoon sun turned the streets golden as he stepped onto the sidewalk, making sure the gate closed behind him like Francesca and Paola had instructed. He reached for his phone to look up restaurants but stopped himself. He was Interesting New Ramin. He didn't need Google reviews. He took things as they came. He did as the locals did.

He turned left and started walking.

His apartment was in Porta Nuova, a cute neighborhood north of the city center, but then again, were any Italian neighborhoods *not* cute? Vespas and Fiats zipped by on the street. Bicycles weaved around and between them.

On every street he passed, folks were closing up shops, pulling down metal shutters, locking doors, turning off lights. On every sidewalk, people sat around little black metal tables sipping spritzes and eating olives off toothpicks, enjoying an aperitivo before dinner. Restaurants were getting ready to open, too: servers flapped out tablecloths, set places, polished silverware.

Another thing Ramin had read: The best way to find a good restaurant was to find one where the menu *wasn't* in English.

His stomach growled at him again. He was supposed to be *Interesting* New Ramin, not *Indecisive* New Ramin.

He rounded the piazza and turned onto a narrow street that curved to the right, obscuring the other end. On the left, a patio caught his eye, lit with fairy lights. A line was already forming by the door, but most of the people waiting looked like actual locals. At least, he didn't see any pairs of tennis shoes.

"Tavolo per uno?" Ramin asked when he finally made it to the host stand, manned by a black-haired twink with a strong tan and an even stronger nose.

"Sì, signor, fuori o dentro?"

"Uh…"

"Outside or inside?"

Ramin *knew* that. But he couldn't translate that fast in his brain. "Oh. Outside?"

The twink led Ramin to a small table up against the rail that separated the patio from the sidewalk. Ramin ordered a sparkling water (acqua frizzante, as the locals called it) and settled in to study his menu. Sure enough, it was entirely in Italian.

A good sign.

At least until Ramin actually tried to read the menu and realized he couldn't. His Italian wasn't up to snuff yet. He pulled out his phone to start translating.

Before he could, though, he heard a voice call his name.

An impossible voice.

Noah's voice.

"Ramin?"

six

Noah

Noah hadn't been on many vacations in his life.

Growing up, "vacation" had just been visiting his grandparents down in the Ozarks or seeing Silver Dollar City in Branson. His parents had been weirdly obsessed with Yakov Smirnoff.

And once he graduated and moved out, there'd been no time for vacation. He'd had bills to pay.

His first true vacation had been his honeymoon with Angela. She'd always wanted to see New York City, and Noah had never been, so they'd spent a week there. Noah had expected fancy restaurants and Broadway shows, making love in a fancy hotel bed, and maybe seeing the Statue of Liberty.

What had followed instead was his first experience with the Death March of Fun.

Angela liked to schedule her vacations to within an inch of their lives, and woe to any human, animal, inanimate object, or act of God that got in her way.

Noah thought Angela might lay off in Italy. She was moving here, after all, so she'd have time to see the sights. Besides, they were all jet-lagged. It was hot out. Jake was getting cranky. But no.

Angela had dragged them out of the gelateria before Noah could even say a proper goodbye and set a rapid pace down the streets of Milan toward the garden in Porta Venezia that had been "highly recommended" by whatever travel blog she'd been following.

From the gardens, it was a long walk down Via Alessandro Manzoni to visit the Starbucks Reserve in Milan, which was—apparently—a big deal. It *was* fancy inside: a huge open-floor plan, almost like a train station, but for coffee. From there, she led them down a side street to see a famous statue of a middle finger.

"You sure this is okay for Jake to see?" Noah muttered.

"It's art." She bit her lip and turned to Jake, who was practically hanging off Noah's leg. "Remember, it's not a very nice thing to do to people, all right? And never in school."

"Okay." Jake nodded and yawned.

"I think we'd better get him back," Noah said, smoothing Jake's hair off his forehead.

Angela looked at her phone, where she probably had another twelve spots pinned to visit, then deflated. "I guess you're right."

Jake was getting a bit too big to realistically carry around on his back. Not weight-wise—between carrying stuff at work and lifting heavy things at CrossFit, Noah was pretty strong—but simply size-wise. Jake was getting taller, his legs were getting gangly, and when they swung they bumped into things. Or other people.

Plus, when Jake fell asleep against Noah's back, he went limp, so it was like trying to stop wet pasta from spilling out of a backpack.

Jake had gone completely dead to the world by the time they made it back to their hotel. Angela wasn't looking much livelier herself. In the elevator he was pretty sure she fell asleep standing, her eyes closing and her chin resting against her chest, until the elevator dinged and she straightened up with a start.

Angela had booked them two connected rooms, so they could both have some privacy and let Jake run back and forth depending on who he wanted to bunk with for the night.

"How are you still awake?" Angela asked through a yawn.

Noah shrugged.

The truth was, he was more awake now than he had been when they'd landed. He was practically buzzing, all because of Ramin. Seeing his old friend had been like a jolt of electricity.

"I can put him to bed if you want to go do something," she said.

Too late for that. The only thing Noah wanted to do was go back to that gelateria. He couldn't even say why. But seeing Ramin had been so unexpected, so joyful. He hadn't felt like that in a long time.

That wasn't Angela's fault, though.

"You sure? I don't mind." Truth be told, Noah was usually better at dealing with Jake's bedtime, but Angela shook her head.

"I need the practice," she muttered. "Especially if he's going to be living with me here."

Noah swallowed away the lump in his throat.

"Okay."

The hotel gym wasn't bad—some free weights, a few machines, treadmills—but no matter how much Noah lifted he couldn't stop his mind from swirling. Now that he was alone, he realized he was annoyed. Annoyed at Angela for running them all ragged, and annoyed at himself for not complaining, and annoyed at his life because he was thirty-eight years old and single and the only good thing in his life, his son, might be moving across the ocean.

A shower didn't help. Neither did spending some time with his sketchbook, which usually settled his nerves.

Plus he was hungry.

He knocked on Angela's door, but the only answer was a soft snore. So he sent her a text, letting her know he was going out, and headed down.

The streets had cooled off a bit as the afternoon shadows grew. Colorful stucco façades lined every street, with apartments above and shops or restaurants below. Every so often, the buildings broke apart for a park, or a hotel, or a church, or a gleaming steel-and-glass tower that looked out of place against its neighbors.

Noah was relieved to be able to just wander without having to stick to Angela's itinerary, but now that he was on his own, he did kind of wish he knew where he was going. He had his phone, so it wasn't like he was in danger of getting lost, but still. He hadn't had time to look up restaurants or sights to see or anything like that.

So he just kept walking. At one point, he passed a child a few years younger than Jake talking to a grown-up in rapid-fire Italian, their tiny, clasped hand raised to gesture emphatically along with whatever they were saying.

Noah smiled but stopped himself from laughing aloud. Even Italian children talked with their hands.

The next block, he passed a row of restaurants. The smell of cheese and pasta and meat slammed into him, setting his stomach to growling and his mouth to watering. He really did need to eat something. One of the restaurants had a little outdoor patio full of people crammed into tiny tables. It smelled so good, but there was a line down the block. Who knew how long it would take?

Noah shook his head and kept walking. Maybe he could find whatever passed for fast food in Italy. But as he strolled past the patio, he stopped and doubled back.

It couldn't be. *It couldn't be.*

There, sitting alone at a little table for two, sat Ramin, studying the menu.

"Ramin?"

seven

Ramin

Once was a coincidence.

No, that wasn't right. Maybe once was an accident?

Whatever the quote was, what did it mean if something happened twice?

"Noah?" Ramin blinked at Noah, standing on the other side of the fence. "What're you doing here?"

Noah smiled, his eyes sparkling in the warm patio lights, and Ramin felt his cheeks heating up.

"I was hungry."

"Uh." The gears in Ramin's brain ground for a second, making a *brrrrrrt* sound.

There was no way. How had they wound up at the same restaurant? Was Noah...asking to join him?

Noah had a family, though. Except where were they?

"Are you, uh, by yourself?"

Noah nodded. "Angela and Jake collapsed. Jet lag."

"Oh." Ramin was determined to make it to bedtime without napping. Apparently Noah had the same idea.

Noah. Who was here. Alone. And hungry.

"Uh. Did you want to join me?"

If anything, Noah smiled even brighter, so bright Ramin nearly needed sunglasses. "You don't mind?"

Ramin shook his head.

Noah glanced around, then hoisted himself over the fence, flexing the cords in his forearms and stretching his jeans with his leg muscles.

Ramin pressed harder at his tattoo. This could not be happening.

Noah settled into his seat and scooted in.

"You're sure you don't mind? If you wanted to eat alone..."

"No! I mean, I'm sure. I don't mind the company."

"Just like old times, huh?"

Twenty Years Ago

"Mind if I join you?"

Ramin looked up from his homework. Noah Bartlett was standing across the table from him, with his big green sketchbook in one hand and a tray of what Northland High optimistically called "the lunch salad" (really just a pile of shredded lettuce, the same kind that went on the tacos) in the other.

Ramin had already eaten his own lunch, leftover kotlet that Farzan's dad had made over the weekend. Farzan's dad was an amazing cook— he and Farzan's mom owned the only Persian restaurant in town. The kotlet had been amazing: spiced meat patties stuffed in pockets of pita with herbs and onions and pickles. But he was relieved he'd finished before Noah sat down.

It had been a while since any of Ramin's classmates had made fun of him for bringing Persian food for lunch—why do that when they could call him fat and ugly?—but still.

Noah wore a gray sweatshirt with NHS WRESTLING across the front, and his Joe Boxer waistband showed where his jeans sagged a bit around his hips. He must've gotten a haircut over the weekend, because his black hair, which usually flopped a bit over his forehead, was now short and stuck straight up. His brown eyes looked right at Ramin, like he was actually happy to see him.

"Ramin?" Noah asked. Ramin realized he hadn't actually answered.

"Oh. Sure." Ramin looked around. All the other wrestlers were at another table, halfway across the cafeteria, laughing and shouting. "Don't you want to sit with your team?"

Noah's brow scrunched up. "Nah."

Ramin's chest gave a weird flutter. Was this a trap? But he didn't know how to say no. "Okay."

"Thanks." Noah plopped down onto the bench, scooted his sketchbook to the side, and frowned at his salad.

"Everything okay?"

Noah sighed and reached for his collar, pulling out a little silver cross necklace. He rubbed at it with his thumb. "Cutting for the meet this weekend. I *hate* cutting."

"Oh. Sorry." Ramin remembered when Arya had wrestled freshman year and been miserable the whole time. He'd switched to swim team after that.

"It's fine. As long as it helps me win, right?" Noah's voice was deep and smooth. Sometimes Ramin wished his own voice had gotten that deep. Or at least a little deeper. He would've rather been a bass than a tenor.

He would've rather been in the kind of shape Noah was, too. Most of the wrestlers were in good shape, but Noah was something else. Ramin had been chubby all his life. Maybe if he started wrestling, he could lose some weight. Be more like Noah. Just because Arya had hated it, that didn't mean Ramin would.

"Sorry," Noah said. "I didn't mean to interrupt you. You can keep studying. I just wanted a little company."

Were Noah's cheeks turning red? No, it was just Ramin's imagination, and anyway, Noah stuffed a huge bite of salad...well, lettuce into his mouth.

Ramin shrugged. "I don't mind the company, either."

Now

While Noah looked over the menu, Ramin studied the wine list. Did Noah even like wine? Ramin needed some or he'd never make it through dinner. His heart would hammer its way out of his chest. Or he'd accidentally rupture his spleen from nerves. Twenty years later, Noah still made him nervous.

He didn't know why. Noah was kind and thoughtful and seemed genuinely happy to see Ramin.

But he was also hot, and he still wore that silver cross, and he had no idea Ramin was gay, and what if he was secretly a homophobe?

So. Wine.

Ramin wasn't nearly as knowledgeable about wine as David—the guy was a freaking master sommelier, after all—but he did know *some*. The problem was, he'd never heard of any of the wines on the list. They were all Italian, and no doubt all amazing, but how he was he supposed to pick?

Finally he spotted one wine he recognized in the Tuscan section— Ornellaia, a super Tuscan he'd heard David talk about with a dreamy look in his eyes. Ramin had never actually tasted it. He didn't usually spend that much on wine. Hell, he never spent *half* that much on wine.

But Interesting New Ramin liked to splurge.

And some small, juvenile part of him wanted to impress Noah.

So after they both ordered—both going for the risotta alla Milanese, short-grain rice with saffron and bone marrow—Ramin said, "And a bottle of the Ornellaia?"

Their server, a young woman with flame red hair, bugged out her eyes. "Sì. Is this a special occasion?"

"Oh. Uh." What was he supposed to say? Yes? But what occasion? No? But then he just looked like some asshole who ordered expensive wine because he could. A typical American tourist. Probably ruining the local economy, too, and—

"It's a reunion," Noah offered. "We haven't seen each other in twenty years!"

"Ah, che bello," the server said. "Allora, we'll bring the wine right away."

Ramin unclenched his butt and looked back at Noah. "Thanks. Sorry, I didn't even ask if you drank. You don't have to—"

"I'd love to try the wine." Noah smiled softly and shifted his legs under the table, but Ramin didn't get out of the way fast enough and their knees bumped.

Noah had changed out of his Royals shirt and jeans into a light pink polo shirt that looked absolutely incredible against his skin (not to mention stretched across his chest, which somehow looked even more perfect than before), and a pair of shorts, because Ramin felt his leg hair brush against Noah's. He fought off a shiver and snapped his legs back together, though he kind of missed the feel of Noah's warm skin. That was the jet lag talking again, no doubt.

"So." Noah leaned in and rested his forearms on the table. Ramin tried his best not to trace the cords there or imagine the texture of the black hairs. Noah had really hairy forearms.

"—anyone from high school?" Noah was saying. Ramin blinked.

"Sorry, say again?" Ramin gestured vaguely toward the road, though annoyingly, no cars were driving past. "I didn't hear you."

Noah didn't seem to notice the lie. "I was asking if you kept in touch with any friends from high school? I haven't talked to *anyone* since graduation."

"I still talk to my best friends. You remember Farzan Alavi and Arya Nazeri?"

"Oh yeah, Arya was on the wrestling team one year. You're still best friends?"

"We own a restaurant together, actually. Shiraz Bistro, up in Gladstone."

"No kidding? That's amazing." Noah blew out a breath. "I couldn't wait to get away from everyone in school. Leave it all behind. Move away from home. Then I realized it was my parents I was trying to escape more than anything."

Ramin raised his eyebrows but kept his mouth shut. He remembered Noah's mom had been...kind of awful. She taught Spanish at Northland, and she certainly hadn't kept her opinions on Muslims and the Middle East and the "Axis of Evil" to herself.

Thankfully, before Ramin could get sucked into an awkward conversation about Noah's parents, their bottle came in the hands of an older gentleman with a bow tie. It was topped with red foil embossed in gold and featured a simple, elegant label with a sketch of the winery on it.

"This looks fancy," Noah muttered.

"This is a very special wine," the sommelier said, emphasizing the *very* and the *special*. "You have excellent taste."

Noah beamed at Ramin, but Ramin just blushed. Impressing Noah had seemed like a good idea at the time, but now he just looked like he was trying to show off.

The somm opened their bottle and poured Ramin a tiny taste.

Sweet fuck.

Okay, fine. It *was* very special. A luscious ruby, notes of raspberry and vanilla, a hint of tobacco that absolutely coated the sides of Ramin's mouth. He sat back in his chair. "Wow."

"Wow?" Noah grinned.

"Wow," Ramin agreed, smacking his lips. The finish kept going and going.

The somm poured them both proper glasses. "Enjoy, signori."

"Grazie," Ramin said, but he kept his eyes on Noah as he tasted the wine. What if Noah didn't like dry wines? Oh God, what if he only liked saccharine Missouri wines?

But no. Noah took a long, slow sip, the muscles of his neck stretching as he tilted his head back. His Adam's apple bobbed. His jaw worked. And when he swallowed, he sighed.

"Wow is right."

"Yeah?"

"Yeah. I've never had anything like it. It's so..." Noah's lips pressed together. They were already turning purple. "Special."

"Yeah."

Okay. This had been a good idea after all.

Noah raised his glass. "Hey, we didn't toast. Here. To..."

Noah studied Ramin for a moment, his brow furrowing and then relaxing as another smile blossomed.

It should be criminal for any straight man to have a smile like that.

"To old friends," Noah finished.

Ramin raised his glass and met Noah's eyes. They were a deep, dark brown, but the setting sun revealed honeyed streaks deep within. Ramin hoped Noah didn't think he was staring, but you *had* to make eye contact when you toasted. Otherwise you'd get cursed with seven years bad sex, and that kind of curse would ruin his plans to get fucked into the European Union.

"This is so good," Noah said after drinking again. "Seriously. You pick all the wine at your restaurant?"

Ramin shook his head. "I'm a silent partner. Farzan's the one who runs it. And his boyfriend does the wine list. He's a master sommelier."

Shit. Ramin hadn't meant to out Farzan like that. Though he supposed he was about to find out if Noah was a secret homophobe.

Please, *please* don't let Noah be a secret homophobe. That wouldn't just ruin dinner. It would ruin some of the only good memories he had from high school. Ones that didn't include Farzan and Arya, at least.

Ramin held his breath.

But Noah just nodded. "That's a big deal, right? Being a master sommelier?"

Ramin exhaled slowly. Was that it?

It was. Relief washed over him like cool mist.

"Yeah. He studied for years."

"Wow." Noah took another taste of his wine. "So—" he began, but the arrival of their risottos interrupted him.

Ramin's looked perfect: a golden circle of rice, with a dollop of rich brown brodo in the center. It smelled like heaven.

Noah's eyes lit up as he beheld his own dinner; he even leaned in to smell it better.

Ramin waited to pick up his spoon—was Noah the kind of guy who'd want to say grace?—but Noah grabbed his own spoon and dug in. As soon as he closed his mouth, he let out a moan that Ramin felt in his taint.

"Oh my goodness. It's so good. Try yours."

Noah was right: It was creamy, savory, the lightness of the saffron playing counterpoint to the richness of the brodo. The fruit and acidity of the wine cut through everything.

"Wow."

"Yeah."

They ate in silence for a moment, Noah digging in with gusto, Ramin taking it a bit slower. He'd had a long therapy appointment after the breakup (and the bout of intense negative self-talk it had brought on). He was mostly okay when it came to his relationship with food. His therapist had reminded him he was literally going to one of the food capitals of the world.

His body was a good body. A strong body. A healthy body. He was allowed to enjoy good food. He was *excited* to enjoy good food.

Even if it did kind of suck, sitting across from Noah, trying not to notice the way his muscles filled out his polo shirt.

Fuck body dysmorphia.

Noah caught his eyes and gave him another smile. Noah was all smiles. And Ramin couldn't help it. He smiled back.

He felt like a kid again, eating lunch with a friend. Except instead of terrible square pizza, it was heavenly risotto and the greatest wine Ramin had ever tasted in his life.

Noah reached for his wineglass right as Ramin did, and their hands brushed briefly. Despite his hairy forearms, Noah didn't have very much knuckle hair, unlike Ramin, who had a few coarse strands on every finger. Noah's hand was warm, especially compared to the night air, and softer than Ramin expected, and—

Ramin snapped his hand back. He was absofuckinglutely not holding hands with Noah Bartlett. Just because he wasn't a secret homophobe didn't mean he wasn't straight. And even if he *wasn't* straight, they were two old friends having a reunion dinner. He wasn't on a date.

Noah Bartlett was completely out of his league. He might as well have been playing a different sport.

Noah quirked his head and pursed his lips, but Ramin just shrugged. "Sorry."

"It's fine."

God, Noah was even *nice* about it.

This was going to be a long fucking night.

But then Noah smiled at him again, and Ramin wished the night would never end.

Ramin cleaned his plate. He hadn't realized how hungry he was, but it was the first real meal he'd had after his flights. Speaking of flights, Ramin had forgotten how easily he got buzzed after being on a plane, but he didn't stop their server when she topped up his and Noah's glasses with the last of the bottle.

"I hope you enjoyed," she said. "This is a very special wine."

Noah smirked. Four different servers—none of them *their* server— had swung by their table to say the same thing as they ate.

"We did," Ramin assured her.

As she cleared away their plates, Noah leaned back and ran a hand through his hair.

Ramin wondered if it was as soft as it looked.

Nope, that was the alcohol talking. Ramin set down his glass and rubbed at his mom's name over his pulse point and tried to remember where he was. This was not a date, and Noah was not interested in him, and he really needed to sit up straighter, because their knees had been knocking under the table for the last thirty minutes, but Ramin and Noah had both gotten too buzzed to do anything about it.

"That was so good," Noah said. He sighed and scratched at his chest, where his collar was unbuttoned enough to show the valley between his pecs. Ramin wondered what it would feel like to rest his head against them.

And then he stopped wondering, because that was inappropriate. Obviously. Noah was his friend, a whole human being with his own thoughts and desires, not one of those anime body pillows. They'd shared a lovely meal. It didn't have to be more than that.

"It *was* good. I'm sorry Jake and Angela missed it," Ramin said.

Noah's hand stilled in his hair. He bit his lip.

"What's the deal with you and her anyway?"

Noah's eyes went wide. He dropped his hand to the table.

Ramin blinked. He couldn't believe he'd just asked that. Yeah, he'd thought it once...or twice...or thirty times tonight. But he didn't mean to *say* it.

"Oh my God, I'm sorry. That's the wine talking. Forget I asked."

Noah shook his head. "It's fine." He took a long sip of his wine, and Ramin tried not to stare at the arch of his neck, the divot in his chin, the glimpse of a wine-stained tongue. Noah puffed up his upper lip before blowing out a breath.

"We were married. Eight years."

"Were?"

"Yeah. Divorced two years ago."

"I'm sorry." That sucked. "Did Jake take it okay?"

Noah's eyes crinkled up. "Yeah. He did. Thank you for asking. I think it helped that me and Angela stayed friends. Granted, we did lots of therapy."

"Thank God for therapy." Ramin raised his glass.

Noah grinned again and clinked with Ramin. "What about you? Any family? Kids?"

Ramin shook his head. "I just got out of a relationship, actually."

"Oh, man, that sucks." Noah leaned in, his eyes softening in sympathy. "Was the breakup bad?"

"I mean, it was bad enough that I flew halfway around the world to get away from it, so..."

"You want to talk about it?"

Ramin shook his head. Noah didn't need to hear about his humiliating proposal.

"That's fair." Noah shifted, and their calves brushed under the table, their fine hairs tangling, sending electricity up Ramin's spine and shorting out his brain.

"I proposed and my boyfriend turned me down," he blurted out.

Fuckety-fuck! He hadn't meant to say that.

Damn this wine! (Not really. The Ornellaia hadn't done anything wrong.)

Ramin tensed all along his back and neck. So much for not outing himself. He braced himself for Noah's smile to fall. For him to frown and make some excuse to leave. Or worse—

But none of that happened. And Noah didn't move away. If his smile dimmed, it was only to curve down in sympathy. "I'm really sorry. What happened?"

Ramin sighed and unclenched. "You don't want to hear about it."

"I do. Really."

And for some reason, Ramin believed him. "He said I was too boring to marry."

Now Noah's smile *did* vanish. His eyes burned and his jaw clenched. "What a jerk."

That was one way to put it. *Fucking asshole* was Arya's preferred epithet.

"You're not boring," Noah insisted. "You're seriously the most interesting person I know!"

Ramin snorted at that.

"Okay, point taken, we've had a gap in the knowing each other part, but really. That guy doesn't know what he's missing."

"Thanks," Ramin said softly. "I'm over it. Mostly."

"Mostly? It's recent then?"

Ramin finished the last of his wine, then reached for his water; his mouth was bone dry. "If three weeks ago counts as recent."

"Three weeks?!" Noah nearly shouted. "I'd still be in bed crying."

Ramin laughed. "Well, I spent the night in bed crying and looking at trips to Italy, so..."

Noah laughed, too, the cloud that had fallen over their dinner breaking. "Okay, I'm really sorry for what happened, but I'm glad you came here." His voice lowered. "I'm glad I ran into you."

"Yeah." Ramin lowered his own voice and looked down at his hands. It was nice, talking to someone who didn't know Todd. Who hadn't known Ramin as part of a pair.

Who didn't think he was boring.

He looked back up. Noah was still smiling at him.

He didn't realize how much he'd missed Noah's smile all these years. "Me too."

eight

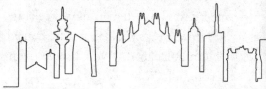

Noah

Noah's head was pleasantly fuzzy. He wasn't exactly a practiced drinker. Not that he didn't like wine—he and Angela used to have a glass each with dinner most nights—but since the divorce he hadn't drunk much. So now, half a bottle—combined with jet lag and probably a little dehydration—had him happy and loose.

He felt young and carefree with the evening breeze in his hair and an old friend beside him, laughing like they were the only two people in the world. For a moment, Noah could almost forget about Angela wanting to move here. About Jake maybe moving with her.

Noah swallowed. Did wine always make him so maudlin?

He was so caught up, he nearly walked right into a busy intersection. He halted, throwing up his arm, because Ramin was following him.

"Oop, careful." Ramin's chest bumped against him before he stopped, but Ramin broke the contact right away. He'd been like that all night, if their legs accidentally brushed under the table, or if their hands touched while reaching for the wine bottle. Noah didn't know if Ramin was worried he was a homophobe—a valid fear, given Noah's parents, though an unfounded one, given Noah's bisexuality—or if he was still hurting from his breakup and didn't want to touch anyone. Or if it was some secret third thing. Noah had showered before dinner, so he knew he didn't smell weird.

"It says don't walk." Noah pointed.

"There's no one coming." Ramin gestured. "And the locals don't wait."

Noah glanced up and down the street; sure enough, there were no cars around. He didn't mind waiting, though. He didn't want to say bye to Ramin just yet, even though he knew he needed to get back.

He cleared his throat. "Well, I try to set a good example for Jake."

"Okay. We can wait."

Noah swayed a bit as they waited, accidentally brushing Ramin's shoulder, and Ramin stepped away again. Noah stuffed down his annoyance. Not everyone was cool with casual platonic touch, even if most men were starved for it. One thing he missed most about his marriage was the cuddles.

Finally the light changed and they crossed. He wished he could've brushed Ramin's hand. Thrown an arm over his shoulder. Anything. But Ramin was freshly heartbroken, and he had to respect Ramin's boundaries. He'd made it clear: no touching.

He could talk, at least. He liked talking to Ramin. Ramin was easy to talk to. He always had been.

Easy to talk to, and smart, and interesting. Screw Ramin's ex for saying he was boring. Ramin wasn't boring. He was funny. He was thoughtful. He was amazing.

"It's really brave, you know," Noah said. "I mean, *you* are really brave. For doing all this."

"It was this or stay home and stare at the missing furniture," Ramin muttered.

Noah imagined it, and a pang lanced through his chest. He couldn't stand the thought of someone breaking Ramin's heart. He wanted to gather up all the pieces and fit them back together. He wanted to frame it, reinforce it, so it was impervious.

He never wanted anyone to hurt Ramin ever again.

He'd always felt protective of Ramin, back when they were in school, back when half the senior class seemed to like picking on Ramin for no reason other than he was Iranian. Noah had tried his best, but he couldn't be everywhere.

And now Ramin was a grown man who had his life together way more than Noah did. So it wasn't like he could really shield Ramin from anything, anyway. All he could do was commiserate.

"I remember when I moved out and into my own place. Everything just felt hollow." Some small part of him still felt that hollowness. The part that spoke in his father's voice, telling him he was a failure of a man for not holding his family together, for not keeping to his wedding vows, for not giving Jake a stable home.

"What happened?" Ramin asked, looking his way, but his eyes widened. Noah tried to fix his stormy face, but Ramin already had his hands up. "God, sorry. Not my business."

Noah shook his head. "It's fine. You told me about your breakup." *With that jerk*, he wanted to add but didn't.

Noah thumbed at his cross. His mom had gotten it for him...he couldn't even remember when. He hadn't spoken to either of his parents in three years, ever since that night he'd gone to pick up Jake and he'd found his son crying because his mother had given Jake an unwanted haircut, complaining his hair was getting *too long for a boy*.

Granted, there'd been plenty of crap before that. They'd judged him weak for leaving their church, finding a new one, a kinder one. And they'd judged him heretical for marrying a Catholic, even though Angela was long-since lapsed. They'd even judged him unmanly for being a stay-at-home dad, when Angela made three times more than him.

All of that, Noah could handle. He was used to his parents' judgment.

But they'd foist that judgment upon Jake over his dead body.

Jake had said no, and they had ignored it, and there was no going back after that.

But still, still, he kept that little silver cross around his neck. It felt like the memory of love, pressed against his sternum.

His parents hadn't been all awful.

Ramin was still waiting for him to explain, his face lit by the glow from a grocery store as they passed. Noah took a deep breath.

"I think we just fell out of love. There was no big thing, and we weren't fighting, but somewhere along the way we stopped making each other happy."

"Did she ask or did you?" Ramin asked quietly.

"She did." She'd been right. And she'd been brave, to finally bring it up, when Noah had been too scared of change to do it.

"I'm sorry," Ramin said.

"It's fine, it—" Noah caught his toe on the uneven cobbles of the street. He nearly fell, but a strong hand grabbed his arm and pulled him back up. The momentum brought him face-to-face, chest to chest with Ramin.

Noah forgot how to breathe.

This time, Ramin didn't spring away. Up close, his eyes were jade fire kindled in the streetlamps, beautiful and sad and keen, like they'd seen all the hurt the world had to offer but refused to give up. Life's pains hadn't turned Ramin brittle but somehow soft and gentle.

And Noah's chest filled with fire again, thinking of the man who'd dumped Ramin for being *boring*. How could any man look at Ramin's stunning eyes, or see the confidence he carried himself with, or hear his clear, strong voice, and think he was *boring*? How could anyone look at Ramin and not want to know *more*, want to know *everything* about him?

Noah still had about a million more questions.

A firm hand squeezed Noah's bicep. Ramin was talking to him.

"You okay?" Ramin asked. His lips were thin, creased in concern, stained plum from the wine. Noah wondered what they tasted like. Which was irrational and inappropriate to think about an old friend you hadn't seen in years and who just wanted to catch up and was getting over a heartbreak.

But they were so *pretty*.

Noah was morally opposed to any form of corporal punishment, but he wished someone would smack him upside the head, just to help him focus.

"Yeah. Just tripped." Noah shook his head. "I think I'm buzzed. I don't usually drink that much."

Ramin blushed and let go of him, leaving Noah chilled at the sudden absence. Maybe Ramin was cold, too, because he shivered as he rubbed at one of his tattoos. "In your defense, none of the sidewalks are even here. I tripped twice on the way home from gelato, totally sober."

Ramin turned down the sidewalk once more, leaving Noah with a view of his strong backside.

Noah shook himself. *Not appropriate!* He took a couple long strides to catch up.

"What were you saying earlier?"

"Hm?" Noah tried to remember.

"About the divorce?"

Noah rewound their conversation as best he could, even though his mental image seemed to go into slo-mo at the part with Ramin's lips.

"I think I was just gonna say it was painful but it got better. For all of us. Jake is happy, Angela's happy." He waved vaguely in the direction of the hotel, to his sleeping son and ex-wife. "I'm doing okay too."

Ramin frowned then, a little line appearing between his heavy brows, shadowing his eyes. Noah didn't like it when he couldn't see the light in Ramin's eyes.

"Just okay?"

Noah hadn't meant to admit that, but somehow Ramin drew the truth like a magnet.

"I just..." He pinched his cross and tried to put it into words. "Angela's a lawyer, so I was a stay-at-home dad. And I knew who I was and what I was supposed to do. I was a husband. I was a father. I was a son, until I stopped talking to my parents. But now..."

Now Jake was getting older and didn't need him as much. And half the time he was mad at Noah anyway. And he might be moving to Italy.

Noah *loved* being Jake's dad. It was the most important thing in his life. But maybe he needed to figure out how to be more than that.

"Now what?" Ramin asked.

"I don't know. I guess maybe I'm trying to find a new me." He sighed. "I need to show Jake there's more to life than just working and parenting and going to the gym."

"It's working for you, though," Ramin muttered, then blushed. "God, I'm buzzed too."

But Noah's chest fluttered. Ramin thought he looked good?

He laughed, and that made Ramin laugh, and the heaviness over them seemed to recede a bit. Tonight was supposed to be fun, not maudlin.

Ramin's steps slowed as they approached another crosswalk. "I'm that way," he said, pointing to the right, but Noah's hotel was to the left.

"I'm that way." Where had the night gone? Why did it have to end? "I'm really glad I ran into you again."

"Me too. I'm glad you got hungry." Ramin gifted him another smile, dimples deeply shadowed in the orange streetlight. "I had fun catching up. Say hi to Jake and Angela for me."

"For sure." Noah rubbed the back of his neck. He didn't want to say goodbye. It wasn't even that late, really. The night was still young, and it felt like magic, being here. Like a second chance he didn't know he wanted. A change he never knew he needed. But he didn't know how to seize it.

Maybe they could keep walking? See the city at night? Noah cursed himself for not being better at drinking, because if he was, maybe they could've gone to a bar, or just stayed at the restaurant, or—

Noah's phone buzzed. Jake's cheesing face flashed on his screen.

"Ah, sorry. Gotta take this." He pressed answer. "Hey, Jake. Did you get some rest?"

"Yeah. But I'm hungry."

Noah caught Ramin watching him, eyes twinkling. "It's okay," he whispered. "I can go."

Noah shook his head. He didn't want Ramin to go. He held up a hand and mouthed, *Wait?*

Then, aloud, "I'm on my way back. We'll get you something. Okay?"

"Okay. Did you know they have American shows here, too? Can I watch TV?"

Noah ran a hand through his hair. He and Angela hadn't even talked about screen time rules for while they were overseas. Plus Jake would still need to go back to bed and try to get on a good sleep schedule.

Was Angela even awake? Or would she sleep straight through?

He turned back to Ramin, who mouthed, *I better go*, and gestured down the street.

Noah wanted to reach out and take his hand, hold him in place, at least get a proper hug goodbye, but—

"Dad? You there?"

"Huh? Yeah, Jakey?"

"Remember how you promised we could have mac and cheese?"

"I didn't promise, Jake. You can't put words into my mouth."

"But you said—"

Noah pinched the bridge of his nose. Ramin was backing away, waving at him.

It felt like someone had poured cold water over him.

He wanted to say a proper goodbye.

He didn't want to say goodbye at all.

But he gave a little wave.

Ramin Yazdani smiled and turned and walked out of his life again.

Noah took a deep breath. Jake had no way of knowing he was

interrupting anything. Noah kept his voice even. "Why don't we talk about this when I get back. Okay, Jakey? I'm not far."

"You promise?"

"I promise we'll *talk*. Okay?"

"Okay."

"Be there soon. Love you."

nine

Ramin

Ramin turned back to stare as Noah walked away, phone to his ear, reiterating to his son that screen time rules still applied overseas. Ramin couldn't help it: It was impossible to ignore the way Noah's back and shoulders filled out his shirt, the way his ass looked in those shorts, the way his deep, smooth voice was full of love and patience.

He shook himself. What was the point in admiring a man he had literally zero chance with? He spun around and power-walked in the direction of his apartment.

After turning a corner, he slowed to breathe. He felt like he'd been holding his breath all night, metaphorically, metaphysically, and literally, for that matter. He'd been engaging his core during the meal so his stomach didn't pooch out too much.

Still, he'd survived dinner. With Noah Bartlett. Who was every bit the kind boy Ramin remembered, but now more mature, more patient, more handsome, more open. He hadn't freaked out when Ramin's hand or leg accidentally touched him; he hadn't flinched when Ramin mentioned having an ex-boyfriend. In fact, he'd leapt to Ramin's defense, just like back in high school, when Noah got mad if people made fun of

Ramin. Honestly, it had bothered him more than it bothered Ramin, but it was still nice to have someone on his side.

Ramin's chest glowed with the memory, but he pushed it away. When he was in high school, he hadn't understood all these feelings. He'd told himself he was jealous of Noah, who'd had everything going for him, but he knew himself better now. He'd been crushing, *bad*.

And now all that crush had come roaring back, twisting Ramin's heart into knots, because Noah was divorced and straight and unavailable and Ramin was never going to see him again, so what did any of it matter? He was here to get dicked down by Italian fuckboys (or fuckmen), not fan the flames of a twenty-year-old infatuation.

He was Interesting New Ramin, not Lovesick Puppy Ramin.

Still, as he pulled his phone out to double-check the way back to his apartment, he couldn't help wishing he'd at least asked for Noah's number.

Just so they could catch up more, back in Kansas City.

"Ramin!" Paola shouted from her doorway.

Ramin dropped his keys. He was only halfway through opening his door.

"Ciao," he said, scooping them back up. "Sorry, did I disturb you?"

"What? Of course not." Paola stepped out in a stunning blue dress, her hair coiffed and pinned perfectly. Francesca followed behind, this time in dark jeans and a sport coat that shimmered with silvered threads. She still had her bolo tie, though. "We're just heading out."

"Oh. Have fun."

Ramin fought with the big lock—it took four full cranks of the weird-looking key—as Francesca locked their door with practiced ease.

"Did you have a date tonight?" Paola said, waggling her eyebrows at Ramin. "Meet any good men?"

Ramin shook his head. "Just dinner with an old friend."

"Ah. 'There's not a word yet for old friends who just met,' " Paola half-sang.

Ramin smirked. "You know *The Muppet Movie*?"

"Sì, who doesn't know the Muppets?" She held out her arm, and Francesca took it. "Well, next time, bring someone home. Italy is for lovers!"

With that, the two of them headed for the elevator, leaving Ramin to finish letting himself into his apartment. He yawned his way through the kitchen, made himself another cup of weak tea, flopped onto the couch, and FaceTimed the group chat.

"Please tell me you've found some dick," Arya said without preamble. Sunlight reflected off his sunglasses, and the Sky Stations receded over his shoulder as he walked downtown.

"Hi, Ramin," Farzan said, giving Arya a pointed look. Ramin recognized David's kitchen immediately. David owned an old house off West 39th, with seventies-style cabinets that he constantly complained about but Farzan insisted he secretly loved. "How are you doing? Did they find your bags yet?"

Arya stuck out his tongue. He had his earbuds in and a crisp white baseball hat covering his bald head. He'd been growing out a short beard for the last month or so, and it framed his sharp jaw and thin, elegant lips.

"Not yet." Ramin set down his mug and swiped at his phone for a second, checking for missed emails or messages. "Nothing. I got some clothes and essentials, though. Where's David?"

Farzan glanced away from the screen for a second. "He's showering. Want me to get him?"

"No, no, it's nothing important. Just wanted to check in."

"Okay, great, yes, we're happy you are clothed. Now, have you found any dick?" Arya narrowly dodged around someone else on the sidewalk with an "Oop, sorry." Ramin caught a glimpse of a scandalized face. "The bigger the better."

Ramin sipped his tea and kept a neutral expression. That had only been a rumor anyway.

But, fuck, he must've done *something* with his face.

"You *did*," Arya said. "Tell us everything."

"I didn't," Ramin insisted.

"Okay, but *something* happened." Fuck, even Farzan could tell?

When Arya and Farzan ganged up on him, he always gave in. He blew out a breath.

"You guys remember Noah Bartlett? From high school?"

Farzan scrunched his eyebrows, but Arya nodded right away. "Hard to forget Noah's Ark."

Well shit.

"Oh yeah," Farzan said. "I do remember hearing some of the girls talking about his...ah. Ark."

"I'm pretty sure that was just a rumor," Ramin muttered. Even though he'd definitely heard more than one girl giggling about Noah being well hung. Part of him had wondered if it was true, but the noble part of him was mad at people talking about Noah behind his back in general.

And the closeted, horny part of him had wondered just how big they were talking, anyway.

But Noah had looked out for Ramin, stood up to bullies for him, and Ramin had always felt just as protective. He cleared his throat. "Even if it's true, it's his body, his business."

"Listen, I agree in principle," Arya said. "But I'm just saying, I *did* see him in a wrestling singlet freshman year, and I don't think he was done growing."

Ramin sincerely wished he had never brought this up. That he had gotten too drunk on wine and jet lag and had promptly fallen into bed and forgotten everything.

"Can we focus, please?" he asked, trying not to think about how his knee had brushed Noah's under the table during dinner.

"On what?" Arya asked. "Why are you asking about Noah Bartlett anyway?"

Ramin sighed and blew out a breath. "Because I ran into him at a gelateria."

Arya dropped his phone, if the clatter and sudden blackness was any indication. Another cracked screen protector, no doubt. Arya was keeping AppleCare in business single-handedly.

"Really? Noah Bartlett?" Farzan asked. "How do you know it was him?"

"Because he came up to me and asked if I remembered him from high school."

Farzan's jaw dropped.

"He was there with his son, who is adorable by the way, and his ex-wife. I guess they went to therapy and stayed friends."

"Gross!" upside-down Arya said before righting himself. "Fuck Todd by the way."

"Fuck Todd," Farzan echoed. "So, *did* you remember him?"

"Of course he did, Ramin had a huge crush on him. How's he looking? Still hot?"

Ramin nearly spat out his tea. "I did not." Except that obviously wasn't true. "Okay, well, I didn't know it back then." He sighed and fell back against the couch. "He's aged like fine wine."

Farzan's eyebrows arched upward. "Ooh, you get a picture?"

Arya cut in. "You get his number?"

"There wasn't time. He had to get back to his hotel."

"He couldn't take thirty seconds?"

"His son needed dinner."

Farzan cocked his head. "I thought they just had gelato."

Fuckety-fuck. Why did he have to have such observant friends?

"Fine. We met at the gelateria and went our separate ways, and then we met *again* when he happened to be walking by the place I was getting dinner at, and he ended up joining me."

"You're killing me! No, not you," Arya called over his shoulder. He turned back and brought his phone closer to his face. "Are you telling me that you, Ramin Yazdani, had a romantic dinner in Italy with your old high school crush?"

"It wasn't—"

"Who's having a romantic dinner?" David poked his head in next to Farzan. A still-damp shower cap hid his sponge twists. "Did you have any wine?"

"Ornellaia, and—"

"You're shitting me. Ornellaia? Really?" David closed his eyes and sighed. "That's a special wine. What year?"

"2020. But—"

"Nice. He must've been pretty special."

"It wasn't like that!" Ramin sputtered.

"It was his old crush from high school," Farzan said, giving David a kiss on the cheek. "You smell good, babe."

Ramin wanted to vomit.

"His big-dicked crush from high school," Arya added. His camera went wonky for a moment as he went through a door, and then Ramin saw the inside of Arya's favorite coffee spot on Wyandotte.

Ramin closed his eyes and wished he'd never opened his mouth. Never made this call in the first place.

He also wished, solemnly, that his friends would never meet Paola and Francesca. He wouldn't have worried about the odds of that happening, except he'd literally run into Noah Bartlett in Italy, so clearly the laws of probability were fracturing around him.

"We were just two old friends. Catching up. There was nothing romantic about it, and there was no discussion of dicks of any kind. Okay?"

His friends all stared at him.

"Listen. I came here to get away from everything. To reinvent myself. Not to rekindle my old crush on a straight boy. Well, man."

Farzan narrowed his eyes. "How exactly do you know he's straight? Did he tell you?"

"Well, no," Ramin said. "But he only dated girls in high school."

"Okay, but it's not like any of us were out then. He could be bi or pan or anything."

Ramin ran a hand through his hair. His friends weren't listening.

"It doesn't matter even if he is. We caught up, and then we said our goodbyes. It's not like we'll run into each other again. Now can we talk about something else?"

"Okay, fine," Arya said. "Just a sec, let me put my order in."

But Farzan muttered, loud enough for Ramin to hear, "Stranger things have happened."

ten

Noah

Light streamed in through the window. Noah blinked and grumbled. His body felt like it was full of sand. Was this jet lag? Or just being thirty-eight?

He rolled over and scratched his chest. Maybe it was both.

Or maybe it was a hangover. Not from wine but from Ramin.

He couldn't remember feeling so happy, so at peace, in a long time. So like the version of himself he liked best. He missed being that Noah. The Noah who smiled easily, who laughed loudly, who was excited for the future. Who had friends and community and more going on than just keeping track of work contracts and Jake's appointments. He liked his job, and he loved his son, but last night was the first time in a while that he'd done something just for him.

And Ramin...Ramin hadn't changed a bit. Well, he had, of course he had, but he was still the same smart, kind guy he'd been when they were teenagers. Except now his shyness was gone, replaced with the sort of quiet confidence that Noah had never quite managed. Confidence to be himself.

What kind of man could look Ramin Yazdani in the eyes—those beautiful eyes—and tell him he was *boring*?

Ramin was the opposite of boring.

And Noah wanted to kick himself for not getting Ramin's number. He'd been too distracted (and, okay, maybe a little buzzed) and hadn't realized until he got back to the hotel that twice, now, he'd failed to ask.

He'd been lucky to run into Ramin twice, but what were the odds he'd get a third chance? And he wanted one. Desperately.

He rubbed his eyes with the heels of his hands. His flirting game was *so* out of practice. Nothing had worked—not the smiles, not the brushes of their legs under the table, not the fleeting hand contact. Ramin just wasn't into him.

Or—oh God—Ramin was still heartbroken from his breakup.

Noah groaned. He was an insensitive jerk. Of course Ramin wasn't over it yet. Even if he liked Noah, Noah had plowed right over his hurt, smashed through his boundaries, made a total fool of himself.

But he couldn't help it. Ramin was there. *Right there.* There was a spark between them. He knew it. There always had been, even if they hadn't entirely understood it. And Noah hadn't sparked with anyone in a long time. He'd let the warmth of it override his better judgment.

And now Ramin was gone again. It had taken all of one evening for Ramin to take up space in Noah's heart again, and now he ached in the shape of that loss. They'd connected, Noah knew they had, even if only as friends, and now those threads were severed.

Again.

And Noah was alone.

Noah had to shampoo twice to get the smell of smoke out of his hair. Seriously, why was everyone in Italy still smoking like it was 1995? Last night's clothes carried the distinct scent of Eau de Smoking Section at Perkins.

While Angela finished getting ready, Noah sat down next to Jake and they both pulled on their shoes. Noah missed when Jake still needed help tying his. Or even when he did bunny ears.

Yeah, he wasn't a cool world traveler like Ramin. Yeah, he was divorced and estranged from his parents. Yeah, life had gone differently than he expected. But he'd never regret Jake. Jake was the best thing he ever did.

"Dad?" Jake's voice was small.

"Yeah, buddy?"

"You're smiling weird."

Noah laughed and mussed Jake's hair. "Just thinking how much I love you."

Jake laughed. But then his face went serious.

"You remember that guy we met yesterday?"

"Ramin?"

"Yeah."

How could Noah forget?

"What about him?"

Jake shrugged. "He had an awesome face."

"He did." He really did. "He was a good friend."

"How come I never met him before?"

"I don't know. We fell out of touch after high school."

Jake frowned. "Are we going to fall out of touch?"

"What do you mean?"

"If I move with Mom."

Whatever the emotional equivalent of stepping on a Lego brick was, that's what Noah felt. Times a million.

"Never." Noah pulled Jake into a hug.

He didn't want his son to move. He didn't want to lose Jake.

But even if they were half a world away, he'd always be Jake's dad. He'd call every day. Twice a day. Whatever it took.

"You promise?"

That was one promise, at least, Noah knew he could keep.

"I promise."

"Okay." And then Jake stood, brushed off his shorts (even though they were clean), and let out a whole-body sigh, like he'd just finished a twelve-hour shift in a coal mine instead of an emotional heart-to-heart with his dad.

Sometimes his son was a complete mystery to him. But he wouldn't change a thing about him.

"Mom! We're ready!"

Noah held Jake's hand and followed Angela to the subway station. Noah thought maybe she'd want to rest more, but no. After a good night's sleep, she was ready to begin the Death March of Fun: Day Two.

Stucco buildings hemmed them in on all sides, painted white and red and pink and amber and occasionally lilac. Heat and humidity pressed in on them, even in the shade, as they dodged bikes and scooters and power-suited business folks talking on phones and smoking cigarettes.

"Are we there yet?" Jake asked with a sigh as they followed Angela down the stairs into the subway station.

"Not yet," Noah said. "I thought you wanted to ride the subway?"

Jake used to like trains, at least.

"I'm hungry."

"We're headed to lunch," Angela said. "A place Nonna recommended. Near the Duomo."

"What's that?"

"The big cathedral." Noah rubbed his cross. He'd never been Catholic—his parents had been firmly Baptist, and he was nondenominational himself—but he was excited to see the Duomo. He loved architecture.

They hopped onto the crowded subway, passed a few stations, until the automated announcement came in Italian and then in English: "This is Duomo. Doors open on the right."

Angela took Jake's hand and Noah followed close behind, up more escalators than he could count, down long corridors, emerging into blinding daylight at the final staircase up to the Piazza del Duomo.

Noah's jaw dropped.

Pinnacles and spires reached for the clear blue sky. White marble with blue-gray swirls shone in the daylight. Statues dotted every flying buttress. High above, barely visible, a golden cross and statue of the Virgin Mary gleamed.

The cathedral was *enormous*.

His own church back home was a converted Popeyes Chicken that had gone out of business (Pastor Josh always joked it would've been too on-the-nose if it had been a Church's Chicken), but it was perfect to Noah: cozy, humble, with room for Jake to play with the other kids, a flagpole out front flying a Progress Pride flag, and, most importantly, a version of God that meant loving everyone instead of controlling them.

Noah loved his church. But the Duomo…well, the Catholics certainly knew how to make a statement.

He wished he had his sketchbook with him. And that Angela had budgeted time for him to sit and draw it.

"So," Angela said. "How was—*ack!*"

She flinched as a pigeon zipped by her head. Thousands of its fellows strutted along the gray and white stones of the piazza. Tourists snapped photos, admired the Duomo and surrounding buildings, tried to feed the birds. Jake clung to Angela's side as another one zipped by, but then he laughed.

"You all right?" Noah asked.

"We're fine." She oriented herself and started cutting through the crowd, a gentle but firm grip on Jake's hand. Over her shoulder she called, "What'd you end up doing last night?"

Noah pulled out his phone to snap a few photos. "I actually ran into Ramin again at a little restaurant. We ended up eating together."

Angela's eyebrows slowly raised, a move he remembered all too well. It meant she could tell there was more there but was waiting for you to say something she could use to pin you down. It was probably why she was such a great lawyer.

"You didn't tell me!" Jake frowned. "I wanted to have dinner with Ramin!"

"Jakey, you were asleep."

"You could've woken me up."

Noah looked from Jake to Angela, whose eyebrows had gone from skeptical to bewildered.

"You're always doing things without me!"

"Jake..." Noah didn't know what to say. His whole life revolved around Jake. The only things he did without Jake were work and the gym.

Where was all this coming from?

"Jake," Angela said. "Your father's allowed to have friends."

"I guess," Jake muttered. But he clung to Angela as they made their way through the piazza.

Noah prayed it was just Jake's hunger talking. Or jet lag. He didn't understand it. Truly.

Noah and Jake had always been close. All through Jake's childhood, Noah had been the one who did most of the parenting. He was around more, and he was more suited to it, too. Angela had never been the most patient. Her decisiveness had always served her well as a lawyer, but Jake wasn't a witness to be deposed. He was a child, and sometimes he needed to get his feelings out, even if those feelings didn't make sense. Sometimes he needed to make his own choices, even if they were different from those Angela or Noah would make. Sometimes he just needed to try and fail at things, because how else was he going to learn?

Noah had always, always done better with Jake. So how had it come to this? Why was Jake suddenly mad at him all the time?

"It's just a phase," Angela said softly as she studied the map on her phone. "Don't take it personally."

"I know." That didn't make it any easier.

They skirted the edge of the piazza and the Galleria Vittorio Emanuele II, an enormous glass-ceilinged shopping center with open arches wide enough to drive a semi through. They passed high-end fashion stores, a gelato cart (thankfully Jake was looking the other way), and even a busker playing an impressive rendition of "Shine On You Crazy Diamond," before turning down a narrow side street.

"Here we are." Angela looked up from her phone. "Oh."

Oh was right. There was a line of people down the block and back up, all waiting to get through a set of double doors leading into a literal hole in the wall.

Angela frowned and looked back at Noah. Had she factored in lines when scheduling the Death March of Fun?

He shrugged. "Nonna said it was good, right?"

Angela nodded and tucked her phone into her tactical satchel. "She said to try the panzerotti."

"Dad?" Apparently Jake was talking to him again. "Did you and Ramin have mac and cheese for dinner?"

"No. We both had risotto."

"Oh." He sighed, like Noah had just dropped the weight of the world on his shoulders. "I guess that's okay then."

"Thanks, buddy. He owns a restaurant back home. Maybe we can visit when we get back."

"Yeah? Do they make mac and cheese?"

Angela met Noah's eyes. Her nostrils flared and her lips pressed together, a sure sign she was holding in a laugh. Noah grinned. Angela always looked cute when she was trying not to laugh, which thankfully didn't work that often. It was the first thing Noah fell in love with, back when they were young and first dating, and she'd made that face when Noah told a terrible joke.

He didn't miss those days. Not exactly. And he didn't exactly miss being married to Angela. But he missed the version of himself that had been married. A man whose life was on course. A man who knew what he was doing.

Not a man dwelling on a twenty-year-old unrequited crush while waiting in line for fried dough.

Finally they made it into the bakery.

"What d'you want, Jakey?" Noah asked. "Mozzarella and tomato?"

"Yeah!"

"What about you?" Angela asked.

"Hot salami?"

Angela ordered for them in halting Italian—when had she picked *that* up?—and Noah collected their orders.

"Don't burn your—" Noah began, but Jake had already bitten into his panzerotti. He curled his lips back and breathed through his teeth.

"—mouth," Angela finished. She met Noah's eyes and they shared a long-suffering sigh at their son's expense.

Noah bit into his own panzerotti—a pocket of fried dough filled with tomatoes and mozzarella and hot salami—far more carefully. The pastry was short and crunchy and salty, the filling spicy and savory, though he could feel the oil escaping the paper wrapping to trail down the outside of his hand. He should've grabbed napkins; instead, he had to lick it off.

They found a quiet spot of sidewalk to enjoy their panzerotti, Jake sitting on the curb, Noah and Angela standing above him.

"This is nice, huh?" she asked.

"Mm-hmm," Jake mumbled around his food.

"I love how walkable it is here. Everything's so easy to get to. Plus the subway."

"Yeah." It *was* nice.

If Milan hadn't been so walkable, he never would've bumped into Ramin again.

"I don't know if I'll move here or close to Bellagio, like Nonno and Nonna. I've still got a lot to decide. Plus I need to figure out the whole school situation."

Ah. She didn't mean *nice* as in nice to visit. She meant *nice* as in *Wouldn't it be nice if I moved here with Jake?*

And maybe it would. It *was* nice here. Milan had a good vibe. Everyone seemed happy, and no one was in a rush (except for other tourists on their own Death March of Fun).

It was nice, but Noah didn't want it to be. He wanted to argue with Angela. He wanted to point out that it was far from home. That none of them spoke the language. That Jake didn't know anyone here. All his friends were back home. His school. Heck, Angela's own parents and siblings were there!

Noah was, too.

But he had to be objective about this. Give Italy a fair shake.

He wasn't his parents. He'd do what was best for Jake. He'd *ask* Jake and let him decide what was best for himself. Even if it hurt Noah.

That's what being a dad meant.

eleven

Ramin

Twenty Years Ago

Ramin was crying.

He never cried at school. *Never.* He'd learned that lesson back in first grade, when he'd cried because the other kids kept getting his name wrong, and they'd switched to calling him a crybaby.

But he couldn't help it. Who *wouldn't* be crying if their mom had cancer?

Fuck cancer.

He hunched his shoulders as high as they would go, slouched as low into his desk as he could, hoped no one would notice.

"Hey," Noah said.

"Hey," Ramin muttered, not looking up as Noah flopped into the seat next to him. Ramin wasn't sure how, exactly, Noah had decided they were...what? Friends? Noah had just started talking to him one day and never really stopped. And then he'd started sitting with Ramin at lunch, too.

It made no sense: Noah was a popular guy. He was a wrestler. All the girls talked about him.

(All the girls talked *a lot* about him. Ramin didn't think about *that*, though.)

Noah was the kind of guy who should've been bullying Ramin like all the other jocks, shoving him into lockers and calling him names. Instead, he told off folks for being mean to him. He shared jokes and borrowed pencil lead and treated Ramin like a friend. Ramin didn't *have* friends. Just Farzan and Arya, and they were more like brothers than anything.

Even they hadn't heard the news about Ramin's mom. He hadn't found a way to tell them.

"You okay?"

He didn't want to talk about it. If he did, the crying would only get worse. "I'm fine."

"Are you crying?" came the soft reply.

"No." But sure enough, he started crying harder.

Noah scooted closer. "What's wrong?"

Ramin shook his head. He couldn't, he couldn't, he couldn't—

"My mom has cancer."

He didn't know why he'd said it. It had slipped out of him. He wished he could snatch the words back from the air.

"Oh." Noah's voice was so gentle, it felt like he'd draped a blanket over Ramin's shoulders. "I'm so sorry."

Ramin just cried harder. Because he could tell Noah really meant it.

He shouldn't have. Noah Bartlett wasn't supposed to be that kind of guy. He wasn't supposed to be nice and compassionate. He should've been making fun of Ramin, like all his teammates did, like every single asshole in their class did.

A hand slipped through the crook of Ramin's elbows, clutching a handful of Kleenex.

"Thanks," Ramin managed through sniffles.

"Anytime."

Ramin blew his nose and wiped at his tears and cried, while Noah Bartlett, of all people, shielded him from the rest of the class.

He didn't know what to make of it.

But he was grateful.

⌒

Now

Ramin woke covered in sweat. He twisted and flung off his blankets. The small air conditioner over the door kicked on, and he eyed it suspiciously; sure enough, it was on some sort of motion sensor. What was the point of an air conditioner that wouldn't keep you cool while you slept?

His morning wood felt like a steel bar trapped in his trunks. He'd noticed over the last few years how he didn't wake up as hard as he used to, but that wasn't the case today.

He'd been dreaming about Noah.

Not a sex dream. Well, they hadn't gotten to that. In his dream, rather than go their separate ways last night, they'd gone back to Noah's hotel, taken a weird glass elevator that went sideways to his room, where Noah had pressed him up against the door. He'd used his strong arms to pin Ramin's wrists above his head, leaned in close, and whispered, *I know you want to know if it's true.* His lips had brushed Ramin's jaw, which made Ramin sweat, which made him realize he was actually sweltering, which made him wake up.

He wasn't sure if he was relieved or disappointed.

He rolled out of bed, figured out how to turn off the air conditioner's motion sensor, took a shower, checked on his bags—still on a European adventure of their own—and got dressed. He didn't let himself think about Noah. He'd never see Noah again. Last night was fun—borderline magical—but it was an anomaly.

He was here to have lots of sex with hot Italian men he'd never see again. Or at least average-looking Italian men, since that was what he could reasonably expect to attract. Hot men didn't go for guys who looked like Ramin. He was soft, with stretch marks and loose skin and gray nose hairs...

Ramin shook himself. He'd gotten better at snapping himself out of dysmorphia-induced spirals, but they still crept up on him sometimes. He'd been fat as a teenager, skinny after his mom died, fat again when his dad died, and then there was the whole disordered eating thing he went through in his mid-twenties, until Farzan and Arya had more or less bullied him into therapy.

The therapy had changed his life—saved it, really—introducing him to yoga and meditation, and helping him unlearn all sorts of harmful shit he'd internalized over the years. His body was strong and capable and beautiful, even if he wasn't (never had been, never would be) a picture-perfect twink.

He was healthy. That's what mattered.

He rubbed at his tattoo and took a few breaths. Then he laced up his shoes, fought with the billion locks on his door, and went in search of breakfast.

Ramin found the tattoo parlor by accident.

He'd eaten breakfast—a croissant (though the cafe called it a brioche for some reason) and a double espresso—and was heading home when he spotted it.

The entry was narrow, nestled between a pharmacy (advertised with a green cross, which had befuddled Ramin at first, because back home that meant a dispensary) and a little general store. The door and windows were covered in art in all different styles: graffiti script, black and white portraits, geometric designs, tribal motifs.

Ramin only had two tattoos, his parents' names in Persian script, one over each wrist, but every so often he thought about getting another. Or maybe several others. He'd always told himself he wanted to get in better shape first, especially before doing his chest, which had been at times bony, at times soft, at times a little flabby, but never muscled.

Nothing like Noah's, which had been much firmer-looking than Todd's, but from what Noah had said last night, he actually *used* his muscles instead of growing them for vanity. Ramin wondered what Noah's pecs felt like...

He shook the thought away. He wasn't here to wallow in an old crush. He was here to reinvent himself.

Maybe it was the drive to be Interesting New Ramin. Or maybe it was lingering exhaustion and jet lag. But fuck it.

He stepped inside and hoped the tattoo artist spoke a bit of English.

twelve

Noah

How long till we get there?" Jake asked, staring out the bus window.
It was forty-five minutes to Como, and from there another
forty-five minutes if they caught the faster ferry to Bellagio, where
Nonno and Nonna had their wine shop.

"That's so long," Jake sighed. "Can I use your phone, Dad?"

"If you use it on the ride, you can't use it again until the ride back.
Deal?"

"Deal," Jake said.

Noah handed the phone over. Thankfully Jake's grumpiness had
eased after another night's sleep.

Angela shot Noah a half-fond, half-amused look across the aisle as
the shuttle rumbled to life and pulled out of the station.

It was exhilarating and a bit alarming as they navigated the streets
of Milan before finally reaching the freeway. While Angela sat next
to Jake, Noah had ended up next to a German backpacker who had
promptly fallen asleep against the window. He peered around them for
a glimpse of the far-off Alps, clusters of villas, parks, churches, a small
university, even a few fields of corn.

Noah pulled his sketchbook out of his pocket.

When he was younger, he used to draw a lot, at least until his parents had told him he was never going to be an artist, so why not focus on something practical instead? But he'd gotten back into it after the divorce. Well, more specifically, after his therapist recommended it.

He used a cheap sketchbook with unlined paper, a soft cover, and an elastic loop for a small ballpoint pen. It was small enough to fit in his pocket, which left no room for the grand landscapes or detailed portraits he preferred, but it was *something*, and it was *his*.

Meanwhile Angela kept pointing things out to Jake in an overly enthusiastic voice, like she was trying to convince him how awesome Italy was, but she was laying it on way too thick. Jake *always* got suspicious if you hyped something up too much, even when he was a toddler and could barely speak. When Noah had tried to convince him carrot sticks were good by playing up how tasty and crunchy they were, Jake had stuck one up his nose just to prove a point.

Honestly, Noah wished he had a picture. Frustrated as he'd been, it was hilarious. One of Noah's favorite memories.

Noah admired Angela's intelligence, but sometimes he wondered if all that college made it hard for her to remember what it was like to be a child, to not know anything about the world except what your own little hands could grab at. She'd been great when Jake was a baby, but once he started developing his own little personality (and once he'd been able to argue), she'd struggled.

Angela loved Jake with her whole heart. On that front, she and Noah were exactly the same. But when it came to the little things—getting Jake to brush his teeth at night, or letting Jake Calvinball the rules of a board game, or helping him build a Lego set—parenting had always come much easier to Noah than to her.

Maybe this whole moving thing was her way of balancing the scales. Noah couldn't blame her for wanting that.

He didn't have to like it, though.

The shuttle dropped them off by the train station, at the top of a tree-lined hill. Angela ushered them off the bus, anxiously checking her phone.

"You need the bathroom, Jakey?"

"He can use it on the ferry," Angela said. "The dock is that way."

Noah pressed his lips together but didn't argue with her. They tried not to argue in front of Jake.

Despite her short legs, Angela had a long stride, and she was walking faster than Jake could manage. Noah took him piggyback to keep up.

"You good, buddy?"

"Yeah." But suddenly Jake let out a huge belch.

"Excuse me."

"Jake!" Angela admonished.

"I said excuse me!"

"Your tummy okay?" Noah still remembered last year's stomach flu. He didn't want to be caught in the blast zone.

"Yeah."

They cut through narrow streets lined with shops and banks, a small park with fascinating sculptures, took another left, and then—

Then Noah saw it.

When Noah was a kid, his dad had loved fishing at Osage Beach. The Ozarks formed the backdrop for what few uncomplicated good memories Noah had of growing up. Quiet days with his dad teaching him to fish, encouraging him to try again instead of berating him for failing. Nights filled with the hum of cicadas, his mom cooking hot dogs on a charcoal grill, laughing as he chased fireflies instead of yelling at him to keep his shoes clean.

Noah loved the Lake of the Ozarks, but Lake Como was a million times better.

Mountains dense with green and orange trees rose on every side.

Vibrant yellow-beige-pink buildings climbed the slopes. Puffy white clouds sailed by, silent barges on an endless voyage through a sky so blue it redefined the word. And stretching into the distance, shimmering in the morning light, lay Lake Como itself.

A cool breeze ruffled Noah's hair. The sound of gentle waves against the docks settled into his soul.

"Wow."

He let Jake down but kept a hand on his head as he stared, slack-jawed, at the water.

He hated to admit it, but maybe Angela had a point.

Italy *was* awesome.

Noah pulled out his phone to snap some pictures, but Angela kept power-walking toward the dock. "Come on, guys, we gotta go."

Noah sighed and took Jake's hand. Angela had always been an *on time is late* type person. Granted, Noah always showed up to work fifteen minutes early—the surest way of getting the other folks in the union to hate you was tardiness—but when you had a kid, sometimes you couldn't help it. Still, he supposed they had a boat to catch.

"Do you think there's fishing?" Jake asked as they headed down the boardwalk. He burped again. "Sorry."

"Just cover your mouth, buddy. And probably, but I don't think we can do it from the ferry."

"Aw man." Jake's shoulders slumped melodramatically.

The line for the ferry—a triple-decker blue and white boat with red awnings—bottlenecked on the narrow gangway as everyone stopped to get their tickets scanned.

"Let's go to the front!" Jake shouted, once they finally made it aboard. He charged toward a row of seats near the metal railing at the bow.

"You sure you don't want to sit in the shade?" Noah asked. The sun was bright and hot, even with the breeze to cool them, but Jake shook his head, and so they all filed in, Noah and Angela sandwiching Jake between them.

A few seats away, a young couple stood against the railing, playing a fairly intense game of tonsil hockey. Noah thought of Ramin, of the weird, inexplicable draw he'd felt as a teenager who thought he was straight, of the soft, quiet attraction that had reignited at dinner the other night.

He wondered what Ramin's lips felt like. Not that he'd ever get to find out. He wished again he'd gotten Ramin's number.

It was okay, though. He was here with Jake, having an adventure. That was enough. *More* than enough.

"I'm glad you're with me, buddy," he said, dropping a kiss onto the crown of Jake's head.

The boat filled quickly. Groups started splitting to find separate seats. Some folks had given up completely and stood around the rails instead. As an announcement in Italian played over the loudspeakers, people jostled to Noah's left, the last folks aboard trying to find what seats they could. A few groups of friends split up. Families stuck their kids on seats and stood hovering over them. Noah scanned the crowd. The seat next to him was still open.

He was about to have them all scoot over, so maybe someone could get in on the aisle, when he heard something.

A familiar voice.

No. It couldn't be.

"Scusi. Sorry. Is that seat taken?"

High and clear. Noah's heart skipped a beat.

It *couldn't* be.

Noah held his breath and turned to find a pair of familiar green eyes, widened in surprise.

"Noah?"

thirteen

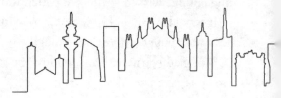

Ramin

It *was* Noah. Sitting there, next to Jake and Angela, in a clean white T-shirt, the kind that Hollywood actors always seemed to be able to pull off.

"Ramin?" Noah gifted him a smile so bright, Ramin squinted behind his sunglasses. "I can't believe it!"

Ramin couldn't believe it, either. He'd looked it up: Once is an accident, twice is coincidence, three times is enemy action.

Ramin didn't *think* he had any enemies, unless you counted Robert in accounting, but that was just a big misunderstanding...

Or maybe third time was the charm. But the charm of...what? It wasn't like anything was going to happen between them.

Maybe this was a tattoo-fueled hallucination. Yeah. Maybe the needle had been laced with drugs and he was on one hell of a trip. Or maybe it was an allergic reaction. Did they use different inks in Italy? Toxic ones? He thought the European Union was usually ahead of the US when it came to removing toxins from things, but who knew?

Noah was still looking at him, though his smile had started to dim into a question. Maybe this was real after all.

"Sorry, I just…was not expecting to see you here. I had a bit of a brain fart."

Behind Noah, Jake let out a giggle.

"I was pretty surprised too," Noah said. "Where are you headed?"

"Bellagio. I heard it's nice?"

He'd picked Como on a whim—it was the next train when he showed up at Milano Centrale—but his seatmate had talked his ear off about how great Bellagio was. She lived in Milan but was headed to Como to catch a soccer game, and after giving Ramin advice on what to see, she'd spent the rest of the ride explaining Italy's Serie B football league to Ramin in intricate (some might say obsessive) detail.

"We are too!" Jake shouted, grabbing Noah's shoulder to pull himself up so he was kneeling on the chair. "Nonno and Nonna live there."

"Nonno and Nonna?"

"My grandparents," Angela said, peeking over Jake's shoulder.

"Oh. Cool." Great. He'd interrupted family time. "I didn't mean to intrude. I'll just—"

He glanced around, though the only seat he could see was the one next to Noah. Then again, standing the whole time wouldn't be so bad. Or being dragged behind the boat in a little life preserver. Or keelhauled.

"What? No, sit with us." Noah thumped the plastic seat next to him. "We're all headed the same way."

Jake was nearly bouncing out of his seat. "Yeah, and you have an awesome face!"

The compliment was so unexpected, so absurd, Ramin couldn't help but smile.

"No one's ever told me that before." He reached for his wrist, but the move chafed his plastic-wrapped chest. Why the fuck did he get a tattoo yesterday? He reached up to twist his studs instead. "You're sure you don't mind?"

"Positive," Noah said.

Ramin covered a wince and sat, accidentally knocking his legs into Noah's before he could snap them together. Noah was wearing longer khaki shorts today, and with the way he was sitting they pooched up in the front. Either that or it was just full, and—

No, nope, definitely not thinking about Noah's Ark. Ramin's own shorts were a proper gay five-inch inseam. He hoped his goosebumps didn't show.

"Dad? Can I have your phone?" Jake asked.

"Remember what you agreed to on the bus?" Noah asked. "No screen time until the way back."

Jack harumphed and crossed his arms, kicking his feet. He looked like the human equivalent of a Muppet, all loose limbs and goofy expressions, especially with one of his front teeth missing.

On Jake's other side, Angela was checking something on her own phone.

"Sorry for crashing your party," Ramin told her. "I know you're trying to have family time."

"It's fine." She gave him a wry smile. "You're in charge of entertaining them, though."

Ramin laughed. "Deal. Jake said your grandparents are in Bellagio?"

"They own a wine store there."

"Really?" That sounded kind of amazing, actually.

"You should come with us," Noah said, before turning to Angela. "Ramin knows a ton about wine."

Angela nodded, but she also gave Noah a *look*, and Noah gave her a *look* right back.

Ramin and Todd used to have their little *looks*, too. What did this one mean?

A final announcement played over the speakers, but Ramin couldn't make it out over the hubbub. Then, with a soft lurch, they were off. Ramin closed his eyes for a moment to enjoy the breeze in his hair, the sun against his face. The water was bottle-green all around them, reflecting the tree-lined mountains hemming them in. He took a deep breath of mountain air and sighed it out. When he opened his eyes, Noah was watching him.

"What?"

"You looked really content is all. You didn't used to smile so much."

"Senior year was tough."

"I remember." Noah's eyes softened. "Sorry for bringing it up."

Damn Noah. Straight people shouldn't be allowed to be so nice.

"It's fine." Ramin swallowed and fought back a blush. "Anyway. I love the water. Lakes, rivers. The ocean. Doesn't matter."

"Really?" Noah shifted, pressing his knee against Ramin's. For someone with ridiculously hairy forearms, Noah didn't actually have much leg hair. There was a manspreader on Ramin's other side, so he couldn't pull away; he waited for Noah to do so instead, but he didn't.

Damn Noah for not being homophobic, either.

"I love the water, too. Growing up, my parents took me to Lake of the Ozarks all the time. I take Jake when I can, too."

At the sound of his name, Jake perked up. He pointed toward a collection of colorful buildings in the distance and asked, "Is that where we're going?"

"It's a little farther," Angela said. "And sit properly, please."

Jake planted his butt on the plastic seat and started in on an endless stream of questions about Bellagio: how big it was, how many people lived there, whether you could fish. Noah gifted Ramin another one of his sparkly eyed smiles.

He looked so beautiful then, his hair fluttering slightly in the wind. He brought a hand up to shield his eyes from the sun, giving Ramin a perfect view of his bicep in action.

Ramin made himself stare out at the lake.

He hadn't believed in God for a long time. Not since his mom got diagnosed with cancer. But it certainly felt like some sort of divine comedy of errors that he was here, stuck on a boat next to Noah. Why couldn't he have found a seat next to a handsome, single Italian man? He could be getting dicked down off the starboard bow or something.

Instead he had to sit here feeling Noah's body heat. Smelling his sweet, woodsy cologne. Listening to his deep, smooth voice as he talked to Jake.

This was going to be a nightmare.

"Are we walking the plank?" Jake asked, reaching for Ramin's hand as they disembarked. Ramin folded it into his, surprised how well it fit.

"Why? Did you mutiny?"

"Arrrr," Jake said, closing one eye and making a hook with his free hand.

Ramin laughed, guiding Jake to the side once they'd reached land so Noah and Angela could catch up.

"Okay, have fun today," he said, but Jake held on.

"Do you have to go?"

"Uh…" He did. Right? They were on a family vacation. He was just…wandering. He looked to Noah for help.

Rather than helping, Noah just smiled. "Don't you want to at least see the wine store?"

"Uh…"

Ramin waited for Angela to object—*someone* had to be the voice of reason—but she was on her phone, turning on the spot so the compass would align. Ramin *did* like wine. And Jake was still holding his hand, and seemed comfortable, and he was so adorable with that mop of chestnut hair.

"Please?" Jake smiled up at him, gap-toothed, brown eyes glowing with warmth. He had his father's eyes.

Fuckety-fuck. Ramin had never been able to resist Noah's eyes.

"All right."

fourteen

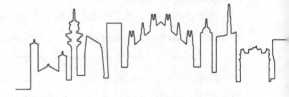

Noah

The dock at Bellagio spilled out onto a curving road where cars and the occasional Vespa zipped by. On the other side, shops and restaurants with colorful awnings glowed in the morning sun. Narrow alleyways marched up the slope, lined with more shops.

It looked like a postcard. Like a painting from someone else's life. It looked perfect.

Noah pulled out his phone to snap a few pictures, but Angela was already moving. "We gotta go!" she called over her shoulder.

Noah met Ramin's eyes for a moment; Ramin shrugged and led Jake up the slope, leaving Noah to bring up the rear.

He sighed and tucked his phone away. He could get photos later.

The town bustled with folks strolling in the sun, popping in and out of shops, laughing and smiling. Noah could imagine Jake happy here. He could imagine himself alone at home, too. He stuffed that down. This was about what Jake wanted, not what he wanted. When Jake glanced back, Noah put on his best smile. If Jake moved here—if this is what he chose—Noah would be heartbroken, but he'd support his son no matter what.

Jake turned forward again, swinging his hand in Ramin's, taking in the scenery with open wonder. The sight warmed Noah's heart.

The sight of Ramin in those short shorts warmed a different body part entirely. Ramin's legs and butt looked amazing as he climbed the slope. Noah almost pulled his phone out, but that would've been totally inappropriate.

And thank goodness he didn't, because Ramin glanced over his shoulder and nearly caught Noah staring. Noah pretended to be looking at the nearest store window. Ramin had made it clear in a thousand unspoken ways that they were only friends. Noah had to respect that boundary, even though every cell in him yearned to smash it down.

The noon sun beat against the back of Noah's neck, and he hoped he'd put on enough deodorant. Ramin always smelled good, like citrus and leather, though now mixed with sun and sweat. The breeze kept sending whiffs in Noah's direction.

He reached down to adjust his tightening boxers.

"What's salita?" Jake asked, pointing to a stone placard hung on the corner of a building—Italy's version of a street sign.

"It means 'climb,'" Ramin said. "That's what they call a narrow street like this that goes up."

Jake nodded sagely. "I'm hungry."

"We're nearly there. We're looking for Salita Serbelloni," Angela said over her shoulder. "Keep up, guys!"

Ramin's eyes widened and met Noah's for a moment, but Noah shook his head. There was no future in getting between Angela and her schedule.

Angela made a right turn that had them going back downhill, then paused in front of a little shop with a dangling metal sign in the shape of a wine bottle. A few oddly angled steps led up to the bright orange door where a sign read ENOTECA ROSSI.

"Here we are!" Angela reached for Jake, who let go of Ramin to take his mom's hand. Ramin rubbed at his tattoo, like he missed the warmth of Jake's hand, and Noah's heart nearly burst. Ramin was radiant. He was brighter than the sun, and Noah had lived too much of his life in shadow.

Ramin caught his eye, and this time Noah was too slow looking away.

"You okay?" Ramin asked. He scratched at his collar, where a few black chest hairs poked out. Noah wondered what they felt like. "Nervous?"

No, but that was a good enough excuse.

"A bit."

Ramin gave him a soft, dimpled smile. His stud earrings sparkled, even though they were in the shade. "You need a sec?"

"Nah."

"You didn't get any pictures earlier."

"It's fine." It was sweet of Ramin to notice, though. "Come on. Don't you want to taste some wine?"

Ramin's smile broadened. "Always."

"Dad!" Jake shouted as soon as Noah opened the door. "Can I get one of these?"

He held up a bottle of bright yellow limoncello. Noah laughed and let Ramin in behind him. "I don't think you're old enough to buy alcohol just yet, buddy. Even in Europe."

Jake studied the bottle with a puzzled look. "I thought it was lemonade."

Noah mussed Jake's hair and stepped in to greet Angela's grandparents.

Nonno and Nonna—Tomaso and Maria Russo—were talking to Angela, but when Maria spotted Noah, she immediately pulled him into a hug.

"Noah! Every time I see you, you get more handsome." Her voice was smoky, her English flawless, though every word ended with a consonant so heavy it nearly became a vowel again. Maria was short and plump, like Angela, with curly white hair piled high on her head. Her face was lined and suntanned, but her hands were strong as she pulled his face down to kiss his blushing cheeks.

"Every time I see you, you get more beautiful," he said in response. Granted, he hadn't seen her since the wedding, but she looked lively and happy and every bit how he'd imagined Angela looking as they grew old together.

Maria let out a musical laugh and swatted his chest. "How was the trip up? Any problems with the barca?" She shook her head. "The ferry?"

"No, it was great," Noah said. "We actually ran into an old friend of mine. Ramin?"

Ramin had tucked himself into a corner, where he was looking over a wall of bottles, a look of pure awe on his face.

"Huh?" Ramin blinked and shook himself. He approached, a shy smile making his dimples pop. "Sorry. Your store is beautiful. I was just looking at all the Gaja you have."

Nonna's limpid blue eyes lit up. "Oh, a man who knows his wine!"

Ramin offered a hand to shake, but Nonna pulled him in and kissed both cheeks. Ramin kissed back, like he'd done it a million times.

"I try."

"Allora, let's open a bottle." Maria dragged Ramin back toward the shelf.

"Nonna, we're supposed to go have lunch!" Angela called.

Maria waved her free hand, swatting the complaint away.

Noah had never been able to derail Angela's plans so smoothly. Angela shot him a look, but he just shrugged and joined Maria and Ramin.

"I don't want to be any trouble," Ramin said.

"It's no trouble." Maria glanced along the rows of bottles, each with GAJA in white block letters at the top of the label. "Noah's family, which makes you family."

Noah's chest warmed, and he looked away to hide his blush. Sometimes it annoyed him how much Angela took her family for granted, when Noah's own was a toxic mess.

"Tomaso! Portaci i calici!" Maria shouted at Tomaso, who was nodding along at a story Jake was telling. "And some chips!"

Tomaso was nearly as tall as Noah, though age had stooped him just a bit. He had kind brown eyes with little baggies under them that gave his whole face a friendly, slightly befuddled aspect. Or maybe it was his bushy dark eyebrows, which were still jet black despite his wild silver hair.

He set five glasses atop one of the wooden barrels that served as tables and pulled Noah into a hug. He smelled like musk and Irish Spring.

"What're you opening, Maria?"

"Noah's friend wants to try the 2016 Conteisa."

Ramin squeaked—actually squeaked—and shot Noah a panicked look, but Noah just shrugged as Angela brought Jake over. With practiced grace, Maria cut the foil and began opening the wine, but as she levered the cork out, it broke in half.

"Ah! Tomaso, grab another?"

"Please, it's fine! I don't mind," Ramin said.

"Nonsense. Don't worry, we'll try this one later. Maybe it's still good."

Ramin gave another one of those squeaks. Noah pressed his lips together to hold in his laugh.

Nonno swapped out the half-opened bottle for a fresh one. This one, Nonna opened with no problem.

While she poured the inky purple wine, Angela caught Noah's eye with a *Let's talk* look. He sidled away while Jake tucked himself between Nonna and Ramin. He looked right at home.

Noah's heart gave a little pang, but he shoved it down.

They retreated to a little corner near a row of those wine-dispensing machines where you could get little tastes of a bunch of different wines.

Angela bit her lip but didn't speak up, so Noah did.

"Nonno and Nonna seem happy to see you and Jake," he said.

"And you," Angela said. "You know they always liked you."

"So what's the matter?"

"Nothing."

But Noah knew that face.

"Angie…"

She sighed and tucked her hair behind her ear, which she always did when she was trying not to be confrontational. Which was funny, given how much of her life she spent in a courtroom, being confrontational on purpose.

"Did you have to bring your friend along?" she finally asked. "This was supposed to be family time."

"I thought you were okay with it," he said. "You didn't say anything. And Jake was so excited."

"I didn't want to be rude. But we're trying to figure out our future. Jake's future. It's hard to do that with an audience."

She glanced back toward the barrel, where the wine tasting seemed to have been interrupted by Jake wanting to examine Ramin's tattoos. Ramin stood with a patient smile on his face as Jake traced the black script with a finger.

Noah wanted to freeze time so he could draw this picture-perfect moment.

But he couldn't.

"I can ask him to leave," Noah said, though everything in him hated the idea.

"No! No. I'm fine with him along. I just don't want this to be our whole trip."

"It won't. I promise."

He caught Ramin watching them, gave a little smile and wave. Ramin turned away and stuck his nose back in his glass.

Noah's heart ached.

It had felt like providence, running into Ramin again, after all these years. Three times, no less! That had to be some kind of miracle. A second chance to rekindle a friendship that Noah hadn't even realized he missed.

Noah needed friends. Especially if he'd be losing Jake.

"Come on. Let's try this wine."

fifteen

Ramin

The Barolo was beyond exquisite. Notes of licorice and dark red fruits basically punched him in the face.

Granted, the bottle cost €600—even more than the Ornellaia—so if it *hadn't* punched him in the face, he would've been shocked. And Maria had just opened it without a second thought, all because he was a friend of Noah's. Who did things like that?

"I love Barolo." Maria stuck her nose in the glass, swirled it, took a long sip herself, then fixed Ramin with a sparkling smile and a wink. "It's a tough life."

"It's a tough life," Ramin agreed. Drinking Barolo on a sunny day in Bellagio. He could get used to this.

He absolutely *should not* get used to this. Wine and potato chips for lunch was not sustainable.

Neither was crashing his high school crush's family trip.

Jake still had his right arm in a gentle grip, tracing the tattoo on his pulse point over and over. Nasrin, his mom's name. His dad's name was on the other wrist. Noah sidled in on Ramin's left, so close their shoulders brushed. Ramin sucked in his stomach and lost another chest hair to the plastic wrap around his tattoo.

"What's that, Jakey?"

"Ramin's mom's name." He looked at up Ramin, his brows furrowed. "Dad says I can't do any body modification until I'm thirteen."

Ramin nearly spat out his wine trying so hard not to laugh. "That's not a bad rule. You have plenty of time."

"I guess." Jake huffed and reached for the crinkle-cut chips.

Noah smiled at Ramin and reached for his own taste of wine. Ramin did his best not to stare at Noah's throat as he swallowed, which meant he saw the pleasure sweep over Noah's face as it happened. His eyes popped open in wonder. "This is amazing."

"Right?" He stuck his nose back in his own glass to hide his blush.

How had he gotten himself into this?

"I can't decide which is better, this or the Ornellaia the other night."

Maria's eyes bugged. "When did you have Ornellaia?"

Ramin blushed. "Ah, we ran into each other at dinner two nights ago? My first night in Milan?"

Maria sighed. "That's a special wine."

"This one is, too," Ramin said, raising his glass. "Seriously. You didn't have to share it. But thank you."

Maria just winked at him again. "It's my pleasure."

Ramin kind of wanted her to adopt him.

"Okay, finish up your tasting, we have to go," Angela said.

"We're fine—" Noah began, but Angela shook her head.

"We're on a schedule."

Noah sighed and tossed back the last of his taste. Maria recorked the bottle and tucked it in the crook of her elbow. "We can finish this with lunch."

Sensing his escape—finally—Ramin set his glass down. "Thank you so much for letting me taste. I'd better—"

But Maria stopped him. "You and Noah can take the Vespa. There's not enough room in the car for six."

The what now?

"Oh, I'm not...I mean, I was going to eat in town—"

"Nonsense! Join us! There's plenty of food."

Ramin wondered if Maria was part Iranian, her taarofing skills were so masterful. How could he politely decline? He was weighing his options when Angela cut in.

"Nonna, none of us can drive a Vespa."

"Why not? It's safe. We just had it serviced. I drove it today."

"We don't have an international permit."

"You don't need that," Nonno said.

"It's recommended—" Angela began.

"I have one."

Ramin clamped his mouth shut. He shouldn't have said that out loud. Everyone turned to stare at him.

"Uh." He wanted to disappear. If only Maria hadn't taken the wine bottle away, he could've drowned himself with it. Or given himself a concussion. Or thrown it through the window and made a run for it.

So much for politely declining.

"I have a permit? If it helps?"

"Here we are," Tomaso announced after a sweaty climb up another salita, on which Ramin definitely did not stare at Noah's ass in his shorts.

Tomaso rested his hand on a tiny silver car. Next to it sat an azure Vespa with a matching helmet on top.

"We've got another helmet," Maria said. She dug in the tiny car's even tinier trunk, then thrust a plain black helmet into Noah's hands.

"You're sure you're okay with this?" Ramin asked one last time.

"You have to come!" Jake said, yanking on Ramin's arm. "Can I ride with Ramin?"

"Absolutely not," Angela spat, so loud Ramin jumped. She looked at him sheepishly. "Sorry, nothing against you, but—"

Ramin shook his head. "I get it." He knelt next to Jake. "It's my first time driving one of these, and it's safer for you in the car, okay?"

Jake pouted at Ramin, but it was so cute it only made Ramin snort. Jake really was like a Muppet in human form.

Jake seemed to realize it wasn't working, too, because he changed tactics. "Okay, what about next time?"

"He said no, Jake," Noah said. "You need to respect it when—"

"Fine!" Jake's face turned red. He spun away from Ramin. "I didn't want to ride it anyway."

Ramin blinked and stood, staring after Jake as he stomped over to the car.

"Ah, kids," Maria said, brushing his elbow. "He'll be fine."

She stood next to him as he mounted the Vespa and made sure he knew how to run it. "Just follow Tomaso. It's not far."

"Okay." Ramin took his seat, pushing down the panic mounting in his chest. Not at driving the Vespa—he was fine with that—but about sharing it with Noah.

"Sorry about Jake. Lately he gets mad at me whenever I say no to him."

"We all said no," Ramin pointed out.

"But I'm the one he's mad at."

The Vespa sunk into its suspension as Noah mounted up behind him. Ramin felt the warmth against his back even before Noah scooted close and brought his hands up to Ramin's side. Ramin sucked in his stomach as hard as he could.

Noah's arms were warm and firm and big. The last six months or so, Todd's embrace had changed, gotten so firm it wasn't entirely comfortable. But Noah's arms felt like being cradled.

Ramin made himself unclench his ass as Noah's powerful chest settled against his back. He breathed in deep. He was fine. Everything was fine. This was for safety, not for cuddles.

"You good?" Noah asked, so close Ramin felt the breath against the back of his neck. He thought about cold water, the lake below, wondered if it had that brain-eating amoeba he'd read was in some lakes in the States. Anything to stop himself getting hard.

Which would've been a lot easier if his brain wasn't trying to calculate exactly how much distance lay between his ass and Noah's Ark.

No, nope, no way. He accidentally revved the engine way too hard. "Sorry!"

"You're fine." Noah's voice resonated all the way through Ramin's chest.

How the fuck had he wound up here, swooning at a straight man's arms around him? Was this a cosmic joke? Had Todd put some sort of curse on him? Worse, had he cursed himself? Had he failed to make eye contact during a toast and consigned himself to seven years bad sex?

Well. Interesting New Ramin was supposed to be doing Interesting New Things. A Vespa ride through the hillsides of Lake Como counted. Even if it was with an old crush.

"Here we go," Ramin said. Noah's arms tightened, digging into his tattoo. Tomaso pulled away, and Ramin followed him onto the sunlit streets.

sixteen

Noah

Noah clung to Ramin as they zipped down the streets of Bellagio, the sun on his skin, the wind in his hair, but Noah barely noticed. He desperately thought about to-do lists at work and emails he hadn't sent and chores he'd neglected back home.

Anything to stop himself from getting hard.

It was nearly impossible, nestled up against Ramin's backside. His hands circling Ramin's chest. Ramin's scent filling his lungs. The Vespa's motor throbbing beneath only made matters worse.

On the one hand, this was the best thing ever. A totally platonic excuse to hold Ramin the way he'd been wanting to.

On the other hand, this was torture, because platonic was all it could ever be. Ramin wasn't into him like that. He was too busy mourning his breakup. He'd barely even looked at Noah the whole day. Maybe Noah should've helped him get away. He was clearly trying to avoid lunch. Angela would've been relieved.

But Noah *wanted* Ramin with them. He liked Ramin's company. Nonna was clearly smitten with him, too.

Plus, if Noah was busy entertaining Ramin, then Angela could have the one-on-one time with Jake she wanted. Give them both an idea of what it would be like, just the two of them. (Not that Noah wanted them to like it, but he pushed that thought away. That wasn't fair to Angela, and it wasn't fair to Jake.)

"You good?" Ramin called back.

"I'm good." As good as he could be when every muscle was tense with resisting the urge to dig his nose into that soft spot behind Ramin's ear, or rest his chin on Ramin's shoulder, or drag his teeth down the cord of Ramin's neck.

He tightened his grip a bit as Ramin hit the gas, and Ramin flinched.

"What?"

"Nothing," Ramin shouted back.

And then: "I might have gotten a tattoo yesterday."

"You *what*?" Noah hoped that didn't come out judgy. He wasn't critical, just surprised. "That's cool!"

"Not with all the chafing!"

Noah laughed, the tightness in his chest loosening. Who was this new Ramin? He never would've imagined the shy, quiet guy he knew twenty years ago would grow up to be a pierced and tattooed international man of mystery. The kind of man that knew who he was and what he wanted.

Noah wished he knew how to be that way.

The drive wound farther into the hills, away from the bustling city center, along a treelined street filled with quaint villas and apartments. People walked along the side of the road, on their way to the city or back home, laughing and talking and smiling in the sun.

Despite himself, Noah loved it. The blue sky above, the blue-green lake below, the friendly locals. Jake probably loved it, too. He really could be happy here, couldn't he? Fishing with Nonno, taking walks with Nonna, going to school, living in some sort of fancy villa with Angela. What did Noah have to offer compared to that? A cramped apartment, public school, no family but what the two of them made?

Unbidden, the image of Jake holding Ramin's hand popped into his mind. Of Jake tracing Ramin's tattoos with a gentle finger, Ramin softly explaining their meanings. Ramin listening patiently, like Jake was the most interesting person in the world, as he told a meandering story about the last time he and Noah had gone fishing in the Ozarks.

Noah shook himself. When had he taken his hands off the driver's wheel of his own life?

Where was the Noah who escaped his parents' house at eighteen? Who fell in love? Who cut off his parents when they became unbearably toxic?

He missed that Noah. He hadn't realized just how much.

But Ramin made him want to be that Noah again.

Tomaso and Maria lived in a small villa painted a cheery saffron yellow, with evergreen awnings on all the windows. As Ramin parked the Vespa, Angela helped Jake out of the car, just in time for him to let out a huge belch. "Excuse me," he said, rubbing his stomach.

"You okay, Jakey?" Noah's foot caught as he hopped off the Vespa, but Ramin was right there to save him from tripping. He gave Ramin a thankful smile and knelt by Jake to feel his forehead. He didn't know why; truth be told he'd never once been able to accurately diagnose a fever this way. But it made him feel better, and it made Jake feel better, too. "Car sick?"

Jake shrugged.

"He needs some food," Angela said. "All he had this morning was a banana."

"It won't take long," Maria said as Tomaso let them into the villa, the wine from earlier tucked under his arm. Noah hung back with Ramin and took in the view. They were near the top of a hill, and through a gap in the trees, they could see the lake below and the sky above. Big puffy clouds were rolling in, a bit gray on the bottoms. The breeze carried a hint of sweet petrichor.

Noah breathed in deep. "Smells like rain."

"I thought so, too," Ramin said. "Sorry for crashing family time. Again."

"Don't be," Noah said. "Just don't tell Jake about your new tattoo."

Ramin covered his face. "I don't know what I was thinking."

"I think it's cool," Noah said. "I hope you'll show it to me sometime."

Ramin's eyes went big. His cheeks turned red.

Noah hadn't meant it that way. But he wouldn't mind seeing Ramin with his shirt off. Or more, for that matter.

He wouldn't mind at all.

But that was no excuse for making Ramin uncomfortable.

"Sorry, that came out super weird!" Noah pinched at his cross. "I meant, maybe you can show me a picture of the design?"

"Oh. Yeah. Of course!" Ramin reached up to twist one of his earrings.

That was one disaster averted, but still, Noah really needed to get a grip.

He'd managed to control himself on the ride—barely—though it had left him feeling aroused and unsettled. He couldn't let his imagination run wild now, even if he really did wonder what Ramin looked like without his clothes on.

"Come on. Let's see if Maria needs help."

He let Ramin go first, so he wouldn't see Noah adjusting himself.

"Nonna!" he called. "What do you need us to do?"

seventeen

Ramin

The Russos' kitchen was magnificent, and roomy enough they could work without bumping into each other. An antique French stove stood in one corner. Blue tile backsplashes wrapped around every countertop. Photos of family hung on every free inch of wall space. Ramin caught some of Noah and Angela's wedding, and a few of Jake as a baby, but before he could find any more, Maria put them to work on a "light lunch."

Apparently, for Maria Russo, "a light lunch" involved four courses.

She put Tomaso to work on a dish of guinea fowl sautéed with leeks and braised in white wine with fresh green grapes, and she tasked Angela with slicing eggplants to fry them up Sicilian style. Meanwhile, Jake was in charge of soaking Pavesini in espresso—Maria swore the tiny cookies made better tiramisu than ladyfingers.

"Allora, you two can help me with the pasta," she announced to Noah and Ramin.

She got Noah cooking spinach and had Ramin help her make the fresh pasta dough.

"Ah, you've done this before?" she asked as Ramin gently whisked his fork in the egg mixture, occasionally using a few fingers to knock in more flour from the sides of the well.

"A few times." He'd gotten into a pasta-making kick a few years ago. In fact, he used to make it once a month, for him and Farzan and Arya. He hadn't done it much lately, though; Todd always said it was too many carbs.

Fuck Todd. Interesting New Ramin *loved* fresh pasta. He loved the soft mixing of egg and flour; he loved the sticky feel of the dough as it came together (even when it stuck to his knuckle hairs); he loved the quiet meditation of kneading until the pasta was a perfect ball with just the right amount of give.

When he was done, he set the dough aside to rest, covering it with a damp tea towel. While Maria went to check everyone's progress, Noah sidled up next to Ramin.

"You doing okay?"

Ramin nodded. "You have a lovely family."

"Yeah." Noah gave a soft smile then, his eyes lingering on Jake, whose fingertips were stained brown from espresso. "Thanks for joining us."

"Thank you for inviting me." Despite his earlier fears, he hadn't felt awkward as he joined in making lunch. He'd felt at home.

He'd felt like it was his family, too.

For so long his only family had been Farzan and Arya.

He didn't have words to explain that to Noah. Or to express just how much it meant to be included. To feel safe and warm and welcome somewhere. So instead he just said, "It meant a lot."

But that was Noah in a nutshell. Taking care of people. Making them feel seen.

Noah bumped their shoulders together. "I'm glad."

Ramin set the pasta machine to #6 and started cranking, keeping his left hand below the rollers to catch the dough. It was his last pass before it would get filled and turned into ravioli.

"You have good pasta hands," Maria said. "Your girlfriend must be very lucky."

Ramin pressed his lips together to stifle a squeak, but he could feel his ears burning, and not from his piercings. Should he just agree? Smile and nod?

He glanced around the kitchen and met Noah's eyes. Noah seemed to know what he was asking, because he nodded.

"Boyfriend," Ramin said. "Ex-boyfriend. We broke up."

"Che peccato!" Maria tossed another handful of flour onto the large wooden table that looked older than the house. "You know, Italy is for lovers. I'm sure you'll find a man."

"Maybe." He looked up and saw Noah watching him, though he turned to help Jake, who was having way too much fun grating cheese.

Todd had never helped much in the kitchen, aside from his meal prep, but here Noah was, getting his hands dirty, helping Jake without ever taking over for him. Letting him make mistakes and have fun.

It was pointless to compare Todd and Noah. Ramin knew that. Noah was straight and definitely not interested. Ramin didn't want that, anyway. He was Interesting New Ramin, Power Bottom. Not Sad Teenage Ramin, Closeted Virgin with an Unrequited Crush.

Still...he could see himself being with someone *like* Noah. Someone kind and thoughtful and present. Someone who laughed and smiled and didn't take himself too seriously.

He thought of Paola and Francesca back in Milan, wondered if they could hook him up with someone. If not for a date, at least for a good fuck. That's what he came here for. Not to be kidnapped by an Italian nonna and force-fed a four-course lunch.

Not that he was complaining. He couldn't wait to taste all the food they'd made.

While Tomaso took Jake and Noah into the yard to admire the lemon trees, Ramin hung back to clean up his work area.

"You do this every day, Nonna?" Angela asked.

"Only if we have company."

"It's so much work, though!"

Ramin silently agreed. Though he could maybe do it once a month, for his friends back home. He'd have to see if Maria would share her recipes.

"It's a joy. You know, life here is slower. We take our time and enjoy things. You'll get used to it when you move here."

"You're moving here?" Ramin asked.

Then realized how personal that was.

"Sorry. None of my business."

But Maria waved her hand. "You're practically family now. Angela's taking over our store. We want to retire."

"Oh. Wow. Congratulations." That sounded like a dream, honestly. "Are Jake and Noah coming too?"

Also none of his business. But why did the thought of Noah moving away bother him? It wasn't like he'd see Noah again. Although at least, with them both in Kansas City, there was a chance. A small chance.

"Jake might," Angela said.

Jake, but not Noah. Ramin had only known Noah again for a few days, but it was obvious Noah loved his son more than anything. Did Noah know about all this? He had to, right? That was the kind of thing co-parents discussed. Wasn't it?

"Wow," he said again. He didn't know what else to say.

"Allora, Ramin, can you get the boys?" Maria asked as she scooped the now-cooked ravioli out and dropped them into a pan of brown butter and sage. "It's time to eat."

Outside the villa, the rain had started, lashing the windows in heavy curtains of silver as they dug into the enormous meal.

Ramin wasn't usually a fan of eggplant (grounds for excommunication from the Iranian diaspora, to be honest), but the fried discs were savory and smooth and magical topped with grated Grana Padano and a garlicky tomato sauce. The guinea fowl melted in his mouth, juicy and complex with just a bit of acidity. The ravioli tasted like rich, heavenly pillows. Jake's tiramisu had come out a little lopsided, but it tasted oh so good.

And the wine, the rest of the Gaja Barolo, was a revelation. Ramin wanted to bathe in it. Shrink himself down and live in the bottle. He didn't know how he could ever love another wine again.

"Everything is amazing," Ramin said. "I can't believe we made all this. Thank you for letting me come."

"Of course, of course!" Tomaso boomed. "If we didn't have to drive, I'd get out the limoncello. Made from our lemons! Forty years and no pesticides."

Ramin's mouth watered. But he definitely wasn't going to risk driving tipsy. A glass of wine—maybe even two—he could handle with a big meal like this, but liquor? Better safe than sorry.

"Next time," Ramin said, then realized there wouldn't *be* a next time.

He'd never see any of these people again.

He didn't know why that made him so sad. Except that, for the last few hours, it felt like having a family again.

But he was Interesting New Ramin. He came through towns and homes like the wind, here and then gone, seeking out adventures. Not planting roots.

He polished off the last of his tiramisu. Everything tasted so good, he hadn't even measured his portions. He'd just taken whatever sized scoop Maria offered and finished every bite.

To his right, Jake's plate was still half full.

"You okay, Jake?" he asked.

Jake shrugged. Ramin frowned. He wanted to rub Jake's head the way Noah always did, but that seemed like a boundary not to cross. Instead he said, "What's wrong?"

"I don't feel so good," Jake muttered.

Noah, who sat on Jake's other side, did start rubbing Jake's hair. "What is it, buddy?"

"My tummy hurts." He swallowed. His face was turning red. "I think I have to *go*."

eighteen

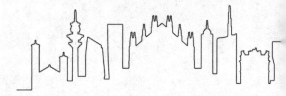

Noah

J akey?" Noah knocked on the bathroom door. "You still doing okay, buddy?"

"Don't come in!"

"I won't. Do you need anything?"

"No." His voice got smaller. "Don't be mad."

Noah dropped his voice, made it as gentle as possible. "I'm not. You can't help it if you don't feel well."

"Okay."

Noah pinched at his cross. Poor Jake. An upset stomach and an upset mother.

Angela was pacing back and forth in the living room, furiously swiping on her phone to check the ferry times. Angela had so many great qualities. She was feisty, intelligent, kind, organized, loving. But she'd never been particularly flexible, and when you had a nine-year-old, you needed to be.

Jake couldn't help an upset stomach. Maybe it was the different food in Italy, or maybe it was the stress of travel, or maybe it was just that sometimes people got sick.

Noah knocked again. "I'll be close if you need me. Just holler, okay?"

"Okay."

Noah popped his head in the kitchen, where Ramin was helping Maria and Tomaso with the dishes. He looked right at home, smiling as he scrubbed the ravioli pot, and Noah's heart swelled.

He shook himself. If he hadn't been so distracted with Ramin, maybe he would've noticed Jake wasn't feeling well sooner.

"All good?"

"Va bene," Maria said, elbowing Ramin. "I might steal his passport so he has to stay here."

Ramin laughed and blushed. Noah made himself turn away, heading toward the living room.

Angela was biting her lip and looking out the window, her phone held limply at her side.

"We'll be okay," he told her. "It's not like we're in Siberia. What's the worst that could happen?"

She sighed. "Nothing. I don't know. We have stuff to do in Milan tomorrow. If we don't make it back, we'll have to cancel, and it was really hard to get tickets to see *The Last Supper*, and I know you wanted to see it—"

"It's fine," he said. "Jake is more important."

"I know he is! You don't think I know that?" Angela snapped.

"Angela." Noah took a deep breath. "If you're going to get frustrated every time you have to adjust your plans because of Jake, you're going to spend your life here constantly frustrated."

"So, what, the answer is him staying with you? What kind of future is that?"

Angela's voice was dripping with disdain. She did that sometimes—in her more self-aware moments, she admitted she was "allergic to being wrong"—but Noah didn't miss that side of her.

Like usual, she regretted it right away.

"Sorry. That was…"

Unkind. Rude.

"Kind of bitchy, wasn't it?"

Noah shrugged. This is how it always went, when they fought. She got mad, said something mean in the heat of the moment, and always, always managed to poke the scabbed-over wound that Noah's parents had left him with. He'd had years of therapy, but that didn't mean he was magically better.

Noah kept his mouth shut. He wasn't going to agree with her, even if some part of him secretly did, because being mad at her wouldn't solve anything. Neither would name-calling. Or swearing.

She finally locked her phone and put it away to look at Noah.

"I didn't mean it that way. It's just..."

"Just what?" Noah was proud of himself for keeping his voice even and not lashing out in return. His therapist would say he was allowed to be angry back. But what kind of example did that set for Jake?

"Jake's life could be full here. With Nonno and Nonna. With a fresh start. He could learn another language, he could visit all of Europe, he could go to school without worrying about guns."

Yeah, that all sounded amazing. Especially that last point. When Noah thought about that, he was ready to sign Jake up for school here himself.

"I don't know how to say this without sounding mean, so I apologize in advance, but, Noah... you don't exactly have friends back home. You don't talk to your parents. You just go to work and go to the gym and come home, and your whole life is just Jake, Jake, Jake. You're going to smother him, and you're going to burn yourself out, and I worry about you. You're lonely, and our son can't be the solution to that. It's not fair to him."

Noah wanted to argue with her, but the knife she'd stuck in his heart was lodged too deep. It was one thing to think it to himself, but to hear Angela say it? How pathetic must he seem? No wonder she wanted Jake to move with her.

"That's not..." Noah began, but then Ramin stepped into the room, carrying a tray with tiny cups of espresso.

"Nonno thought you might like some," he said, way too brightly.

He must've overheard some of the conversation. But he didn't react, didn't do anything but smile his dimply smile at Angela as she took a cup, before turning it on Noah. It wasn't just his smile, it was his lake-green eyes, which were so full of kindness, Noah wanted to hide.

He wanted to hide and he wanted to pull Ramin out into the rain and do unspeakable and inappropriate things together, things Ramin wasn't ready for because he was still getting over his heartbreak, and maybe he didn't find Noah attractive the way Noah found him attractive anyway.

Instead, he managed to grunt out a "Thank you." He dropped a lump of sugar into his cup, gave it a stir, and took a sip. Some part of him registered that it was good, the roast dark but not too bitter, the crema nice and foamy, but he was too worried about Jake, too hurt from arguing with Angela, too worried she was right to taste much else.

"There's more if you want some," Ramin said, turning back, but he paused. His voice brightened. "Oh. Jake! You feeling better?"

In a flash, Noah was crouching next to his son, feeling his forehead. "Hey, buddy. You all better?"

Jake nodded. And then he let out another big burp.

Noah thought he was going to run back for the bathroom. But he just excused himself and asked if he was in trouble.

"Of course not. As long as you feel okay, that's all that matters," Angela said. But she pulled out her phone to glance at it, then nodded at Noah. "We'd better get going, though."

The rain had blown out, though the roads were still wet, misting Noah's face on the ride back into town. He closed his eyes and enjoyed the coolness on his skin. The warmth of Ramin in front of him. He wished he could stop time, that life could always be this—a lazy day, a delicious lunch, a beautiful man to wrap his arms around—but of course it couldn't. And besides, if life was always like this, then Jake would always be sick, and he would never wish that.

When Nonno pulled over to park, Ramin did as well, bringing them to a smooth stop.

"You sure this was your first time driving one of these?" Noah asked.

Ramin shrugged. "It wasn't so hard once I got used to it."

Noah wished he could say the same about the situation in his shorts. He let Ramin get off first and pretended to stretch his lower back to give himself time to deflate.

"Don't be a stranger," Maria said, cupping Noah's face before kissing his cheeks. "You're always family. Always. Don't forget."

Noah's chest tightened, his cheeks turning warm beneath Maria's hands. "I won't."

He wouldn't forget. But he wouldn't be back here, either. This was Angela's future, not his.

"Next time we'll go fishing!" Tomaso added.

Noah smiled. "That sounds nice."

He caught Maria holding Ramin's elbows. "Have a beautiful time here," she told him.

"I will. Thank you for your hospitality." Ramin's eyes twinkled. His earrings shone in the setting sun. "It's a tough life."

"It's a tough life!" Maria said with a laugh, pulling him in for another hug.

On the other hand, if somehow Ramin was here, too, then Noah wouldn't mind coming back.

They waved as Nonno and Nonna drove off, then joined the line for the ferry, which snaked back and forth across a wide piazza before extending down the street.

"We can still make it," Angela said, though Noah recognized the barest hint of anxiety in her voice, the little wobble that she fought so hard to hide from everyone.

And maybe they could have made it, if they'd been let onto the first ferry that came. Or the second. Or the third.

"They said they'll get everyone back to Como who wants to go," Angela said when she bustled back into line, her lips pressed flat. "As many ferries as it takes. But no guarantee on arrival time."

"We'll be okay." Noah played with Jake's hair while Jake peppered Ramin with questions about whether he had pets, and whether he *wanted* pets, and what kind of dog he would get.

"We will," Angela agreed, though she bit her lip. "We'll figure something out."

They were halfway to Como when the rain began again.

They had finally made it onto the sixth (or was it the seventh?) ferry. It was much smaller and much faster than the one they'd caught that morning. They'd found seats inside, so they managed to stay dry, though Noah could still hear the rain pounding the deck above.

Angela spent the ride on her phone, trying to figure out how to get back to Milan. They'd already missed their bus, but hopefully there would be more. Or the train, maybe, though it would be a miserable ride in rain-soaked clothes.

Jake had fallen asleep against Ramin's side. He was going to ask Ramin if it was okay, but one look at Ramin's face kept him quiet. Ramin smiled down at Jake with such fondness, Noah wanted to cry.

How could he live with his son halfway across the world? How could he endure it?

Finally the ferry docked in Como. The cold rain smacked Noah in the face as soon as he stepped onto the boardwalk. Big, fat droplets slid down his collar. Ramin stifled a curse as he stepped into a huge puddle and nearly tripped, but Noah caught him.

"Thank you." Ramin wiped at his face. "Where are you all headed?"

"The train station." Noah nodded ahead, where Angela was waiting for the walk signal at the crosswalk, huddled against the rain. Jake was awake again, already wet and shivering.

A silent war raged across Ramin's face. Noah had the unreasonable urge to smooth out the little furrow in his brow. But then Ramin nodded to himself and ran after Angela. Noah jogged to keep up.

"I've got a hotel for the night," Ramin said, raising his voice above the rain. "It's only a couple blocks away. We can see if they have more rooms."

Noah was surprised—shocked, really—when Angela actually agreed. Her voice was resigned as she said, "We missed the last train. Which way?"

Ramin gestured down the lakefront. The streetlights were on, bluish haloes marking the rain-darkened streets. Noah scooped up Jake as they made a run for it, ignoring the twinge in his lower back. Carrying Jake after that Vespa ride didn't feel great.

The rain was so heavy, it felt like blows against his neck and face as they hurried down the street. The lake rippled in silver swirls. He started once, when a car cut the curb right in front of them—without its headlights on—but they finally made it. A lit sign above the hotel doors, blurry in the rain, spelled out PALAZZO DEL COMO.

A bright and cheerful lobby greeted them, though the sodden black rain mats covered half the coral-colored marble tiles. Noah tried to dry his soles, but he just squeezed out more water onto the floor instead. Jake shivered in his arms, looking around the lobby with wide eyes, while they all followed Ramin to the receptionist's desk.

"Welcome back, Mr. Yazdani," the receptionist said. "Sorry you got caught in this weather!"

"It's okay. Um, these are my friends. Do you have any rooms available for them? Our ferry from Bellagio was late and they missed their bus."

"Just a moment, Mr. Yazdani..." They clicked away on their computer. "I'm sorry, Mr. Yazdani, it's not looking good..."

"Are you sure there's nothing?" Ramin leaned closer over the desk. Noah didn't see what he pulled out of his wallet, but the receptionist's eyebrows lifted.

"Ah, of course. It looks like we do have one room available."

"Just one?" Angela asked.

"Yes, I'm sorry, just the one. Queen bed."

Angela turned back to him. A queen bed would be tight with the three of them, but it was better than sleeping in the train station in their wet clothes. Or heading back into the rain to try to find a room somewhere else.

He could sleep on the floor. Or maybe they had a sofa. His back wouldn't like it, but as long as Jake and Angela were comfortable—

"Why don't you and Jake take that one," Ramin said. "And Noah can room with me? If you don't mind, that is?"

That last part practically came out as a squeak, and he turned to Noah with a question in his eyes.

Noah swallowed. His stomach gave an uncomfortable swoop that had him worrying he'd end up like Jake.

How was he supposed to share a room with Ramin Yazdani?

Ramin, who was beautiful and kind and had just put a roof over his cold, wet son's head?

Ramin, who shied away from every touch like Noah was lava. Who was getting over a breakup and wanted nothing to do with Noah.

How could he share a bed with the man he wanted more than anything else?

"That would be amazing," Angela said. "That work for you, Noah?"

He swallowed again. Pinched at his cross.

This was going to be torture.

"Of course."

nineteen

Ramin

What. The Actual Fuck. Had he been thinking?

Sharing a *bed*? With *Noah Bartlett*?

He held Jake's hand while Noah and Angela gave their passports and information to the receptionist.

"You cold?" he asked.

Jake shivered and said, "No."

Ramin made himself shiver too, though he *was*, in fact, cold. Someone had set the lobby air conditioner so cold, the rain in his hair was in danger of freezing. But he said, "Me neither."

Jake's shy smile actually did warm him a little.

Angela and Noah returned with handfuls of single-use toiletries.

"Thanks for waiting," Noah said, barely catching a tiny tube of toothpaste before he dropped it. "For everything. Really."

"I didn't do anything," Ramin pointed out.

"Then what was all that at the front desk?"

Ramin blushed. "Uh, I travel a lot for work, so I have loyalty status here? And I showed them my card?"

Noah whistled. "Well, you didn't have to do that for us."

"I don't mind." How could he *not* do that? Noah and his family had wined him and dined him and made him feel welcome for no other reason than that they could. Flexing his Diamond Membership was a poor way of making it up to them.

They crowded into the elevator. This one, at least, seemed made for more than one person at a time.

As soon as the doors shut, Angela blurted out, "My sister's a lesbian."

Noah made a choking sound.

Jake giggled.

Ramin just blinked at her.

"Uh...okay?"

Angela's cheeks reddened. An embarrassed smile slashed across her face.

Suddenly she seemed a lot less intense.

"Sorry. Just, my sister's a lesbian, and she's my best friend."

"Oh...kay." She might've been less intense, but Ramin still didn't know where she was going with this.

They reached the fourth floor to let off Angela and Jake. Angela stepped out but held the door.

"Just, I wanted you to know I don't have a problem with gay people. If I came across gruff today, it's because of family stuff, and not anything you did. You've gone above and beyond to help us out, and I wanted you to know how thankful I am. And sorry if I ever made you feel unwelcome."

Ramin could feel Noah practically shaking from holding in a laugh.

"Plus you have an awesome face," Jake added.

That broke the tension, and Ramin managed a smile. "I was glad to. Really. And no worries." It had never even occurred to him that she might be homophobic. Just...intense.

"Uh, have a good night."

When the doors finally closed, Ramin let out a breath. "Was it just me, or—"

Noah barked out a laugh. "That was super weird. But she's always like that. She gets stressed and cranky and then gives the most weirdly sincere apologies."

The elevator let them out on the fifth floor. Ramin led the way to their room, keenly aware of Noah at his back. He'd never been well and truly alone with Noah before. His back tingled. His heart raced.

This was not good.

"Here we are," he said, way too brightly, as he tapped his keycard and let Noah in first.

"Oh, Ramin," Noah sighed as he took in the room.

It wasn't the fanciest room ever—Ramin had stayed in some truly ridiculous hotels for work over the years—but it *did* have huge floor-to-ceiling windows facing the lake. The last bit of daylight had turned the sky a murky blue. From up here, the rain rippling across the surface of the lake looked like the result of some giant child, twirling their finger in the water.

"Is this okay?" Ramin asked. The view was great, but there was still a problem.

A single queen-sized problem.

"I bet this'll look beautiful at sunrise," Noah said, turning back to Ramin. "Huh? Did you ask something?"

"Is this okay?" Ramin gestured around the room, toward the single queen bed.

Noah's eyes softened. His voice dropped low and gentle. "It's amazing. I can't thank you enough. Really."

But then he let out a little shiver. Rain soaked his shirt. The white fabric clung to his torso, translucent where it stuck to his shoulder blades and collarbones.

"You want the bathroom? You're cold and wet." Also, Ramin desperately needed a moment to reset his brain.

"So are you. It's your room. You go first."

Normally Ramin would've taarofed. Insisted Noah go first. Deployed any number of very effective Persian deflections to make sure Noah was taken care of.

But this wasn't a normal situation, and Ramin desperately needed to escape.

Ramin had dropped his backpack off earlier in the day, and the bell staff had left it on one of the stuffed armchairs in the corner. He grabbed it and locked himself in the bathroom, grateful to finally have some sort of barrier between him and Noah.

Part of Ramin wanted to hide in the shower forever, but the other part was conscientious enough to remember Noah waiting, wet and cold. He kept it quick. The thought of being naked with Noah on the other side of the door wasn't arousing; it was terrifying, much too terrifying to jack off in the shower. Not that he didn't try. The last thing he wanted was to spring a RAB while sharing the bed—God, it wouldn't even be all that random-ass, with Noah literally in bed next to him—but the fear gnawing at his chest kept him from getting hard.

He dried himself off with the fluffiest towel he'd ever used in his life. Then he pulled out his wound wash to take care of his earrings. He carefully unwound the plastic wrap from his tattoo and studied the design in the mirror: a faravahar, the Zoroastrian winged man symbol that had come to more broadly represent Iranian identity. His artist had, surprisingly, done one before, and this one was perfect, centered over Ramin's sternum. He looked kind of funny with part of his chest shaved, but whatever.

He liked it. Even if his chest was soft and his pecs sagged a bit and there were stretch marks on his stomach below. Even if his belly dunlopped a bit over his waistband. Even if his skin was cherry red from the hot shower.

He washed and dried the tattoo and applied the second skin the artist had recommended, wincing as he stretched the wrong way. Why the fuck had he gotten a tattoo, of all things?

He was Interesting New Ramin, that was why. Apparently Interesting

New Ramin liked spur-of-the-moment body modification, consequences be damned.

Now Interesting New Ramin just had to survive sharing a bed with Sad Teenaged Ramin's old crush.

Ramin pulled on one of the shirts he had packed for tomorrow. Usually he slept naked, but that was out of the question with Noah here. He pulled on a pair of underwear too, plain black trunks. He flossed and brushed his teeth and did his skincare. Took a deep breath.

He could do this. He could share a room, a bed, with Noah.

He could.

Except when he opened the door, Noah was standing there.

Right there.

Hand raised, like he was about to knock.

"Oh!" he breathed. Ramin felt it across his cheek. "Sorry."

"It's okay." Ramin breathed back. When did his voice turn all husky? But Noah was *right there*. He could feel the warmth of him, even through Noah's cold wet shirt. Ramin was a hair taller than Noah, but he didn't feel like it, pressed up like this. Noah loomed over him somehow.

The smell of Noah's rain-soaked skin wound its way straight to Ramin's core. His ass clenched.

Noah had said something, but damned if Ramin had heard.

"Huh? Sorry?"

Noah's hand came up. Ramin held his breath. Licked his lips. Swallowed. But Noah's eyes weren't on Ramin's mouth. They were to the side.

Noah tweaked Ramin's left earring. It must've been off-kilter.

"Fixed it," Noah said.

Ramin shivered again.

"D-did you need something?"

"Sorry. Uh, do you have a shirt I could borrow?" Noah plucked at his own, pulling it away from the swell of his pec.

"I think so." Ramin knew so. He always packed like he was going to spill a pot of chili and shit himself three times a day. He tugged down the hem of his own shirt as he dug through his bag and pulled out a pink T-shirt he'd picked up the other day.

"My favorite color!" Noah said. "Thanks."

Noah's fingers brushed Ramin's as he handed the shirt over. Ramin felt it like a shock.

What the fuck what the fuck what the fuck?!

He darted past Noah, holding the backpack in front of his underwear. "The bathroom's all yours!" he squeaked.

He didn't breathe until he heard the door close and the lock click.

Thank fuck.

Maybe he could fall asleep before Noah came back out. That would be best, right? Ramin tucked himself into the far side of the bed and closed his eyes.

Except he still needed to charge his phone. Shit.

He reached over and dug through his backpack to find his charging cable and adapters, but there was no place to plug it in on the bedside table. So he got back up and found an outlet next to the floor lamp.

He tucked himself back in bed and immediately started sliding toward the middle. He slid his hand under the cover and felt the seam in the middle of the mattress—or rather, two mattresses, pressed together, but with a single sheet over them.

He shifted to make sure he was firmly on his side. Was sleeping on his back best? That was safe, right? No chance of accidentally touching. But what if he got hard and his erection tented the covers? Side, then. He was usually a side sleeper, so that worked out. Should he have his back to Noah or his front? Back was normal, right? Front meant you might kiss, or cuddle.

Outside, darkness had truly fallen, though the rain still hammered the window. He realized with a start he hadn't eaten dinner. Normally he wouldn't let himself skip, even if he wasn't hungry—he used to skip all the time when he was in a disordered eating phase—but he was so full from lunch, the thought of eating anything else made him cringe.

But, shit, he hadn't said his nightly prayers.

Ramin was an atheist. He had been since he was twelve or so. But his parents had both been Bahá'í. Ramin didn't believe in an afterlife, but his parents had. He prayed for them every night. Prayers for the departed. One for his dad, one for his mom. Just in case.

It didn't make Ramin feel any closer to any sort of God, but it did make him feel closer to his parents. To the memory of them sitting side by side on their bed every night, silently reciting their Obligatory Prayers together.

Ramin pulled back the covers, sat up, and closed his eyes, muttering the words under his breath.

When he finished, he sighed and began to get back into bed.

"Hey," Noah said.

Ramin startled. He hadn't heard the shower turn off.

"Hey." Ramin glanced over automatically and then immediately wished he hadn't. Noah was standing in the bathroom doorway, in Ramin's pink T-shirt and a pair of ugly, baggy plaid boxers, haloed in the glow from the bathroom.

On the one hand, Ramin was almost offended that Noah wore such terrible, formless underwear.

On the other, he was extremely grateful for that fact, because the heinous boxers obscured any possible sign of Noah's Ark.

"I took this side, is that okay?"

"Of course."

Ramin slid himself back into bed, facing away from Noah.

"What were you doing?"

"Oh." Ramin felt heat creeping up his cheeks. "I was, um . . . praying. For my parents."

"Did I interrupt?"

"No. I was done."

"Oh. Okay."

Ramin closed his eyes, but he still felt the shift in the bed as Noah slid under the covers. The heat rose immediately.

Ramin tried not to think about that.

Or about how Noah smelled like soap and clean skin and just a little lingering remnant of sugared birch.

Or about his erection. He really should've jacked off.

That seam in the middle of the bed threatened to pull Ramin into its gravity well. He clung to the edge as the bed shifted. The light clicked off. And then Noah settled.

His breath ghosted the back of Ramin's neck. Was Noah on his side, too? *Facing* Ramin? With his Ark pointed right at Ramin's ass?

This was torture.

"Ramin?"

"Yeah?

"I'm sorry I didn't keep in touch."

"Me too." Ramin swallowed. "We were kids. It happens."

"Yeah. But still. You were going through something awful, and I . . . I should've been there for you."

"It's okay. You were going through your own stuff."

Ramin couldn't see Noah, could only imagine the warmth in his eyes, but that made it easier to talk somehow. Noah couldn't see him blush.

The darkness protected them both.

"Thanks for inviting me along today. For making me feel like part of the family. I haven't had that in a long time."

"I was glad to. I had fun. We all did." Noah's voice dropped so low Ramin could barely hear it. "I don't think you're boring at all."

Ramin chuckled. It was nice of Noah to say, but he'd only seen Interesting New Ramin. He'd missed the last twenty years.

But he liked being not-boring to Noah.

"Thanks. I think you're pretty cool too."

"Thanks." It was Noah's turn to chuckle. The laugh made the hairs on Ramin's neck stand up. "I try."

"Seriously. You're kind and you're"—Ramin was about to say *hand-some* but that was definitely not appropriate—"you're patient and you're thoughtful. You always have been."

Noah went quiet for a long moment.

"Thanks." He sighed. "It's nice to have someone that knew me before. Before Angela and Jake, I mean. Sometimes it feels like that's all I am to people. Jake's dad. Angela's ex. But to you, I'm an old friend."

Ramin's chest heated. He slid his feet around to find a cooler spot. "I'm glad."

The rain kept falling. Noah kept breathing. Eventually, Ramin relaxed enough to breathe himself, too.

"Night, Noah," he whispered. He didn't even expect an answer.

But Noah whispered back, "Night, Ramin."

twenty

Noah

Twenty Years Ago

Y ou going to Sweetheart?" Noah asked, leaning against the locker next to Ramin's. Students filed past on the way to seventh hour, but Noah's (and Ramin's) was just down the hall.

Ramin shook his head and avoided Noah's eyes.

Noah didn't know much—Ramin didn't really talk about it—but he knew Ramin's mom wasn't doing well. He thought maybe talking about the dance would cheer Ramin up, at least a little bit.

Not that anything seemed to do that these days.

Over the last few months, Noah had watched as the light went out of his friend's eyes. He hadn't been able to do a thing about it. Every night he prayed for her to get better. He'd asked his parents to pray, too, but his father said prayers didn't work on Muslims, and his mother had gotten angry he was even hanging out with someone from "that part of the world." Even though Ramin was born here in the States and he wasn't Muslim. That hadn't mattered.

So Noah had stopped talking to his parents about it. And he didn't mention that he still hung out with Ramin anyway. If it was at school then they couldn't complain.

Noah gently elbowed Ramin's arm. "Come on, you should go. It'll be fun."

"No one asked me," Ramin muttered.

Noah bit his lip. He'd been asked by...well, technically, just Stacy, but he'd had a bunch of girls ask if they were still together "just to check." It didn't seem fair he got so much attention when a nice guy like Ramin didn't.

"You can always go with friends," Noah said. "Or solo. You don't have to have a date."

"It's fine."

It wasn't fine, though. Noah wanted Ramin to go. He wanted his friend there. He wanted to see Ramin smile and laugh and dance and forget about the world and just...just be there.

He liked it when Ramin was around. Noah's heart beat quicker, his chest felt lighter, his smile came easier when his friend was nearby. He'd never had a friend like that before, one who made everything better just by being there. Who looked Noah in the eyes and really saw him. Who didn't want anything from him, didn't expect anything of him, didn't tease him about all the rumors or ask him how many girls he'd slept with. (Just Stacy, and they hadn't even gone all the way. Not because he was waiting for marriage or anything; they were just taking things slow.)

"Come on. Say you'll come."

"I'm good. Really." Ramin closed his locker and slid on his backpack.

"But it'll be fun!" Noah wrestled Ramin into a mock pin, though it was really more of a standing bear hug from behind, swaying Ramin side to side.

"Stop!" he wheezed between bursts of laughter. Noah hadn't heard Ramin laugh in a long time, and he laughed along, too, though he made sure to keep his hold loose so Ramin could get away if he really wanted to.

"Say you'll come to the dance!"

"You can't make me!"

Ramin squirmed but didn't take the obvious out of just pushing Noah's arm away, so Noah gave him a gentle shake, which got another squeal of laughter out of Ramin.

But suddenly Ramin went stiff in his arms. Noah let go, looking for a teacher, but there was no one but the usual press of bodies. Ramin's face had gone all red.

"You okay?" Noah asked.

"Fine." But Ramin wasn't laughing anymore. He tugged on the hem of his shirt. "See you in class."

And then he took off down the hall.

Noah swallowed the lump in his throat. And adjusted the lump in his jeans. He hadn't realized... well. That happened in wrestling sometimes, it was a normal reaction, though he thought he'd grown out of it.

His heart sank. He'd wanted to cheer Ramin up. And he'd thought it was working.

He didn't understand what he'd done wrong.

Now

Noah woke but kept his eyes closed. He was too warm, too cozy. He just had to keep his eyes closed and drift off again. He snuggled deeper into his pillow, into the warm arms holding him, into—

Wait.

Warm arms.

Noah cracked his eyes open. He was in a dimly lit room. In Como. He remembered. The rain had finally stopped, and the clear moon lit the lake outside.

Here, now, Ramin was holding him.

Noah's heart hammered.

Ramin was holding him.

He'd spent the last three days wondering what it would feel like if they touched, and now... now he knew. He felt himself growing harder in his boxers and breathed a soft sigh that at least he was the little spoon so Ramin wouldn't notice.

Ramin.

Did he know?

"Ramin?" Noah whispered.

Ramin didn't make a sound, but he did hold Noah a bit tighter. His grip was strong yet gentle. He smelled like hotel soap and lemons and minty toothpaste and just a little bit of sweaty skin. He smelled like heaven.

"Ramin?"

But Ramin didn't stir. And Noah couldn't bring himself to wake him.

He hadn't been held in so long. Not since the divorce. He'd tried dating, but it had never gone anywhere, certainly not to a soft bed after a long day.

Noah slowly reached down to adjust himself where he was caught on the seam of his boxers. He should wake Ramin up. Right? Ramin didn't know what he was doing.

Or did he?

Noah didn't *think* he was that out of practice at flirting. Surely Ramin knew he was interested, right? At first, Noah thought Ramin was still hurting from his breakup, or was just not that into him, but then last night, outside the bathroom, with Ramin all pink and clean from his shower, Noah had thought... well. He thought maybe Ramin saw him the same way he saw Ramin.

He'd felt his mouth go dry. Had licked his lips, in case Ramin leaned in for a kiss. Or he did. But then the moment had broken, and he'd gone to shower frustrated, and then gone to bed frustrated, and now here he was, with Ramin's arms around him and a rock-hard erection in his boxers.

He didn't know what this meant.

But he was going to enjoy it for as long as he could.

He took a deep breath and relaxed deeper into Ramin's arms. The valley in the middle of the bed pulled them both in deeper, made them cuddle closer. If this was all that would happen, this was enough. It was innocent. It was friendly.

And if Ramin wanted more...well.

Maybe Noah would have to be the one to make a move.

twenty-one

Ramin

Ramin woke to an azure sky and a streak of golden sunrise reflecting off the lake below. He squinted.

He'd shifted during the night, and something heavy lay upon his arm, and *oh holy fuck* he was holding Noah. *Spooning* him. Arms wrapped tight around Noah's strong, warm chest. Hips tucked snugly against Noah's. Feet tangled at the foot of the bed, still wrapped in the soft, cozy blankets.

And disaster of disasters: He was hard.

Not just morning wood. This was morning iron. Morning titanium. Morning diamond, tucked up against Noah's ass.

He tried not to flex it but couldn't help it.

Fuckety-fuckety-fuck! He'd been so careful to face away last night. When did he start spooning Noah? Damn that gap in the bed. It had sucked him down like quicksand in a nineties movie.

He never should've shared a bed. He should've slept on the floor. Hell, he should've grabbed a blanket and slept in the bathtub or something.

Ramin thought about spreadsheets. He thought about his inbox at work. He thought about that time Todd tried a new chemical peel and he was allergic to it and it left his face all red and weird.

Nothing worked. If anything, he was getting harder, his dick throbbing with the beat of his bounding heart.

As if things couldn't get any worse, Noah shifted back against him. He snuffled and smacked his lips.

"Morning."

Noah's voice rumbled, low and scratchy and pure sex, reverberating right through Ramin's core. Ramin clenched up, swallowing a whimper as his dick flexed again.

Noah had to notice.

"I'm so sorry. I don't know how I...I mean, I didn't mean to..."

Ramin tried to pull away, but Noah held on to his arms, kept him close.

"It's okay." Noah backed up again. "I'm hard too."

Ramin's brain short-circuited.

Noah took Ramin's hand and twined their fingers, guiding Ramin to rub soft circles on his chest. Even through Noah's borrowed shirt, Ramin could feel the warm, firm swell of his chest muscles.

"You feel so good holding me," Noah murmured. "Is this okay?"

Ramin's breath hitched. "Uh. Huh?"

Was it okay?

It was *everything*.

"You can touch me more."

Whatthefuckwhatthefuckwhatthefuck!

Ramin was still asleep, that's what it was. He was dreaming. Having a sex dream about Noah. It wasn't the first time, after all, though this one was more realistic than the last one had been. Yeah, that's what this was, just another sex dream. He'd wake up with wet sticky underwear, and oh God please don't let Noah notice—

Ramin bit his lip but didn't wake. Noah was still moving Ramin's hand in circles around his firm stomach. But then they stilled.

"Ramin?"

Ramin was amazed he could make his voice work. His throat felt like sandpaper. "Yeah?"

"Do you...not like this?"

Noah released him.

"I'm sorry, I thought...I mean, I just..."

Ramin brought his hand back to Noah's stomach. Was this really real?

Who cared?

"I like it."

He'd wanted to touch Noah ever since he saw him.

"I like it too." Noah let out a rumbling sigh. And then: "You can go lower."

Fuck if Ramin needed to be told twice.

Heat rose as Ramin reached the waistband of Noah's boxers. His fingers moved on their own, stroking the skin of Noah's waist, playing with his happy trail, before slipping under the elastic.

Holy shit.

"You sure?" Ramin paused with his hands in Noah's soft, silky hair.

"I wanted you since I saw you in that gelato shop."

Ramin could barely breathe. "Really?"

"Can't you tell?"

Ramin slid his hand lower, and fuck.

Fuck.

He could tell.

Noah's breath hitched as Ramin wrapped his hand around his cock. It was hot and hard, the tight skin silky smooth. And it was big.

Very big.

Ramin's fingertips barely met around it.

"Fuck, it's true," he murmured.

Noah shivered at his touch. Ramin gave him a tentative stroke down his full length to cradle his heavy balls.

"What's true?"

Ramin swallowed. His own dick jumped.

"Your dick is huge."

Noah huffed. "You heard about that?"

"*Everyone* heard about it."

"You never said anything."

Ramin stroked Noah again, tighter this time, a languid slide up to twist around Noah's head. Noah gasped.

"What was I supposed to say? I thought I was straight." Ramin fought with Noah's waistband to finally free him. Gave him another long stroke. "I thought you were, too."

"I'm bi," Noah sighed. "Oh, Ramin..."

Noah was bi? Holy shit. Ramin needed to process that. Needed to reevaluate every single interaction he'd ever had with Noah.

But first he needed to get him off.

"You like this?" he whispered in Noah's ear.

"Uh-huh."

Ramin traced his thumb along Noah's circumcision scar. Ran it up to collect the honey that had begun oozing. God he wanted to taste it.

Fuck it. He was on PrEP.

Noah whimpered as Ramin released him, licked the salty sweetness off his thumb. "How long has it been since someone did this for you?"

"I haven't been with anyone since the divorce."

Two years? That was practically a crime against humanity.

It was Ramin's solemn, moral duty to break that drought.

"That's a long fucking time, Noah."

Ramin hocked up as much saliva as he could and spat into his hand before reaching for Noah's cock again.

"Oh," Noah purred as Ramin's slick fist wrapped around him again. "Oh. Ramin."

Ramin stroked farther down, trailing wetness onto Noah's balls. He unclenched his fist to rub them with every downstroke. He wished his other hand was free—aside from Noah being a two-hander, he could've given his balls more love—but his arm was still trapped under Noah and falling asleep.

Ramin didn't care. Let it fall asleep. Let it fall off.

He. Had his hand. On Noah's cock.

He built up speed, added a little twist to the end, as Noah bucked and his dick surged. Ramin's own dick was leaking into his underwear now, the warm dew turning cold, and he didn't even care.

The bed had turned into a sauna around them. Noah's dick kept getting harder and heavier, the warm skin yielding to Ramin's touch, the tacky sweet smell of Ramin's saliva mixing with Noah's sweat.

Noah was glowing. So was Ramin. No, that was the sunrise, spilling over them, turning the bed to liquid gold.

Ramin freed Noah's dick again to gather more spit, and Noah let out another groan of protest, but Ramin got right back on him, jacking harder. Noah's dick was flexing more rapidly now, practically jumping out of Ramin's hand, and he held Noah tightly by the base to hold off his climax.

"Ramin, please," Noah gasped. His voice had gone high and breathy.

"Please what?" Ramin gave Noah another long, slow stroke.

"Let me finish."

Ramin chuckled. Apparently Noah was too shy to say *Make me come*.

But that's what he was going to do.

He kept his pressure even but picked up his pace, focusing on Noah's full head, adding a solid glide down to Noah's balls every fourth stroke or so, going for more saliva when things got too dry. If only his bags weren't in Amsterdam or Istanbul or wherever the hell they'd landed now, he would've had his good lube. But this was okay.

This was better than okay.

He was giving Noah Bartlett a handjob.

Noah Bartlett wanted a handjob. From him.

Ramin's heart raced. His taint tingled. His ass clenched.

If this was a dream, he never wanted to wake.

Noah whined as Ramin gripped his head and rubbed it with his palm. He shuddered as Ramin varied his strokes. He sighed as Ramin tugged on his balls. His dick jumped with every breath.

"Ramin," he gasped. "Ramin, I'm..."

Noah's dick began pulsing in Ramin's hand, thrashing, nearly surging out of Ramin's grip. He grunted a long, low breath as he came, shaking in Ramin's arms, while Ramin stroked him through the entire orgasm, relishing every spasm, feeling Noah's hot seed on his hand.

Ramin's ass tightened. Ecstasy sparked in his core. He nearly came himself when Noah ground back against him, but he bit his lip and clenched his Kegel muscles and kept it in.

He didn't want anything to distract him from the feel of Noah spurting in his hands.

When Noah was finally spent, Ramin gave him one final strong, lazy stroke, milking the entire length of his cock before releasing it.

Noah sighed. "That was amazing."

Ramin nearly purred with pride.

Fuck yeah it was.

Ramin just gave Noah Bartlett a handjob.

Ramin just had his hand on Noah's huge cock.

Should he...kiss Noah? Would that be okay?

Now that the haze of sex had lifted, a thousand questions and worries and insecurities rushed in. This wasn't a dream. This was real life.

What was he supposed to do now?

He settled on tucking Noah back into his boxers and planting a feather-soft kiss on his shoulder.

In response, Noah scooted back.

"What are you doing?"

"Scooch back, I don't want to get your shirt messy," Noah said.

"But—"

Noah gave another scoot. The problem was, there was no more bed.

Ramin tumbled off the end with an *oof*.

But then Noah was right above him. Legs around Ramin's. Arms bracketing Ramin's shoulders. Eyes glowing with desire. His silver cross had escaped his shirt and dangled down, resting against Ramin's collarbone, warmed by Noah's body heat.

"You okay?"

Ramin nodded.

"Good." Noah's smile turned cocky. "I needed room to do this."

And then he leaned down and pressed his lips to Ramin's.

Noah's lips were soft, full, luscious. Perfect. The kiss was chaste at first, gentle pressure against Ramin's lips as lightning danced across every inch of his skin. Until something inside him cracked and he opened his mouth to sigh in relief, in ecstasy. Noah took the opening, plunging his tongue in to tap against Ramin's teeth. Ramin opened further, let Noah in deeper, slid his tongue along Noah's, felt Noah rumbling in pleasure above him.

Noah's stubble scratched against Ramin's chin. Ramin's hands rose to clutch at Noah's shoulders. Ramin's dick, which had deflated when he fell off the bed, came roaring back to life.

Noah shifted his weight to one hand and used the other to reach for Ramin's waistband. Ramin clenched his stomach as Noah's knuckles brushed the skin there.

Noah Bartlett wanted to touch him.

His fingertips had just slid below the elastic when someone knocked on the door.

The room snapped back into focus. Bright light. The muffled ding of the elevator in the hallway. A rapidly cooling pool of cum in the bedsheets. Their bodies tangled on the floor.

Noah reared back, brows furrowed in confusion.

Another knock.

"Dad?"

They both froze.

"Dad? You up?"

Noah's eyes widened in panic. He swallowed.

"Yeah, Jakey," he said, but he sounded like a Muppet. Noah cleared his throat and tried again. "I'm up."

"Can I come in?"

Ramin didn't think Noah's eyes could get any wider, but he'd been wrong. Before, Noah had looked alarmed. Now he looked like he needed to vomit.

Ramin shook his head. *Say no!*

"Uh. Ramin just woke up," Noah lied, then winced.

God, Ramin wanted to curl up and disappear.

God, he wanted to pull Noah down and keep kissing, taste the hot skin of his neck, the dip of his collarbone...

"What's up, buddy?" Noah called. "Everything okay?"

"There's breakfast downstairs. Mom says to hurry. She found a bus back."

A bus back.

Fuck. Noah had to go.

Noah was here *with his family*.

It was so absurd, Ramin stifled a laugh. Was this what it felt like, getting caught by your parents? Ramin had never experienced it.

Noah kept his voice even. "I'll be down soon, buddy. Okay?"

Noah stared at the door a second—they both did, waiting for the coast to be clear—and then Noah brought his hand to Ramin's chin, rested his thumb right below Ramin's lip. Came in for another kiss, smooth as silk.

"Talk about bad timing."

Ramin nodded. He shifted to kiss the pad of Noah's thumb. "It's okay. You can go."

"I can't just leave you like this."

He very much could. Jake had been such a bonerkiller, Ramin's dick might've actually inverted all the way into his abdomen.

But the way Noah was looking at him, maybe he could—

"Dad!" Jake's voice came again, and Ramin nearly jumped out of his skin. "They've got waffles!"

Noah's arm gave out, and he collapsed onto Ramin, covering his *oof* with his own low laughter.

"Sorry," Noah whispered.

"I told you. It's okay. Go be with your family."

Actually, that wouldn't be the worst thing in the world. Ramin needed a moment to process everything that had just happened. Actually, several moments.

After all, a *lot* had happened.

"I'll be fine. Really."

Noah looked doubtful, lips drawn into a pout. Ramin wanted to kiss him again, but then Noah might never get down to breakfast, and then Jake—or Angela—would interrupt them again, and Ramin would die of embarrassment.

Noah got off him, ducked into the bathroom, and pulled on his shorts. Ramin only let himself be a little disappointed he'd never actually laid eyes on Noah's Ark.

"Can I 'orrow dis?" Noah mumbled around the flimsy hotel toothbrush, plucking at his borrowed (and thankfully un-cum-stained) shirt.

"Of course."

Ramin managed to pull himself up to sit on the edge of the bed. He watched as Noah scurried around the room, grabbing his things, slipping on his shoes, patting his pockets, tucking his cross into his shirt.

"Text me when you get back into town. Yeah? Or I'll text you?"

Noah wanted them to text. Did Noah want to see him again? Or just sort out returning Ramin's shirt? What did this mean? Had this been a one-time thing, a horny morning mistake? Did Noah *like him* like him, or had he just been a warm body and a talented (if he did say so himself) hand?

Everything had made perfect sense while they were having sex, but now, in the cold light of day, what the actual fuck had Ramin been thinking?

This wasn't the plan.

Well . . . getting dick was definitely the plan. But not a familiar dick. He should've been waking up in some Italian stranger's bed, taking a walk of shame. Getting over his breakup by getting under a revolving door of men. He was supposed to be rebounding!

Not watching Noah tie his shoes.

Noah swooped in for another kiss. Two.

A third, letting his lips linger, his forehead resting against Ramin's.

Ramin leaned in.

Fuck. Whatever Noah was thinking, Ramin was along for the ride.

Noah hesitated at the door, looking back, giving Ramin one last, perfect smile.

"See you soon."

The door swung shut.

Ramin let out a breath.

Had that really just happened? It had. He could feel his precum all sticky and cold in his underwear. The room smelled of sex and Noah.

Noah Bartlett had kissed him.

The tiniest of smiles dawned across Ramin's face, soft and subtle, before exploding into a laugh.

Noah Bartlett had kissed him. He'd kissed Noah back.

He'd kissed Noah Bartlett. And he thought—he hoped—he might get to do it again.

twenty-two

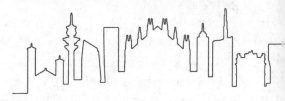

Noah

"You sleep okay?" Angela asked across the aisle as their coach sped back to Milan.

"Hm?" Noah shook himself. "Yeah. Why?"

"You seem a little out of it."

"Sorry. Just enjoying the view."

That wasn't true. Noah hadn't taken in a single mile of the drive.

He was too preoccupied with the tacky feeling in his shorts, where Ramin's saliva had dried all over his skin. Too distracted by the full-body tingles that kept sweeping over him, like he was still back in that bed. Too overwhelmed by the glow in his heart.

"It's gorgeous, huh?"

Noah nodded, but that wasn't why he couldn't stop smiling.

He'd kissed Ramin.

Ramin had kissed him back.

Ramin had *touched* him.

He wanted to run through the streets. He wanted to shout it from the rooftops! He wanted…

He didn't know what.

The truth was, though Noah was bisexual, this was still new to him. He'd been with guys before, but both times had played out more or less the same way. A guy who was fascinated by Noah's size, but didn't see him as a person beyond what he had in his pants. A one-time thing, no kissing, no chance for Noah to even reciprocate.

He hated that he hadn't gotten to touch Ramin back. Hated that they'd been interrupted.

But kissing Ramin? That had been magical.

Noah's lips still burned with the memory of it. He traced them with his fingertips. Were they swollen? They'd kissed hard but they hadn't been kissing for very long when Jake interrupted them. Had Angela noticed anything while they ate a quick breakfast and ran for the bus?

She hadn't said anything.

Noah pulled his phone out to see if Ramin had sent anything, but it was dead.

Crap. It must've died during the night. His charger was back in Milan, and he hadn't thought to borrow Ramin's last night. He'd have to wait till they got back.

At least he'd finally managed to get Ramin's number yesterday, while they took a break from rolling out ravioli.

When would Ramin get back to Milan? When could Noah see him again?

Did Ramin even want that? Noah thought he did, but maybe he was reading the situation wrong. Maybe he was just projecting his own hopes and wishes. Maybe—

"Dad?"

Noah shook himself. "Yeah, buddy?"

"What does 'good pasta hands' mean?"

Noah nearly choked. Ramin's hands had been good for more than pasta.

"Uh. I think Nonna meant that Ramin was good at making the ravioli."

"Oh." Jake frowned thoughtfully. "How come he has dimples and I don't?"

"Well, that's just the way he was born," Noah said. "Like how you were born with brown eyes."

"Aw, man." Jake poked at his cheeks, like he was trying to give himself dimples, though all he really did was make himself look like an evil chipmunk. Noah chuckled and ruffled Jake's hair.

"Hey!"

"You like Ramin, huh?"

"He's cool," Jake said, glancing out the window. But then he looked back at Noah. "Are you *sure* I can't get a tattoo yet?"

"Your mom and I are both sure," Noah said.

Jake sighed. "Ramin said he got another tattoo. He said he couldn't show me because it was still healing. I bet it's cool."

"He didn't show me either," Noah said as heat crept up his neck. They hadn't had the chance, this morning, to really see each other.

"Do you think he'll show me next time?"

"Maybe, buddy." If there *was* a next time. What was this to him? A one-time hookup? A rebound from his breakup? Curiosity?

Or was it the start of something like a relationship? Did Ramin want that?

Did Noah? *Could* he want that? Should he even be worrying about that now, when they were trying to figure out their family's future? Should he tell Angela what happened? Would she be happy or mad? She kept saying she was worried Noah was lonely. But she *also* wanted him to focus on their family this trip.

But what if this thing between him and Ramin was real?

Twenty years ago, Noah had had a crush on Ramin. He just hadn't known what it was. He wouldn't figure out he was bi for another few years. At the time, he just…liked being around Ramin.

He still liked being around Ramin.

"Dad?"

"Huh? Sorry, buddy. I was thinking."

Jake shrugged. "Can we get gelato when we get back?"

Noah laughed. "If it's in your mom's schedule, sure."

Unfortunately for Jake, gelato wasn't on the route for The Death March of Fun: Part III. (Or was it Part IV? Noah couldn't decide if yesterday counted, since while they'd definitely done some marching, they'd also spent hours with Nonna and Nonno.)

Angela gave them just enough time at the hotel to change clothes. Noah grabbed a quick shower, though he hated the thought of washing Ramin's smell off him. He consoled himself by sniffing Ramin's pink T-shirt. It smelled like the both of them, like sweat and lemons and sugar and lust.

It smelled like heaven.

But then Jake knocked on the bathroom door and he nearly dropped the shirt into the open toilet. He hung it carefully and told Jake he'd be done in a few minutes.

"Hey, is your battery pack charged?" Noah asked Angela once he'd gotten dressed. "My phone is dead."

Thankfully, iPhone and Android had finally started using the same connectors.

Nothing in the divorce had felt so final as when Angela had switched from iPhone to Android, turning her and Noah's years-long text chain green.

Angela shook her head. "Sorry. But my phone is charged. We'll be okay if you need to leave yours here."

Noah didn't want to leave his phone. He wanted to text Ramin, be ready to get a response. But he couldn't tell Angela that; she'd ask too many questions, extract a confession from him. He'd been relieved to see her warm up to Ramin a little yesterday—if making awkward small talk about her lesbian sister counted as warming up—but still, he didn't want Angela thinking he was distracted.

So he plugged his phone in next to his bed, waited for it to power on, and shot off a quick message. Well, messages.

> **Noah**
>
> Made it back to Milan!
> When do you get back?
> Thanks for everything last
> night.
> And this morning.

Noah stared at his phone. Was that too forward? Or not forward enough?

How were you supposed to text someone you'd had sex with? Especially if you wanted to have sex with them again, but not *only* have sex, because you wanted to kiss them too, and talk with them, and go on dates, and just spend time together.

Noah was so out of practice at this.

He held his breath, waiting for Ramin to answer, but Angela popped her head through the open door connecting their rooms. "You ready? We've gotta go!"

"Yeah." He started typing out a message to let Ramin know he'd be without his phone, but before he finished, Jake ran into the room.

"Dad! Have you seen my Spider-Man socks?"

"We'll find them, buddy."

He set his phone on the nightstand and went to help his son.

The whole time they'd planned the trip, there was only one thing Noah truly wanted to do: He wanted to see *The Last Supper*.

To her credit, Angela had made sure to get them tickets, scheduling the Death March of Fun around their entrance time.

The church of Santa Maria delle Grazie had a redbrick façade, a steepled roof, and a green arch over the entrance. Beyond, the apse of the church rose several stories, with more intricate white and yellow stonework and arches supporting the exterior.

Before they could go in, though, they had to show their IDs and pick up their tickets, then wait in the small piazza for their group to get called. A group of Swiss tourists huddled on one side, all wearing matching lanyards.

Jake stalked around the piazza like a disgruntled pelican, scowling at the ground. Noah hoped it was just the lingering aftereffects of being sick yesterday, but still, it didn't make dealing with Jake's mood any easier.

"Do we have to see this?" he muttered. "It sounds boring."

"I really want to," Noah said. "It's one of the most famous paintings in the world."

"Painting is dumb."

"Jake," Noah warned. They didn't use that word.

Noah tried hard not to police Jake's words, but some were off-limits. The ones that could be used to hurt other people, for instance.

"What? It is. Why do we have to be here?"

"Because we all got to pick things to do," Noah said, keeping his voice as even as he could.

How had he ended up here, arguing with a nine-year-old, when just this morning he'd woken up in Ramin's arms? Well, that was his life now, wasn't it? He would always be a dad first. A dad with a son who was mad at him for no reason he could figure out.

"You picked the San Siro." Jake had been excited to see a soccer— well, football, here—match at Italy's largest stadium. "I picked this."

"Well, you picked a dumb thing," Jake muttered.

Before Noah could say anything, Angela jumped in.

"Jake. That's not how we talk to people."

Noah was ready for Jake to argue. For them to have to step away from the line and deal with a meltdown. But to his surprise, Jake muttered, "Sorry, Dad." He kicked at the ground and then tucked himself in the shadow of a wall, studying his hands.

Noah had never seen Angela handle him so masterfully. When had that happened?

"Sorry about that," Angela said. "I don't know what's gotten into him."

"Don't be." Noah shoved down his pride. He was supposed to be the one that was good with Jake. "You handled that well."

Angela shrugged. "I just do what you do, to be honest."

Then why didn't it work when he did it?

When their group was finally called, they passed through a modern-looking lobby with tile floors and metal detectors and plexiglass barriers, and then a windowed hallway looking out into the convent's inner courtyard, and then finally, finally, they were let into the refectory.

The vaulted room was dimly lit. High, narrow windows let in filtered daylight. A few strategically placed spotlights illuminated the murals.

To their left, a huge mural depicted the crucifixion. Noah took a moment to feel bad for the painter who had to share a room with Leonardo da Vinci. But not that bad, because to the right: *Wow.*

Goosebumps spread up Noah's arms, crept along the angles of his neck muscles. Euphoria pooled in his belly.

It felt like when Ramin had touched him.

But no one was touching him. No one except a long-dead artist, who'd painted his soul up on a dry stretch of cracked wall.

The Last Supper was gorgeous. Breathtaking. Perfectly imperfect—faded paint, cracked wall, and all. Its age only made it more beautiful.

Noah didn't remember making his way to one of the benches sitting a few yards back from the barricade that stopped people from getting too close, but suddenly he was seated, and staring, rubbing his cross.

Angela sat next to him and leaned to bump his shoulder.

It felt like old times.

"What do you think?" she muttered. It was quiet in the refectory, a reverent quiet, some unspoken agreement keeping their voices down.

"It's breathtaking."

Sitting here, staring at Leonardo's work, Noah felt the whispered awe of everyone else who'd ever come through here. Every art lover. Every historian. Every penitent. Everyone who wanted to feel connected to something bigger than themselves.

Angela leaned her head against his shoulder. He wrapped an arm around her and sighed.

He could stay here for days.

"This is pretty cool."

Then he pulled out his sketchbook and began drawing, the scratch of his pen echoing in the silence.

twenty-three

Ramin

Ramin had grand plans for the weekend. He was going to explore Como. Take the funicular up to Brunate, this little town on the mountain overlooking Como. Check out the Grindr map.

Instead, he found himself canceling his second night at the hotel, buying a train ticket, and hurrying back to Milan.

This was ridiculous. He *knew* it was ridiculous. Tiny angel Farzan flapped his tiny angel wings over his shoulder once more, chiding him for getting dicknotized, arguing with tiny devil Arya, spinning his tiny devil tail as he told Ramin to buy some lube on the way back to his apartment.

But fuck it.

It wasn't just the dick (though if Ramin was being honest with himself, he *did* want to get a look at it and not just feel it). It was Noah.

Noah, who was bisexual.

How had Ramin missed that? Had Noah been flirting with him this whole trip, and Ramin just missed it? Had he been reading every signal completely wrong? Why was Noah interested in him, anyway?

He shoved that thought aside.

Noah kissed him. Noah *wanted* him. Maybe some part of him had always wanted Noah to want him.

So now Ramin was changing all his plans and rushing back to Milan. Back to Noah.

Just like the lovesick teenager he'd been all those years ago.

Fuckety-fuck. If this wasn't Boring Old Ramin behavior, he didn't know what was.

When the train reached the outskirts of Milan, Ramin's phone began buzzing nonstop. It finally had signal again.

> **Noah**
> Made it back to Milan!
> When do you get back?
> Thanks for everything last night.
> And this morning.

> **Ramin**
> I get back later today. Glad you made it. And I was happy to help.

Ramin bit his lip. He *was* happy to help them find a place to stay.

He was also very happy to give Noah a handjob, but he couldn't just say that. What if Jake was borrowing Noah's phone or something? He typed and deleted and finally settled on:

> **Ramin**
> With everything

There. That was subtle and had plausible deniability. Right?

He waited, fiddling with his studs, but Noah didn't answer. Which was fine. Noah was busy. And Ramin had lost signal again.

He sighed, locked his phone, and watched the Lombardian country-side fly by.

Francesca caught him as he stepped off the elevator. She wore another power suit, maroon pinstripe this time. "Ciao, Ramin! You're back! How was Lago di Como?"

"Good. Beautiful."

"I hope the rain didn't catch you."

Ramin shrugged. His sodden clothes from yesterday were at the bottom of his backpack. Along with Noah's white T-shirt. Which he had only sniffed a few times before jacking off in the shower.

"Francesca, dov'è la—Ah, Ramin!" Paola stepped out of their apartment in a slinky blue dress, a mascara wand clutched in one hand. "Your luggages came!"

"Really?"

"They said you didn't answer your phone, so we just signed for them." Paola disappeared for a moment, then came back with Ramin's two purple suitcases. "Here. We got you this, too."

Paola handed Ramin a black plastic card with a stylized blue A on it.

"What's this?"

"An ARCO card. For the clubs!" Francesca said. "So you can go have fun tonight."

Ramin slipped the card into his pocket. He wasn't sure how much fun he'd be having at a club. But Noah still hadn't answered him. What if it was just a one-and-done thing? What if Noah *didn't* want him, just a warm hand, any hand. *Any hole in a storm*, little devil Arya whispered into his ear. Ramin waited for little angel Farzan to offer a rebuttal, but he just whispered, *Get in, get off, get out—those are the rules.*

Great. The cartoon versions of his friends that lived over his shoulder might've been cute, but sometimes, they gave absolutely useless advice.

Ramin was loading his dinner plates into the dishwasher when his phone buzzed. He sprang up, stubbed his toe on the kitchen table with a hissed *fuck!*, and hobble-ran to the living room.

Finally, *finally*, Noah was getting back to him.

Except it wasn't Noah calling.

It was *Todd*.

On FaceTime.

Ramin slumped onto the heinous red couch and stared at the screen. At some point someone (probably Arya) had changed Todd's contact to *Fucking Todd* and his photo to the poop emoji. Ramin was tempted to ignore the call, but on the off chance Todd had left something at the house, or had some other inane question about the logistics of breaking up, he answered.

"Hello?"

Todd's face came into frame. He was growing out his beard, and it framed his cheeks and jaw nicely. He must've colored it, too, since the brown was richer and deeper than Ramin remembered, auburn covering the gray whiskers that had started to pop up. Ramin had liked Todd's grays, liked his smile lines, too, though now Ramin got a good look, he seriously wondered if Todd had gotten some Botox, because his face was too smooth.

"Hey, Ramin. Uh. Hi." Todd scratched the back of his head. "How are you?"

Desperate to be anywhere else. Even the dentist's office. Without modern painkillers.

"I'm fine...uh, you?"

"I'm good." Todd lowered his arm. "I'm good."

"Good." Actually, some of those painkillers sounded great right about now. "Did you need something?"

"Sorry, yeah, I couldn't find two of my winter coats, and I wondered if you could check for them?"

"Ah. Sorry. I can't."

"Really?" Todd cocked his head, like he was really looking at Ramin for the first time, noticing the bright blue accent wall behind his head. "Where are you?"

"Milan."

"Milan." Todd blinked. "Like, Italy?"

Ramin nodded.

"For work?"

"No, I just needed a change." Ramin tried to keep his voice light. Fun. And not like he'd drunkenly booked the trip after spending the night crying about their breakup.

Todd's mouth dropped.

"Farzan and Arya have keys, though. They can let you in if you need to check."

"They're not the biggest fans of me right now," Todd muttered.

Ramin tried not to snort. But that's what ride-or-dies were for. Holding you up when your ex-boyfriend let you down.

He wanted to show Todd he was okay. He wanted Todd to know he was thriving.

"Well, I better let you go. It's late, and I've got to get to the club."

"The club?"

Ramin nodded.

"Yeah. Have a good day."

"Oh. Okay." Todd looked absolutely bewildered. Ramin wanted to laugh. "Bye."

"Byeeeeeee," Ramin said, drawing out the vowel. He ended the call and flopped back onto the couch. Why had he said that?

The truth was, he wasn't the biggest fan of clubs. At least going by himself. Todd had loved them—naturally—but Ramin had only really gone along to make him happy. His first time at a club, back when he was only twenty-two, a drunk twunk had told him "Straight skinny is gay fat," and he'd meant it, too.

So, yeah. Clubs weren't exactly his scene. But fuck. It was nearly nine o'clock, and Noah still hadn't gotten back to him.

Maybe he wasn't going to. Maybe it really was just a random hookup.

Maybe Ramin hadn't given him a good handjob. No, fuck, that was ridiculous, Ramin had turned in A+ work as usual. He might have a beautiful mosaic of hangups about his own body, but damn it, he knew his way around a dick.

So what was it? Why was Noah ghosting him, not twelve hours after they'd hooked up?

Well, whatever, he was Interesting New Ramin. He gave men handjobs in hotel beds. He navigated the Italian rail system on a whim.

He went to clubs, by himself, and danced with hot Italian strangers.

Boring Old Ramin might not have liked clubs, but Interesting New Ramin had different ideas.

twenty-four

Noah

Noah grunted, hoisting Jake's sleeping form a bit higher on his shoulders, as Angela fought with the keycard. It was nearly midnight, way past Jake's bedtime, but the restaurant Angela had booked for them hadn't even opened until eight o'clock, and they hadn't gotten their food until nine, and Jake was nodding off by the time it was done.

Then their subway stop had been closed for some reason, and after a miserable half hour of walking around they finally managed to find a taxi to get them back to their hotel.

Jake had promptly fallen asleep against Noah's side, and Noah hadn't wanted to rouse him.

Now he tucked Jake into Angela's bed. "This okay?"

She nodded. "Thanks. I'll take care of him."

"You sure?"

"Positive. Night."

"Night."

Noah let himself into his own room, locked the door, flopped onto his bed, kicked his shoes off, stretched. Had this day really begun with him waking up in bed with Ramin? That seemed like a lifetime ago. A beautiful dream he was desperate to recall.

Ramin. His phone.

He'd been in the middle of texting Ramin when he got distracted with Jake. And then spent all day out. *Crap.*

He rolled across the bed and nearly yanked his phone off its charger. Sure enough, Ramin had finally responded to him.

A lot.

> **Ramin**
>
> I get back later today. Glad you made it. And I was happy to help.
>
> With everything
>
> I'm back now! What are you up to?
>
> Everything okay?
>
> Sorry. You're probably with your family.
>
> I didn't mean to interrupt. I know it's important. Tell Jake hi!
>
> Sorry, didn't mean to blow up your phone
>
> I hope I wasn't weird or anything.
>
> Sorry

Noah groaned. The last message was from two hours ago.

Ramin probably thought he was a jerk. That Noah had just been taking advantage of him. And Noah couldn't blame him. He'd left Ramin high and dry this morning. Unsatisfied. And then he'd ghosted him to run off with his family.

What else was Ramin supposed to think?

Crap. He hadn't meant to. But he'd never had to juggle seeing someone with his family obligations. *Was* he seeing Ramin? Did Ramin want that?

Oh no. Had he already ruined it?

Please, please, please...

He had to explain. Had to apologize.

His thumbs were jittery as he tried to type out an acceptable response, but as he did, Ramin started texting again.

Noah's heart leapt into his throat.

> **Ramin**
>
> Hey it's coool i get it
>
> Didnt mean to be all needy or whatever
>
> It's cool
>
> I'm cool
>
> Don't worry about meeeee
>
> I'm at a club!!!!!!
>
> Enjoy the rest of your vacayyyy

Noah's thumbs froze. That sounded like goodbye.

A very drunken goodbye.

Was Ramin...drunk texting him?

From a *club*?

Shame filled Noah's chest. He'd driven Ramin away. All because his phone wasn't charged.

Ramin had given up on him.

It wasn't fair. He was new at this. Well, not *new* new, but out of practice. He'd never had to juggle having a child with...well, whatever this was with Ramin. He was figuring it out. That didn't mean he didn't want Ramin. That didn't mean he didn't want Ramin to want him back.

He deserved a chance, didn't he?

He had to find Ramin. Had to make him understand. This morning wasn't some random hookup, and Ramin wasn't some random guy. Ramin meant something to him. He wanted them to figure this out.

But how?

Noah

Where are you? Which club?

To Noah's surprise, Ramin answered, though not the way he expected.

Ramin didn't send the name of the club. Or the address. Or a little map pin.

Instead he sent a photo.

Despite everything, Noah laughed. Ramin was holding a drink, standing at the bar, posing in front of the lower half of some sort of go-go boy in gold booty shorts. The faceless bulge was perilously close to Ramin's head.

Something burned its way through Noah's chest, something primal and dangerous and perhaps even a bit problematic. But he didn't want Ramin dancing with other guys. Or looking at their bulges.

Ramin was his.

It wasn't a mature thought. He knew that. It was selfish and reductive and it didn't matter, because after twenty years he was finally getting a chance with Ramin, and he wasn't going to let some muscled Italian in booty shorts come between them.

Noah sprang off his bed and pulled his shoes back on. He started googling clubs nearby to see if he could find photos, find some clue—the shape of the bar, or the lights or, ugh, even evidence of gold-booty-shorted dancers. He had to find Ramin.

He had to.

Noah had never been to a gay club before.

He'd never been to any kind of club at all. His twenties had been spent working, saving money. Not hanging around Westport testing the limits of his liver. Part of him had wanted to, but he'd been careful with his budget, desperate not to have to ask his parents for anything.

Though now that he thought about it, he had been to *one* club: the Green Lady Lounge, a famous jazz club off Grand. Angela had taken him when they were first dating. They'd had overpriced drinks and danced until closing. She'd been so beautiful, so full of life, Noah had fallen in love that night.

This club was nothing like that.

Neon lights painted the walls of the entryway. Bass-heavy EDM thundered in the air. He wished he'd brought his earplugs. He took his hearing protection seriously.

Still, he was almost certain this was the right club. He'd spotted Ramin's bartender—a shirtless guy with a truly epic mustache—in several of the photos of this place. Hopefully the guy didn't work at other clubs, too.

Noah didn't know the protocol—the folks he'd followed had flashed some sort of card to get in—and there wasn't a bouncer. Instead there was a front counter, where a young guy with a shock of pink hair explained to him in shouted, accented English he could pay for a one-club membership or do a three-month pass instead.

He handed over a few euros, took his card, and slipped into the dark club.

The bass thrummed in his chest, so loud he could barely make out the actual music. Pink and purple lights strobed. He weaved his way through the press of bodies—some clothed, some half naked. Some fat, some skinny, some muscled and smooth, some burly and hairy, all painted with color and light and shadow. For a second Noah imagined letting himself get lost in here. Dancing the night away.

He'd finally figured out he was bisexual when he was twenty or so. Started telling people a few years after that. But for a multitude of reasons—ranging from heteronormativity to convenience to his parents to how expensive gas was when he was in his mid-twenties—he'd never really gotten to live a queer life the way he wanted to.

On his own terms.

He wanted to dance, wanted to touch, wanted to laugh.

But he didn't want to do any of that without Ramin.

To his relief, he did indeed find the mustachioed bartender, spinning bottles and smiling. Ramin's picture had been too blurry to show the guy's pierced nipples, though. Noah wondered if they'd hurt.

If this was the right place, then where was Ramin? Noah made a circuit of the dance floor, checked the bar on the opposite end, dipped into the bathroom and then immediately dipped back out because it was *extremely* occupied in a way Noah thought was just a myth.

Had Ramin left? Or worse, left *with* someone?

Noah clenched his fist. No. Ramin wouldn't do that, would he? Just because Noah didn't get back to him fast enough? They were both adults. It wasn't like Noah ghosted him. Not on purpose, at least.

He angled his way toward the DJ stand. Maybe he could beg them to make an announcement or something.

Ramin Yazdani, please report to the front office.

But then Noah spotted him.

Ramin swayed on the dance floor, eyes half closed, wearing a teal T-shirt and the most sinful pair of orange shorts Noah had ever seen in his life. His mouth went dry. His whole body flushed.

Ramin looked like heaven.

And he moved like heaven, too. Noah had no idea he could dance like that. Ramin was a good decade older than most of the other folks on the dance floor, folks with sculpted abs showing through mesh shirts, or firm butts exposed by shorts somehow even shorter than Ramin's, but Ramin was the most beautiful person there.

He opened his eyes and saw Noah. His head cocked to the side, almost comically, before a smile stole over his features, catching rainbows in his dimples.

Noah stepped up, but he didn't know what to do. This wasn't like prom, where you just spun in a circle with your hands on your girlfriend's butt.

Then again, Ramin did indeed grab Noah's hands and plant them on his butt.

"What're you doing here?" he shouted, though it was almost a slur. And up close, Noah could tell Ramin's eyes were droopy.

"Looking for you."

"Whyyyyyy? I'm being interesting!"

Ramin slipped out of Noah's hands, dancing more feverishly, grinding up against the other guys nearby, and that primal flame roared in Noah's chest once more.

Oh. He was *jealous.*

He hadn't been jealous in a long time.

"I want to talk to you," Noah shouted.

"What?"

"I said—" But someone bumped into Noah, slid between him and Ramin. A young guy with the lower half of his butt cheeks literally hanging out of his shorts. He rubbed up against Noah's front for a second, before turning and looking at Noah, eyes wide and interested.

But Noah shook his head, brushed him aside, found Ramin again.

"Can we go?"

"What?"

"I said, let's get out of here!"

Ramin stared at him for a moment. Noah took his hand, tugged him toward the exit. Not a hard tug, just enough to show what direction he was trying to go.

"But what if I'm not done dancing?"

"You're done," Noah said, with more force than he meant to, but Ramin was drunk and Noah didn't like the thought of Ramin here all alone without someone to watch his back, guard his drinks, make sure he got home safely. "We're going."

Ramin gave a full-body shiver as Noah led him off the dance floor, out the club, and into the blessedly silent streets.

Ramin tripped on the sidewalk, but Noah caught him. When Ramin straightened up, they were chest to chest. Ramin's face was flushed. He blinked, his head sagging a bit to the side.

"You came for me," he said. "I thought you were done with me."

After the shouting in the club, Ramin's voice had gone soft and sad. Noah ached that he'd made Ramin think that.

"My phone was dead," he explained. "And then I was out with Jake and Angela while it was charging. I'm sorry. I didn't mean to leave you hanging. I didn't want you to think I don't want you. Because I do. I…"

Before Noah could explain more, Ramin was leaning into him, enveloping Noah's mouth with his own. His kisses were forceful, needy, a little bit sloppy, but Noah could feel the smile in his lips.

Still, they had to talk about things first. He broke the kiss, held Ramin at arm's length.

"Hey. Hey. You okay?"

"I don't usually have gin," Ramin admitted. He rested his head against Noah's shoulder. "I think I'm drunk."

"Let's get you home. Which way?"

"Uh." Ramin looked around, confused. Pulled out his phone, but the screen stayed dark. He blew a raspberry. "Now *my* phone is dead. Cockblocked by an iPhone."

Noah's chest fluttered, but he wasn't thinking about that right now. "We can go to my hotel. I have a charger."

"Okay."

Noah kept hold of Ramin's hand as he led the way back to their hotel. As they passed a pharmacy, Ramin snickered.

"Look. The vending machines sell condoms."

Sure enough, a large silver vending machine stood outside the dark, locked pharmacy. It had more than just condoms: There were lubes, vibrators, tampons, pregnancy tests, even little bottles of soap for washing your butt when you used the bidet.

"Guess what! My luggage showed up!" Ramin sighed. "I didn't bring any condoms in your size, though."

Noah blushed, but his heart skipped a beat. He liked knowing that Ramin was thinking about him like *that*.

He really, really liked it.

Ramin rested his head against the lit-up glass of the vending machine and heaved a sigh that would've made Jake proud. "And the pharmacy is closed."

Noah smiled.

He wanted to do more with Ramin. But not now, while he was drunk.

"We'll figure something out," he said, hoping to get Ramin moving again.

It worked. Ramin pouted, but he started walking again.

Noah let Ramin in as quietly as he could. The walls were thick enough, he didn't think they'd disturb Jake and Angela, but on the off chance they woke up, he didn't want to have to explain this. Not when he was still trying to wrap his head around it himself.

"You want some water?"

Ramin nodded. He could hold his head up straight again, and his walking had improved. He was sobering up, at least a little. He scratched at the center of his chest.

"I better. Thanks."

Noah grabbed a bottle, handed it over. Ramin cracked it, took a huge glug, and immediately spat. He coughed and wheezed as Noah patted his back and winced at the noise.

"The bubbles," Ramin sputtered.

Crap, Noah hadn't meant to grab the frizzante one.

Ramin wiped his mouth with the back of his hand.

Why was that so sexy?

He took another, slower drink, as Noah self-consciously assessed his room. It was smaller than the one they'd shared in Como. And messy, too. Who could keep a neat hotel room when you sometimes shared it with a nine-year-old?

Noah gestured for Ramin to sit on the bed, then settled down next to him.

"Thanks for coming to get me." Ramin sighed. "How'd you even find me?"

"Your picture."

"I sent a picture?"

Noah's eyebrows raised, and Ramin blushed.

Noah liked it when Ramin blushed, liked the way the pink spread all the way down his neck, toward his collar.

"No more gin," Ramin muttered.

"At least you didn't book another international trip."

Ramin snickered, giving him a mischievous grin.

More than anything, Noah wanted to tackle him to the bed and kiss him all over. He had to wait, though. Ramin had to be completely sober before they did anything else.

"But *why*?" Ramin asked. "You could've waited for the morning."

"I didn't want you going home with any of those other guys," Noah growled. He blinked, surprised at himself. He hadn't mean for it to come out so gruff.

Ramin's eyes danced.

"Oh yeah?"

"I mean..." Noah swallowed. "You're a grown man, and you can do whatever you want. Sorry."

"Don't be," Ramin said. "I liked it when you—"

He snapped his mouth shut so hard his teeth clicked.

Noah's heart sped up. Ramin liked it when he *what*?

He had to know!

Ramin finished off the water bottle, his blush growing more intense. He kept avoiding Noah's eyes.

So Noah took Ramin's free hand and rubbed his thumb along Ramin's tattoo. Ramin shuddered at the touch.

"Come on," Noah said. "Tell me."

But Ramin clamped his mouth shut in a shy smile.

That smile of his was going to get Noah in trouble.

Noah didn't know what came over him, but in a heartbeat he lunged, pinning Ramin to the bed. The empty water bottle bonked to the ground as Noah held Ramin's hands against the mattress, using his hips to trap Ramin's legs.

Suddenly they were eighteen again, horsing around in the hallways. Noah kept his laughter as quiet as he could.

"Tell me!"

Ramin laughed and struggled, but Noah didn't let him up. Not until he heard Ramin's breaths get ragged, felt Ramin's arms shaking beneath him.

Noah felt like he'd been dunked in a cold tank. He let go of Ramin in an instant, retreating to his side of the bed.

"I'm sorry," he said. "I'm so sorry."

Ramin blinked. "Sorry? For what?"

"You were trying to get up, and I wasn't listening, and—"

Ramin shook his head. He sat up, adjusting his erection. Noah tracked the movements and realized he was licking his lips.

He had to stop perving. Ramin had been drinking tonight. *Everything* was off-limits.

"I liked it," Ramin whispered, rubbing at one of his wrist tattoos.

"You what?" Noah had to have heard wrong.

"I liked it." Ramin finally met Noah's eyes. "When you held me down. I really liked it."

And then he squinted.

"I also really have to pee."

Noah snorted as Ramin slipped into the bathroom and closed the door. Noah followed and knocked. "There's extra toothbrushes in my bag." He always traveled with extras for Jake.

"Thanks."

Noah paced, trying to make sense of what Ramin had just told him. He liked being held down? Noah had spent his whole adult life being careful with people in bed. Because of his size, because of his strength, because he was a white man and there were always power dynamics to consider.

"Thanks," Ramin said, emerging from the bathroom smelling fresh. "I think I'm sober enough to make it home."

"You don't have to go."

"I really should."

"Please." Noah knew it was risky. Angela and Jake were right next door. But after sharing a bed with Ramin last night, he couldn't help wanting to do it again. "I liked cuddling."

He liked what they'd done this morning, too, but that was a conversation for when Ramin was totally sober.

Ramin looked down, but he couldn't quite hide his dimples. "I liked it, too."

Noah let Ramin get settled while he took care of his own nighttime routine. He brushed his teeth and popped in his night guard. He'd ground his teeth off and on most of his life.

He peeked out and saw Ramin still in his shirt, so Noah kept his on too. Normally he'd sleep in just his boxers, but he didn't want Ramin to be uncomfortable.

Noah slid into bed behind Ramin. "Is this okay?"

"Why does your voice sound weird?"

Ramin twisted to get a look. Noah opened his mouth.

"Night guard."

Ramin's face softened so sweetly. He leaned in and planted a kiss on Noah's nose.

And then he snuggled into the pillows.

Noah clicked off the light. He was facing Ramin's back, but they weren't touching. Should he reach out? Pull Ramin in closer to spoon? Did Ramin only like being the big spoon? Noah didn't mind either way. He'd turn over if that's what Ramin wanted.

"Ramin?" Noah asked.

"Yeah?"

"You...want to cuddle?"

Ramin scooted back and let Noah wrap an arm around him.

They breathed quietly for a moment. Beneath Ramin's shirt, Noah felt something smooth and slick. He rubbed his thumb against it and Ramin flinched.

"That's my tattoo. It's still healing."

"Sorry." Noah planted a soft kiss on Ramin's shoulder. That seemed safe, right? He wanted more, wanted to peel off their clothes, feel Ramin's skin against his. Wanted to pin Ramin down to the bed and make him talk. Wanted...well. *Wanted.*

He couldn't do all that, not right now. Instead he asked, "What did you mean earlier?"

"Huh?"

"When you said you liked it when I held you down."

"Oh God." Ramin's voice was small. Embarrassed. "Forget I said anything."

"Come on."

Noah jiggled Ramin.

"Just...sometimes I like being...dominated."

"Dominated?" Noah's heart beat faster. Why did that excite him?

"Ugh." Ramin twisted around. Noah could barely make out the green of his eyes in the dim light filtering in from the window. "Don't freak out, okay? It's just a kink."

"Okay." Noah hadn't given much thought to kink before. He didn't even know if he had any. What was a kink and what was just...what you liked? Or what your partner liked?

And why did he want to pin Ramin to the bed again?

"I'm not freaking out."

He was, however, making a mental list of things to google.

"Can you explain a bit more?"

Ramin sighed. His minty breath washed over Noah's face. "I like being...told what to do. Held down or bossed around or made to...not literally made to, but just kind of...I don't even know how to explain it."

"Huh." Noah tried to bite his lip, but he only managed to smoosh it beneath his night guard. "How come?"

"I don't know? Maybe my therapist would say it's because I have to be in control of so many things in my life so I like it when someone else takes control? But I think I've always liked it. When I used to dream about you—"

Ramin's voice choked off.

Noah grinned. "You used to dream about me?"

"Ugh. I'm still drunk."

Ramin might have been buzzed, but Noah didn't think he was drunk anymore.

"Uh-huh. Sure." He tightened his arms. "Come on, tell me."

Ramin whined and closed his eyes.

"I won't judge," Noah said.

Ramin groaned. "Fine. Remember how I used to be on newspaper? Back in school?"

"Yeah."

"I dreamed I was covering one of your wrestling matches, and then I had to pee, and you came in to the bathroom, too, in your singlet, and you...I can't believe I'm telling you this."

"I'll keep your secret." Noah's heart was hammering. Could Ramin feel him getting harder in his boxers? Maybe Noah was a little kinky, too. "So. What happened?"

"You shoved me into a stall, and told me you'd seen me checking you out, and you...pushed me down to my knees and made me give you a blowjob."

Noah felt like Ramin had splashed cold water over him. Consent was the most important thing. "I would never—"

Ramin's hand came up to shush Noah with a finger. Noah's lips tingled where they touched.

"I know you wouldn't. But it was...really hot. In the dream, I mean. I woke up wet." Ramin snickered. "Also, in the dream your dick reached the floor."

Noah snorted. "You're a menace."

"So. You don't think I'm weird?"

Ramin said it lightly, but there was a quaver there. Did he honestly think Noah would judge him?

Noah would never do that.

"I don't think you're weird." Honestly, Noah had liked holding Ramin down. And he'd liked it, back at the club, when he'd told Ramin they were going, and Ramin had obeyed.

Maybe Noah liked being in charge, sometimes. What did that mean?

Maybe Ramin's therapist would say that Noah spent too much of his life making other people happy, listening to what others wanted, letting people steamroll him, first his parents and then Angela, twisting himself inside out to make sure Jake was happy and healthy and taken care of.

Or maybe he just liked it because he liked it.

Noah had never had sex dreams about Ramin when they were younger, and certainly not ones involving bathroom blowjobs. But looking back, in his limited experiences with guys, he *had* enjoyed taking charge. The feeling that he could be rougher.

Yeah. He was definitely a little kinky.

"I can't believe I told you all that," Ramin said.

"Me neither," Noah teased.

He leaned in and kissed Ramin's nose.

Ramin giggled, but the laughter turned into a yawn, which set off Noah's own yawning. It was past two in the morning. Noah was exhausted. And Jake liked to wake up early.

He rested his forehead against Ramin's for a second.

"Get some sleep. I'll take care of you."

"I know you will," Ramin said. He turned over, letting Noah spoon him again, and sighed.

Noah breathed deep until he could feel their heartbeats sync up. His penis lay warm and heavy in his boxers, but it wasn't even half hard, and if Ramin noticed it, he didn't mention anything.

He could stay like this forever.

twenty-five

Ramin

Ramin's mouth tasted like the inside of an old car. It felt like it, too, that fuzzy, scratchy feeling that cars from the nineties always seemed to have. Actually, that might've been the pillow mashed into his face. He'd turned in his sleep, onto his belly, and he almost never slept that way.

A heavy arm still lay across his back. It took him a moment to realize where he was. He groaned. He'd made a complete and total ass of himself.

"Good morning," Noah rumbled.

"It's definitely a morning," Ramin muttered.

Noah chuckled. Ramin twisted to find beautiful eyes peering at him, catching the morning light, a smile tugging their corners.

"You feel okay?"

Despite the horrible taste and dry mouth, Ramin didn't feel all that gross. Not hangover-gross, just regular dehydrated.

"Yeah. Thanks for taking care of me last night. I should get out of your hair."

Ramin made to slide out, but Noah's arm around him tightened. "You don't have to go."

Ramin shook his head. He'd embarrassed himself last night. Getting drunk and acting a fool was bad enough. But spilling all his kinkiest secrets? By that point he'd been . . . well, not exactly sober, but definitely sober enough he should've kept his mouth shut.

He wanted to curl into a ball and hide. Or maybe live in the rafters of one of the churches here. There were so many to choose from. He could hang out with the gargoyles.

"I never did get to make it up to you," Noah mumbled.

Ramin scrunched his face. What was Noah talking about?

"Back in Como. In the morning." Noah tugged Ramin closer. "We got interrupted."

Oh.

Ramin's heart lurched.

"You don't have to—"

"I want to. I owe you."

"You don't owe me anything."

"But you got me off, and I didn't . . ."

"No one's keeping score."

Noah huffed. His brows drew down. He looked genuinely upset. Ramin reached out to poke the little crease between Noah's eyebrows.

"What's wrong?"

"You'll think it's silly."

Ramin snorted. "I literally confessed my teenaged wet dreams to you last night."

Noah smiled and hid his face in the pillow. But when it poked up again, he said, "I haven't actually been with many guys. In fact, only two others before you."

"Okay? So?" Ramin's body count was higher than two, for sure, but it wasn't like he was in Arya's league.

"So both times it was really . . . uneven between us." Noah's cheeks were getting pink. "Like, it wasn't reciprocal."

"Reciprocal how?" Like, Noah didn't like them back? Or Noah liked them, but they didn't like *him* back? How could anyone not like Noah back?

"Like, this guy I used to work with at the Hollister up at Metro North—"

Ramin snorted. "You worked at *Hollister*?"

"At least it wasn't Abercrombie, okay? I was twenty-two. I had bills."

Ramin imagined Noah standing shirtless in a haze of cologne at Metro North Mall, with the balloons hovering over the fountain in the distance. Maybe wearing one of those puka shell necklaces. He stifled a laugh. "Sorry. Go on."

"So this guy, one of my coworkers, I think he was gay, though he never said anything. Just the vibe, I guess? Anyway, somehow he'd heard about my...uh..."

"Your *uh*?"

"He'd heard I was hung, I guess."

"Ah." Ramin tried not to smirk. Noah was so *proper* sometimes. It was endearing. He wondered what Noah would be like if he let loose.

He hoped he'd get to find out.

"And one day we were in the stockroom and he asked if it was true, and I tried to get out of the conversation because I didn't want to get in trouble—I really needed that job—but he kept asking, and he was pretty cute, and one thing led to another and he ended up giving me a blowjob."

Ramin's dick lurched at the thought. He bit his lip.

"Then when it was done, he got up and was like 'Thanks' and just left."

"That's really hot," Ramin whispered. He imagined himself in that guy's place, getting on his knees, worshipping Noah the way he deserved, and—

"It didn't feel like it. It felt like being used."

Ramin's mouth went dry.

Of course it did. Noah was a person, not just a dick. He deserved to be treated better. Ramin swallowed back his shame. "I'm sorry. I didn't think of it that way."

"It's fine."

It wasn't fine, but Noah shook his head and kept going. "I asked him out after. Told him I was bi. He got this look on his face. He said if he'd known I wasn't straight he wouldn't have gone for it. That it wasn't nearly as hot."

Anger reared up in Ramin's chest. What kind of asshole says things like that? *Does* things like that?

"That's fucked up. I'm sorry."

Noah shrugged.

"Was it like that for the other guy, too?"

"Worse. It was another guy at Hollister, actually..."

Ramin wished he'd known to shop at the Metro North Hollister back then. Maybe he and Noah could've run into each other all those years ago. Maybe he could've shown Noah that not all guys were assholes. That there were guys out there who'd like him for every part of him.

But then, if they had, Noah wouldn't have had Jake, and he knew without a doubt Noah would never want that.

"This guy actually saw me changing one day, and he started acting weird, and then said he wanted to compare, and ended up giving me a handjob. But when I tried to touch him, he jerked away, said he wasn't gay, said it was just an experiment, and he never talked to me again. He quit a few days later. Didn't even give notice. At least I got overtime for covering his shifts."

"Fuck him. Fuck both of them." Ramin pulled himself closer to Noah. "You deserved a lot better. I'm sorry you had to deal with that."

"It's fine. Lots of people had it worse than me."

"It wasn't fine. That first guy was super biphobic, and the second guy was just a dick. And not the good kind."

Noah giggled at that. Giggled, like a little kid, all high pitched and everything. Ramin had never heard anything like it. Now he knew where Jake got his laugh from.

"But still," Noah said, "I'm a white, bisexual, cisgender man. I'm sure you've dealt with—"

"That doesn't matter," Ramin said. Noah acted like he wasn't allowed to be hurt. Or worse, deserved it. "I'm glad you have the perspective to understand your privilege, but that doesn't make what happened okay. It doesn't mean you don't get to be upset."

Noah furrowed his brow, but finally nodded.

"Good. Also, I hope you know I'm not keeping track of orgasms like... like some sort of point system."

"But—"

Ramin put a finger on Noah's lips. Noah kissed the pad of it, but Ramin didn't let himself get distracted.

"Whatever this is between us..." What *was* it? They'd spent the last two nights together. They'd kissed and had sex, and apparently Noah wanted more.

But Noah had also just confessed he was inexperienced with guys. And his two prior experiences had both used him. Was Ramin truly any better than them? He'd been lusting after Noah half his life.

Shame at his own behavior warred with tenderness for Noah, a desire to protect him.

He'd sort that out later.

"Whatever it is, our obligation isn't to get each other off. It's to be honest with each other. Yeah?"

"Okay." Noah swallowed. "In all honesty, I really want to get you off."

Ramin snorted, but in a flash, Noah was on top of him, pinning his hands above his head.

"You said you liked this," Noah said. His cock lay warm and firm atop Ramin's, pulsing when he flexed it, heavy enough to feel even through the layers of their underwear.

Ramin's skin hummed with desire. His mouth went dry. "Uh-huh."

"What about this?" Noah ground his hips against Ramin's. Ramin whimpered as his own dick hardened swiftly. He nodded and bit his lips and pretended to struggle. It didn't take much pretending: Noah was *strong*.

Noah reached for Ramin's shirt. Ramin clenched his stomach, engaged his core out of instinct as he drew in a swift breath.

"I really want to see this tattoo of yours." Noah's eyes sparkled. He began to tug on Ramin's shirt, but—

Knock knock knock.

Noah froze. Ramin did too. He stared up at Noah. Noah stared down at him.

"Noah?" Angela called through the door. "You up?"

"You've got to be fucking kidding me," Ramin muttered.

He meant what he told Noah—that they weren't keeping score of orgasms—but being cockblocked by Noah's family yet again did feel like a huge cosmic thumb on the proverbial scales.

It was like the universe hated him. Why? He'd never done anything particularly nasty to it, had he?

Noah was still staring at him, and seemed to be trying to communicate something silently, but Ramin didn't know what. They couldn't talk with just gestures and expressions. They barely knew each other, when it came down to it.

So Ramin shrugged, and then Noah called out, "I'm up. Give me a sec."

Noah rolled out of bed. He pulled on a pair of shorts (sadly out of Ramin's view—seriously, when was Ramin going to get a proper look at Noah's Ark?) and went to answer the door connecting his and Angela's room.

Ramin sunk lower into the bed and pulled the covers up and over his head.

"Hey." Noah's muffled voice still carried through the duvet. "Is everything okay?"

The door closed with a snap. The room went silent. Ramin peeked out.

Alone, thank God, and his boner was, once again, thoroughly killed.

He got up and searched for his own shorts. He had a vague memory of throwing them over his shoulder last night. Maybe he'd been drunker than he thought.

He finally found them caught between the lamppost and the wall. He'd just slid them back on when the door opened again and Jake charged into the room. He launched himself onto the bed, then came up short, staring at Ramin.

Ramin stared back.

Caught.

What was the proper procedure when your hookup's son caught you before you could make your walk of shame?

Was Noah just a hookup? What *was* he? What was any of this?

Jake was still looking at him. Shit, how long had Ramin been standing there like a deer hoping for an insurance payout?

"Hey, Jake," he finally mustered.

Jake unfroze and a huge smile broke over his face. "Ramin!" He scrambled up and came to sit cross-legged on the edge of the bed, right where the covers were rumpled from Ramin and Noah's attempt at a little morning excitement.

Jake wore a pair of Spider-Man pajamas. He cocked his head to the side, and his messy hair flopped over. "Are you here for breakfast?"

"Ah, no." Ramin cleared his throat and scrambled for an answer. "I wasn't feeling very well last night, so your dad came to help me out, and, uh, he let me stay here since I was so sick."

That was age appropriate and not technically a lie, right?

Ramin didn't really believe in lying to kids, but he didn't know if Jake knew what *gin drunk* was.

"Aw man, we could've had a sleepover!" Jake bounced on the bed.

"It was pretty late, you were already asleep. And I was too sick for company."

"Dad's good at taking care of people when they're sick," Jake observed. That didn't surprise Ramin. Noah struck him as the kind of guy with a strong nurturing side. "He makes the best grilled cheese."

"Oh really?"

"Yeah. Do you like Spider-Man?"

Ramin grinned. "Of course. Who doesn't?"

"Total losers," Jake said dramatically. "We walked by the Lego Store yesterday and they had this huge Spider-Man set, but Mom and Dad wouldn't let me get it. They said they could get it cheaper back home and not have to fit it into our suitcases."

Ramin nodded sagely. "I guess that makes sense. The exchange rate isn't great right now."

"I suppose," Jake muttered. He looked down and started plucking at the duvet. He might've only been nine, but he looked like he had the weight of the world on his shoulders.

Ramin gave him a little nudge. "Whatcha thinking?"

Jake shrugged. "Just boring stuff."

"Oh yeah?"

"Yeah." He sighed. Jake had the biggest sigh, and he looked so serious, his brow furrowed over his brown eyes, just like his dad's did. "My mom is moving here."

"I heard."

"But my dad's staying back in Kansas City."

"Yeah."

His voice got smaller. "What's going to happen to me?"

"What do you want to happen?" Ramin asked. At the end of the day, that was what mattered most, right?

Jake's face screwed up. "I don't know."

"I'm sorry." Ramin wished he knew what to say. But it wasn't like Noah and Angela had figured this out, either. If the grown-ups couldn't work things out, no one could expect Jake to. "That really sucks."

"Yeah." Jake nodded solemnly. "It does suck."

Uh-oh. Ramin tried to remember if he'd heard Jake saying that before, or if he'd just taught him a new way to complain about things. Nine-year-olds knew *sucked*, though, right?

"Your parents both love you, though. I hope you know that."

Ramin could see it in the way Noah played with Jake's hair. In the way Angela laughed at his cheesy jokes.

"I guess. Can I see your tattoos again?"

Ramin nearly got whiplash from the change of topic.

"Uh, sure." Ramin offered his wrists.

Jake's little fingers tickled Ramin's pulse points as he traced the Persian script. "Can you write like this?"

"Only a few words. I'm taking classes, though."

He'd signed up for online Persian classes last year. He'd finally found a teacher from Yazd, the city his family came from. Most teachers taught you to speak like you were from Tehran, but Yazd had its own idiosyncratic dialect.

Ramin had never told anyone about his classes before. Learning his parents' language—the language he remembered snatches of from his childhood—felt so personal. Plus he didn't want to disappoint people if he never made much progress. Somehow, though, he didn't mind telling Jake.

"You write Farsi right to left, and it's all in cursive. Have you done cursive in school yet?"

"Not yet."

"Okay. Well, most of the letters join up. That's an *n*, and *s*, and *r*. And then *ee* and another *n*. Nasrin."

"What about the *a*?"

"You leave it out. For short vowels you have to just know what goes where." Ramin sighed, doing his best Jake impression. "It's really tough."

"I bet."

Ramin switched wrists. "And this is Sina—"

The door cracked open. Ramin and Jake both looked up to find Noah peering at them with a soft smile. "Jakey, can I talk to Ramin a sec?"

"Okay."

Jake offered Ramin a fist bump, then scurried back to Angela's room. Noah closed the door behind him.

"You two were cute," Noah said.

"He's a good kid."

"Yeah. When he's not being a pill, at least."

Ramin didn't know what to say to that. But being a parent was probably a lot harder than just showing off tattoos and talking about Spider-Man. And explaining to your ex-wife why there was a strange man sleeping in your room.

"Sorry if I made things complicated."

"Don't be." Noah swallowed. "I told Angela we might be kind-of-sort-of...seeing each other."

Ramin's chest tightened.

Were they seeing each other? Was that what all this meant? If that's what Noah wanted, was that what Ramin wanted, too?

Seeing each other?

It also freaked him the fuck out, but one crisis at a time.

"How did she take it?"

Noah snorted. "She's not always good with unexpected changes, but she'll come around."

That sounded like it went badly, then.

"But she already knew you were bi...right?"

"Oh yeah."

On the one hand, good, she wasn't freaking out about Noah being with a man.

On the other hand, shit, because she *was* freaking out about Noah being with Ramin, for whatever reasons.

"I feel like maybe I should let you three process all this?" Ramin said, standing.

To be honest, maybe he needed to process it, too.

"And now that we both have phones that are charged, we can figure out what's next?"

Noah chewed his lip as Ramin stuffed his phone and wallet and chunky keychain into his pockets.

"See you?"

Noah nodded. But then, before Ramin could open it, Noah had him backed up against the door. His arms were on either side, hemming Ramin in.

Ramin inhaled. Noah still had morning breath, but beneath that, he smelled like he always did, of sugar and wood and sweat and sun. His lips made a perfect heart, until his smile turned wolfish.

"Noah," Ramin warned. Jake and Angela were in the other room, after all.

"Ramin," Noah growled, before enveloping Ramin's mouth. His tongue plunged in without preamble, and Ramin would've melted, slumped to the floor, if Noah wasn't right there holding him up.

Ramin's blood pounded through his ears as they kissed and kissed and kissed. His skin hummed. His lips burned. His knees weakened.

He never wanted to move, never wanted to do anything but explore every bit of Noah's luscious mouth. He was getting hard again. But finally he put a gentle hand on Noah's chest.

Noah was breathing hard. His pupils had dilated.

He looked like he wanted to devour Ramin, and Ramin really, really wanted to be devoured, but they had to be responsible adults.

"I better go," he said.

"I'll call you."

Wow. Moving to calls already? Were they just going to skip the awkward texting phase?

Ramin couldn't bring himself to complain. He gave Noah one last kiss. "Okay."

He only looked back once (all right, twice) as he let himself out and headed for the elevator.

twenty-six

Noah

Noah closed his eyes and rested his forehead against the door. He could still smell the tiniest bit of Ramin's cologne. Could still taste Ramin's lips on his tongue. Could still feel the warmth pooling in his belly, between his legs, as he breathed.

This was...not how he wanted Angela and Jake to find out about him and Ramin.

Him and Ramin. Despite himself, he smiled.

He and Ramin were a thing now. A real thing. Right? That's what he'd told Angela, at least. He thought Ramin was on the same page.

But maybe that's what Ramin had meant by *processing.*

Please let Ramin be on the same page.

And once again, they'd been interrupted before he could actually get his hands on Ramin. Make him feel the way he'd made Noah feel.

Still, even though he hadn't been able to touch Ramin the way he wanted, it was worth it to see Ramin and Jake together. Sitting on the bed, heads bowed in conversation, two co-conspirators in the making.

Jake was clearly smitten with Ramin. That was one thing he and his son had in common. And thank goodness. Jake might've been butting heads with Noah, but at least he got along with Ramin.

Now, if only Angela could be so easily swayed.

Noah straightened up, adjusted himself, and knocked on Angela's door.

"You didn't have to make him leave," she said.

"He needed to get home." Noah looked around. "Where's Jake?"

"Bathroom." She frowned. "I don't think the food here agrees with him."

Noah bit his lip. Jake's stomach had been shakier the last few days, but it wasn't like he was eating anything he didn't eat back home.

"So…" Noah began, right as Angela said, "I just—"

Noah nodded. "You go ahead."

Angela pulled her hair tie off, stuck it between her teeth, and started regathering her ponytail. It had started to curl without the rigorous straightening routine she used back home. It had bounce to it. It reminded Noah of when they first started dating.

"What're you smiling at?" she mumbled around the elastic.

"Your hair looks nice."

Angela rolled her eyes, but her cheeks turned pink. She was in a turquoise sundress today, one that hugged her wide hips and the swell of her stomach just right. She looked…

It took Noah a moment to realize she looked *relaxed*. He couldn't remember the last time he'd seen her looking relaxed.

"Italy agrees with you."

He didn't want it to be true. He wanted her to tell him no, it was just the humidity. Or no, it was just her not having time for her hair.

But instead, she finished tying her hair and smiled.

"You remember what Nonna said, about life being slower? I think I needed that. I've been going-going-going for years, and I…I can breathe here."

Noah's heart couldn't decide if it wanted to clench or unclench.

Angela was *happy* here. And Noah was glad for that. He always

wanted her to be happy, and he'd always be a little sad he couldn't make
her happy himself.

But he wished she hated it here. He wished she was rethinking
everything.

He wished they didn't even have to have these conversations.

"Anyway." She took a deep breath. "I was going to say…you're a
grown man. You can make your own choices about who you see and
who you sleep with, and I don't get a say in that anymore. I'm sorry
if I came across like I don't approve or don't want you to be happy
or…whatever's going on."

"Thank you."

"That said, I really don't think this is the right time for either of us
to be embarking on anything new, relationship-wise, not until we get
things more sorted out. We're already asking Jake to accept a lot of
change. I don't know if we should be adding to it."

Noah swallowed what he wanted to say: *You get to change, but I don't.*
You get to reinvent yourself, but I don't.

That wasn't fair, though. This wasn't about him. This was about
Jake. About what was best for him.

At the end of the day, Noah's feelings didn't matter.

Angela took his hand. She hadn't done that in such a long time.
Her hands were practically strangers. He used to know them as well as
his own.

"Listen. I *am* happy that he makes you happy. He does make you
happy, right?"

Did Ramin make him happy?

A thousand times yes.

"You've seen him. He's a good man."

Angela laughed. "I've seen him. And I've seen the way you look at
him. And I've seen the way he looks at you."

Noah covered his face. "You make us sound like lovesick teenagers."

They were at heart, though. Weren't they? Maybe they always had
been.

"It's sweet. You used to look at me that way." She glanced toward the bathroom. The door was still closed, and the fan was still running, and Noah wished he could gather up all of Jake's pains and take them for himself, so Jake wouldn't have to feel them. "Jake likes him, too."

"Better than he likes me these days."

It escaped his lips before he could stop it.

He hadn't meant to say it out loud.

"It'll get better."

"Yeah." Or Jake would decide it was too much and move away. Noah's chest clenched up again. But even so, he couldn't stop hoping.

"You should've seen them, Angie. When I walked back in they looked like they were planning world domination. Either that or Jake was trying to talk him into buying him something."

Angela smiled. "Probably that Lego set from yesterday."

"Probably." Noah sighed. It wasn't fair. Angela was moving forward with her life. Why couldn't Noah?

"Listen. I know the timing isn't the best. I know there's a lot we need to figure out as a family. But I need to see where this goes." He swallowed and waited for Angela to argue—she always had a counterpoint to make—but for once, she acquiesced.

"All right." Angela took a deep breath. And then she smirked. "I guess I can hardly blame you for taking my advice."

"Your advice?"

"Yeah. I told you I was worried you'd be lonely. So here you are. Fixing it."

That wasn't what this was. Ramin wasn't some . . . some balm to ease him losing Jake.

He didn't *want* to lose Jake.

Still. This was progress, at least.

He glanced toward the bathroom. "Jake's been in there awhile. You mind staying? I'll go find him some medicine."

❦

"Grazie," Noah told the pharmacist. He'd picked up medicine for nausea and for diarrhea to cover all the bases. Well, all the bases he could think of right now.

As he turned his steps back toward the hotel, he passed another one of those condom vending machines, the sun nearly blinding him as it reflected off the glass front. Noah slowed his steps. Ramin had mentioned not having condoms in Noah's size. And Noah hadn't brought any himself. He hadn't expected to need them.

Not that he was expecting to now. It just seemed like maybe he should have his own bases covered, too. But this vending machine didn't have XXLs.

Plus he wasn't going to buy them on a street corner in broad daylight. He was going to buy them in a store, awkwardly avoiding eye contact with the shopkeeper and praying he didn't run into anyone he knew, like a proper Midwestern boy.

He went straight at the crosswalk, since his sign was lit, and ended up on a slightly different route back to the hotel. He passed a bustling coffee shop, a cute clothing boutique, some kind of home goods store, and a fancy butcher shop. One storefront caught his eye. The windows had blackout curtains on them, all except one, which had a Pride flag instead. The door was covered in blackout, too, but it had a bright APERTO sign.

The back of his neck prickled. Was this...an adult store?

He'd never actually been in one. Not out of prudishness. He'd simply always gotten what he needed from pharmacies. Or better yet, online shopping, where you didn't have to avoid eye contact with anyone at all.

When he was a teenager, he'd driven by the Priscilla's in Gladstone often enough, and his dad had always muttered darkly about it being on a "family street" as he was learning to drive. But he'd never actually stepped inside.

Noah bit his lip and checked his phone to see if Angela had messaged him. Jake was out of the bathroom now, and supposedly feeling better. So Noah had a few minutes. Right?

His curiosity got the best of him. He pulled the door open and was immediately overwhelmed with the scent of leather. His mouth hung open as he looked around.

He wasn't sure what he expected, honestly. Maybe red lights and dark walls and dirty floors.

This store, though, was more like a Target. Bright lights, clean tile floors, and aisles full of just about everything Noah could imagine, plus plenty of stuff he definitely could not.

One aisle was nothing but lubricants and condoms. Including his size. Noah's heart hovered in his throat as he pulled out his phone to try and translate some of the lube packages to make sure they were condom safe. He wondered if he should text Ramin to check if he was allergic to latex, but that was *way* too forward, right? Maybe he wouldn't even need them. Maybe they wouldn't get together again like that.

Or maybe they would, but they'd get interrupted again.

Noah nearly snorted a laugh. It had been awful in the moment, and beyond frustrating, but looking back it *was* kind of funny.

Noah grabbed what he needed and was about to head for the inevitably awkward checkout—made even more awkward by the language barrier—but when he turned down the next aisle he finally figured out why it smelled like leather in here.

Caps. Collars. Pants. Chaps. Some...he'd call them harnesses, he supposed, but all the harnesses he wore for work went around the thighs. These were thin, and bright red, and displayed across a mannequin's chest, and the only place he saw to clip in was right in the center of the chest, but it looked more like the ring on a dog collar than a proper D-ring. Definitely not OSHA-approved, but then, these were clearly not meant for fall arrest.

And opposite all the leather was a bunch of athletic gear. Some tame, like regular jock straps, and some less so, like jock straps that were just...straps. No jock. Just a loop of elastic that went around the whole package.

But there were singlets, too.

Noah's blood thundered in his veins and crept into his neck and cheeks as he thought about Ramin's wet dream. Or dreams. Ramin hadn't been clear on that part, and now Noah was kicking himself for not getting clarification, because it was...kind of hot, honestly.

Exhilarating.

He half-hardened, imagining Ramin's dream. Imagining he *had* dragged him into a bathroom stall, pushed him to his knees, made him...

Noah shook himself. Okay, maybe he got why Ramin found it so sexy after all. He'd spent most of his life being cautious, but the thought of throwing caution to the wind, of taking what he wanted...well, it was exhilarating.

But he'd think about that later, when he wasn't surrounded by leather and spandex.

As long as he was here, though...

Noah reached for one of the singlets, felt the sleek material beneath his fingers. Could he really buy one? No, of course not.

He was being ridiculous. Even if he *did* want to do something like that, eventually, it would make more sense to buy it at home, where the exchange rate was better.

But then he imagined Ramin's eyes, green and needy. His mouth, pink and hungry. Before he could stop himself, he grabbed a blue and silver one—their old high school colors—balled it up, and scurried to the checkout, hoping he wouldn't see anyone he knew. Yeah, he was in Italy, so the chances were low, but he'd already run into Ramin. *Thrice.* Clearly his luck was all over the place.

The last thing he wanted to do was buy condoms and lube and sex gear in front of his dentist.

twenty-seven

Ramin

Ramin knew it was after midnight back home. He tried—he really tried—not to call or text too late. But Arya's schedule was erratic, and David and Farzan both worked in restaurants and kept later hours, so he decided to risk a text.

> **Ramin**
> Something happened

He stared at his phone as he power-walked back toward his apartment until he nearly dropped it, stubbing his toe on a particularly tall cobble, and stuffed it back into his pocket.

He needed a shower. He could still feel Noah's hands all over him. Noah's mouth on his. And once again, he had a spot of cold precum in his underwear, smearing around his dick as he walked, and he'd put that sensation up there with wet socks as far as unpleasant clothing-related experiences.

Once again, he was making the walk of shame, and once again, he hadn't even gotten off!

Which was fine—he meant what he told Noah about not tallying orgasms—but damn.

Ramin was a block away from his apartment when his phone began to buzz. The sidewalk was more even here, so he risked taking it out. Arya was FaceTiming him.

"Are you okay?" he asked as soon as Ramin answered. He was dressed in a dapper blue suit, though he'd left his collar undone. The lights of Kansas City's downtown backlit him, twinkling through the floor-to-ceiling windows of his swanky apartment in the Power & Light District.

"I'm fine," Ramin assured him. "It's nothing bad. Sorry, didn't mean to worry you. I just thought you might be up still."

"Just got home," Arya said. The image juddered, and Arya muttered a *shit*. Probably banging into the furniture like usual. Arya always had the randomest bruises. "Making some herbal . . . wait."

Arya narrowed his eyes and brought the screen so close, all Ramin could make out was the expanse of his bald head.

"Why is your hair all messed up?"

Ramin reached up to fix it. Fuckety-fuck—

"You finally got laid!"

Damn it. Of course Arya could tell. Arya could always tell.

Ramin sighed. Before he could figure out what to say, Farzan joined the call, lounging shirtless in bed. The bedside lamp turned his brown skin golden. His own hair was longer, curly, and *definitely* showing signs of being freshly fucked.

"How am *I* the only one not getting any Vitamin D?" Arya lamented. The picture went shaky again; Ramin heard the beeping of Arya's kettle.

"Wait, Ramin got laid?" Farzan said, scratching his chest hair. "When?"

"Last night."

"I didn't have sex last night!" Ramin interrupted, way too loud, because some of the folks passing by swiveled to look at him. He lowered his voice and pulled out his keychain to get through the gate.

"You didn't have sex *last night*," Arya muttered, and then his eyes widened. "You had sex *this morning*?"

Ramin groaned. Why oh why was *that* the conclusion Arya had drawn? And why oh why did he text his friends in the first place?

Because he loved them, that's why. He loved them and he was a mess and he needed advice. He needed someone to help him figure out what to do. He needed his real friends, not their little miniature angel-devil versions.

"Okay, can we pause on that, at least until I get into my apartment?" Ramin muttered. "How are you both doing?"

Arya sighed. "Ugh. Some days I don't know why I do this job."

"Because you love it and you're good at it," Farzan said. "What happened?"

"We had a big wedding at Union Station," Arya said. "And *apparently* the father of the bride picked flowers his future son-in-law was allergic to. On purpose. For a hundred floral arrangements."

A deep, rich laugh preceded David as he flopped onto the bed next to Farzan, equally shirtless, with a black silk cap protecting his hair. "No shit?"

"No shit," Arya said.

Ramin finally made it off the elevator and into his apartment. He went straight for the kitchen to grab a saucepan for some tea.

"Okay, dude, are you back now? Out of earshot of nosy Italians?" Arya asked. "Wait, I thought Italians loved sex. Why are you so worried?"

"Can we focus?" Ramin asked automatically, then wished he hadn't, because fuck, the focus was on *him*.

"Exactly," Farzan said. "Spill."

"Wait, what're we spilling?" David asked.

"Ramin had sex with someone this morning." That was Arya.

"I didn't!" They only made out. A lot. And did some light grinding. And definitely intended for it to happen.

"Then why are you blushing so hard?" Arya asked.

Ramin *was* blushing. Part of him wanted to protect this fledgling thing with Noah, whatever it was. But part of him wanted to shout it from the rooftops. He wasn't usually the one with stories to share. He was usually the . . .

Well. The boring one.

"We only kissed this morning," Ramin admitted. "We had sex yesterday morning."

"I knew it!" Arya shouted, and promptly dropped his phone again.

Ramin's face burned so hot, he thought he might catch fire. Farzan and David were grinning at him.

Finally Arya picked his phone back up.

"Okay, dude, spill. What? Who? Where?"

"Promise not to make fun?"

"Make fun?" Farzan asked. "We're happy for you!"

That was fair. His friends really did want him to be happy. Ramin took a deep breath and then let it spill out of him.

"I kind of gave Noah a handjob."

Arya whooped.

Farzan's eyes went wide. "Wait, really?"

"Really." While Ramin waited for his water to boil, he leaned against the kitchen table and told them the story.

"Wait," David interrupted when he got to the wine shop. "You had 2016 *Gaja*? Which one?"

"Conteisa?"

David groaned in appreciation, closing his eyes like he was drinking it himself. He probably had before. "First the Ornellaia, now some Gaja. And a handjob too? You're living the dream."

"Hey!" Farzan smirked and elbowed David.

David gave him a big smooch. "Don't mind him. Keep going."

Ramin went down the whole thing—the wine shop, getting strongarmed into lunch, the rain, the hotel—

"Waitwaitwaitwaitwait," Arya said, steepling his fingers over his mug of herbal tea. He'd moved to his couch, jacket slung over the back, phone propped up against something on his coffee table. "Are you trying to tell me that you, Ramin Yazdani, engineered an only-one-bed scenario with your big-dicked high school crush?"

"I didn't *engineer* anything," Ramin said. "It just happened. How was I supposed to know he was bisexual and had a crush on me, too?"

Arya cackled. Farzan sighed, but it was a fond one.

"Are you kidding? You're a catch. You know that."

Ramin shook his head.

"Anyway, we got interrupted before anything else happened, and then he had to come back to Milan but his phone was dead, so I thought he was ghosting me, and then Todd called and I got into a weird headspace—"

"*Todd?*" David asked. "Like, *Fucking Todd* Todd? That Todd?"

"He's the only one we know," Arya said. "What did he want?"

"Uh, stuff from the house. I told him to call you guys."

Farzan snorted. "I think he's afraid of us."

"Good," Arya said. "Okay, so Todd called, and I assume you told him to go fuck himself—"

"I told him I was in Italy, and then I went to a club and got drunk and then somehow Noah found me and took me back to his hotel because I was too drunk to find my way home. And we didn't do anything, just cuddled, and this morning we talked, and I think we're... seeing each other now?"

All three men on his phone stared at him. Ramin scratched at his new tattoo. He loved the piece, but he hated the itching.

Arya was the first to speak. "Dude. This is perfect. You went to Italy to drown in foreskins but this is *better*. This is your second-chance romance!"

"This isn't a movie," Ramin said. "This is real life."

"I don't know," David said, scratching at his chin. "I think you should go for it."

"But what if this is just... just a rebound? For me, or for him, or for both of us? What if it all falls apart?" Ramin could tell he was spiraling, but he couldn't stop himself. "He's divorced and has a kid and his kid might be moving here and either way he's going back home in like a week and I'm here for two months and I don't know if I can just cancel the rest of my trip and go home and I don't even know if I want to and—"

"Whoa-whoa-whoa," Farzan said. "Hey. Calm down."

Ramin huffed.

Farzan's expression softened. "What's this really about?"

Damn it. Why did Ramin have to go and have such perceptive friends?

"What if he gets bored of me, too?"

He felt silly for even saying it. For admitting how much Fucking Todd had gotten into his head. But what if this thing between him and Noah fizzled? What if this was just a flashback of teenage hormones and Noah's two years of celibacy and Ramin's (admittedly very talented) hands?

What if Noah realized there were more interesting people out there?

The guys were all quiet for a long moment.

"If he does, fuck him, too," Farzan finally said. "But I really don't think he will. I don't remember him being an asshole when we were younger. And you're a good judge of character."

"But Todd—"

"Todd made you happy for two years. Just because he turned into an asshole at the end, that doesn't mean you made a mistake."

"Yeah," Arya said. "Look. I know you're the cautious one of us, but this time you really need to embrace your inner Arya and be brave."

Ramin rolled his eyes, but smiled just a bit.

"You look happy," David said. "Every time you talk about him. It's a good look on you."

"Really?"

"Really-really. I think Arya's right. Be brave." He yawned. "Sorry."

"No, God, I'm sorry. It's late for you."

"We love you," Arya said. "Don't apologize."

"Yeah. Seriously. We're here for you any time. Even if we're asleep," Farzan added.

"Okay. But I will let you go. Love you guys, too."

Ramin hung up and grabbed his tea, but it had gone cold. He went to go heat up more water.

Maybe Arya was right. Maybe he needed to just go for this.

He could be brave. He could take a chance.

While he waited for the water to boil, he pulled his phone back out.

Ramin

When can I see you again?

twenty-eight

Noah

Noah pressed his ear against the door, but his room was silent. He didn't know why he was sneaking around. It wasn't like you could tell the bag was full of condoms from the outside. But Jake had a habit of thinking any unmarked bag *might* contain something exciting for him, and Noah really didn't want to explain what lube was to his son.

Not right now, at least, not unless Jake asked. He knew one day he would be doing that. His own father had given him absolutely zero sex education, just a bunch of fire and brimstone and shame, and Noah was determined that he'd never make Jake feel uncomfortable or ashamed talking about sex. Well, no more than the usual awkwardness. They *were* from Missouri, after all.

Though, if Jake moved here, who knew where he'd be getting his sex ed? Maybe Europeans taught it better. Maybe Jake would become friends with a bunch of sophisticated Italian children who wore scarves and striped shirts and sat around smoking and drinking espressos and drawing in Moleskines, even though the texture of Moleskines was all wrong for sketching.

Noah shook himself, unlocked the door—all clear—and ran to his dresser to hide his evidence. Just in time.

"Noah? That you?" Angela knocked on the door connecting their rooms.

"Yup! Got the medicine!" He double-checked he definitely had the medicine bag in hand, *not* the sex bag, and yes, he was good. "How's Jake doing?"

"I'm fine," Jake huffed, opening the door and practically stomping in. "Not that you care."

Where in the world had *that* come from?

"Jakey. Of course I care."

But Jake crossed his arms and refused to so much as glance at Noah.

Noah met Angela's eyes. *What happened?*

Angela's eyebrows raised. *Beats me.*

Noah shook his head and knelt by his son.

"Jake? Buddy? Will you look at me?"

Jake did, and then looked away again. "What?"

"I care about you more than anything in the world. That's why I went to get you medicine."

Guilt gnawed at Noah's insides, though. He *had* taken a detour.

He'd thought Jake was fine. But this is what he got for being selfish.

"I'm sorry. I love you, buddy."

"Love you, too," Jake muttered.

Noah bit his lip and tried not to take it personally.

He left Jake on the bed and stepped into Angela's room, closing the door and keeping his voice low.

"What is going on with him?"

"I don't know. I'm sorry." Angela retied her ponytail. "I hate to ask when he's in this kind of mood, but can you take him for the day? I've got some things to take care of."

"You do?" Noah had figured, now that Jake was on his feet again, it was back to the Death March of Fun.

"Nonno recommended an immigration lawyer for me to talk to, and she had an opening today, and I just thought...well. Better to take the chance while I have it."

An immigration lawyer.

Noah's mouth went dry. Suddenly Angela's move felt a million times more real.

"Oh. Okay." Noah swallowed. This was happening way too fast. "I'll find something for us to do."

Assuming Jake would actually go with him.

He stepped back into his room to find Jake still sitting on the bed, looking all glum, his hand under his chin like *The Thinker*.

"You want some medicine, buddy?"

Jake shook his head.

"You sure?"

"I'm sure."

"Okay."

Noah sat next to Jake, chanced a hand on Jake's shoulder. At least he didn't pull away.

"What's going on, buddy? What did I do?"

"Nothing." But Jake sniffed. Wiped at the corner of his eye.

Noah's heart threatened to snap in two. He never wanted Jake to hide his tears. He'd told Jake time and time again it was okay for boys to cry, for them to cry in front of *each other*. So why was Jake hiding them now?

He couldn't hold them for long, though. Noah pulled Jake in closer as he cried.

"I don't want Mom to move."

Noah winced.

"Me neither, buddy." He wished he knew what to say. Wished he could make everything better. Wished he knew how to keep their lives from changing. But he couldn't.

All he could do was hold his son and let him cry.

Once Jake had cried himself out, Noah convinced him to take some of the medicine for diarrhea.

"Want to go out somewhere? We can do whatever you want," he said.

Jake gave him a sly look. "Can we go to the Lego Store?"

"We can go, but we're not buying anything. All right?"

"Yes, yes, yes!" Jake ran for the door to grab his shoes. Noah sighed. What was he going to do with his son?

At least it sounded like he wasn't sold on this whole Italy thing. A spark of hope flared in Noah's chest. Maybe Jake would want to stay with him. Maybe...

Noah's phone buzzed.

Ramin

When can I see you again?

Noah held back a grin, but not very successfully.

When *could* he see Ramin again?

But no. He needed to focus on Jake. He'd have to ask for a little time. He'd have to—

"Is that Ramin?"

Noah hadn't even noticed Jake clamber back onto the bed until Jake grabbed onto him to look over his shoulder.

"What? Uh. Yeah, buddy. I was just about to tell him you and I were busy."

"Can he come to the Lego Store with us?"

"You just saw him this morning," Noah said automatically. He needed to focus on Jake. Spend this time together, just the two of them.

"So? I can see him again. I bet he likes the Lego Store."

Noah was ready to say no. Though if he and Ramin were going to have any kind of future, Ramin would have to get used to being flexible, to shifting plans if they needed to shift, to taking Jake's needs into account, too.

Maybe it was better to find out if he could do that sooner rather than later.

Noah thumbed his cross. "You like Ramin, huh?"

"Yeah. He has an awesome face. And awesome tattoos!"

Noah laughed. He liked Ramin's face and tattoos, too. And his hands. And his mouth...

Noah needed to rein himself in.

He glanced toward Angela's door. She'd just told him she was worried about throwing too much change at Jake.

But she was doing the same. And she hadn't been the one to hold him while he cried about it.

Noah deserved to move forward too, didn't he? And unlike Angela, he was inviting Jake along for the ride.

"All right, buddy. I'll ask him."

"Tell him they probably have Spider-Man ones!"

> **Noah**
>
> Depends. Want to go to the Lego Store this afternoon? With me and Jake?
> He says they probably have Spider-Man.

A light rain had swept through around lunchtime, but the streets were already dry again. The air smelled crisp and fresh as Noah strolled down the streets, Jake's hand in his.

"I like your socks," Jake said.

Noah was wearing bright pink ankle socks with his white sneakers, along with a white polo shirt and black shorts that fell below his knee. He thought they might try to take a tour of the Duomo after the Lego Store; they'd only walked by the outside on the Death March of Fun. The Duomo's dress code said no knees or shoulders showing. With a start, he realized he hadn't mentioned it to Ramin. What if Ramin showed up in those shorts of his, the ones Noah liked, the ones that were definitely above the knee and technically against the dress code?

Not that Noah didn't *want* to see him in those shorts again. Or out of them.

Except he was with Jake. This was a family outing. Not a... *hookup* felt crass. Rendezvous?

Afternoon delight?

Whatever. It didn't matter. It wasn't happening.

"You look sharp too, buddy." Jake was in a white polo shirt of his own, with jean shorts and a pair of Spider-Man socks peeking above his sneakers.

"Thanks."

Noah finally spotted the bright yellow brick sign for the Lego Store at the end of the block; Jake saw it a moment later and took off running.

"Jakey! Wait!"

But Jake had too much of a head start. And besides, Noah realized who he was running to: Ramin stood beneath the big yellow brick, waiting for them.

He wore an azure button-up short-sleeved shirt and white shorts that definitely hit below the knee but somehow still made his legs and behind look absolutely delicious.

Before Noah could stop him, Jake ran up and threw his arms around Ramin's waist. Ramin's eyebrows popped up above his sunglasses, and he looked toward Noah for a second before wrapping Jake in a hug. Apparently they'd moved past fist bumps.

Noah thought he would melt into a puddle on the spot as Ramin hugged his son.

"Hey," Ramin said. He let go of Jake and pushed his sunglasses up into his hair. His eyes sparkled in the sun.

Noah wanted to reach for him and pull him into a kiss hello, but he didn't know if they were doing that yet and he didn't know if they were doing that in front of *Jake* yet. He hadn't dated since the divorce, and as far as he knew, Angela hadn't either, so they'd never really talked about how to introduce new partners to Jake.

A thrill ran up his spine. *Partners.*

Him and Ramin.

It could happen, couldn't it? Maybe. If the stars aligned. If they figured all this out.

In the end, Noah settled for a one-armed hug, and if his lips happened to graze Ramin's cheek, well, that was just how Italians did it.

"Come on. Let's see what they have!" Jake said, grabbing Ramin's hand and dragging him into the store.

Ramin gave Noah a look that either meant *This is hilarious* or *Help me!*—he wasn't sure yet.

Noah half expected Ramin to get impatient as Jake slowly went from shelf to shelf, admiring Lego sets he'd admired a hundred times before, at the Lego Store back home. But if Ramin was annoyed, he didn't show it. He nodded sagely as Jake explained which sets he already had and compared notes about the Lego themes he'd had when he was a child himself.

"What about you?" Ramin asked.

Noah blinked. "Me?"

"Yeah. Did you have a collection growing up?"

"Not really." He'd had a few sets, but his mother always complained about finding stray bricks, and his dad thought Noah should've been playing with G.I. Joes or He-Man figures instead. Even though, looking back, He-Man was pretty homoerotic. "But Jake lets me help him build, sometimes."

"Dad's a good assistant," Jake said. "He's good at sorting out the pieces."

"A man of many talents," Ramin said, though when Noah caught his eye, he could've sworn Ramin wasn't just talking about sorting bricks anymore.

Jake managed to spend a good thirty minutes browsing, and to Noah's surprise, he didn't even ask to buy anything.

"Sometimes it's just nice to window shop," Jake told Ramin.

"Yeah. Thanks for letting me tag along." He glanced Noah's way. "So what now?"

"I thought maybe, if you both wanted, we could take a tour of the Duomo? But only if you want."

"I've heard it's beautiful," Ramin said. "What d'you think, Jake?"

"Okay."

⌇

It was Noah's second time seeing the Duomo, but it was no less impressive. The sun gleamed off the marble. Pigeons swooped around the piazza. Noah even spotted a person standing stock still, arms outstretched, as someone trailed birdseed along their sleeves to attract pigeons.

Jake gasped as a pigeon landed on the person's arm. "Can I try?"

Noah had a horrible flash of trying to get bird poop out of Jake's clothes or, worse, his hair. "Uh. Maybe later."

Noah bought them all tickets and led them toward the visitors' entrance on the southwest corner. A snaking set of metal barricades stretched from the heavy wooden doors to the small shaded stand where two guards were checking people's tickets—and enforcing the dress code.

"I want one!" Jake said as one of the guards handed over what looked like a folded trash bag to a woman with a spaghetti-strap shirt on.

The trash bag turned out to be a gauzy white poncho, and Noah couldn't tell if it was fabric or paper. Another strip of gauze made a belt the woman tied around herself, which left the stiff gown looking slightly ridiculous as it flared out below her knees and around her shoulders.

"I don't think they come in your size."

"Plus you're already dressed properly," Ramin said. "Nicely done, Jake."

Jake stood up straighter at that, keeping close to Ramin's side as they followed the line toward the doors. They each got wanded with a metal detector before being allowed inside.

After the sunlit brightness of the piazza, it took Noah's eyes a moment to adjust to the Duomo's interior, which was lit by high windows and stained glass. He kept one hand on Jake's head and the other on his phone, snapping pictures as they moved into the cathedral.

The arches of the ceiling high above looked like the ribs of some enormous whale. And ahead, column after column marched toward the apse, each topped with carved figures all the way around. Noah ached to grab a seat on one of the pews, pull out his sketchbook, and start drawing, but he had to keep up with Ramin and Jake.

Jake kept to his tiptoes, stepping carefully in the blank spaces of the tiled floor, which was laid in intricate patterns of alternating red and black flowers.

"Which way do we go?" Jake asked, his voice soft. Everything in the cathedral was quiet; even the sounds of footsteps upon tile seemed muted by the majesty of the space.

"We could follow them," Ramin said, pointing to a tour group wearing little wireless headsets as their guide spoke softly into a small microphone.

Noah didn't know whether to look up or down, left or right: Everywhere the church's beauty surrounded him. What would it be like to worship here, instead of a converted Popeyes? Not that Noah was considering converting, but still, it was hard to ignore the splendor of a place like this.

The aisle led them past a series of alcoves on their right. In each, a stained glass window illuminated them, intricate scenes from the Bible laid out in glowing detail. Beneath the windows, each alcove hosted paintings, or sculptures, or even beatified cardinals.

"Cool," Jake whispered, stepping closer to read the placard. Noah kept a hand on his son's head and watched; with a start, he realized Jake wasn't moving his lips as he read. When had he stopped doing that?

A strange ache formed in Noah's chest, grief mingled with pride, because this amazing human he and Angela had made was growing up into his own perfect little person. It was happening so fast.

Everything was. Jake growing up. Angela moving here, maybe taking Jake with her.

Noah and Ramin.

As much as all three scared him, Noah couldn't find anything to regret in that last one. No matter how many times he told himself to focus on Jake or to listen to Angela's advice, every time Ramin smiled at him, he forgot everything. Everything except how beautiful that smile was. How it settled deep into his soul. How he'd give almost anything to see that smile every single day.

They made a circuit around the edge of the church, passing stately dark wood confessional booths with intricate metal grilles, and paintings of the Virgin Mary and Jesus Christ, dodging around individual tourists or large groups huddled together listening to a guide speaking in hushed tones. At the apse, three enormous stained glass windows, bigger than any of the others they'd seen so far, stretched to the ceiling, filling Noah's vision with a hundred glowing scenes. He wondered how many hours had gone into making those images. How many hands had crafted the designs, cut the glass, soldered the pieces together. Whether they knew they were making something special.

Noah could feel them. All those hours of devotion. Different from his own devotion, but no less beautiful, to be in service to something greater. Something that you loved.

Noah pinched at his cross and basked in the feeling. His own journey with religion had been long and fraught and complicated, but here, it was easy to remember that for him, it all came back to love.

The back of the cathedral was closed for renovations. Noah wondered, with a building this large and this old, whether there was ever a day when there were no renovations going on.

They wove their way through the pews, paused in front of the altar, admired the enormous pipe organ, and made their way back down the north aisle. Some alcoves were barricaded off for worshippers only, but others were open. Rows and rows of votive candles flickered. All those prayers.

"Can we light one?" Jake asked.

"Sure." Noah dug out two euros, let Jake drop them in the copper box and pick the candles, helped him light them and bowed his head to say a short prayer, keenly aware of Ramin waiting behind them. He almost felt self-conscious, but he'd seen Ramin pray, too.

He didn't mind sharing this.

twenty-nine

Ramin

Noah had bought them tickets for the terraces atop the Duomo as well, but a heavy rain had blown in while they were still inside, so loud they could hear it echoing all through the cathedral. It reminded Ramin of their flight from the docks in Como, of their cozy hotel room, of their morning together...

Good lord, he could *not* think about sex in a cathedral. Just because he didn't believe in God, that didn't mean he was willing to risk getting smote.

They ended up making a dash across the piazza to the shelter of the Galleria on the north side. The rain continued to hammer on the huge arched glass ceiling above, and wet shoes left the tile floor slippery, but at least they could stay dry.

"Can we get gelato?" Jake asked as they passed by a gelateria with a line winding its way past several high-end clothing stores.

"Let's get some real food first."

All the restaurants in the Galleria seemed to be tourist-driven chains, but Jake was ecstatic with his cotoletta di pollo—a crispy fried chicken cutlet—and fries. Noah got a pizza with a huge ball of burrata in the middle, and Ramin got a salad, because some fucked-up instinct told him that if he and Noah *were* seeing each other, then this *was* a date, and he still defaulted to getting salads on dates, out of a combination of lingering body dysmorphia and hard-learned practicality.

Not that he expected to be bottoming tonight, but just in case…

"Try this," Noah insisted, cutting an uneven wedge of pizza and trying to get it onto Ramin's plate without all the toppings slipping off. He scooped up a big dollop of the burrata—it was slowly oozing out all over the pizza—and dropped it onto Ramin's slice.

"Uh. Thanks."

Noah was right, the pizza *was* better than Ramin's boring salad. He chided himself. He was supposed to be interesting.

"Look what I can do!" Jake said, sticking a french fry in the gap left by his missing front tooth. "I'm a narwhal!"

Ramin nearly spat out his burrata, he laughed so hard.

"Jakey does that whenever he gets a new audience," Noah muttered. "Hey, buddy, don't play with your food, okay?"

"Fine," Jake said, but he didn't look contrite. He gave Ramin a sly smile that had Ramin nearly choking on his salad. "Can we get gelato after?"

They did, in fact, get gelato after. Ramin enjoyed a lemon sorbetto, Noah went for a stracciatella, and Jake got hazelnut. They strolled and window shopped, nearly losing Jake to the lure of a chocolatier, but thankfully they were able to distract him with a big Spider-Man cutout in the window of a nearby bookstore.

The rain slackened and finally died. The sun returned. Noah got a text from Angela. Apparently she was stuck at a lawyer's office.

"Looks like we're on our own for dinner," he announced.

"Guys' night!" Jake crowed.

Noah looked at Ramin, a question in his eyes.

"I'm game if you are."

Which is how they ended up lost in the middle of Milan, strolling slowly so that Jake could look at every single storefront they passed, sometimes running ahead, sometimes hanging back to hold Noah's or Ramin's hand, occasionally insisting on swinging between the two of them. Jake told stories about school, his friends, his soccer team, and even his bowling league. Ramin had no idea that was even a thing for nine-year-olds.

Ramin told Noah and Jake about the queer kickball league back home that all his friends (and his ex-boyfriend) played in. He didn't play himself, but he went to cheer them every game. He talked about Shiraz Bistro and how much work it was and how much fun it was and how grateful he was to be part of something so important to his community.

Noah, in turn, regaled Ramin with a series of increasingly bizarre anecdotes about his work as a carpenter back home, about the weird projects he'd worked on, the unrealistic expectations of clients, the fights he'd gotten into about safety.

And of course, he told hilarious stories from Jake's childhood—to Jake's amusement and occasional consternation.

"It wasn't *that* funny," Jake grumbled as Noah reenacted the time Jake walked right into a shopping cart return because he wasn't looking where he was going.

"You looked like a cartoon, buddy," Noah said. "But if you had gotten hurt I wouldn't be laughing. I hope you know that."

"I know," Jake muttered.

They walked for hours, stopping once for espressos and waters, another time for a bathroom break, popping into whatever stores Jake wanted to investigate. The sun was westering, and the late afternoon was warm and muggy from all the rain, when they reached Navigli, the neighborhood built around Milan's canal system.

Ramin hadn't imagined Milan with canals, but apparently they'd once been used to move goods around the city. Now, though they featured the occasional gondola, they mostly seemed to be an excuse for a dining district. Restaurant after restaurant lined both sides of the wide canal. Bridges crossed it every few blocks or so.

Mosquitos buzzed around Ramin's legs.

He couldn't stop smiling. Couldn't help imagining that *this* was his life. His real life. Not some artifact of trying to reinvent himself.

Being with Noah and Jake felt right.

It felt terrifying.

He was barely a month out of a two-year relationship. The last time he'd tried to imagine a life like this, tried to make it come true, it had blown up in his face. He should've still been grieving the breakup, right? He should've been a mess.

But every time Noah looked his way, all he knew was he had to give this a chance. Even if it scared him.

The sun set, and the streets along the canal came alive with lights and music and vendors plying a thousand things that caught Jake's eye, but thankfully Noah navigated Jake around the souvenirs, because Ramin probably would've given in at the first instance of puppy-dog eyes.

They found a quiet restaurant and sat on the patio overlooking the canal. Their tables had paper placemats printed with Italy's wine regions. Ramin could still remember the taste of the Gaja they'd shared in Bellagio, so rather than try to top it, he decided to be interesting and picked the first wine he didn't recognize.

Their server brought them a bottle of Grignolino, a red wine from Piedmont. It was lighter than Ramin was expecting, almost like a Pinot Noir, rusty-red and oh so perfect.

He and Noah shared a toast, along with Jake, who clinked his glass of Limonata.

"It's a tough life," Noah said.

"It's a tough life," Ramin and Jake agreed.

While Noah ran to the restroom, Jake put down his drink, steepled his hands, and gave Ramin a *look*.

"Are you and my dad in love?"

Ramin nearly spat his wine out his nose.

"What?" He coughed. "What makes you ask that?"

"You're both acting weird."

"Sorry about that."

Jake shrugged. "It's fine. So are you?"

"No." That was ridiculous. They hadn't spoken in twenty years. Had met again just a few days ago. No one fell in love that fast.

Ramin wished Noah was here. He was the dad. He knew how to handle the hard questions.

But Jake seemed to trust him, and Ramin owed Jake some honesty, as best he could give it. Ramin wanted to be the kind of grown-up that Jake could trust. That Noah could trust with Jake.

"We're just getting to know each other again. But we *do* like each other. I hope that's okay. And if you have any questions, we'll try to answer them." That was good, right? And honest. And gave Jake autonomy and respect. "I like you, too, by the way. You're pretty cool."

Jake beamed at him. "I like you, too. You have an awesome face."

"What'd I miss?" Noah asked, taking his seat.

Ramin waited until Noah had a sip of his own wine.

"Jake was asking if you and I are in love."

Now it was Noah's turn to sputter and cough, while Ramin laughed.

"You are evil," Noah said, without any real heat. "Jakey, would you be mad if we did fall in love?"

Ramin swallowed his wine and stared. Noah was so nonchalant about it. Like he thought they really *could* fall in love.

Jake shook his head. "Can I get triple presents if you do?"

"We'll see." Noah ruffled Jake's hair. "You drive a hard bargain, buddy."

If you do.

Could Ramin fall in love with Noah Bartlett?

Yes.

Ramin knew, deep down, he could.

thirty

Noah

Noah had forgotten it could be this way.

The ease of walking side by side with someone. The little smiles as you thought of each other. The unbridled joy when a new text came in.

It had been that way with Angela, for a long time. Before they drifted apart. Before they fell out of love.

Falling out of love had been its own strange ache. Noah hadn't realized how long he'd carried it around.

But now his chest was light. His heart was full. He couldn't stop smiling.

He really liked Ramin.

He really, really, *really* liked Ramin.

After their day together—and after Angela's meeting with the lawyers—the Death March of Fun had resumed, so Noah had been limited to hurried texts, late night calls, or once, a quick breakfast together.

He couldn't get enough.

Still, just knowing Ramin was thinking of him made it better.

Angela took them to museums, and parks, and famous landmarks.

She took them to lunch spots she'd found on Google, pasticcerias Nonno and Nonna had recommended, a Michelin-starred restaurant she'd booked them reservations for even before she bought their plane tickets.

Noah loved every minute of it, even if he wished Ramin was there, too.

Jake seemed to wish the same. He kept asking Noah to text Ramin on his behalf. (Noah and Angela both agreed: no phone until Jake hit middle school.)

Angela covered her annoyance as best she could, but Noah could tell she was frustrated.

He couldn't help it if Jake liked Ramin, though. Noah was on his best behavior, not texting Ramin at the table, not calling him, being focused and present during the day.

Nights were another story. He and Ramin would stay up way too late talking. Ramin would tell him about whatever remote work he was doing, what he'd seen in the city, what he'd eaten. They'd talk about nothing until it was Jake's bedtime.

Then Noah would retreat to the bathroom with his phone and a private browser to do some research. He knew Ramin had more experience, but that didn't mean he was a babe in the woods. He might not've had much sex with other men, but he had a data plan, some mental notes about what Ramin liked, and an anonymous account lurking on the r/kink subreddit, just to be sure.

He had a right hand for when his research got a little too stimulating, too.

Twenty Years Ago

"What're you working on?"

Noah looked up from the charcoal portrait of Stacy he'd been drawing for the last week. Her birthday was coming up soon, and he thought it'd be a nice gift. More personal than another pair of earrings from Claire's, at least.

"Just a sketch," Noah said, suddenly shy. He didn't know why the thought of Ramin looking at his art made him so nervous. They swapped notes all the time. Ramin helped him with his homework. He filled Ramin in when he missed a class for one of his mom's appointments, which seemed to be growing in frequency.

"All right, you don't have to show me." Ramin said it lightly, but there was something under the surface, some lingering hurt. Noah didn't want to hurt Ramin. Life was doing that enough as it was. His mom wasn't getting better.

Noah would've done anything to change things.

"I don't mind," he said. "Here."

He slid his sketchbook over. Ramin studied it for a long time, so long Noah's heart started racing. He'd never been a nail biter, but all of a sudden, he wondered what his cuticles tasted like.

"Wow," Ramin said. "You must really love her."

"Huh?"

"You put so much care into this. It's beautiful. She's lucky."

Fire crept up the sides of Noah's neck, trailed along the shells of his ears, blotted his cheeks.

"Thanks," he muttered.

"You should be an artist," Ramin said.

"Huh?"

"For a job. You could draw stuff."

"Nah. It's not practical," Noah said automatically. His dad had made it quite clear this wasn't a career. Just a hobby.

"So? If you like it, that should be all that matters. What do *you* want to do?"

Noah licked his lips. What *did* he want to do?

He'd never thought about it that much. What his parents wanted him to do had always loomed so much larger. Or what Stacy wanted him to do. Or what his teachers wanted him to do. Or his coaches.

Ramin was the only one who ever asked him what *he* wanted. And he couldn't even give an answer.

"I don't know," he admitted. "I guess I'd better think about it."

Now

"Dad?"

"Yeah, buddy?" Noah helped spoon scrambled eggs onto Jake's plate. "You want some cheese, too?"

"Sure."

Noah grabbed the tongs. "What were you gonna ask?"

"When can we have another guys' day out? With Ramin?"

Noah smiled. Ever since their day with Ramin, Jake seemed to have mellowed some. He'd stopped being so cranky with Noah. Had held Noah's hand as they crossed streets, or even when they were just taking in the art in a museum.

He still wasn't sure why Jake had been so surly with him for so long, but he was glad they'd finally turned a corner.

"Tell you what," Noah said. "I'll ask him when he's free. Maybe we can do something this afternoon. That sound good?"

Jake beamed. "Yeah!"

Jake took his plate to the table, then ran for a second one. When it came to breakfast buffets, Jake always separated his savories from his sweets. And there were a *lot* of sweets on offer. Noah nearly got a cavity just looking at the pastry table.

Still, a few cavities would be worth it. The pastries were so good here. He selected a tiny croissant coated with apricot glaze for himself.

"I was thinking," Angela said, sidling up to Noah at the fruit station. "I want to take Jake on a trip."

Noah scrunched up his face. They were already on a trip.

"I mean, I want to take him to another city here. By train."

"Oh." Noah frowned. Their days were already pretty full, and now Angela wanted to tack on another city? Still, when it came down to it, this was her vacation. She'd paid for the tickets, the hotel, everything but what meals Noah had managed to snag the check for. If she wanted to go, they'd go. "Where did you have in mind? I can look at tickets."

Angela's cheeks reddened. "Uh, I was thinking, just me and Jake. The two of us."

Noah nearly dropped the pineapple he was scooping onto his plate. "Really?"

He couldn't remember Angela ever taking Jake anywhere solo, other than school or the occasional doctor's appointment. Not out of town, and certainly not on a train or plane or anything like that.

"It would be good practice for if he moves here. Plus it would let him see more of the country. Get a sense of what it would be like, living here with me."

Noah wanted to tell her no. Pull the plug. Sabotage this.

Do everything he could to stop Jake from even considering staying here in Italy with his mom.

He couldn't do that, though.

"When were you thinking?"

"Today."

"*Today?*" They finally had a free day. Jake wanted to see Ramin. They were going to—

"Why not?"

Noah couldn't think of a good reason. Except that he didn't want her to. Because he was petty and selfish.

"All right," he finally said.

"Good. Thanks." Angela swallowed. "I also thought you might like the chance to spend some actual time with Ramin."

It was Noah's turn to blush. Was it that obvious? He'd stayed in the moment. He'd paid attention to Angela and Jake and focused on their family. He'd only texted on breaks, or while they were waiting for the subway, or late at night.

"Angie, I swear, I—"

"I know, I know, you've been with us and you've been present and I'm not mad. But this is your vacation, too. I want you to have a good time. And you do, when you're with him. Don't you?"

Noah pictured a flash of green eyes. A dimpled smile.

A pack of condoms stuffed in the bottom of his dresser.

He shouldn't want this. But he did.

He really did.

Unfortunately, Jake very much did *not* want it.

"But you *promised*," Jake said. He dropped his fork and looked at Noah with big, hurt eyes. "You said—"

"I said we'd *try*, Jake," Noah said. "I haven't even talked to Ramin yet."

"But...but..."

Noah reached for Jake's hand. At least he didn't pull it away.

"Jakey. Sometimes you have to be flexible. That's just part of life. We try, and sometimes we have to change our plans. It's not the end of the world."

If Jake's sniffling was anything to go by, it *was* the end of the world.

"Your mom really wants to take you to Turin. Don't you want to see it?"

Jake shook his head. Noah fought a sigh.

"I'm sorry, Jake. We'll have a guys' day another time, okay?"

"Fine," Jake pouted. He pulled his hand out of Noah's and crossed his arms. "I don't care."

Noah looked toward Angela, who was getting another espresso.

Maybe he should've let her be the one to break the news. Then she'd be the one dealing with Jake's meltdown.

After breakfast—and after calming Jake down—Angela took him up to her room to pack an overnight bag. Noah hung back at the table, finishing off his tea.

He should've felt guilty. He *did* feel guilty. He'd ended up being the bad guy. *Again.*

And he didn't even know if Ramin was free. If he was up for some *alone* time. Just the two of them. No random knocks on the door. No interruptions.

The thought fluttered in his chest on little golden wings as he pulled out his phone.

Noah had seen Milano Centrale when they caught their bus to Como, but he hadn't had time to really appreciate it. A huge, imposing stone building—part Art Deco, part who-knows-what—supposedly it was the largest station in Europe. In the courtyard out front, skateboarders practiced grinds on stone benches, people filed into and out of the Metro entrances, and tourists took pictures of an enormous statue of an apple with a bite taken out of it and stapled back on.

He swallowed against the tightness in his throat. Ignored the anxious churning in his gut.

It had seemed like a good idea a few hours ago, when he'd texted Ramin and asked if he wanted to hop a train and go somewhere. Ramin had said yes right away.

But could he actually do this? Or would his nerves get the best of him?

His phone buzzed.

> **Ramin**
> I'm here! Inside!
> Meet by the bookstore across from the platforms?

The platforms were on the third level. Noah rode the long moving walkways up, thumbs tucked around his backpack straps, as he dodged travelers wheeling their luggage around. He found Ramin next to a window display, head down, looking at his phone.

He looked perfect.

He wore a striped green-and-white tank top, which showed off his lovely shoulders, and a pair of light pink shorts that weren't sinfully short but were certainly enticing. He looked so cosmopolitan, with his sunglasses pushed up into his hair, and a gray backpack slung off one shoulder.

Noah licked his lips. He'd dressed his best, too, in a long-sleeved white linen shirt he'd bought specially for this trip. He'd had to check three times to make sure it covered what he had on underneath, especially when he'd unbuttoned the top three buttons like the locals did. He had blue chinos on below, not as short as Ramin's but still breezy.

He tried to adjust himself without Ramin noticing. He was much more used to boxers.

When Ramin noticed him, he smiled so bright it outshone the sun streaming in through the skylights.

All Noah's nerves melted away, replaced with joy, with excitement, with the scent of Ramin's cologne and the sparkle in his eyes.

He stepped in close, chest to chest, pressing Ramin back against the window. Ramin's nostrils flared. His eyes widened.

Noah smirked. "Hi."

Ramin's cologne smelled fresh, clean, like lemon verbena and spring rain. Noah wanted to taste his collarbone, but they were in public.

That could come later.

"Hi." Ramin looked around, then leaned in for a peck on the lips. "You look amazing."

"You too. I like the way you smell."

Ramin smiled brighter, though he tugged at the hem of his tank. "Not too much? There's a stereotype about Persian men and too much cologne."

"Just right." Noah cleared his throat. "So. How does Genoa sound?"

"Genoa?" Ramin quirked an eyebrow.

"You said you liked the water."

"You remembered?" Ramin seemed almost surprised.

"Of course I remembered."

Noah remembered every moment with Ramin.

"That sounds perfect."

"Good." Noah had spent the morning looking up which seaside towns they could get to on a single train ride, and Genoa had been the best option. Plus there would be pesto.

Pesto was the besto.

"I already got us tickets."

"You did?"

Noah nodded. "The train leaves in forty minutes. Which leaves us just enough time…"

Noah's heart hammered. This was it. He could do this.

He could do this.

Ramin cocked his head. "Enough time for what?"

Noah ignored the sandpaper in his throat as he leaned closer to whisper in Ramin's ear.

"See those bathrooms over there?" He nodded to his right, where a bright blue sign said TOILETS in bold white letters.

"Yeah?"

He fished in his pocket for a one-euro coin and slipped it into Ramin's hand.

"Why don't you go in there. Find the last stall." Noah kept his voice steady, even though it wanted to shake with the hammering of his heart.

Ramin said he'd dreamed about this.

"Get down on your knees."

Ramin stiffened next to him, drew in a sharp breath.

"And suck my cock."

thirty-one

Ramin

Ramin was stunned.

Noah had taken charge. Gotten tickets. Picked out a place. He'd even remembered that Ramin liked the water.

His skin hummed as he power-walked to the bathroom.

Noah wanted him to suck his cock.

He'd even said *cock*. Out loud.

Was this even real? Maybe Ramin was hallucinating. Maybe his plane had depressurized on the way to Italy, and he was still in the air, and his entire trip had been a figment of his oxygen-starved imagination because he hadn't gotten his mask on in time. Maybe he was dying and all of Milano Centrale around him was some sort of metaphor for him moving on to the next life.

Ramin dropped the euro in the coin slot and pinched his leg as the plexiglass doors parted to let him into the bathroom. A huge stick-figure MEN's sign to the left pointed the way.

Noah. Wanted him. To suck his cock.

And God, Ramin wanted to suck it. Sucking cock was his favorite.

Bringing a guy pleasure, mapping the skin of his dick, finding all the little things that made him moan.

Making him feel *good*.

The bathroom had nicely tiled walls. And it was surprisingly clean. Ramin wasn't above getting dirty for sex, but this was way nicer, even if the scent of disinfectant tickled his nostrils. The stalls were floor-to-ceiling, big wood-grained things, with red-green lights above them to indicate if they were occupied.

Best of all: No gaps.

Though with his own dick hardening in his shorts, he wasn't sure a gap would've stopped him. Did Italy have public indecency laws? Fuck it. If they did, Ramin would just have to get Noah off in time for them to make a run for it.

He didn't mind a challenge.

The last stall was blessedly unoccupied, so he took it like Noah had ordered. He turned around, banging his backpack against the stall. Should he hang it on the hook, or would that be in the way? The door wouldn't open all the way, and he didn't want Noah to get stuck outside.

His heart was pounding. He never wore tank tops, but he was glad he had today, because otherwise the flop sweat would've showed in his pits.

How long was Noah going to keep him waiting? He swallowed against his dry mouth, because he absolutely could not go into this with a dry mouth. He took a few deep breaths, tried to work up some spit. He needed to bring his A game.

He. Was going to suck. Noah's cock.

It could've been seconds, or it could've been hours, or, hell, it could've been years, but finally, *finally*, the door swung open. Noah stepped inside, forcing Ramin back until his calves pressed against the toilet. They jostled each other a bit until Noah could get his own backpack inside and close the door. Noah flipped the lock and turned back to face Ramin, his eyes molten.

His voice was molten, too. "Pretty sure I said on your knees. Nerd."

Ramin's entire body shivered. He obeyed.

He grabbed some toilet paper on the way down, though. If he was at home, he'd put a pillow under his knees. He wasn't twenty anymore.

Noah spread his feet a bit to make room, framing Ramin with his legs, stepping forward once Ramin was situated. He pressed the fullness in the front of his shorts against Ramin's face.

Ramin looked up at Noah. Noah looked down at him. Time stood still.

Something crossed Noah's face, a fleeting look that Ramin couldn't place, but it was banished as Noah's dark eyes sharpened.

"Are you just going to stare at me?"

Ramin swallowed again. He was hot all over. Feverish. He shivered again as he reached for Noah's waistband. The chinos were smooth and cool, despite the warmth emanating from Noah's skin. He popped the button, fought the zipper for a moment before finally pulling it down, opening the shorts—

Ramin forgot how to breathe.

Noah wasn't wearing his ugly plaid boxers.

He wasn't wearing nice trunks or briefs or a sexy jockstrap. He wasn't even commando.

No.

Shiny blue spandex waited for Ramin, trimmed in silver, disappearing up into Noah's shirt and down into his legs. Ramin pulled the shorts farther down to behold Noah's bulge, trapped in the singlet.

"Oh my God," he moaned.

"Shh," Noah said, and he actually sounded a bit nervous. But he didn't move as Ramin brought his hands up to frame the warm length hardening just behind the sleek fabric. One hand left Noah's cock just long enough to run up the singlet, finding the straps that framed his firm chest; the other pressed hard against Noah's cock until Noah let out a soft gasp of pleasure.

He wanted to touch every inch of Noah. Feel every ridge of muscle, every divot, every dimple. Trace them with his fingers, with his lips, with his tongue. He loved worshipping his partner. Had always tried to do it with Todd. Todd's body had been beautiful, but he had never let Ramin worship him. Every time Ramin picked a spot, he complained about how it wasn't as developed as he wanted to be.

Fuck Todd and his insecurities.

Ramin wanted to feast on Noah. He would have, too, if Noah let him, if they had time before the train, if Ramin didn't already feel the tingle in his legs as they started to fall asleep.

He satisfied himself with another squeeze of Noah's pec.

Noah cleared his throat. Ramin looked back up.

Noah's voice had gone gentle. "If you want to stop, say 'red light.' Okay?"

Ramin couldn't believe Noah knew what a safe word was.

Ramin couldn't believe he *needed* a safe word with Noah.

He nodded his understanding. Gripped Noah's cock harder. It was still growing beneath his hand.

"Good." Noah's voice hardened again. "I thought I said suck it."

Every one of Ramin's nerves lit up like the Plaza lights. He couldn't stop himself as he jammed his face against Noah's bulge, planting his mouth on the warmth hiding beneath the thin fabric. He tasted polyester and sweat, smelled skin and musk, felt the growing heat against his face.

He imagined Noah's sweat soaking into the singlet after a hard match. His honeyed precum leaking as Ramin worked him over. Ramin planted his lips around the outline of Noah's head and sucked hard.

Noah let out a soft hiss and pushed his hips forward to meet Ramin's desperate mouth.

"Not too wet. I still have to wear this on the train."

Ramin leaned back. "Sorry." He had to remember to breathe. "This is so hot."

"Did I say stop?" Noah growled. "Take it out."

Ramin's own cock ached in his shorts, flexing uncontrollably.

He'd been waiting for this.

He trailed his fingers along the silver trim of Noah's left leg hole. He slid his hand in, felt the heat grow as he gripped Noah's trapped cock and finally freed it.

There should've been angels singing. Sunlight bathing the scene through a hole in the roof. Confetti falling in slow motion. Hell, even a balloon drop.

Noah's cock was a thing of beauty.

It twitched and pulsed and grew before Ramin, lifting itself toward his mouth as it reached its full hardness. It was perfectly shaped, well proportioned, the skin smooth, slightly darker than Noah's face. A vein traced down the top, slightly off center.

And fuck was it big.

Not an asswrecker—not something truly frightening—but not far off, either. Ramin's heart sped up. His ass puckered in anticipation.

Ramin had never been a size queen. Todd's dick had been average, and they'd had a fulfilling and delightful sex life. But damn. Maybe it was time for a coronation.

Ramin inhaled Noah's musk. Honey and wood and sweet-and-sour ball sweat. His whole body was buzzing. A droplet of sweat traced a path behind his ear and down his neckline.

He looked up at Noah again. Had he said something?

"Huh?"

"Condom?" Noah held up the foil packet.

Ramin stared at the XXL in black block letters.

On the one hand, safe sex was important. Really fucking important.

On the other hand, he was negative across the board.

And on the third leg, he thought he might die, literally die, if he didn't taste Noah's cock.

"You really haven't been with anyone since the divorce?"

"Really."

"I'm on PrEP. I'm good without it if you are."

Noah cocked his head for a second, then slipped the condom away.

"All right." His eyes sharpened again, his brows furrowed, his voice lowered to a growl. "I've seen the way you stare at me. When you think I'm not looking. You want this?"

He hefted his cock and smacked it against Ramin's face. Ramin hoped it wouldn't leave a mark.

Actually, fuck that. He hoped it *would*.

He wanted Noah to mark him.

He stuck out his tongue, met Noah's piercing gaze.

Fuck his legs falling asleep. He could stay like this forever.

As long as Noah gave him his cock.

"Then get to it. We've got a train to catch."

Fuck, this was really happening.

Ramin leaned in. He started with little kisses of Noah's inner thighs, but Noah gave a grunt of impatience, so Ramin moved to kissing his balls, bathing them with his tongue, sucking gently on the tender skin. Noah tasted like man. Like hard work. Like sun and salt and heaven.

Ramin released Noah's balls and ran his tongue in one long, slow move up the underside of Noah's cock, paying close attention to the way Noah's breath hitched. He made out with the tip, collected the thread of precum before it could escape, traced the dark line of Noah's circumcision scar. Then he worked up as much spit as he could and wrapped his lips around Noah's head.

"Yeah," Noah murmured. "Just like that."

Ramin's dick felt like it was going to snap in two. He reached for it, but Noah kneed his arm out of the way.

"Did I say you could touch yourself? You get off when I say you get off."

Ramin's chest tightened and he nearly came in his pants. Holy shit, Noah was into this.

Ramin was too. He sucked harder and brought his hand up to stroke the part of Noah's cock that didn't fit in his mouth. *Yet.* The skin was warm and smooth, Noah's hair soft and a little wild as it tickled the back of Ramin's hand.

He caressed Noah's length with his lips, increasing the pressure with each stroke. He traced his tongue against the firm tube on the underside, felt the steel beneath the velvet. Noah's cock flexed and jumped in his mouth, so hard, so sudden he caught Ramin's teeth. But Noah just grunted and moaned again as Ramin corrected the problem.

Ramin drank in every sound Noah made. Savored every twitch of his cock. Relished the shifting of Noah's balls as he cradled them in his free hand.

He vaguely saw Noah rolling up his sleeves before he brought a hand down to Ramin's head, running his fingers through Ramin's hair before gripping the back of his skull. Somehow firm and gentle at the same time. Noah was in total control, but Ramin knew, with absolute certainty, Noah would never hurt him.

He was safe. He was cherished.

He was wanted.

He was ready to be used, and God, did he want Noah to use him.

"So good," Noah said with a sigh as he pumped into Ramin, taking over the pace, Ramin's mouth wet and sloppy around him. "So good."

Ramin hummed against Noah's cock, and Noah shuddered at the vibrations. He added a twist to his stroke, tugged a bit on Noah's balls, sucked harder, lashed his tongue more ferociously, until Noah's hand in his hair gripped harder. Not hard enough to hurt, but hard enough to bring Ramin up short.

He met Noah's eyes as best he could without taking his mouth off his cock.

God. Noah was looking down at him, his pupils dilated, his cheeks flushed. He was breathing hard, mouth hanging open in a blissed-out half smile.

Ramin's cock spasmed again. He was leaking so much, he worried it would stain his shorts.

"You okay?" Noah breathed.

"Mm-hmm," he managed, keeping his lips around Noah's head, flicking the underside with his tongue, which got another twitch of pleasure out of Noah.

"I guess the safe word isn't much use with your mouth full," Noah murmured. He chuckled to himself. "Um. Pinch me in the leg if you need to stop, okay?"

Ramin let out another "Mm-hmm."

Noah sighed, but then shook himself.

"Good boy." He cleared his throat. Grabbed Ramin's head with both hands. Sharpened his voice. "Now then, let's see if you can deep throat."

Ramin could. In theory. Though he was about a decade out of practice.

It took a couple thrusts to get his alignment right. For muscle memory to come back to him. But God, he wanted this. He wanted all of Noah. Every inch.

He needed to be used.

He needed Noah to use him.

He sank deeper into his haunches to get a better angle. Inside-smiled to relax his throat. Released his grip on Noah's cock and balls, clenched one hand into a fist to suppress his gag reflex, rested the other on Noah's thigh to keep his balance. Controlled his breath.

He let Noah's hands guide him, hold him, as he went down, down, down.

Finally his nose met Noah's bush. His chin met Noah's balls. His lips met Noah's hot and shuddering skin.

"I was only j-j-j..." Noah stuttered. His legs shook; he steadied himself by holding on to Ramin's head. "Only joking. I didn't think...No one's ever..."

Fuck yes. Ramin was going to ruin Noah for anyone else. Ever.

He swallowed against Noah's cock, massaging it with his throat, and managed to get his tongue out to lick at Noah's balls. He was pretty fucking proud of himself that he could still pull that move off. Especially with Noah, who was bigger than the last guy he'd done it on.

"How are you doing that?" Noah gasped.

Ramin didn't answer, but he did let up to catch his breath and wipe his tears. His stamina was shot.

He hoped Noah would help him build it back up.

Ramin took a deep breath and caught what slobber he could in his palm, reaching for more toilet paper to wipe it off, sucking up what he could from Noah's balls before it dripped into his shorts. He gave Noah's dick another languid lick along its full length.

Then he went back down on him.

He wanted to feel Noah's cock surge and spurt as he came. He wanted to hear the little noises Noah made.

He wanted everything.

Noah's hands in Ramin's hair grew slacker. His dick flexed erratically as Ramin brought him to the brink.

"Ramin," he grunted. "I'm close."

Ramin's body was on fire. His nerves were buzzing. His ears were full. There was only him and Noah, only skin and tongue and lips and lust.

"Ahhhhh," Noah hissed, and then he was coming, his dick swelling and pulsing against the confines of Ramin's throat. He ground his hips against Ramin's face. Ramin's dick clenched in his pants, but he fought back his orgasm, focused on Noah, on swallowing the load he'd worked so hard for, on making Noah's every moment the best he'd ever had.

When Noah was finished, he ran his fingers through Ramin's hair again, gently this time, then slowly withdrew his length from Ramin's mouth. It was wet and shiny and red. Ramin leaned in to clean it. He'd missed tasting Noah's cum, but there was always next time.

Please let there be a next time.

Noah tucked himself back into his singlet, pulled up his shorts, and then reached down to help Ramin stand. Ramin's left leg roared back to life in pins and needles. He stared at Noah, breathing hard, tears streaming down his face, nose running.

He felt like a total mess. A satisfied, glowing mess.

Before he could say anything, Noah pulled him into a bone-crushing hug. He couldn't move, couldn't speak, could only breathe and feel Noah's breaths against him as he came down from the high of whatever the fuck had just happened.

"Thank you," Noah whispered. And then he loosened his grip just enough to pull back, look Ramin in the face, and kiss him.

He kissed him long, and hard, and deep, forcing his tongue into Ramin's mouth like he wanted to taste himself.

"You did great, baby," he said softly. He kissed Ramin once on the tip of his nose and then stood back, looking at Ramin, waiting for him to say something.

But all that came out was "Holy fuck, Noah."

Noah's smile turned sheepish. "Was that okay?"

Ramin's mouth hung open, even though his jaw ached. "Are you kidding? That was the hottest thing that's ever happened to me."

Noah smiled, a small, gentle thing. "I'm glad. I wanted it to be good for you, too."

"It was," Ramin assured him.

"Good." Noah unlocked the door, stepped out and surveyed the bathroom, then gestured for Ramin to follow. Ramin adjusted his dick to the right to try to hide his rampant erection. He tugged the hem of his tank top down to cover the growing precum stain.

They went to wash their hands, and Ramin stared at himself in the mirror. His lips were swollen, his neck was flushed, his face was wet. He cleaned himself off, dried his tears, blew his nose. Ran wet fingers through his hair to fix it. Tried to scrub the wet spot out of his shorts.

Next to him, Noah was washing his own hands. His sleeves were still rolled up, and something caught Ramin's eye.

"What's this?"

There was writing, in blue ballpoint ink, on the underside of Noah's left forearm.

Safe word—Red light
Call him a good boy
Degrading but not mean
Ask if he can deep throat?
AFTERCARE!

Ramin gaped. "Did you make *notes?*"

He didn't know whether to laugh or pull Noah in for another kiss.

Noah's ears were turning red as he met Ramin's eyes in the mirror. "I've never done anything like this before. I had to do some research."

"I want to know more about that," Ramin muttered. The thought of Noah on his phone, looking up how to be a dom...

"But it was good?" Noah sounded like he needed reassurance. As if Ramin devouring his cock hadn't been enough indication.

"It was..." Ramin went quiet as someone passed behind them, on their way to the urinals. He turned to smile at Noah for real.

"It was perfect."

thirty-two

Noah

"What did you mean by *research?*" Ramin asked, leaning closer to Noah.

They were seated next to each other in the business-class car, enjoying the spacious seats and ample leg room and general vibes on the train. Noah couldn't believe he'd gone his whole life without knowing how awesome trains were.

A tiny part of him felt guilty that Jake wasn't with them. But Jake was on his own adventure, with Angela, probably having the time of his life, so Noah shushed that part. He was here with Ramin, finally getting time together, and he was going to savor every second.

Noah cocked his head. "Research?"

Ramin traced his index finger along Noah's forearm, where he'd rolled his sleeve down to cover his notes. His thoroughly exhausted member twitched in his singlet, remembering Ramin's touch.

Oh. *That* research.

Noah reached for his cross, but he didn't grab it. "Um. Just looking up best practices." He swallowed. "And maybe some examples. Like... scripts."

"That's really hot," Ramin whispered.

Noah grinned. It *was* hot. He didn't know how much he'd like it until he was—well, *they were*—doing it. Literally.

He shivered and tried to keep his body under control.

The Italian countryside sped by outside the windows, sunlit fields reflected in Ramin's green eyes. Noah would never get enough of them. His hands itched to sketch them, but even more, his hands itched to touch Ramin, to hold him, to pick up where they'd left off in that bathroom, but that was definitely not appropriate in the middle of a train.

Instead, he leaned over and gave a peck on Ramin's exposed shoulder. He loved seeing Ramin in a tank top. A few times, he'd even caught a glimpse of ink on Ramin's skin.

"I like you in this," he said. "You should wear it more often."

Ramin blushed and tugged it lower. He was always doing that, tugging on his hem. Noah reached for one of Ramin's hands, laced their fingers together. Ramin's hand was warm, smooth, strong.

Perfect.

"This okay?" Noah asked, when Ramin glanced around.

"Yeah, just making sure..."

"Making sure?"

Ramin's voice dropped. "Making sure it's safe? For two guys?"

Noah wanted to smack himself on the forehead.

He'd never even thought about that before. At least not in anything more than the occasional hypothetical. He'd certainly never looked over his own shoulders.

"Got it. Sorry." He felt himself getting warm all over. "Can I ask another question?"

Ramin lips quirked. "Sure."

"What's prep? You mentioned it earlier, when we were...you know, with the condom?"

"Oh. Pre-exposure prophylaxis. It prevents you getting HIV if you're exposed. I started taking it again before I came here. I thought I was going to…well." Ramin's voice dropped lower. He reached up to twist one of his studs. "Meet lots of men."

"Should I be on it, too?"

"I mean…" Ramin took a long breath, and Noah couldn't help feeling like he'd stuck his foot in his mouth somehow. Ramin scratched his chest with his free hand, pulling the tank top down just enough for Noah to get another glimpse of ink.

Ramin caught him staring.

"What? I'm curious." Noah reached for Ramin's shoulder, but Ramin swatted him away.

"Don't!" he whined, but his dimples were popping. "It's peeling."

"I don't mind."

Ramin shook his head. "*Behave.* Anyway, with PrEP…it's a good thing to be on if you're worried about HIV exposure. It's preventative. And I've been on it ever since it came out, even when I was with Todd and we were completely exclusive. I only really stopped it the last year or so, when I thought…well. Doesn't matter."

"When you thought he was the one. And you were gonna get married," Noah finished for him.

He was glad that hadn't happened. So glad. Otherwise he and Ramin never would've found each other again. But he still wished Ramin hadn't been hurt. Noah would've taken that pain for him, if he could've.

"Yeah. So, anyway, I'm on it again, but it's a personal choice, and you can talk to your doctor about it if you're worried."

"Okay." That all made sense. Another thing Noah hadn't ever really thought about before. Condoms had always seemed like enough for preventing STDs (not to mention birth control), but HIV was definitely scarier than most things.

"But if you're not, you know, sleeping around…I mean, if you and I are going to be exclusive…that *is* what you're thinking, right?"

"Absolutely," Noah said. The thought of Ramin with anyone else made his hackles rise. He leaned in so he could growl in Ramin's ear. "You're all mine."

Ramin laughed and shoved him. "Down, boy."

Noah giggled too.

"Anyway, growing up gay, hearing stories about AIDS... I guess it's always been a lot bigger fear for me than it was for you. I don't say that to guilt you, just so you can understand where I'm coming from. Does that make sense?"

It did. It made a lot of sense. Even after realizing he was bisexual, Noah had never given much thought to what sex with men really meant. His only two encounters had been so disastrously one-sided, he'd never ended up learning more. Learning what he needed.

He didn't regret the path his life had taken, all things considered. But sometimes he wished things had gone differently with one of those guys, or both. That he'd found more queer folks to talk to about this stuff, to learn what he needed to know.

Then he wouldn't feel like Ramin was having to tutor him in Gayness 101.

"I'm sorry so much of this is new to me. I promise you don't have to hold my hand through every little thing."

"I like holding your hand," Ramin murmured.

"I like holding yours, too."

They sat quietly for a moment, watching the verdant Padan Plain speed by, but then Ramin sat up straighter.

"Hey. Where did you get that singlet, anyway?"

The last half hour or so of the train ride was mostly dark as they took a series of tunnels through the Apennines and toward the coast. Noah plugged his nose and exhaled to try and relieve the pressure in his ears.

Finally, the train slowed, and an automated voice announced their arrival at Genova Piazza Principe.

Noah had imagined stepping off the platform onto a hill overlooking the Ligurian Sea, feeling the salt breeze on his face, seeing Ramin's eyes widen in wonder at the expanse of ocean before them. He'd been looking forward to that moment ever since he booked their tickets.

Instead, the underground platform led them through a cramped hallway before they found the exit and emerged in a bright piazza. There were buildings all around them, a traffic circle, and, ahead, a huge statue of Christopher Columbus.

No ocean in sight. No gull cries. No wind off the water.

It didn't matter, though, because Ramin smiled at him, eyes sparkling. Then he hiked his backpack higher, turned—and flipped Columbus the bird.

Noah giggled—the embarrassing one he sometimes let out—but Ramin turned back and his smile only got brighter. The sky stretched high and blue above them, full of tall, puffy white clouds. It was cooler than Milan, but more humid. At least the breeze cooled Noah's skin.

"Where to?" Ramin asked.

"The hotel's not far," Noah said.

"Hotel?"

Noah nodded. He didn't have much experience traveling, especially internationally, but he hadn't *only* been researching how to be a dom. He'd looked up hotel reviews, too.

"You didn't have to do that."

"I wanted to," Noah said. "Let me take care of you for once."

"You're always taking care of other people," Ramin pointed out.

Noah grumbled. It wasn't the same as taking care of Jake. This was . . . this was a partnership. They each took turns caring for the other. "You got the hotel in Como. I want to do this for you."

"Okay. Thank you."

Noah pulled out his phone and led the way.

Genoa reminded him of Bellagio: full of colorful buildings—some freshly painted, others faded by sun and salty air—narrow streets and steep hills, tight alleyways and hidden staircases. All the windows were covered by forest-green shutters.

"Do you think it's in, like, the HOA rules that they have to have those?" Noah asked.

"I don't know. I like them, though."

Noah checked his phone again and turned down a salita so steep, it probably should've been a staircase. The alleyway was gray and dim, like it had never seen the sun, and given how narrow it was, that might've been the actual truth.

"This kind of reminds me of Seattle," Ramin said. "All hills and curves."

"Yeah? I've never been." Noah imagined visiting it with Ramin and Jake. Of traveling all around the States with the two of them. Having family adventures together.

The thought nearly made him lose his footing.

Family adventures.

Him and Ramin and Jake.

A family.

It was way, way, *way* too soon to be thinking thoughts like that. Wasn't it?

He'd only known Ramin again for, what? Ten days? Or was today eleven? Was he even counting right?

You couldn't decide to make a family with someone after ten days. Even if that someone was the most beautiful man you'd ever seen in your life. Not to mention the kindest.

And gave the most amazing blowjobs.

Noah gave his leg a step-shake to try to unstick himself from his inner thigh.

The alley opened onto a sunlit street that faced the old port. In the distance stood huge, colorful shipping containers, tall blue cranes, and enormous cruise ships in a row. One of them had, of all things, Bugs Bunny on it.

But there, finally, was the sea.

It was a rich, dark blue, lightening as it stretched toward the horizon, until it was impossible to know for sure where the water ended and the sky began.

Seagulls cried, or did they laugh? One swooped from a light post across the street, its white belly marked with gray spots. The salt breeze caught in Noah's hair.

Ramin stopped abruptly, and Noah paused beside him. Ramin's eyes went wide and beautiful as he gazed out over the port and the water beyond, squinting slightly in the sun. His smile dawned slowly. First it lifted the corners of his eyes, and then it pierced his cheeks to form the deep wells of his dimples, and then it curved the heavenly bow of his lips, his face transported with wonder.

Noah wanted to kiss him a million times.

"This was a good choice," Ramin said softly.

"Yeah?" Noah's heart fluttered with pride. He'd made Ramin happy. He really liked making Ramin happy.

"I'm glad."

Noah hadn't managed to find a hotel that was actually on the waterfront (not for lack of trying), but they still walked along the boardwalk to get there.

They passed a huge maritime museum, a set of bouncy castles (Noah spotted an Avengers-themed one and immediately thought of Jake), an old galleon, and an impressive aquarium before taking another narrow salita back uphill. Noah hung back to enjoy the sight of Ramin's butt in those pink shorts of his.

He'd made Ramin wait for his own satisfaction back at the train station, but he had every intention of making it up to him at the hotel. In a nice, comfy bed. Doing anything and everything that Ramin wanted.

Noah guided them to a lavender building with the same forest-green shutters as all the others. Its walls were smooth but frescoed to seem like they were built from huge stones, with highlight and shadow giving a three-dimensional effect. Painted-on reliefs bordered the windows.

He held the door to let Ramin into the lobby.

"Good choice," Ramin said, looking around.

It *was* fancy. Noah had balked a bit at the price, but Ramin was worth it. Besides, he hadn't been on a date in two years. He could afford it.

Marble floors, leather armchairs, and a huge red velvet sofa sat to the right of the check-in desk; farther in lay a sitting room with a grand piano, a crystal chandelier, and more ridiculously ornate furniture.

"Got your passport?" he asked.

Ramin unslung his backpack, exposing more of his chest and another tantalizing hint of ink, and dug his passport out.

Faint music played over hidden speakers; the lobby smelled of vanilla and lavender from some sort of scent diffuser. It was the fanciest hotel Noah had ever been in.

Noah had never been poor, but he certainly hadn't grown up rich; his mother was a teacher and his father a mechanic, so they'd never gone hungry, but they'd also never taken trips like this. When they traveled—driving to Branson or Colorado or, one time, Minnesota, to see the Mall of America—they stayed at Holiday Inns. He'd gotten a taste of splurging while he and Angela were married, especially on their honeymoon, but truth be told, they'd both been more intent on making sure Jake's college fund was in good shape than on staying in nice hotels.

"Prego, Mr. Bartlett," the front desk clerk said as Noah handed over their passports. "It looks like your room isn't ready just yet. But if you want, you can check your bags, and we'll deliver them for you."

Ramin made a little sound, and Noah suddenly remembered his whole baggage debacle.

"We don't have to," he said, but Ramin shook his head.

"It's fine."

Noah handed over his backpack, suddenly painfully, awkwardly aware that there were condoms and lube in it. Surely they wouldn't search his bag, but he couldn't help feeling like he should be avoiding eye contact with the receptionist. He glanced around to make sure his dentist hadn't suddenly appeared.

"What now?" Noah asked as they stepped back out into the sun.

Ramin pulled on a slick pair of aviators. Noah wore his own Walmart plastic sunglasses.

"You hungry?" Ramin asked.

"Starving." Breakfast felt like a lifetime ago, and after Jake's meltdown, he hadn't had the appetite to finish. "You know, Genoa is famous for focaccia."

Ramin licked his lips. Those sinful lips. That perfect, talented tongue.

Noah's penis twitched in his singlet. He swallowed a groan at the memory. He needed to keep it in his pants until they got back to the hotel and could check in properly.

And then . . .

Then he could finally have his way with Ramin.

thirty-three

Noah

They headed east through the old town, following the boardwalk before cutting north a bit. They passed little convenience stores and cafés, shops and restaurants, and even a store selling nothing but typewriters.

Sometimes, as they walked, their hands would brush, and Noah would ache with the desire to link them together, but what Ramin had said about safety made sense. He'd never thought much about that before. He was going to learn, but until he did, he was going to let Ramin take the lead.

He also let Ramin take the lead on finding them lunch, following him to a small piazza—Piazza di Fossatello—lined with dark gray stones and full of metal tables clustered beneath large umbrellas. The smell of hot bread and olive oil filled the square.

Noah's mouth watered.

"Uh-oh." Ramin pointed to the bakery. The line was out the door and down the block.

"It smells amazing, though," Noah said. "I'm good to wait if you are."

The line moved quickly—thank goodness for small blessings—and it was absolutely worth the wait. The golden slabs of focaccia were crisp on the outside but soft and toothsome on the inside. They were practically oozing olive oil, salty and spicy and fruity.

Noah couldn't help it. He moaned. "This is so good."

Ramin sighed. "It really is."

Noah polished off both his slices way too quickly, but good gravy, they were delicious. Ramin took longer, picking at his single slice, as they basked in the crowds, in the flow of life around them.

It was a slower life, like Maria had said. No one was in a hurry. They could take their time, enjoy their focaccia. Ramin leaned over and thumbed a crumb away from the corner of Noah's mouth. Noah took that as encouragement, leaned in and gave Ramin a quick kiss on the lips.

Ramin smiled at him, eyes twinkling.

Noah could get used to this.

This life—long walks, leisurely lunches, fresh baked bread dripping with oil and coated in flake salt—but this man, too.

Sitting next to Ramin felt as natural as breathing. Maybe it was some distant sense memory of being desk neighbors back in school. Maybe it was pheromones, Ramin's intoxicating scent gripping Noah's senses in a vise. Maybe it was the magic of Italy.

Or maybe, just maybe, it was something simpler.

Something exhilarating and frightening, something totally impossible yet utterly inevitable.

"What?" Ramin asked.

"Nothing." Noah reached across the table for Ramin's hand. Ramin let him rub it. "Being with you makes me happy."

Ramin shook his head, blushing hard.

"It makes me happy too."

They visited the Doge's Palace, and the Cathedral of San Lorenzo, and the fountain in the Piazza de Ferrari, its water sparkling in the sun, trying to rival Ramin's earrings. Noah and Ramin stuck to the porticos for some shade.

They lost themselves in the little side streets and alleyways of the city center. They found an old medieval gate, a bronze statue of Elvis on a bench, a gelateria—of course, they stopped in for some.

"There's one other thing they recommended at the hotel," Ramin said. "It's a bit of a walk, though."

"What is it?"

"The Lanterna, the big lighthouse?"

"I'm game if you are."

Noah was game, but it turned out Ramin's definition of "a bit of a walk" was different than Noah's. He was properly sweating by the time they reached the wooden path up to the Lanterna. His underarms were wet, and he was terrified the ballpoint ink on his forearm would stain his shirt. Or worse, transfer right through, and then everyone would see his notes about blowjobs.

His singlet wasn't particularly breathable, either. It had been made for looks, not for moisture wicking, so now his sweat was mixing with the remnants of Ramin's saliva, and he just felt sticky and gross.

Ramin was sweating, too, the exertion making his skin glow a rosy tan-pink. Noah could smell the sun on his skin, and it was getting harder and harder not to drag him into a dark corner and lick him all over.

To his surprise—and utter delight—Ramin had reached over and taken his hand partway through the walk. Noah wasn't sure what had his heart hammering more: the uphill climb or the feel of Ramin's hand in his.

They drew closer and closer, the white and red tower growing ever larger, jutting out over the harbor. The path wound higher, past a security booth, switching back a few times, up a cobbled path and onto the promontory. It took them through a small (unimpressive, if Noah was being honest) park, a little museum about the history of the Lanterna (more impressive, and Noah was entranced by a display of how Fresnel lenses worked—Jake would've loved it), then up to the huge ivory-colored lighthouse itself.

Noah craned his neck to look up, up, up toward the top, where the little viewing deck that was their goal lay.

"There're a lot of stairs," Ramin warned.

"I'm good."

Noah *thought* he was good, but there were *a lot* a lot of stairs. One hundred and seventy-two, the sign said.

Their day had been pretty easy so far—no Death March of Fun—but these stairs might give Angela's travel planning a run for its money.

Noah was in good shape. Great shape, even. He was at the top of his age bracket in his CrossFit classes. He could still run an under-seven-minute mile. He could bench press nearly a hundred pounds. But these stairs might actually be the death of him. His right knee gave an awkward *crackle* as they passed another cramped landing.

"Oof," Noah muttered, more from surprise than discomfort.

"You okay?" Ramin paused, concern written across his face.

"I'm fine. Don't you have any spots that just *snap-crackle-pop* these days? Once I hit thirty-seven I started finding them everywhere." He sighed, rubbing at his knee. "I can squat four hundred pounds, but apparently I can't handle a hundred stairs."

"Wait, really?"

"I mean, yeah." His personal best was 450, but that had been back in his late twenties.

"No wonder you have such a nice butt."

"Not as nice as yours." The one redeeming part of this climb had been the view of Ramin's behind in those pink shorts of his.

Noah was obsessed.

He wanted to knead it. Kiss it. Worship it. Celebrate Ramin's whole body the way he deserved. He wanted Ramin to feel precious and beautiful and wanted, because he was all of those things, and Noah needed him to know it.

Ramin was blushing, but he cracked a grin. "My eyes are up here, buddy."

Noah giggled—which made Ramin laugh—and followed.

He'd read once that the more positive you were about aging, the better you aged, and Noah had taken that to heart. In fact, he was looking forward to being an eccentric grandfather (or even great-grandfather), like a cross between Nonno and a mad scientist.

Still, the last couple years, he'd definitely felt his body changing. He spent more time with sore muscles after a heavy lifting day. The younger members at his gym had started finishing their WODs before him, when he used to be one of the first ones done. Before he'd gotten on the plane to Italy, he'd even plucked a gray eyebrow hair.

But he was wiser now, too. More content.

He had a life. He had Jake.

He had—or at least hoped he had—Ramin.

"Nearly there," Ramin panted. Noah took no satisfaction that Ramin was finally out of breath, too.

The air had gotten progressively warmer as they neared the top. Blinding sunlight streamed in ahead. A breeze stirred, twisting the ends of Noah's hair, cooling the sweat on his forehead and the back of his neck.

A few more steps, one last corner, and they stepped out onto the terrace.

"Oh," Ramin said, so softly it was nearly lost to the wind. He was already moving to the rail, staring south across the docks and out to the endless curve of the blue, blue sea.

Noah shook his legs out before stepping up next to him. From up here they could see the city to their left, climbing up into the mountains, and to their right, the hazy horizon. The clouds had blown away, leaving the sky a brilliant azure canvas that Noah could nearly reach out and touch.

None of that compared to Ramin, though.

His face—his beautiful, awesome face—was totally open as he stared at the water. His pupils had contracted in the sunlight, revealing a broad expanse of green. His cheeks had gone slack, erasing his dimples. He was totally relaxed, lost in the view. The studs in his ears sparkled in the sunlight.

He was perfection.

He was everything Noah had ever wanted.

Noah's heart squeezed, so suddenly he worried he'd overdone it on the stairs. Despite the climb, his limbs felt light, so light he could float away into the sky, fly like the butterflies fluttering a storm in his stomach.

He stepped behind Ramin, wrapped his arms around him from behind. Rested his chin on Ramin's shoulder and took in the Ligurian Sea below them, because if he kept looking at Ramin, he was going to say something foolish. Embarrassing. Terrifying.

True.

"It's perfect," he said instead. "I love it."

He couldn't say the other thing growing inside him.

Ramin sighed and relaxed back against him. His voice was low, reverent, half a prayer.

"My mom grew up in the north of Iran. This city called Rasht. Which is funny, because my dad is from Yazd, and Yazdis are always making fun of Rashtis."

Noah's Iranian geography was terrible, but he hummed so Ramin would know he was listening. He could look at a map later.

"That doesn't matter. Anyway. Rasht is close to the Caspian Sea. My mom grew up visiting the seaside in summers. But when she moved to the States, she ended up in Kansas City. She always said she missed the sea. And my dad always said, 'We'll go next year.' But they never did. I didn't see the ocean myself until after college."

Noah squeezed Ramin tighter. He knew Ramin was strong, knew he didn't need Noah's support—but Noah wanted to give it anyway.

"It makes me think of her, you know?"

"I get it," Noah murmured against Ramin's neck. Life had taken so much from Ramin. But he could still look out at the sea and find beauty. Find connection. Find love.

It would've broken Noah's heart if it didn't bolster it instead.

Ramin sighed. "It's like every time I see the ocean, a little bit of her gets to see it, too. I'm living her dreams for her."

Who said things like that? Who thought things like that? Ramin did.

Noah kept his arms tight and swayed a little. Ramin swayed along with him.

Noah had encountered a few perfect moments in his life. Like the day he married Angela, no matter what had come after. Or the day Jake was born.

But this—holding Ramin, with the sea below, and the sun above, and the wind in their hair—this was perfect, too.

He never wanted to let go.

thirty-four

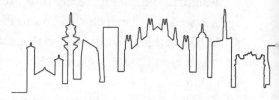

Ramin

Noah beeped them into their room on the hotel's fifth floor, and Ramin sighed with relief. The air-conditioning felt like heaven against his sweaty skin. He rubbed at his tattoos; his wrists were warm, his pulse racing just beneath the skin.

The bell desk had indeed dropped their two backpacks off, and they rested on two armchairs in the corner, next to a bay window looking out toward the port. A pair of towel swans sat on the large bed, heads bowed toward each other to make a (slightly misshapen) heart.

"Oh, Noah," Ramin sighed. "It's perfect."

"I'm glad you like it." Noah leaned in and gave Ramin a swift peck on the lips. "I'll be right back."

Noah disappeared into the restroom as Ramin stepped up to the window to take in the view. It was nothing like the Lanterna—their view was more roofs and streets than port and sea—but still. Noah had done all this. Made this happen. All because he remembered Ramin saying he liked the water.

Had anyone ever truly done something like this for him before? If so, he couldn't remember it.

He could get used to this. Even though he knew he shouldn't.
His phone buzzed in his pocket, and he slid it out.

Farzan
Got Todd's stuff all sorted
He's 100% moved out

Arya
Until the next time he
"remembers something"
Miss you dude

Ramin
Thanks for dealing with it
Miss you both
Love you

Ramin sighed. Today had been...perfect. Absolutely perfect. As far as dates went, he'd never had better. As far as blowjobs, he'd never *given* better. And as far as men...Ramin had never been with better. Yeah, Noah was handsome (and extremely hot), but he was also kind, and silly, and thoughtful, and a good father.

So why couldn't Ramin shake Todd out of his mind? Todd's voice, calling him boring. Todd's eyes, trailing over his stretch marks when he thought Ramin wasn't looking. Constantly asking Ramin to go to the gym with him. Pestering him to join the kickball league.

Ramin felt the tsunami of self-loathing like a physical thing, crashing in from the sea, knocking aside all the cruise ships and boardwalk attractions and locals walking around with their slices of focaccia. He felt it and breathed through it and reminded himself his body was beautiful, his body was strong, his body was capable, his—

"Sorry," Noah said, wrapping around Ramin from behind. He hadn't even heard the bathroom door.

"It's okay." Ramin made sure to keep his voice even. He wasn't going to project his insecurities onto Noah. Insecurities were *definitely* boring. "That was quick. I thought you were showering?"

"Why shower if we're just going to get dirty again?" Noah rumbled in his ear.

Before Ramin knew it, Noah was dragging him away from the window, toward the bed. He knew Noah was strong, but *damn*. Ramin felt his feet leave the floor as Noah heaved him onto the bed and climbed on top of him, framing him with his hands and knees.

"Hi." Noah leaned down for a long, lingering kiss, claiming Ramin's mouth, and Ramin let himself be claimed. His head rolled, his back arched. How could Noah turn him to putty with a single kiss?

"Hi," he gasped back when Noah broke the kiss and he could think again. He managed to find enough strength in his neck muscles to actually look at Noah. "What was all that for?"

"I warned you I was going to have my way with you."

"No you didn't." Ramin definitely would've remembered that. His ass would've been puckered all day.

He was definitely in favor of it, though.

Noah's lips drew down into a pout. "Huh. Well, I definitely thought it."

He slid off and stood at the foot of the bed, gave Ramin a scorching grin, and began unbuttoning his shirt. "Now get naked."

Ramin's breath lodged in his throat.

Noah tossed his shirt over his head, slid down his shorts, so he was standing there in nothing but blue spandex, the heavy tube of his cock bulging to the right. He looked like a dream. Ramin's wet dream.

Ramin just stared, mouth dry, pulse racing, until Noah's voice cracked like a whip.

"I said, get naked."

Noah pulled his arms out of the singlet's straps, rolling it down to reveal his chest. Noah's pecs were firm, round, crowned with nubby little pink nipples, dusted with hair in the valley between. And below, he had abs. Actual abs.

Even Todd had never had abs, something he'd constantly lamented.

Noah's abs weren't cut like a movie star's. Or carved like a model's. But they were there, strong ridges and shadowed valleys. They looked like Noah actually *used* them, like they braced his core while he built a cabinet or framed a house or picked Jake up for a hug. Even now, they flexed and relaxed with his breath.

Noah was a work of art. He was stunning. And Ramin was just... Ramin. What if Noah saw him, stretch marks, dunlop and all, and was disappointed?

Or worse, *bored*?

Ramin knew his heart couldn't take it.

"Ramin?" Noah's whole demeanor softened. His voice gentled. His face opened in concern. "Baby, what's wrong?"

Baby. Ramin's heart squeezed. How could Noah call him that?

Noah clambered back onto the bed.

"Red light?" he asked.

Ramin shook his head and bit his lips.

"Talk to me."

Ramin couldn't. It was too embarrassing. Too messed-up. It was his problem, not Noah's, he knew that. It was his own fears, his own insecurities, swirling and building until they burst from his mouth before he could stop them.

"You have *abs*."

Noah's stomach barely sagged down, even when he was above Ramin like this. Ramin clenched his own core, like that would make any sort of difference.

"Yeah?" Noah's brow drew down. "Does... does that bother you?"

Ramin closed his eyes tight, shook his head.

"You're beautiful." So beautiful. More beautiful than Ramin could stand. More beautiful than he deserved. He tried to silence that voice inside him, the one that sounded like Todd, like the assholes he'd hooked up with in college, like the mean boys in high school who'd teased him for being a chubby crybaby. Usually he could.

But now, looking up at everything he ever wanted, those voices were all he could hear.

"Baby." Noah's quiet voice cut through the storm, a lighthouse beam through the fog. The tenderness framing that word made Ramin's heart crack in two.

"Tell me what's wrong?" Noah pleaded.

Ramin let out a shaky breath.

And then he said, "I don't look like you."

"So?"

Noah didn't get it. How could he? He'd always been handsome and fit and hung. He'd never been the ugly kid in class. He'd never been the fat guy at the club. He'd never been ghosted after a first date because he didn't fit some fucked-up beauty standard.

"I just don't want you to be disappointed," Ramin muttered.

"Why would I be disappointed?"

Ramin choked out a laugh. "Because I've got stretch marks? Because my stomach dunlops over my waistband? Because I've got loose skin? Pick your poison."

Noah leaned back and sat up.

Ramin held his breath, waiting for Noah to get up, to walk away. To shatter Ramin's heart.

But Noah didn't go far. He just shifted his legs a bit so he could pull Ramin up to sitting, too. He held Ramin's hands and looked into Ramin's eyes.

Ramin sniffed and blinked. When had he started crying? He'd tried to hold it in.

He hated Noah seeing him like this.

Noah reached up and thumbed away his tears before any more could fall.

"Hey," he said. "Um. Not to psychoanalyze you, but do you know what body dysmorphia is?"

Ramin snorted. "Yeah. I see a therapist."

"Oh. Okay. Good." Noah breathed deep. "I don't know what it's like to deal with that. And I know queer men have different kinds of body standards. But I don't care about any of that. I care about *you*."

"But—"

"No buts. Ramin, you met Angela. You know she's fat. She was fat when I fell in love with her, and she was fat when we married, and she's fat today, and she's the most beautiful woman I've ever seen. I worshipped her."

"It's different, though." *Straight skinny is gay fat.*

Even if they didn't want it to be, it would always be different.

"I know it is." Noah squeezed Ramin's hands. "You know how I recognized you, in that gelato place back in Milan? Our first day?"

Ramin shook his head. That felt like a lifetime ago. He'd been too stunned to even question it.

"It was your eyes. It was your dimples when you smile. It was your voice. It was the way you carry yourself. The way you make everyone around you calmer, happier, just by being there."

Ramin's throat closed off.

"You are beautiful and perfect the way you are. There's only one thing I'd ever want to change about you." Noah leaned in and kissed the teary corners of Ramin's eyes. "I'd give you a thousand more smile lines, if you let me."

Noah thought he was beautiful.

Ramin let out a shaky breath, but it turned into a snotty laugh.

"I'm sorry. I ruined the moment."

"It's okay, baby." Noah yanked Ramin closer, into his lap. Noah's naked chest was hot, sticky with sweat. Ramin breathed in Noah's musk, nuzzled into the crook of his neck to drink in even more, as Noah cradled the back of his head, walked his fingertips along Ramin's spine.

Despite it all, he could feel Noah getting hard beneath him. He shifted his hips, ground into Noah's dick.

Noah's breath hitched. Ramin could hear the smile in his voice. "The moment's not *that* ruined."

Ramin chuckled.

"You okay?" Noah said.

"I'm okay." Well, maybe *okay* wasn't exactly right. He'd need to sit with what Noah said. Later. Right now, he wanted to keep going more than anything.

"Good. Now." Noah's hand on Ramin's neck tightened. "Are you going to get naked, or do I have to pin you to this bed and make you?"

"I think you have to make me," Ramin said.

Noah's voice went husky. "I was hoping you'd say that."

Ramin knew Noah was strong, but he wasn't prepared for just how fast he was. Ramin barely had time to laugh before Noah had him pinned to the bed, wrists held above his head, hips tucked under Noah's. He felt the hot, hard weight of Noah's erection bearing down on his own hardening dick.

"I'm pretty sure you said I could see this new tattoo of yours," Noah said, and before Ramin could even brace himself, Noah had peeled Ramin's tank top off and over his head.

Ramin reminded himself to breathe. To let Noah look at him. To not reach up and cover himself.

He was desired.

Noah's eyes were dark chips as he took in Ramin's chest. Ramin knew it was doughy, a little pale, though maybe a bit tanned in places from today. In the center of his chest, his faravahar lay, red and tender and still peeling a bit.

He knew it couldn't distract from the silver-pink stretch marks on his sides, though. Or the pooch around his belly button.

He desperately wanted Noah to say something. Anything.

Instead, Noah leaned down and kissed Ramin right over his heart, his lips ghosting the faravahar's wing. And then his mouth trailed down, down, toward Ramin's navel, then along to his sides, kissing every bit of skin.

"I can't believe I get to do this to you," Noah murmured. "Do you know how long I've wanted to?"

Ramin couldn't believe it, either. Noah's mouth was electric, his lips setting off fireworks in every one of Ramin's cells. Ramin felt like a bow-string about to snap. He felt like one of those plasma balls they'd played with in middle school science, the ones that made your hair stand on end.

He felt alive in a way he never had before.

Noah lifted up a bit and grumbled as he tugged on Ramin's shorts. "These are in the way."

Ramin wiggled his butt so Noah could pull them off, revealing his rainbow-colored trunks beneath, trapping his hard dick to the left.

He wondered if Noah could see the precum stains from the train station.

He flexed his dick, and Noah hummed in satisfaction. He couldn't move if he wanted to. Noah's gaze had him pinned, like a butterfly to a board. He had no fight left in him. No voice in the back of his head. No fear.

Just Noah, Noah, Noah.

"You don't have to go any farther if you don't want to," Ramin said when Noah didn't move. He didn't want Noah to feel pressured.

"I want to." Noah was staring down at him, with a look Ramin had never seen before. Ramin couldn't help his cock flexing again. Noah's mouth curled into a smile. "I want to more than anything."

Before Ramin could react, Noah lunged back in, planting his lips on Ramin's inner thighs. Kissing, sucking, tugging on the hairs. Ramin nearly arched off the bed as Noah's face grazed his aching cock.

He heard Noah take a deep breath and murmur against Ramin's skin. "I like the way you smell."

"Even when I'm sweaty?"

Noah lifted his face to meet Ramin's eyes. "Especially when you're sweaty."

Ramin liked the smell of Noah all sweaty, too. His nostrils flared. If he could move, he would've buried his face in the valley of Noah's chest, licked every drop of sweat from between the swell of his pecs.

As it was, Ramin could only feast with his eyes, savor the musk, relish the tingles Noah was raising along every patch of skin he touched.

And then, oh God, then Noah planted his mouth on Ramin's underwear.

His lips traced the shape of Ramin's erection. Ramin didn't think he could get any harder, but he was wrong. If he'd been steel before, he was diamond-hard now, still trapped up and to the left. Then Noah's mouth found his head, hidden beneath the sticky fabric, and the shock traveled straight up Ramin's spine.

"Noah," Ramin gasped as Noah breathed on him, bit lightly, sucked on him through the cotton, wet and warm and wild.

Noah jerked up, an untamed, hungry light in his eyes. "Can I take these off?"

"Yeah."

He did, the pads of his fingers grazing Ramin's sides, ghosting along Ramin's hips. Ramin's cock bent down with the motion, then sprang free.

He held his breath. He wasn't anywhere near Noah's size.

What if Noah didn't like it?

What if Ramin wasn't what he wanted?

"Oh my," Noah purred. "You're perfect."

Ramin's whole body flushed, his skin so hot he was surprised he didn't set the duvet on fire.

Noah's hand came up and gently, oh so gently, cradled Ramin's balls. Ramin kept them smooth—his hair was annoyingly coarse— and Noah's short fingernails sent a ripple of pleasure across the taut skin. Ramin's taint pulsed with anticipation. He shivered.

Noah noticed, because he did it again, holding his breath as he played Ramin like a violin. "I've wanted you since the day I saw you."

His hand finally wrapped around Ramin's leaking cock, thumbing at the head to spread the precum around. His calloused fingers curled around Ramin's length, and Ramin's dick flexed again, because *holy shit*, Noah was touching him.

Noah squeezed tighter, smiling as Ramin gasped, looking down at him like he was the only star in a dark sky. Ramin couldn't take it. His cock spasmed, hard, and he clenched his Kegel muscles as hard as he could before he came.

"Red light," he gasped, and Noah let go right away.

"What?" he asked. "Are you okay? Did I hurt you?"

"Felt too good," Ramin grunted. "Give me a second."

He breathed deep once, twice. Thrice. Tried to calm down.

Except it was nearly impossible with Noah right there. Looking at Ramin like he was ready to devour him. Like he was counting down the seconds until he could touch Ramin again.

Ramin spasmed again and nearly tipped over the edge.

"That's hot," Noah whispered.

Ramin shook his head, gritted his teeth and fought back the orgasm. He wouldn't be so on edge if he'd gotten off while he was blowing Noah. Or at least ducked into a bathroom to jerk off at some point. Instead he'd been left with his horniness building all day. He couldn't take it much longer.

He took a long, shuddering breath and forced his dick to relax.

"Okay. Sorry."

"Don't be," Noah said. "Can I do more?"

"More?"

In answer, Noah smirked at Ramin. Then he dove right down and took Ramin into his mouth.

Oh, fuck.

Noah was giving him a blowjob.

Noah Bartlett was giving him a fucking blowjob.

Noah's mouth was warm and slick. The pressure was...well, a little wrong. And the suction was nearly nonexistent. And Ramin hissed a time or two as Noah had trouble curling his beautiful lips over his teeth. But his tongue...well, it seemed to know what to do, caressing Ramin like a spoonful of gelato.

And it didn't matter, anyway, because it was *Noah Fucking Bartlett* going down on him.

"Fuck, Noah," Ramin hissed, threading his fingers through Noah's hair, luxuriating in the thick strands. "You feel amazing."

Noah hummed in satisfaction, which just sent vibrations right into Ramin's cock, and it jumped again, against the roof of Noah's mouth.

Ramin's breath came in fits and spurts. He might hyperventilate. He might die and go to heaven, if heaven wasn't right here, right now, with Noah's mouth on him.

Noah didn't take him all the way in, focusing mostly on the head, using his hand on the rest. He slowly developed a rhythm. And got his teeth under control. And learned how much Ramin liked having his balls lightly scratched.

Ramin felt the pinching deep behind his taint and clenched up again. "Red light!" he gasped.

Noah popped off Ramin's dick with a suck so hard, Ramin nearly lifted off the bed. He had a sheepish grin slashed across his pink lips. "Am I doing okay?"

"Uh-huh," Ramin said through heavy breaths. "I'm nearly there. You don't have to keep going."

Noah let out one of his giggles, the light, silly ones that Ramin loved so much. "I told you. I want to."

"But I'm going to finish."

Noah's hand was still playing with his tight balls. "That's the point."

"Have you ever..."

"Tasted semen before?"

Ramin nodded.

"My own, a few times. It doesn't bother me."

"You're sure?"

"Ramin. Baby." Noah gave him a rough stroke that had him shuddering for control. "Let me do this. Please?"

Fuck it was sexy when Noah said *please*.

Ramin nodded.

And then Noah's mouth was around him again, and some sort of lightbulb must've gone off because all of a sudden he'd figured out the right amount of suction, and Ramin's body was turning to jelly. He was sweating all over, cooing as Noah's hot saliva trailed down over his balls and toward his hole. And when Noah's tongue found that spot beneath his head, he let out a cry he couldn't stop.

Did they have neighbors?

Who cared?

"Fuck, Noah," Ramin said. "Fuck."

Pleasure mounted again, sparking along his spine, between his legs, deep inside, until he couldn't hold back anymore.

"I'm coming," he gasped, breaking apart, but he didn't fall, because Noah was there to catch him, grunting as Ramin rode the waves of delicious ecstasy.

Noah stayed with him, cradling his balls, pressing a thumb against his taint, humming along until Ramin got too sensitive and begged him to let go.

Ramin collapsed onto the bed with a sigh.

Before he could even catch his breath, though, Noah was on top of him, his own hard cock, trapped in the singlet, now pressed against Ramin's thigh. He looked Ramin in the eyes, rested his forehead against Ramin's, leaned in for a kiss.

Ramin was weirdly disappointed Noah had already swallowed, because he kind of wanted to share his load as they kissed. But on the other hand, holy fuck, Noah swallowed. Ramin could still taste himself as they kissed, as he plundered Noah's mouth with his tongue and Noah fought him back, pinning his tongue as effortlessly as he'd pinned Ramin's body beneath him.

A full-body shiver came over Ramin one last time, all his senses lighting up like fireworks. His back arched off the bed before he finally crashed back into it like a wave upon the shore.

Noah's kissing slowed. His tongue withdrew. He placed one last kiss, right at the corner of Ramin's mouth, and leaned up.

"So." His smile was somewhere between cocky and shy. "How was that?"

thirty-five

Noah

Noah cuddled Ramin for as long as he could, but they were both hot and sweaty, and Ramin was scratching at his peeling tattoo. While Noah liked the way Ramin smelled, he had a feeling they didn't want the bedding to absorb it.

So he dragged Ramin to the shower, kissing him over and over as he waited for the water to warm up. Which took a weirdly long time.

The shower was great, though: big enough for four, with a frosted glass door, blue LED lighting, and a waterfall head that felt like heaven as Noah held Ramin beneath it.

He knew he'd just had his mouth around Ramin's member, his lips on as many parts of Ramin's skin as he could reach, but gently scrubbing him felt even more intimate. Tender. With none of the breathtaking anticipation of sex, he had time to really admire Ramin's skin. The way he curved in spots. The soft bits, the firm bits, the ones with sexy tufts of hair.

Ramin's hands were on Noah too, soaping him up. Noah was worried Ramin would feel weird about showering together, or get self-conscious again, but Ramin seemed quite content, lingering on

Noah's chest, massaging his armpits with soap, lathering up his heavy penis.

"Careful," Noah said. "I don't want to get worked up before dinner."

Ramin whined. Truth be told, Noah wouldn't have minded a shower handjob, but they had a reservation. When they were both clean, Noah stepped out and grabbed a fluffy white towel to wrap Ramin in. He knew he'd said it aloud, but he hoped Ramin could tell, from every one of Noah's actions, just how beautiful he was. How precious. How irresistibly sexy.

"So," Ramin said, once they were both dressed in fresh clothes. Ramin had pulled on a short-sleeved button-up—no more tank top, to Noah's disappointment—and Noah himself had managed to scrub the ink off his arm, so he'd changed into a polo. "You said something about dinner?"

"I've already got us reservations."

Ramin's eyebrows shot up. His eyes sparkled. "Really?"

"Really-really."

They didn't have far to go—just the elevator to the rooftop. The doors opened onto an open-air restaurant lit with fairy lights hung from the trellises. The sun was nearly set, turning the sky above a rich velvety purple. The wind off the darkening sea had turned cool and crisp. The city was lighting up all around them, and in the distance, the Lanterna—Noah still couldn't believe they'd climbed it—shone out to sea.

Ramin took it all in with wonder, the fairy lights reflecting in his eyes, and Noah's heart squeezed so hard he nearly doubled over. How did he get to be so lucky, to be here, at this moment, in this place, with Ramin?

"Buonasera," the host said. "Table for two?"

"We have a reservation," Noah said. "Under Noah Bartlett?"

"Prego, Mr. Bartlett, this way."

Their table was a small thing, covered by a white cloth, nestled up against the rail that hemmed in the rooftop. Noah held Ramin's chair for him before taking his own seat.

"I picked the place, but you still have to pick the wine," Noah said. "Nonna would never forgive me if I picked something bad."

Ramin laughed. "That woman clearly loves you."

"She loves you, too."

Ramin blushed hard and hid behind the wine list.

He ended up ordering a rosé, but it was darker than any rosé Noah had ever seen before, almost ruby-colored. It smelled like candied cherries and children's cough syrup, and it tasted tart and bright and perfect.

"Oh, wow," Noah said. "This is good."

He'd never tasted anything like it. It seemed like Ramin hadn't, either, because he kept sniffing it, sipping it, taking photos of the bottle.

"Everything okay?" Maybe it wasn't good. Maybe Ramin was thinking of sending it back. Maybe Noah's palate was too pedestrian.

"Yeah, it's amazing," Ramin said. "I need to talk to David about it. He's—"

"The sommelier. Farzan's boyfriend. Right?"

"Right." Ramin lifted his glass. Noah clinked. "To…What should we toast to?"

"To no more stairs," Noah joked.

He'd climb a thousand more stairs as long as it was with Ramin. But he was just as glad to be off his feet.

Noah ordered the trofie al pesto Genovese—twists of fresh pasta in a verdant basil pesto, with tempura-fried green beans, served atop a disc of mashed potatoes.

Noah could've eaten two. Maybe even three. The pesto was bright, fresh, and balanced, the green beans crisp and perfect. The silky mashed potatoes melted on his tongue, buttery and rich. And for dessert, Noah picked the pineapple carpaccio, thinly sliced rings of pineapple with an orange sorbet on top.

"Are you trying to tell me something about how I taste?" Ramin asked.

Noah nearly spat out his wine. "No! No, it just looked good. I didn't mean—"

But Ramin was shaking from holding in laughter.

Noah pursed his lips. "That was mean."

Besides, he was more worried about how *he* tasted. Though Ramin hadn't complained, so . . .

They stayed well past sunset, admiring the silver sickle of the moon over the sea, the sounds of the city below them, the breeze in their hair. Noah lost track of time. He could've talked to Ramin for hours. For years. Forever.

But eventually the breeze turned cold, and the wine ran out, and the candle in the center of their table guttered.

They tumbled back into their bedroom, laughing. Noah caught Ramin against the bed, pulled him into a long, lingering kiss that tasted of cherry candy and citrus.

"Mm," Noah hummed, as Ramin angled his head to dip his tongue deeper into Noah's mouth. Noah wrapped his arms around Ramin and pulled him onto the bed, rolling onto their sides, as they kissed, and kissed, and kissed, until Noah was lost, until all he knew was Ramin, Ramin, Ramin.

He ground their hips together, savoring the freedom now that he was out of that singlet. It had been hot—sexy hot and also temperature hot—but now, his erection grew down the leg of his boxers.

"You're already hard," Ramin muttered, breath ghosting along Noah's ear.

"Uh-huh."

"You didn't let me take care of you before."

"You already did at the train station."

"That was this morning," Ramin said, trailing kisses along Noah's jawline. "What about now?"

Yes yes yes.

This time, when Noah ground against him, Ramin pressed back, his own hot length singing against Noah's through their shorts.

"Tell me what you want," Ramin said.

I want you, Noah wanted to say. *I want us. I want forever.*

Just like when he'd stood atop the Lanterna, gazing at Ramin in the sun, his mouth wanted to run ahead of his brain. Tell Ramin everything that was in his heart. But it was *way* too soon to say something like that. He didn't want to scare Ramin off.

"Noah?" Ramin's brow furrowed. "Hey. Here. Let me up."

Noah did, sliding off to Ramin's side. Ramin scooted back so he was leaning against the headboard. He pulled a pillow over to cover his stomach.

Noah wished he wouldn't. Ramin was beautiful, his stomach just right for grabbing, his limbs soft in all the right places, hard where it mattered.

"Today's been a lot for you. It's okay if you need a while to process."

Noah shook his head. "I've wanted all this longer than I can say."

"Then what?"

Noah swallowed. He couldn't say *I think I'm falling for you*. Even though it was true.

Instead he blurted out the next true thing he could think of.

"I wanted to try some butt stuff?"

Butt.

Stuff.

Noah's cheeks started heating. What was wrong with him?

What's wrong was, he was new at this. He was new, and Ramin had a wealth of experience, and he probably thought Noah was ridiculous.

Ramin smirked a bit, but he didn't laugh. The knot behind Noah's chest loosened. Ramin ran a hand down Noah's arm. Noah scooted closer. "Okay, so, I guess we haven't talked about this yet. I'm mostly a bottom, but I don't think I can do that, for you, tonight. You're big, and that takes more prep work."

"Oh," Noah said.

On the one hand, the thought of making love to Ramin brought his erection raging back from its embarrassment-induced flagging.

On the other hand . . .

Noah swallowed. He needed to be brave. "I meant me. My butt."

Also, he really, really wanted Ramin to touch his butt.

"Oh." Ramin licked his lips. "You sure?"

Noah nodded. He'd never explored the back door. Angela hadn't been into it. None of his other partners had, either. And he'd always been too nervous to try it on his own.

No, that wasn't it. Noah was adventurous, but in this... he wanted someone to show him.

He wanted someone who cared about him to be the first.

Yeah, virginity was a social construct, and it wasn't like Noah had been a virgin for decades, anyway. But vulnerability still mattered, and this made him feel *very* vulnerable, and he wasn't going to share that with just anyone.

He wanted to share it with Ramin.

Noah met Ramin's eyes. "Really sure."

Ramin was the first one to look away, but only for a second. His beautiful skin was flushing, from his forehead all the way down to his chest. When he spoke, his voice came out husky. "You need to prep?"

"Prep? I don't have a prescription yet."

Ramin raised an eyebrow.

It only took Noah a second for it to hit him. Different prep.

"Oh! Right. Yeah. Uh, be right back."

Noah *had*, in fact, researched this bit too. He knew how to do it with a plastic water bottle, though now that he thought about it, why had he left that sex store with condoms and lube and a singlet and absolutely nothing to help with prep? He'd walked past an aisle full of enema bulbs.

He finally emerged from the bathroom, feeling clean and relatively confident, only to behold the most beautiful sight in the world:

Ramin, naked, lying on the bed with his ankles crossed, fiddling with a bottle of lube.

He saw the flinch, the way Ramin clenched his core for a second, before relaxing. He knew he couldn't fix Ramin, knew Ramin didn't *need* fixing, but he swore to himself he'd spend every day telling Ramin just how beautiful he was.

Ramin's gaze fell on Noah's skin like a blow, trailing up, up, up, from Noah's toes, lingering on his twitching erection, caressing his chest, and on to his face. Ramin's eyes burned like jade fire.

"Fuuuuck me," Ramin whispered, low and slow, and Noah hardened even more.

Noah shifted his weight, tried to give a cocky grin, but it probably just looked goofy. "I thought we agreed that was off the table."

Ramin snorted. "Grab a towel."

"A towel?"

"Just in case."

"Right." Just in case of mess.

Noah reached back into the bathroom, grabbed a clean towel, flung it into the bed, and jumped on top. He pulled Ramin onto him so they could kiss, so they could grind their naked bodies together, so he could feel every bit of Ramin. And Ramin was feeling every bit of him, too, hands tracing Noah's chest and stomach, following the valleys of his abdominal muscles. They weren't as cut as they used to be back in Noah's Hollister days, but then, he actually used them now. He didn't work out to look a certain way. He worked out so he could do the work he needed to do, have the fun he wanted to have. Load and unload lumber. Chase Jake around a park.

Make love to a beautiful, beautiful man.

"You're so fucking sexy," Ramin said as his hand slid farther down, teasing Noah's bush. It was a lot fuller than Ramin's, and he suddenly wondered if he should start trimming, but before he could ask, Ramin's hand wrapped around his erection.

Ramin's hands were perfect. Warm and strong and dexterous, trailing smooth pleasure in their wake. Noah groaned.

He reached for Ramin's sex, too, found it waiting for him hard and leaking. He stroked it with one hand, while his other held Ramin's neck, keeping their lips locked together. This wasn't like Milan, where they'd furtively kissed and hoped Jake didn't hear them. It wasn't like the train station, where the kissing was part of aftercare. It wasn't even like this afternoon, when they'd crashed together, desperate to finally, finally be alone.

No, this was a slow, simmering passion that finally had time to blossom. To take its time.

Noah traced Ramin's lips and jaw, seeking out every spot that made him tremble. Ramin discovered that spot below Noah's jaw that always made him tingle with euphoria.

Noah's core was clenching, his erection pulsing in time with their kisses. If they kept this up, they'd never get to the butt stuff. He'd come all over Ramin.

Actually, that sounded kind of hot. He wouldn't mind the chance to paint Ramin's face, but not tonight.

He sighed and broke the kiss. Ramin's lips chased his for a moment as he fell back to the bed.

"Hey," he said, trying again for a cocky grin and getting a little closer this time. He didn't want Ramin to see his nerves, only his excitement.

Ramin licked his lips. "Hey."

"How do you want me?"

Ramin stared down at him, exposed and flushed and breathing hard, his penis lying heavy and twitching against his right thigh. Ramin looked like he wanted to devour Noah.

Noah was ready to be devoured.

Finally Ramin spoke. "Are you comfortable on all fours?"

"Like doggie style?"

Ramin quirked an eyebrow.

Noah rolled his eyes. "I *do* know what doggie style is."

Just because Noah had never had a finger up his butt, it didn't mean he was *that* sheltered.

He rolled over and got onto all fours. His knee only crackled a little bit. "This okay?"

"Perfect," Ramin said softly.

Noah wished he could see Ramin's face. What did Ramin see? He was clean, right? Did he look weird? What if he had a misshapen butthole? Was he hairy? Should he have trimmed? How did one go about trimming their butthole anyway?

Then Ramin's warm hand rested on his lower back, lightly massaging the valley of his spine. Noah shivered and stopped worrying about the shape and hairiness of his butthole.

Ramin was touching him. Nothing else mattered.

"I'm going to try rimming you. That okay?" Ramin's breath ghosted across his shoulders. "Tell me if I do anything you don't like."

"Okay."

Noah's heart hammered. Ramin's hands moved down, cupping his glutes, kneading them before pulling them apart.

Ramin let out a soft gasp.

"Is everything okay?"

Noah could barely make out Ramin's throaty voice over the pounding of his own heart. "Everything's perfect."

Noah didn't know what could make a butt perfect. But then he pictured Ramin's, and yeah, perfect might really be a thing. Maybe he could—

He forgot what he was thinking when he felt Ramin's breath. Warm air, but it felt cool against Noah's burning skin. Heat rising, the whisper of Ramin's skin against his. The lightest scrape of stubble.

And then Ramin's mouth was on him.

Oh.

Oh.

Noah groaned. His arms gave out and he smashed his face into his pillow.

He didn't know it would feel like *this.*

Sensation mounted, like nothing Noah had experienced before. He never knew he had so many nerve endings back there. It was warm yet cool, it was sharp yet soft, it was gentle yet intense.

It was pure pleasure. Teasing pleasure. Sparkling pleasure. Limb-quaking pleasure.

Ramin's mouth was indescribable. Scratchy stubble, soft lips, delicate movements. His hands pried Noah's glutes farther apart, the point of Ramin's nose resting on the little divot at the bottom of Noah's spine, and then—

Then Ramin started using his tongue.

"Oh!" Noah didn't mean to yelp, but the intense, unfamiliar sensation caught him off guard.

Ramin paused and drew back, and Noah ached at the absence.

"Green light, green light!" he grunted into his pillow. *Please don't let Ramin stop.*

Ramin chuckled, and the breath against Noah's most sensitive spot made him flex his erection, clenching hard. His perineum pulsed over and over. He clenched his teeth.

"Relax" came the whispered command, and Noah tried.

Ramin's tongue was on him again. Hot and slick, slow and methodical, and any self-consciousness Noah had left was obliterated by the electric current running up his spine. His core flinched and shuddered and shook.

He couldn't wait to try this on Ramin.

He'd always liked giving Angela oral sex. Liked seeing her lost in pleasure that was hers alone. And now, wow.

Wow.

Ramin's tongue left his hole, tracing downward to press against Noah's perineum, gently massage him there, and then it kept going down, a long wet slide along Noah's balls, and then Ramin was pulling back his erection so he could trace the underside of it, too.

Noah whined, from the pressure of having his member bent backward, from the scintillating pleasure radiating from his core, from wanting more, more, more.

Ramin took Noah's head into his mouth, sucked the dew off the end, but he didn't linger, and he certainly didn't go all the way down like he had back in the train station, when Noah thought he might die and go to heaven in Ramin's throat.

He sucked, he licked, and then he was kissing his way back up, and nuzzling Noah's balls, grazing teeth along Noah's soft skin, and then he was right back where he started, and Noah thrived around Ramin's mouth. Something in him gave, and he let out a heavy breath, and then Ramin's tongue somehow went even deeper.

He moaned into the pillow. He was pretty sure he was drooling.

Then Ramin paused. His ran his hands from Noah's butt up to his back, gently massaging.

"Fuck, you're so beautiful," he muttered. "You think you're ready for a finger?"

Noah's legs quaked. "Green light," he gasped. His erection flexed, swinging back and forth beneath him like some fleshy pendulum. He'd never been so hard, never been so achingly aware of his own arousal.

Noah heard the soft plastic click of a bottle, felt himself clench up a little, tried to breathe, but his heart was beating too hard and fast for him to find any calm.

Wet. Cold. Noah flinched.

"Just relax," Ramin cooed somewhere above him. "Push out a little if you can."

Noah breathed deep and pushed out, though he had the sudden, vivid mental image of accidentally farting. It was so strong he clenched up and started giggling.

"What's so funny?" Noah could hear the smile in Ramin's voice.

"I hope I don't fart on you."

Ramin snickered. "Bodies are weird. Don't worry. I've got you."

"Okay." Noah took a deep breath and tried to relax again. He only jolted a little bit as a wet finger touched him, circled his hole. His breath hitched as Ramin's thumb massaged his perineum. Noah savored the touch, even as one of Ramin's slender fingers found his opening and pressed.

Noah did what Ramin suggested, pushing out just a bit, and *oh*. With a single gasp, Ramin was inside him. It was a strange sensation. Not bad, but different. Different even than Ramin's mouth had been.

Full. Noah's body didn't quite know what to do about it, except squirm a bit, and then clamp down involuntarily.

"Okay?" Ramin asked. "That's normal."

"Okay," Noah agreed, as Ramin moved in and out, gently but firmly, angling his finger to press against Noah's walls, and okay, yeah, that was feeling good. Foreign but good.

Ramin pressed at him with another finger, and this time the pressure was a little uncomfortable.

"Yellow light," Noah said. Ramin waited, his fingers inside Noah. Pain and pleasure mingled, and deep inside something was sparking. Noah didn't know how to describe it.

He only knew he wanted more.

"Green light."

All the world contracted to those two fingers inside him.

Those fingers *hooked*, and that spark got brighter.

"Oh!" Noah gasped as his insides lit up. He thought he might levitate off the bed.

Ramin did it again. Noah's erection flexed so hard it smacked his abdomen. He felt his balls drawing up.

"Is that my prostate?" Noah managed to gasp.

"Yup." Ramin kept moving his fingers. Massaging. Teasing.

Holy crap. Noah had no idea. *No* idea.

None of his doctors had ever given him a prostate exam, even at his physicals. Apparently they could do that sort of thing with a blood test now instead.

If only Noah had known, he wouldn't have waited so long.

Pressure mounted inside him. Warm and sharp, and Noah was flexing hard, his muscles contracting on their own, goosebumps breaking out along his skin, something shimmering deep inside him, building and building, a pinch, and—

"Mmmmmfuck," Noah grunted, and then suddenly he was coming, he was coming, how on earth was he coming? He managed to open his eyes just enough to see himself unloading into the towel below, his penis flailing as it spurted his pleasure.

"Oh fuck, Noah," Ramin groaned above him, and then he felt something hot and wet on his back too, and he came harder, nearly bursting apart with the feeling, with the knowledge that Ramin was getting off, too, coating Noah's back with his lust.

Eventually Noah came back down to earth. Became aware he was a person, with limbs and skin and blood and twitching muscle and nerves that could deliver pleasure like he'd never known.

Ramin slowly withdrew his fingers.

"How was that?"

"That was..." Noah tried to find the words. "That was..."

Noah's legs gave out, and he splayed out on the towel, right in his own mess.

"That was amazing," he muttered. "And now I'm all sticky."

"Yeah, you are," Ramin said. "I hope it was okay that I..."

"Painted me?"

Ramin snorted.

"It was really hot." Noah managed to get his hands under him. Push off the bed. The towel came with him in spots. "But I need another shower now."

"Hm. If only there was someone who could help you with that."

Noah carefully turned so he could see Ramin without spreading his mess everywhere. Ramin's skin was flushed. He was shining, radiant.

They both were.

"So. How was your first *butt stuff*?"

Noah groaned and covered his face. "Don't."

"It was cute," Ramin said. "Did you like it?"

"I did," Noah said. He couldn't wait to do it to Ramin. "I really did."

"Good. Now come on. Let's get cleaned up."

thirty-six

Ramin

Ramin wasn't much of a sex-twice-a-day person anymore, much less thrice-a-day. So he was shocked (and a little proud of himself) when he got hard again in the shower. He and Noah ended up kissing and grinding their erections together, Noah gripping them both with a soap-slicked hand, until they came again, spilling all over their stomachs, and Ramin's dick felt like someone had taken sandpaper to it.

They behaved after that, though, barely even kissing as they washed and dried. Noah let Ramin have the sink first, so Ramin brushed his teeth, then moved on to his skincare while Noah started brushing, and they shared little glances in the mirror.

It felt cozy. Domestic. The kind of thing Ramin used to do with Todd. But fuck Todd. (Not literally.) Ramin always felt like he was trying to keep up with Todd, somehow. With Noah it was easy. Just sharing a nightly routine with someone you enjoyed spending time with. Laughing as your elbows bumped, as you made weird faces while you flossed, as your eyes met in the mirror and you smiled for no other reason than you were happy to be together.

Ramin left Noah in the bathroom and pulled on some underwear, because he felt weird saying his prayers naked. He still had his eyes closed when Noah emerged, voice muffled by his night guard.

"Will it bother you if I call Jake?"

Ramin finished his prayer and shook his head. "Let me pull on a shirt."

He found the shirt from dinner in a wrinkled heap on the floor and pulled it back on. "Should I . . . say hi?"

Ramin knew Jake knew about them, but he didn't know how much. Did he know they were sharing a bed, and not out of necessity?

Noah smiled. "I bet he'd like that."

Noah had pulled on a plain white T-shirt. Ramin already missed the all-access pass to Noah's chest. They sat together against the head-board, shoulder to shoulder, as Noah called Jake.

Jake's face popped up on the screen right away.

"Hey Dad! Hey Ramin!" Jake seemed to be in his own bed, wearing a plush white robe over his Spider-Man pajamas.

"Hey, buddy. You ready for bed?"

Jake shrugged. "Almost."

"Did you brush your teeth?"

"Not yet. We're getting gelato from room service!"

Noah laughed, but Ramin suddenly wondered if their own hotel had room service gelato.

He'd already brushed his teeth, though.

Noah asked Jake about his day. Apparently, he and Angela had gone to Turin, which it turned out (a) had a Lego Store and (b) was where Nutella was made. It was everywhere, even in their hotel lobby.

"There was this thing with a big spike on it, and you could stick your croissant on and pull the lever and it filled it with Nutella!" Jake explained. "It was the best thing ever."

Noah laughed. "That sounds great."

Ramin mostly listened, jumping in with a "Wow!" or "Cool!" at the appropriate point. He desperately wanted to rest his head against Noah's chest, feel the rumble of his voice, but even this, just this, was nice. He loved the way Noah's voice sounded when he was talking to Jake. The tenderness. The boundless joy. The soft laughter. The unconditional love.

Ramin's heart swelled. It made him miss his own parents. But he was grateful to share in this moment.

Jake sat up straighter in his bed. "That's the gelato! Gotta go!"

"Okay, good night, Jakey. Love you."

"Night."

"Night, Jake!" Ramin added.

"Night, Ramin!"

The phone went dark. Noah sighed.

"Good luck to Angela. He's never going to sleep if he has gelato this late."

Ramin laughed. "You're a good dad. You know that?"

Noah shrugged. "I try."

Ramin blinked. Noah was just being self-effacing, right? "Really. You are."

Noah shifted to pinch at his cross. Ramin put his hand over Noah's.

"Sometimes I don't feel like it."

"Why?"

"I can be pretty selfish."

Ramin furrowed his brow. He couldn't imagine anyone less selfish than Noah. "Why do you say that?"

"I don't want Jake to move here." It came out as barely more than a whisper. Noah squeezed his eyes shut. "I should want him to have a good life. To be wherever he'll get the best opportunities. And goodness knows, schools are safer here than back home. I should want all that for him, but I don't. I want him to stay with me."

"You love him," Ramin said. "What's wrong with wanting him to stay?"

"What kind of father does that make me, choosing my happiness over his future?" Noah huffed. "Like I said. I'm selfish."

It didn't sound selfish. It sounded like Noah was punishing himself.

"What if Jake wants to stay in Kansas City?" Ramin pointed out.

"Why would he? He could be having adventures here."

Ramin ached. He couldn't imagine Jake not wanting to stay with Noah. Jake adored his dad. Didn't Noah see it?

"Noah..."

"It's fine. It is what it is. I'm not going to let my selfishness ruin this opportunity for him."

That was bullshit. Ramin twisted so he could look at Noah full on.

"You ever think you might have...kind of a martyr complex?"

Fuck, that was *not* what Ramin meant to ask. But now that he'd said it...well, it was blunter than he meant, but he didn't think he was wrong.

Noah shrugged and stared at the bedcovers. He let go of his cross to pick at a little pill on his T-shirt. "I don't know. Maybe." And then he let out a dry chuckle. "My parents messed me up real good."

"Your parents?"

"Yeah." Noah shrugged again.

"Back in Bellagio, Angela said you don't talk to them anymore?"

"Went no contact a couple years ago."

"Oh." Ramin had a hard time imagining having parents and not speaking to them. They must've done something really fucked-up to push Noah to that point.

"And I always promised myself I'd be a better parent for Jake than either of them ever had been for me. You know?"

"You are."

Noah huffed. "Some days it doesn't feel like it."

"You *are*," Ramin repeated. "I promise, you are."

He rested a hand over Noah's heart. That beautiful, bounding heart. Ramin wished he could reach inside Noah and scoop this...this self-loathing out of him. Ramin had never met anyone more giving and thoughtful and kind than Noah. He was always taking care of people, always pushing aside his own wants and needs for others. He'd seen it over and over with Jake. Noah would do *anything* for Jake.

He bent over backward for Angela, too. And, God, he'd done it for Ramin today, hadn't he? Planning this whole trip, just because Ramin said he liked the sea.

But who was out there taking care of Noah? Who was putting aside their own desires to focus on his?

Ramin wanted to be that person. If only Noah would let him.

"Sorry." Noah dropped a kiss on Ramin's forehead. "I don't know why I got so maudlin. We should get some sleep."

Ramin knew when someone was trying to change the subject, but if that's what Noah wanted, then Ramin was going to give it to him.

He slipped back out of his shirt and tossed it onto the floor, then burrowed under the covers.

Noah clicked the light off and wrapped his arms around Ramin.

"I had a nice day today," Ramin murmured. "Thanks."

"Me too." Noah sighed and pulled Ramin closer. "I wish we could just stay like this forever."

"Why can't we?"

"Hm?"

"I mean...I don't have anywhere else to be. Jake's off with Angela. We could just...stay a little extra. You and me."

Noah's mouth brushed the base of Ramin's neck. "Yeah?"

"Yeah." Ramin could feel the smile on Noah's lips. "We're still getting to know each other again. Time to focus on us could be nice. Right?"

Noah rumbled out a sigh. Ramin's back resonated in sympathy.

"Right." Noah was quiet for a second. "I'll talk to Angela tomorrow. See how long we can take."

"Really?" Ramin had just been wishing. He didn't think Noah would actually go for it.

"Really-really," Noah said. "I like you a lot, Ramin."

"I like you a lot too, Noah."

Maybe more than *liking* a lot, but Ramin wasn't ready to deal with that yet.

"Now come on. We should get some sleep."

"Okay." Ramin settled into the bed, into Noah's arms. Everything was cozy and perfect. Noah's soft cock pressed against his butt.

Hmm...there was something Ramin liked doing, if the guy he was with was up to it.

"One last question."

"Yeah?"

"What are your thoughts on being woken up by blowjobs?"

thirty-seven

Noah

Twenty Years Ago

"Hey, Jayhawks. Rock Chalk!"

Ramin was wearing a blue KU hoodie, even though it was unusually warm out for March.

Noah gave Ramin a friendly elbow nudge. "I didn't know you liked basketball."

Ramin blinked at him like he'd started speaking Russian. "Huh?"

"Rock Chalk, Jayhawk? Your hoodie?" Noah's dad had gone to K-State, and his mom had gone to MU, so both of them hated KU. That wasn't why Noah loved the Jayhawks, though it certainly didn't hurt.

"Oh." Ramin blushed, giving this weird, closed-lip smile that didn't show his dimples. "My dad got it for me. I got accepted. Full ride."

"Really? That's awesome!" Noah had some friends who'd gotten full rides for wrestling at SMSU and CMSU. "Congrats, man."

"Thanks." Ramin twirled one of the hoodie's tassels around his finger and went quiet again. He'd been a lot quieter since his mom died. Noah hated that Ramin's mom had died. And he hated even more that he hadn't been able to go to the memorial. He was still mad at his mom about that. If he had to hear about the "Axis of Evil" one more time…

"What about you?" Ramin asked.

"Me?"

"Where are you going?"

"Oh." Noah rubbed his head. He'd buzzed his hair a couple weeks ago, and now it was at that stage where it was soft and messy and sticking up every which way. "I'm not."

"Not what?"

"Not doing the whole college thing." Noah said it quickly, like if he got it out of the way he could skip past the weird looks people gave him. Or the disapproval. Or the shouting, in the case of his dad, but he was eighteen now, and they couldn't make him.

"Oh." Ramin didn't sound disapproving, though, just curious. "How come?"

Noah chewed on his bottom lip but stopped himself. It was still tender from where Stacy had gotten a little rough with their making out last weekend. He started smiling at the memory, then realized Ramin was still looking at him.

Ramin's eyes were so much greener than Stacy's. And he looked at Noah, really looked at him, like he cared what Noah thought. Noah hadn't realized how few people did that sort of thing.

"I just don't think it's for me," Noah said. "I'd rather get out there and work, save some money. Figure out what I want to do."

"That's cool. More time for your art too, right?"

"Yeah." The lie came easily to Noah's lips, even though it curdled his gut. But he liked that Ramin liked his art. He didn't have the heart to tell him he'd given it up. He needed to be saving money.

Noah hated it, but in this, his dad was right: He needed to do something practical. Especially if he was going to get out of his parents' house.

Still, a small part of him wished he was going off to KU, too. He and Ramin could take classes together, go to basketball games, maybe even carpool out to campus to save on gas, unless Ramin was going to live in the dorms. It was an hour away, so not *that* far, but Noah would hate making the drive there and back five times a week or more.

Heck, he and Ramin could've roomed together. Then both of them could've had a built-in friend on campus.

But that wasn't Noah's life. That wasn't Noah's future.

Ramin was smart. He was going places.

Noah was running from them.

He'd never live up to Ramin, no matter how hard he tried.

Now

Noah had been convinced Ramin was joking about waking him up with a blowjob, until he blinked awake with the sunlight framing the curtains and a warm mouth around his morning wood.

"Oh, baby," he groaned, voice sandy from sleep. "That feels so good."

Ramin's mouth was so talented, Noah didn't know how he'd ever compare. But he was determined to practice, as often as Ramin would let him.

Ramin hummed against him, and Noah felt it in every nerve he had. Ramin's mouth was slick and hot, and as Ramin moved to take Noah into his throat, things only got slicker and hotter. The sounds coming from beneath the blankets were downright obscene.

It only made Noah harder. He flexed involuntarily. Ramin made a *hrk* sound but didn't stop. Didn't even slow down.

Noah's breath hitched. A spasm of bliss rocked his core.

"How do you do that?" Noah sighed when he could breathe again. He didn't know how long Ramin had been at this, but he was getting close already. "You're a miracle."

Ramin just hummed some more with Noah buried to the hilt. He did that trick where his tongue snaked out to caress Noah's balls.

Noah's back arched in pleasure. Lightning crackled down his spine. He closed his eyes and rode the waves of euphoria crashing over him.

"I'm close, baby, you're so—"

Noah's phone started buzzing on the nightstand, loud against the hardwood surface. Not the single sharp buzz of a text, but a constant thing. A phone call.

Noah had heard of bonerkillers before, but he'd never had his own killed so quickly, so thoroughly, as when he saw Angela's name.

"It's Angela."

Ramin came off his now-limp sex and crawled out from under the covers, face wet and shiny in the morning light. He wiped his mouth with the back of his hand. "Everything okay?"

Noah wanted to kiss him, but his phone kept buzzing.

"She doesn't usually call this early." Noah's heart twisted with anxiety as he answered. "Hello?"

"Hi," Angela said, breathing hard. "Do you have a minute?"

Her voice was cracking and tired. Noah's throat clamped up immediately.

"Are you okay? Is Jake?"

"We're both okay," she said. "I promise. Jake and I are both fine."

There was something in her voice that set his heart to hammering, though.

"But...?"

"But Jake is in the hospital."

Noah's world cracked in two.

He'd read once—Elizabeth Stone, he wanted to say—that when you're a parent, your heart lives outside your body.

His heart wasn't just outside his body; it was in another city, squeezing and beating out of tempo as he paced in front of the bed.

Jake was in the hospital. His *son* was in the hospital.

He'd woken up in the middle of the night with stomach pain.

Angela had blamed the late-night gelato at first. But when the vomiting started, she'd taken him to the nearest hospital, where he was diagnosed with appendicitis and sent in for emergency surgery.

"Don't worry. It went fine. He's already in recovery," Angela assured him.

"He's in…" Noah grasped his hair. "Angela, when did you take him?"

"A little after midnight."

"A little after…"

Noah glanced at the clock on the bedside table. It was past eight.

Jake had been in the hospital for *eight hours*. And Angela was only now telling him.

Noah clamped down the anger that threatened to burst from his chest. He clenched his teeth. "Why didn't you tell me?"

Angela's voice was light. Careful. "It was late. There was nothing you could do. We had things under control."

That wasn't good enough. This was his *son* they were talking about. He wasn't there when his son needed him.

"I'll be there as soon as I can. We're not done talking about this."

"Breathe," Ramin said as he tried to fold Noah's singlet into something that would pack nicely. "Don't forget to breathe."

He was right. Noah *was* holding his breath. From anxiety, from anger, from a million feelings all at war within him, and maybe if he didn't breathe he could smother them. Better that than letting them burn everything down.

He pinched his cross so hard he was surprised it didn't snap in two, then took one steady breath. "Thanks."

Noah shoved the last of his stuff into his backpack and zipped it up. "I've gotta get to the train station."

"Just let me pack my stuff too, I won't take long."

"You don't have to come with me." This was Noah's problem, not Ramin's. Yesterday had been so perfect, and now he was ruining everything. His plans for today, a lazy breakfast, visiting museums, drinking wine. Or just staying in bed, lost in each other. It had all gone out the window.

"I don't mind," Ramin said.

"I'm good. Really. You stay."

Ramin stared at him, and Noah had the sinking feeling that he'd said something wrong, but when he tried to figure out what, his brain kept showing him images of Jake in a hospital bed, hooked up to machines, crying for his dad.

He shoved his feet into his shoes. Ramin gave up on packing and grabbed his own.

"At least let me walk with you."

"I'll call a cab," Noah said.

"You saw the roads. We'll get there faster walking. Come on."

Ramin was right, of course. Power-walking took less than ten minutes, climbing uphill the entire way. Sweat drenched Noah's back, leaving a huge wet oval beneath his backpack. Ramin somehow managed to walk and use his phone at the same time.

"I found you a ticket on the next train," he said. "It's boarding in fifteen minutes. We can slow down a bit."

"Thank you," Noah said. It hadn't even occurred to him to check the time tables. He didn't slow down, though. He couldn't. His legs wouldn't stop.

His son was in the hospital. Fear clawed at his throat. Why had he let Angela take Jake? Why hadn't he insisted they go together?

He was selfish, that's why. He'd wanted to get away with Ramin.

And most selfish of all, every time he looked at Ramin, a really messed-up part of him knew that he'd make the same choice again.

They reached the station, scanned the screens, found the right platform. The train wasn't even there yet.

"It's probably coming from somewhere," Ramin said as Noah paced. "It'll be okay."

"I know. I'm sorry." Noah ran a hand through his messy hair. He looked down and stopped. "How long has my shirt been backward?"

"Since you put it on," Ramin said, lips pressed together to hold in a smile. "I didn't want to slow you down."

Noah managed a little bit of a chuckle. "Thanks."

As Ramin helped him sort it out, they heard the whistle, then watched as the train slowly pulled in.

"Thank you. For everything. Really." Noah pulled Ramin in for a kiss. He didn't even stop to see who was watching.

"Thank you," Ramin murmured against his lips. "Yesterday was magical."

"And today's a disaster." Noah sighed. "I'll make it up to you."

"It's okay. Go be with your son."

"Thanks." The doors opened, and a few folks got off the train, but even more got on, jostling Noah as he stood looking at Ramin.

He needed to go. He needed to be with his son. But he couldn't tear himself away from Ramin's eyes. Deep green pools, overflowing with endless kindness. Noah never wanted to look away from them. He never wanted to be parted from them.

Everything in him screamed to get on the train. Everything in him screamed to stay.

Why didn't he give Ramin a chance to pack? They'd had time. Why hadn't he waited? Why hadn't he begged Ramin to come with him?

Ramin had offered, hadn't he?

But this wasn't Ramin's problem. This was Noah's. Jake was his son. He was responsible for him. He had to be there. Had to go.

He'd been living in a dream with Ramin. A beautiful dream where he could have everything he ever wanted. But this was real life. And he had a son to take care of.

"I better go."

He could only hope Ramin would forgive him.

thirty-eight

Ramin

Twenty Years Ago

The last day of Ramin's senior year was on a Monday.

It was a half day, too.

Apparently state law dictated a minimum number of school days you could have in a year, and they'd had so many snow days this winter they had to make up one. Hence the half day. On a Monday.

Freaking global warming.

Ramin didn't know how a half day was supposed to make up for a snow day, especially tacked on to the end of the year after graduation, when no one really cared, least of all the teachers. But whatever. The Missouri Department of Education worked in mysterious ways, or something.

Arya had tried to convince Ramin and Farzan to skip. It was a Monday! They'd already gotten their diplomas!

Well, they'd gotten the little blue frames. The actual diplomas were supposed to come in the mail. But whatever. They were graduates!

They were off to college in the fall! What did it matter if they missed a half day?

But Farzan had announced his parents would kill him if he skipped. Even now.

And Ramin...well, Ramin wasn't ready to say goodbye just yet. He'd see Arya and Farzan over the summer, over college breaks. They'd email and chat online and stay friends forever. But there were other people Ramin would probably never see again. Classmates who'd signed his yearbook wishing him luck or lamenting that they hadn't known each other better. Even a few apologies for bullying over the years.

But half of *them* had skipped, so now Ramin sat in seventh hour, alone and wondering what the point of any of this was, when he and Farzan and Arya could've played hooky and gone to get breakfast at Perkins or something.

Noah had probably skipped, too.

Except—

"Hey, Ramin!"

Ramin slipped into a small grin. "Hey, Noah."

"Decided not to skip, huh? You're such a nerd."

Ramin laughed. "You're here, too."

"Well, I'm an even bigger nerd." Noah dropped into the seat next to Ramin. "Got any plans for the summer?"

Ramin shrugged. "Not much. You?"

"Going to Branson with Stacy's family. Working. You know. The usual."

"Cool." Ramin had been so relieved to see Noah, but now he just felt annoyed. Jealous. Noah had a girlfriend, and Ramin was still single, headed off to college as a virgin.

Whatever.

Thankfully their teacher didn't actually try to make them learn anything. They all sat around joking and talking and sharing stories until the last bell rang. Ramin and Noah and the other seniors cheered and headed toward the student parking lot.

"Well," Noah said. "We did it."

"We did it," Ramin agreed.

He looked at Noah. Noah looked back at him.

He didn't know what to say.

He wanted to ask for Noah's number. Promise to keep in touch. But they'd never been that kind of friends.

Noah seemed to think so, too. Because he looked past Ramin and waved, smiling, as Stacy skipped over and wrapped him in a hug.

Ramin felt cold all over. "See you," he called, and Noah waved good-bye, and then that was it.

Ramin didn't dwell on it, though.

Arya and Farzan were waiting for him.

Now

Ramin stood on the platform long after Noah's train had steamed away. He stared at the dark tunnel.

"I better go." That's all Noah had said.

And what did Ramin expect, really? Noah to ignore Jake being in the hospital? Ramin wouldn't like Noah nearly so well if he was the kind of man who could do that.

Wait for him? Well, maybe. Ramin understood panic. He didn't really blame Noah for that, either.

That didn't stop the ache in his chest, though. The sourness in his stomach. The burning in his throat.

Yesterday had been everything Ramin ever dreamed of. Not the sex (well, not just the sex, because fuck had that been good, every single time), but just being with Noah.

That's all Ramin really wanted. To be with Noah.

Shit. He had it bad, didn't he? There was no getting away from this. Maybe there never had been.

The truth had been bubbling in him for twenty years, building pressure until, like a bottle of Prosecco, fate had popped the cork and all Ramin's feelings had come exploding out.

Eleven days. Half a lifetime.

A single look.

That's all it had ever truly taken for Ramin, wasn't it? One look and he was a goner.

Granted, at the time he'd been walled into the closet "Cask of Amontillado" style. *For the love of God, Montresor!*

But Noah had gone anyway. Ramin wasn't enough for him to stay. No, that was wrong; it was Noah's *son*, what kind of monster would Ramin have to be to want Noah to stay?

He didn't want Noah to stay. He just wanted Noah to say *Come with me.*

To share the burden. That's all he wanted.

But it wasn't enough.

He wasn't enough.

Ramin shook himself. He was probably just feeling this way because of all the sex. Sex released oxytocin, and oxytocin made you feel close to your partner, made you feel euphoric, made you feel like you were in... well. Either way, he was crashing after a huge high. He was blowing everything out of proportion. He and Noah were barely together. This whole thing was new. Hell, Noah had never even done *butt stuff* before. Noah was probably reeling from hormones, too.

That's what Ramin kept telling himself as he headed back to the hotel to check out.

thirty-nine

Noah

Turin was like a smaller, cozier Milan—similar architecture, similar vibes, similar weather—only more closed off. The streets were narrower. The people were quieter. The city had secrets it wasn't willing to give up.

Or maybe Noah just didn't have time to figure them out, running out of the station and into a cab, breathlessly giving the hospital's address to the driver.

Noah kept checking his phone, and he couldn't honestly say if he was waiting to hear from Angela or Ramin. Or both. His neck and shoulders were tight with worry about Jake, even though Angela had insisted everything was fine. And his stomach was heavy with how he'd left things with Ramin.

He'd messed up, he knew that, but he didn't know what he could've done differently. He didn't know how he could fix this.

He texted Angela when the cab finally dropped him off.

> **Noah**
> Here

Angela
Room 1701
He's awake

The elevator moved like molasses. Noah's head swam with the smell of antiseptic. His skin turned to gooseflesh in the cool air. His heart hammered. He hadn't been to a hospital since...goodness, had it really been Jake's birth?

When the doors opened on the seventeenth floor, Noah beelined to Jake's room. Or he tried to, at least. He got turned around twice, his anxiety mounting steadily, until he finally found it.

It wasn't until he saw his son, alert and awake and sitting up in bed reading the latest Ellie Engle book, that his lungs started working again.

"There's my guy." Noah crossed the room in two large strides to hold his son. He stopped himself from crushing Jake with the hug he wanted to give and settled instead for a gentle embrace, a kiss on the forehead, a ruffle of Jake's soft hair. "How are you feeling, buddy?"

"I'm okay," Jake said without looking up.

"The doctors said the surgery went perfectly. No complications." Angela stood by the couch, rolling out her neck and grimacing. Noah let go of Jake to give her a hug.

"I'm sorry it took me so long."

"Why? You made good time." She cocked her head. "Where's Ramin?"

"Ramin's coming?" Jake perked up.

Noah swallowed. "No, buddy. He wanted to, but I..."

What could he say?

Jake's face fell. Noah tried not to think about why.

"We were in a hurry. Sorry."

Angela gave him a bewildered look. "A hurry? I told you, everything was fine."

Everything was *not* fine.

"Jake, you mind if your mom and I step outside for a second?"

Jake shrugged. Noah gestured.

Angela crossed her arms but led the way into the hall. As soon as he closed the door, Noah rounded on her.

"Why didn't you tell me the minute he got sick?" He kept his voice as even as he could, though Angela had to hear the shake in it. Everything in him wanted to scream and shout, but this was a hospital, and no matter what, Noah didn't shout to get his way.

"Because it was a minor surgery. Because you were hours away and it was the middle of the night. Because Jake was safe and being taken care of. And because I was afraid you'd do exactly what you ended up doing."

"What's that supposed to mean?" Anger flared in Noah's chest, but he shoved it down, packed it tight. Except it wouldn't pack. He'd been stuffing down everything he felt so long, there was no more room. "I'm his *dad*. I deserved to know. This whole trip you've been acting like your opinion is the only one that matters, but it's not. I'm allowed to be upset about this."

Angela opened her mouth to argue—like always—but to Noah's surprise, she snapped it shut again. She took a deep breath, her nostrils flaring, but when she exhaled, she seemed to deflate a bit. Soften.

"You're right."

Noah blinked. He could probably count on one hand—two, tops—the number of times Angela had said that to him. Granted, she usually *was* right, but still.

"I'm sorry. I was doing what I thought was best for you, but I don't get to choose that. You do. It's just...you put everyone's needs and wants ahead of your own. All the time. And it probably doesn't help when I steamroll you, and that's something that *I* need to work on. But, Noah, it's okay to put yourself first sometimes. You don't have to be such a martyr."

Noah shook his head, but his ears rang with the truth of it. Hadn't Ramin said the same thing, just last night?

"And now," Angie said, holding his eyes. "You found someone who cares about *your* needs, who puts *you* first, and what do you do? You leave him behind."

"There was no time—"

"Five minutes wouldn't have made a damned bit of difference in getting here, and they sure as hell wouldn't have made Jake recover faster. You could've brought him with you. So why didn't you?"

Noah opened his mouth to explain, but nothing came out.

Why *didn't* he? He'd ached every mile as the train steamed toward Turin. He ached for Ramin now. Wished he could take Ramin's hand and twine their fingers together. Find some strength in Ramin's solid, steady presence.

"I don't know."

Except he did know, deep down.

He had panicked. Plain and simple. He'd spent every day since Jake was born trying to be the best father he could be, and some lizard-brain part of him said *Go-go-go*. So he had.

"I freaked out," he admitted.

"I understand. But I *told* you Jake was all right. What kind of example are you setting for him? To always put everyone else's needs before his own? That's no way to live a life, Noah. Not for him, and not for you."

Noah shook his head. His eyes burned. "I know." It all made perfect sense, now that he was here, now that he could see Jake was okay, but that didn't undo what an absolute fool he'd been. "I just never want him to doubt that I love him with all my heart. Exactly how he is. And I'll always protect him."

"He knows," Angela said. And then, more quietly, in answer to the thing Noah was thinking but hadn't said aloud: "You're not your parents."

Noah let out a low breath. He *knew* he wasn't. But the wounds ran deep, and sometimes he forgot.

"I know," he managed. He was crying, and he hated crying, not because it was weak or bad or because his parents had said that boys don't cry. He hated it because he was the snottiest crier on the face of the planet. He sniffed and tried to spot a Kleenex box through his tears before things got *really* gross.

To her credit, Angela didn't bat an eye, just pulled a little packet of tissues out of her tactical satchel and handed them over.

"Thanks." He blew his nose.

She nodded. "So. What now?"

"I don't know." Another thing Noah hated about crying: It gave him the hiccups. "I really messed up with Ramin."

Angela rested a warm hand on Noah's chest, right over his heart, which was still threatening to claw its way out his chest and shoot across the room.

"You really love him, huh?"

"What?" Hiccup. He liked Ramin. Liked him a lot. Could see a future with him. But *love*?

"You used to look at me the way you look at him."

It was impossible. It was unimaginable.

It was inevitable.

He loved Ramin. Loved him more than he knew he could. Loved him like he'd never loved before.

Maybe he always had.

"You're right," he muttered. "You're right."

Angela tried her best not to smirk, but it didn't work.

"But I left him."

"You can go back."

Noah hiccupped again. He nodded.

"Now come on. Jake's probably wondering what we're talking about."

Angela moved for the door, but Noah tugged her back.

"Angie? Thanks."

A lively nurse in purple scrubs brought Jake his lunch. Noah stayed to help him eat while Angela took a break.

Jake looked so small in the hospital bed, propped up with what looked like a dozen pillows, Noah ached at the sight. He ran his hand over Jake's hair again and again. It was so soft. Sometimes, it was hard to separate the Jake before him, the one devouring a plate of ravioli, from the little baby he'd held to his heart and rocked to sleep.

But Jake was growing up. He was strong. He was mischievous. He'd had a minor procedure, but he was healthy.

"Hey Dad?" Jake looked up from his empty plate.

"Yeah, buddy?"

"What's a martyr?"

Noah chuckled. Jake was a masterful eavesdropper.

"You heard that, huh?"

Jake shrugged.

"It's someone who gives their life for something they believe in."

Jake's eyes widened.

"But what your mom meant is that sometimes I try too hard to make other people happy, even if it makes me *un*happy."

Jake looked at him with those big brown eyes of his. His lip quivered. "I don't want to make you unhappy."

"What? Buddy, you could never. Why would you ever think that?"

"Then why don't you want me to stay with you?"

Something cross-threaded in Noah's brain, made a horrible grinding sound. "What?"

"I'm sorry for fighting with you so much. I don't mean to."

"I know, buddy, I know. That's just part of growing up." Noah brushed Jake's hair back. "What do you mean, why don't I want you to stay with me? I'd love it if you stayed."

Jake sniffed. "I thought you wanted me to move here with Mom."

"Oh, Jakey." Noah's chest squeezed. How many times could his heart break in one day? "I want you to do what'll make you happy. If that means moving with your mom, I'll miss you, but I'll support you."

"But what if I want to stay with you?"

"Then I'd be the happiest dad in the world." Noah looked at his son. His beautiful son. "I'm sorry if you thought I didn't want you to stay with me. I didn't want to pressure you. What *you* want is what matters most to me and your mom."

"I thought you were mad at me," Jake whispered.

Noah caught Jake's tears with his thumb. He kissed Jake on the forehead.

"Buddy, everyone gets mad sometimes. But even if I *was* mad at you, I'll never stop loving you. And I'd never want to send you away."

"You promise?"

Noah chuckled. Jake and his promises.

But this was a real one. One he could keep.

"I promise."

forty

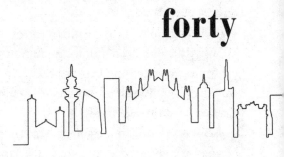

Ramin

A drizzle coated the windows of the train back to Milan. Ramin stared out at the rain-soaked green, listening to a podcast to practice his Italian. He'd meant to listen to it every day, but Noah was way more entertaining than a podcast.

Noah.

His hands itched to pull out his phone and text. See how things were going. Check in on Jake. But he needed to let Noah deal with this. And after that...

Well, after that, they could figure out where to go from here.

Ramin's seatmate returned from the bathroom, jostling him as they sat. Ramin sighed.

This was going to be a long ride.

Strange how quickly he'd gotten used to having someone with him. Being able to turn and tell a story, or point out an interesting view, or share a smile at the experience, or split a bottle of wine. Now that he thought about it, he'd barely been alone this entire trip. Noah and his family had been around. Or Francesca and Paola.

He'd planned to come to Italy alone. Reinvent himself. Find himself under a different man every night. Now that he was actually alone again, listening to a podcast and watching the rain, he realized what a terrible plan that was.

Traveling alone really fucking sucked.

What had he been thinking, anyway? How was cutting himself off from everyone supposed to make him Interesting and New? Who would look at his pierced ears and new tattoo and see something in him that they didn't see before?

Noah had seen him, though. Noah had never thought Ramin was boring, or ugly, or not enough. He'd panicked and run off, but who wouldn't? Now that he'd had time to think, now that the sting of it had worn off, Ramin could see that. Noah *wasn't* Todd.

Fuck Todd, anyway.

So yeah, Ramin had never been boring.

But right now, he was *bored*.

It was raining harder by the time Ramin pulled into Milano Centrale, big fat drops that painted the world in gray. His footsteps sloshed on the wet sidewalk as he power-walked to his apartment, darting from awning to awning as best he could. His clothes were sodden by the time he made it home. His shorts dripped onto the elevator floor. His hair hung damp over his forehead. His shirt stuck to his chest and under his moobs. No matter how many push-ups he did, how carefully he ate, he never seemed to make them go away entirely.

Noah hadn't minded them, though. He'd enjoyed Ramin's body. Ramin had felt that every time they touched, every time they kissed, every time Noah looked at him like he was a work of art that belonged in some fancy Italian museum.

He was still blushing at the memory when the elevator door opened to reveal Francesca and Paola.

"Ramin! Ciao!" Paola said. Today she wore an emerald dress with a white sport coat over it. Next to her, Francesca clutched a rolled-up umbrella under her arm. She was in a sport coat too, with a scarf draped around her neck, even though it was still hot out. The rain had made everything humid but far from cool.

Still, Ramin had seen lots of people dressed like winter was coming. Maybe Italians were immune to the heat.

"Ciao," he said.

"How was Genova?" Francesca pulled him out of the elevator and swiped at his shoulders like she could brush off the rain.

"It was really nice." Ramin felt himself blushing. "Really nice."

"But where's your *friend*?" Paola's eyebrows danced at the word.

Ramin might have told them—in the most general terms—about Noah.

"Paola, he's soaked. Allora, come in, let's have a coffee and you can tell us everything."

"It's fine, really," Ramin said, but Francesca already had a grip on his arm and was dragging him toward their door. She grabbed a towel for Ramin while Paola went to make them espressos.

Their apartment was laid out similarly to Ramin's, but where his rental was minimalistic, theirs was an explosion of color. Oil paintings of flowers adorned every wall. Throws and pillows clashed with the furniture, but somehow, they made a unified whole. The apartment looked homey. Cozy. Perfect.

"Allora, tell us everything," Francesca said, spinning her chair around to sit backward.

Ramin didn't tell them *everything* everything, but he did tell them the broad strokes. What they'd seen, what they'd eaten, what they'd done (not counting the sex).

"Sì, but where is he now?" Paola asked, looking toward the door like Noah might be just outside.

"Turin."

Paola drew back and frowned so deeply it gave her a double chin. "Torino? Why?"

"His son's in the hospital."

"Che disastro!" Francesca said. "Is he all right?"

"He's okay now. But Noah went, and when I asked him if I could go along with him, he said no."

"Ah." Paola and Francesca shared one of those inscrutable couple's *looks*, made even more inscrutable because Ramin didn't know if they were *look*ing in Italian or English.

"But you wanted to go?" Paola asked.

"Yeah. I…yeah." Ramin sighed. "I just don't like how we left things."

"Well, you can talk it out when he comes back," Francesca said. "When you love someone, you have to have faith."

Ramin sputtered. "I didn't say anything about—"

"You Americans," Paola said, but she had a twinkle in her eye. "It's written all over your face. Just because you're afraid to say it, doesn't mean it isn't real."

Something was clawing at the inside of Ramin's rib cage, desperate to get out.

"But I can't love him. It's only been a week and a half. You can't fall in love with someone in a week and a half."

"Why not?" Francesca reached for Paola's hand and twined their fingers. "We fell in love in a day. And every morning for the last twenty years we fall in love all over again."

Ramin stared at them.

Twenty years ago, he was in high school, crushing on Noah, closeted and lonely and grieving and afraid.

No, not just crushing.

He'd loved Noah.

Loved Noah to his core.

So it was the easiest thing in the world to fall in love with him again. Even if it had only taken a week.

Ramin loved Noah. Fuck. He loved him.

"Allora, there's the little lightbulb," Francesca said. She stood abruptly and brushed off the front of her dress. "We'd better go. Tell us how it goes, will you?"

Ramin's head spun. They couldn't just...just drop a logic bomb on him and then leave. Could they?

They could, kissing him on the cheeks and ushering him out the door and then leaving him staring after them, gobsmacked, as they squeezed into the elevator, gave a little wave, and descended.

forty-one

Ramin

Ramin managed—barely—to wait until the afternoon before calling his friends back home. He hoped he didn't wake them. But even if he did, this was kind of an emergency. They'd understand.

Arya answered the call first, nestled in rumpled gray pillows and bedding. Ramin didn't recognize what glimpses of the bedroom he could make out. It wouldn't be the first time Arya had taken a call from some random man's bed, and it probably wouldn't be the last, either.

"Hey, Ramin. You okay?" He brushed the sleep out of his eyes. "What time is it?"

A muffled voice out of view said, "A little after eight."

"Not you, I'm on the phone," Arya said, looking to his left. "It's my friend, sorry, I've gotta take this."

The background whipped around, though Arya's head stayed more or less stationary, as Arya got out of bed shirtless. Probably naked on the bottom too, but thankfully Ramin couldn't see. He'd never actually seen Farzan or Arya naked, and he had no desire to start now.

"Okay, sorry," Arya said as he settled in an unfamiliar living room. "Everything okay? Oh, is that Farzan?"

Sure enough, Farzan popped up. Unlike Arya, he was dressed. Ramin recognized the *Final Fantasy* posters and filing cabinets of Farzan's office at Shiraz Bistro.

"Sorry, I was grinding spices. Didn't hear the phone. What'd I miss?"

"Nothing yet," Arya said. "What's up, Ramin?"

"What about David?"

"He's out with his mom, he probably won't answer," Farzan said. "Everything okay? It's early. Well, for us."

"I know," Ramin said.

Now that the moment was here, he hesitated. A cold fist closed around his heart.

About a year and a half ago, he'd been out at brunch with his friends when he told them he loved Todd. They'd been happy for him, excited and supportive. But it turned out they'd seen the red flags long before he did.

What if Noah had red flags Ramin couldn't see? What if two years from now they were saying *Fucking Noah* over glasses of wine?

Ramin shook the thought away. This was different. *He* was different.

And he was tired of waiting.

"I'm in love," Ramin blurted out. "With Noah."

Farzan and Arya both went so still, so quiet, Ramin thought the connection had frozen. At least until a pair of naked legs passed right behind Arya's head, dick flapping in the wind.

"Guys?" he asked.

Farzan chuckled. "It took you long enough."

"What?" Ramin sputtered. "What's that supposed to mean?"

"Dude." Arya glanced away for a second. "No thanks, I don't drink caffeine." He turned back. "We're your best friends. We know."

"How did you know? *I* didn't know."

Farzan ran a hand through his hair. "That's because you were too busy telling yourself you were too boring to love."

Ramin chuckled. Who needed tiny devil Arya and tiny angel Farzan when he had the real thing?

"Well, I was going through something. But I don't think that anymore."

"Good," Arya said. "We love you."

"Have you told him?" Farzan asked.

"No, not yet. Things have been . . . complicated."

Ramin filled them in on everything while Farzan stepped into the kitchen to make tea. Arya turned off his camera for a bit; when it came back on, he was fully dressed and walking down Summit Street; Ramin recognized one of their favorite brunch spots over his shoulder.

"Sorry about that." Arya gestured over his shoulder. "I can't believe he showed you guys his dick."

Ramin snorted. "So, anyway. I guess I'm just waiting to see him in person again to tell him. I don't want to just, like, text him."

Farzan sipped his tea and nodded. "When's he coming back?"

"That's just it. I don't know." Ramin scratched at his chest. "Part of me wants to just hop on a train to Turin and go find him."

He knew that was ridiculous. He didn't know what hospital Jake was at. Or how long he was even going to be there. How long did it take to recover from an appendectomy? What if Noah and his family were already on their way back? Or what if they were driving?

"Don't," Arya said. "I know you love him, but you need to let him come back and apologize."

"I don't want him to apologize," Ramin said. "I get why he left. I get why he panicked."

Ramin had dealt with enough medical shit in his life to know sometimes all you could focus on was getting to that hospital.

"Still," Farzan said. "Maybe at least talk to him before you go making any travel plans?"

"You're right." Ramin let out a low breath. He was like a wrung-out sponge. "Anyway. Enough about me. What's new with you guys?"

"Hm. Well, David's friend Rhett's coming to visit next week. And he's bringing Titus with him."

"Is that—" Arya began.

"The world's ugliest dog, yeah."

Ramin laughed and settled onto his couch to let his friends catch him up.

He'd figure out what to do about Noah after.

The next morning, Ramin finally worked up the nerve to text Noah.

> **Ramin**
> How's Jake doing?

> **Noah**
> Better thanks.
> He's out of the hospital. Nonna came to drive us all back.

> **Ramin**
> I'm glad!
> Can we talk when you get back?

> **Noah**
> Absolutely
> See you this afternoon?

> **Ramin**
> Great!

Ramin stared at his texts. Did he sound weird? How were you supposed to text when you loved someone but hadn't told them yet, but also didn't want to stress them out, but *also* didn't want them to think you didn't care about how their son was doing?

And was it just him or did Noah sound kind of odd, too?

But whatever. He needed to stop being nervous. He loved Noah. And he thought—well, hoped—Noah loved him, too. That they could figure this thing out.

Meanwhile, his fridge was running low. He grabbed his shoes and headed for the grocery store.

Upon reflection, Ramin probably didn't need to buy six bottles of wine.

But everything at the store was so cheap, and he kept finding things he wanted to try, more Grignolinos from Piedmont, Verdicchios from Marche, Cesaneses from Lazio. Table wines, to have with dinner, to drink and watch the sunset, to explore the world of Italian wine or maybe—just maybe—to share with Noah.

They couldn't all be Ornellaia, after all. Ramin would go broke.

He'd just finished putting the groceries away—he might've gone overboard on cheeses to try, too—when his phone rang.

He grabbed it, expecting to see Noah's photo pop up to tell him he'd returned to Milan. Or maybe someone from work, who'd forgotten he was out of the country. Or hell, even another one of those annoying SPAM RISK calls.

It wasn't any of those, though.

It was Todd.

"Hello?"

Todd's bearded face popped up, though he was a bit patchy at the corners of his mouth. Ramin recognized the collar of one of his neon-blue gym shirts, stained with sweat. Todd must've just gotten back from a workout. "Hey, Ramin. How are you?"

The greeting was casual, but his voice sounded conspicuously deeper. Todd used to use that same register while he whispered dirty nothings into Ramin's ear. What was he doing with it now?

"Uh. Fine. You?"

"I'm good." He licked his lips. "I'm good."

"Cool." Ramin didn't know what else to say. Once upon a time, looking at Todd's face had been one of his favorite things. But that was the past. "Did you need something else from the house? Farzan or Arya can—"

"No!" Todd's voice was so emphatic, Ramin nearly dropped his phone.

But now he was quiet. He ran a hand through his hair, fixed his beard.

And then: "I miss you."

Ramin was so surprised, he *did* drop the phone. "Sorry. Uh. Say again?"

Surely he'd heard Todd wrong.

"I miss you."

Okay, he'd heard right, but what the actual fuck? Ramin glanced at the wine bottles lined up on the counter. Maybe he should open one for this.

"You miss me?" he repeated.

"I hate how things ended between us."

"You ended them," Ramin reminded him, keeping his voice even. A statement of fact, not an accusation.

"I know. I just . . . I was feeling insecure and, I don't know, trapped, and I projected a lot of that onto you. And I'm sorry. I didn't mean to hurt you."

"Trapped? By me?" What the fuck was that supposed to mean? Ramin had never done anything but support Todd. Listen to him. Give him space to live his own life, even as they tried to build a life together.

Once, Ramin would've wondered if he was wrong, if he'd been suffocating Todd and not realizing it, but no. He could see himself clearly, more clearly than he had in a long time.

He'd been a fucking great partner.

Todd frowned. His forehead turned ruddy.

"Trapped by turning forty soon," Todd said. "I guess I just didn't expect my life to be going this way. And then you jetted off to Italy, and you're having adventures there, and I realized it wasn't you. It was me. I was the one who was boring. I'm sorry. And I was thinking . . . maybe we could give this thing another chance? I could even come join you there. We could go clubbing together."

"Cl—" Ramin sputtered.

Todd. Wanted to come to Italy. To go clubbing. With him.

He'd dumped Ramin in the middle of a restaurant, told him he was too boring to marry, and now he wanted to go *clubbing*.

Fucking Todd.

Ramin cleared his throat. "Hey. You remember *Legally Blonde*?"

"I'm a gay millennial. Of course I do."

"You remember how you dumped me in the middle of a restaurant?"

Todd's flush grew darker. "Of course I...oh."

Ramin saw the lightbulb go off.

If Ramin was Elle, then Todd was Warner. And there was no way Ramin was getting back with such a complete bonehead.

"I guess I deserve that."

Ramin didn't argue.

"I'm sorry," he said again. "I do want you to be happy. I hope you know that."

"I want you to be happy, too," Ramin said. And to his surprise, he found it meant it. He wanted Todd to have a good life. Just not with him. "I better let you go."

He set his phone down and stared at the dark screen, his heart hammering like he'd just climbed another lighthouse. He thought he might feel relief. Or sadness. Or vindication. But all he felt was impatience. Todd was his past. And Noah was his future.

So when would—

Knock. Knock-knock.

Ramin frowned. No one knocked on his door. No one could even get in the gates without a key. Maybe Paola and Francesca needed something.

He shook his head, fumbled with the twelve different locks, pulled the door open—

And froze.

It couldn't be.

"Noah?"

forty-two

Noah

Ramin stood before him, surprise and delight written across his face. Noah's shoulders relaxed.

He'd worried Ramin wouldn't be happy to see him.

He clutched a bottle of wine in one hand. Nonna had helped him pick it out—a red wine similar to Nebbiolo called Ruchè.

In the other hand, he cradled a bouquet of red roses. Ramin's lesbian landlords, who'd let Noah in, had nodded approvingly before pointing him toward Ramin's door and hiding around the corner.

Noah held his breath. Did Ramin even like flowers? Was he allergic?

A smile blossomed over Ramin's face, and relief washed over Noah. He'd buy a million flowers if they made Ramin smile like that.

"Hey," he said. "I'm back."

"Come on in."

Ramin closed the door behind them. Noah wanted nothing more than to push Ramin up against it and kiss him until he couldn't remember his own name. But they needed to talk first. He knew they did.

Noah had never been good at talking. For Ramin, though, he'd try. "These are for you."

Ramin laughed, a tinkly thing, and took the roses. He smelled them deeply, his smile turning softer.

"You know, every week my mom was in the hospital, my dad brought her a dozen roses."

Noah's heart clenched. Crap. He was trying to be romantic, but instead he'd dredged up bad memories.

"I'm sorry, I didn't..."

"My mom loved flowers. And every time Baba showed up with a new bouquet, it was like she forgot all about the chemo, and the surgeries, and all the other treatments. She just knew that Baba loved her, and she loved him, and that's all that mattered."

Noah had a hummingbird in his chest. No, that was just his heart, beating faster than it ever had.

Did Ramin mean...

Noah swallowed.

"I'm sorry."

Ramin looked up at him, eyes twinkling.

"I'm sorry. I had my head up my butt." No, it was more than that. "I panicked. I thought if I didn't drop everything to be there for Jake, I'd be a bad dad, and that's the one thing I'm most afraid of. Failing him. Like my parents failed me."

Ramin set down the flowers and reached for Noah's hand. Noah let him take it, stepped closer, so close he could feel Ramin's breath ghosting along his skin.

He wanted to kiss Ramin more than anything. But he had to get this out first.

"I've made my whole life about Jake for so long. Cut myself off from a making new friends, from trying new things, because I thought that's what I had to do. But you opened me back up again. You made me want more."

Ramin still hadn't said anything, but he hadn't moved away. Noah leaned in and rested his forehead against Ramin's.

"I love you, Ramin."

Ramin closed his eyes. His breath slid across Noah's lips.

He kept going. "I love you, and I'm sorry and I hope you'll forgive me. I hope you'll give me another chance."

Noah waited. He waited for Ramin to open his eyes. He waited for Ramin to say something.

Ramin's smile was like the dawn. Subtle, quiet, but then suddenly blinding.

"I love you, too," Ramin said. "And there's nothing to forgive. You never lost your chance to begin with."

"But—"

"You're Jake's dad. You always will be. And I wouldn't love you so much if you didn't care about him the way you do. I don't need you to apologize for choosing him over me. I don't want you to even think about doing that. I love you, Noah. All I want is to share with you. To help you. To be with you. Even when things get hard. That's all."

Noah's eyes burned, but he fought back the tears, because he could *not* get all snotty now.

He laughed, and finally, *finally*, he crashed his mouth into Ramin's.

Ramin opened for him immediately, drawing in Noah's tongue, trapping it, caressing it. Noah wrapped his arm around Ramin's back. Ramin dug his hands into Noah's shoulders and held on for dear life.

Noah stole Ramin's breath, kissed him with every ounce of strength he had, because he loved Ramin, because he knew Ramin was strong enough to handle it. He sought every warm, secret spot in Ramin's mouth. He staked his claim, silently shouting *mine, mine, mine*.

Ramin was his.

He guided them toward Ramin's living room, shoulder-checking one of the walls, dodging a floor lamp, forcing Ramin back onto the bright red couch, but Noah caught Ramin before he could fall, laid him down gently. And all the while, he never stopped kissing Ramin. Never stopped loving on him.

Finally Ramin broke their kiss, breathing like he'd just run a marathon. Noah's heart was beating in double-time. His growing erection was trapped down the left leg of his shorts, the same shorts he'd worn to Genoa, because he hadn't even stopped by the hotel to change.

Angela was right. He had to go for what he wanted. And what he wanted was Ramin.

"I love you," Noah said again.

He'd never get tired of saying it.

"I love you, too." Ramin blinked at him, eyes heavy lidded. One glance at Ramin's shorts told Noah he was just as excited. Was that a wet spot growing? Noah felt himself leaking, too.

They'd been apart for barely more than a day, but Noah would never get enough of Ramin's body.

Ramin's eyebrows danced. "You know what else people do when they're in love?"

Noah's erection twitched in his boxers. He'd come here to bare his soul, to fight for their future, not to have sex. But now that he'd won, well . . . How could he turn down what Ramin was offering?

"I have an idea," Noah murmured, dragging a teasing kiss along Ramin's jawline. "I hope you know I don't only love you for your body . . ."

"I know."

"But I do really, really, really love your body, too."

Ramin beamed up at him. Noah dropped another kiss onto his collarbone.

"You are a miracle."

He shifted them so Ramin was lying lengthwise on the couch, then lowered himself to pin Ramin down. He trailed soft kisses along Ramin's jaw, along his neck, up to the corner of his mouth.

Sunlight turned Ramin golden, and Noah felt like he was full of light, too. Like it was spilling out of his heart.

He was in love with Ramin, and Ramin was in love with him, and he was going to show Ramin just how much.

Ramin's skin tasted of clean soap and citrus cologne. His mouth had hints of espresso and butter and pastry and sex.

Noah could kiss Ramin forever and never get tired of it.

He cradled Ramin's face, but Ramin twisted and sucked Noah's thumb into his mouth. Noah felt the hot, wet sensation between his legs. He fought back a grunt of pleasure.

"Oh, baby," he said instead.

"Tell me what you want," Ramin said around Noah's thumb.

"I want whatever you want."

"That's not an answer."

"I don't—"

"Trust me to be honest with me. Trust me to be selfish with me." Ramin's eyes burned into him. "Take what you want. It's yours."

Noah shuddered.

Noah had spent so much of his life never asking for what he wanted. And Ramin *did* ask him.

Noah hardened his voice.

"Get on the floor and suck my cock," Noah said, embarrassed and turned on by his own vulgarity. Ramin shivered beneath him. He liked it when Noah talked dirty. "Use your throat and get me ready to fuck you."

Noah couldn't believe what had just come out of his mouth. But the look Ramin gave him just then?

Noah felt it in his blood.

Ramin slithered out from under him. Noah sat up, arms splayed over the back of the couch, as Ramin sank to the floor in front of him, taking a moment to stick one of the decorative pillows under his knees. He reached for Noah's zipper, but Noah was too hard in his shorts, his erection caught at a weird angle, and the zipper wouldn't go down.

Ramin let out a little whine then, like he needed this. And maybe he did.

Maybe Noah did, too. He lifted up his hips, and that was all the help Ramin needed.

"Good boy," he said, once Ramin got his fly open.

The words were barely out of his mouth before Ramin planted his warm lips on Noah's boxers, right where his erection was trapped against his thigh. He flexed against Ramin's lips. Ramin traced the shape of him, kissing, sucking, gently biting, until he found Noah's head and gave a harder suck that had Noah nearly floating off the couch cushions.

"Ramin," he whimpered. But then he remembered who was in charge here. Ramin liked being told what to do. And Noah liked telling him. He liked the way Ramin reacted when he talked dirty, even though it was unfamiliar and thrilling. He liked that he could give Ramin everything he had, that Ramin *wanted* everything he had.

Yeah, maybe he did have a bit of a martyr complex, sometimes. But here? Now?

He'd take what he wanted and trust Ramin to tell him if it got to be too much.

He summoned up a growl from deep within his chest. "You little tease. I said suck it."

Ramin let up and looked at him, panting. His lips were red and puffy from all their kissing.

Noah needed to feel them on his bare skin.

He cupped the back of Ramin's head. Ramin flashed him a look then, a look of such heat, such intensity, that Noah forgot how to breathe. All he could do was press gently, inexorably downward, driving Ramin toward his boxers until his teeth clenched around the elastic and pulled down.

Noah's erection popped out, swinging back and forth before resting heavy and hot and twitching against his abdomen. Ramin pushed his shirt up, running his fingers along Noah's stomach and chest, scratching lightly as he ran his slick tongue from Noah's balls all the way up to his crown.

Noah sighed in ecstasy. How was Ramin so good at this? He was finding pleasure centers Noah didn't even know he had.

"I love when you do that."

Ramin looked up at him and gave him a smile that made Noah's pulse race. Noah nearly lost himself in those luminous eyes. Maybe he would have, if Ramin's soft lips weren't still cradling him.

"Do that again."

Ramin did, even slower this time, patiently caressing each sensitive inch. Noah never realized just how many nerve endings he had. He could feel the rasp of Ramin's taste buds against his skin, the strength of the slick muscle as it traced his veins.

Noah melted into the couch.

"Yeah, baby, just like that."

Ramin hummed with pleasure as he worked on Noah. Warm tongue, soft lips, gentle suction. Wet saliva coating him. When Ramin had done this back in the train station, Noah had been too distracted with playing his role right, too worried about getting caught, to notice just how messy it was. How obscenely hot. And then, yesterday morning, Ramin had been hidden beneath the blankets.

But now Noah had a front row seat as Ramin's spit glistened across his skin, trickled down to his balls and farther below. He could see how Ramin's cheeks hollowed with the suction. Take in the sloppy, sinful sounds of Ramin's mouth as it spread his saliva all around.

Noah had a brief moment of worry for the couch, but it was quickly forgotten as Ramin cradled Noah's head in his mouth. He looked right at Noah, holding his eyes, as he moved his head in a slow circle, letting Noah rub against the pillowy softness of his inner cheeks. Noah gasped at the sensation.

Ramin was playing him like an instrument. Noah wanted to sing out, but his throat was too tight. Instead he thrust his hips upward, driving himself deeper into Ramin's mouth, grunting as he felt the tightness in the back. Ramin let out one of his little *hrk* noises. Things got sloppier, slipperier, hotter as Noah held Ramin's head down for a long second.

When he let go, Ramin popped off him with a gasp, but before Noah could check in—make sure Ramin was doing okay—Ramin planted his mouth on Noah's balls.

"Oh, holy…" he murmured as Ramin played with the sensitive skin there, tugged, kissed, licked. He stuck his nose into the crease of Noah's inner thigh, gave a heady sniff, and Noah felt it like a shot up his whole spine. "That feels so good."

Ramin worshipped him. Coated every bit of his skin with tongue, with spit, with anticipation, before he came back up to Noah's leaking, angry erection.

He held it upright. Looked up at Noah with hunger in his eyes.

Noah's heart hammered in anticipation. He nodded wordlessly.

Slowly, in one long, smooth movement, Ramin took Noah all the way in. He felt the folds of Ramin's throat seize and then part. Felt Ramin's exhale from the nose in his bush. Felt the heat and pressure as Ramin deep-throated him.

Noah's limbs went numb.

Wet. Hot. Tight. Slick.

Euphoria.

Noah's world contracted to a single point between his legs. Ramin's throat contracting in waves around him. His tongue slipping out to tickle Noah's balls.

Those sinful *glk-glk-glk* sounds as Ramin swallowed around him.

"How are you even doing that?" Noah sighed.

No one had ever done that to him before. He'd always thought it was something people only did in porn.

Ramin hummed, setting Noah's nerves on fire. He could feel it all around him, buzzing, the sensation hooking behind his navel, the plea-sure curling up his spine like smoke rising into the night sky.

He was getting close, but it couldn't end here. There was so much more he wanted to do.

Noah curled his fingers through Ramin's hair, not roughly, but enough that Ramin paused. He tugged, gently, and Ramin pulled off him with a pop that had Noah shuddering. Noah's penis shone with its coating of saliva. So did Ramin's face, though some of that might've been tears. He wiped himself off with the back of one hand. The other stayed wrapped around Noah's erection.

"Everything okay?"

"It's perfect," Noah said. "I don't want to finish. I told you. I'm going to fuck you."

Ramin whimpered. "Please."

Noah pulled Ramin up to kiss him. Ramin's shirt slid against Noah's exposed skin. "Take this off," he growled.

He helped Ramin peel it away from his skin, and there he was, the soft curves of his chest, the silvery stretch marks catching the light, the sharp lines of his tattoo. Noah traced them with his fingertips, relishing the goosebumps that sprang up in their wake.

Ramin was radiant.

"Which way is your bedroom?"

"Hallway, to the left." Ramin's voice came out hoarse. Had Noah done that to him?

Yeah, he had.

"Second door on the right."

Noah stood and scooped Ramin up, cradling him. Ramin yelped in surprise.

"You okay?"

"Are *you*?"

Noah chuckled. "I'm good." What was all that CrossFit for, if not to carry the man he loved over the threshold?

"Fuck me," Ramin muttered.

"That's the idea." Noah angled in to seal his mouth over Ramin's smile. His tongue danced against Ramin's. He could taste his own sweaty skin, but more than that, he could taste Ramin.

Heaven.

Noah bumped into the first door, but that was just a bathroom. A strangely long and narrow one. Noah kept his mouth on Ramin, sucking on the tender skin right below the angle of his jaw, as they crashed through the second door.

The bed was smaller than the one they'd shared in Genoa, but Noah didn't care. He'd make love to Ramin on a cot if he had to. As long as Ramin was happy, that's all that mattered.

Ramin laughed as Noah tossed him onto the bed. His erection was tenting his shorts.

"Take these off, too," Noah grunted, going for the button, yanking them down, leaving Ramin in a stunning pair of bright green trunks. Ramin's beautiful erection was trapped beneath a quarter-sized wet spot.

Ramin was leaking for him.

"You are so sexy."

"Yeah?"

"Yeah. But you'll be sexier out of them." Noah dragged them off, and then there Ramin was. Naked. Glowing. Perfect.

Noah finished unbuttoning his shirt and let it fall to the floor so he was naked, too.

He leaned in for another kiss, laid himself atop Ramin, ground their hips together. His skin flared. His heart pounded. His senses screamed *Ramin, Ramin, Ramin!*

"Fuck me," Ramin pleaded.

"How do you want me to get you ready?" Noah breathed.

"You don't... I can do it."

Noah paused his grinding and pushed up so he could actually see Ramin's face.

"What?"

"It's all still new for you, you don't have to..."

"Baby." Noah's chest clenched. "You take care of me. I take care of you. That's how it works."

"I know, but eating ass..."

"I want to." Noah held Ramin's eyes. "I want to make you feel good the way you made me feel good."

Ramin bit his swollen lips, but he nodded.

Noah grinned and dove in.

Not for Ramin's hole, not yet. First he licked along Ramin's jaw, down into his collarbone. He kissed Ramin's chest, tracing the wings of his tattoo. He found his way to Ramin's left nipple and gave it a hard suck. Ramin didn't respond, though, other than a grunt.

Interesting. Noah's own nipples were pretty sensitive.

He'd have to experiment more.

But not now, not when his erection was aching and leaking onto the covers.

"Crap!" He leaned up. "Towel!"

Ramin furrowed his brow. "Huh?"

"Uh. Sex towel?"

Understanding dawned on Ramin's face. He chuckled. "Bathroom."

Noah moved faster than he'd ever moved in his life. He grabbed the first towel he could find, snagged his backpack for condoms and lube while he was at it. He laid the towel down and helped Ramin settle onto it.

"Now. Where was I?"

He sucked on Ramin's other nipple—more for completion's sake than anything, because that didn't seem to do anything for Ramin, either—then followed a path down Ramin's stomach to his happy trail. He traced Ramin's erection, planted kisses in the valleys of his thighs, nuzzled his balls. Ramin's breath hitched at every touch of Noah's tongue, every soft kiss and languid lick. Noah felt Ramin leaking against his cheek, leaned up to suck off the dew as he stared into Ramin's face.

He loved the way Ramin's eyelids fluttered. The way his face opened up. "Please," Ramin pleaded, and Noah's core clenched at the sound.

So he moved lower, kissing Ramin's dimpled hips before hiking them upward to get at Ramin's hole.

Noah's breath hitched as he took in the slick ring of muscle awaiting him. It fluttered with Ramin's breath, nestled in coarse black hair, then winked as Ramin tensed. It smelled clean and sweaty and earthy and so utterly Ramin.

Noah forgot how to speak.

"Is it okay?" Ramin asked softly, nervously.

It was beautiful.

It was perfect.

Noah didn't have the words to answer. Instead, he dove in and planted his mouth on Ramin's tender flesh.

Ramin drew a sharp breath and then let it out in a low moan. Noah hummed in delight. He remembered the way it had felt when Ramin rimmed him. The teasing passes of the tongue, the jolts of pleasure from a particularly sensitive spot, the heat, the rasp of stubble against secret skin.

He'd always liked eating Angela out, back when they were together, and was pleased that his skills translated here, though things were different, too. Ramin didn't turn wetter as Noah worked, but Noah could still feel him relaxing, unclenching, blossoming. His opening pulsed and twitched with Noah's every move. His legs quivered in Noah's hands.

"Noah," he sighed.

Noah smiled, rolled his tongue to plunge it in, and Ramin cried out, struggling against Noah's grip, but Noah held him firm. He only relented when Ramin whimpered.

Noah trailed kisses up Ramin's thighs and stole a glance at Ramin's face.

His eyes were rolled back. His cheeks glowed red. His nostrils flared. His mouth was slack. His pink chest rose and fell.

Noah just grinned in satisfaction before going back down, drinking in Ramin's guttural groans, his fevered cries, his ecstatic yelps.

"I'm ready," Ramin gasped.

Noah paused. "Hm?"

"Fuck me."

Noah lowered Ramin's hips and placed his thumb at Ramin's warm entrance. "What about fingers?"

He really wanted to feel Ramin wrapped around his fingers.

But Ramin shook his head. His voice dripped with need. "Please, Noah."

Noah's erection flexed, snapping the string of precum dripping to the towel below. His core clenched up in anticipation.

"How do you want to do this?"

"Lie down. Let me ride you." Ramin leaned up a bit, then muttered, "Shit."

"What?"

"Condoms. Lube."

"Right here, baby." Noah leaned over to grab them from his backpack.

"I love you." Ramin guided Noah down onto his back, fixed the towel where it had bunched up. "So much."

"I love you," Noah said, flexing his penis as Ramin grabbed it. He'd dried up some, but he was still achingly hard. Ready.

Ramin straddled him, and Noah relished the weight, the feel of skin against skin, the heat as his crown grazed Ramin's hole. Ramin plucked the condom from Noah's hand, swallowed as he unwrapped it and rolled it down Noah's length. Noah sighed with bliss as Ramin smeared lube all over it.

"Gimme some of that," he said, wetting his fingers and reaching back. Ramin said he didn't need to be fingered, but he couldn't begrudge Noah lubing him, could he?

He could not, as his erection flexed and leaked against Noah's stomach.

"Okay." Ramin braced his hands on Noah's chest. "Ready?"

Noah had never been more ready for anything in his life.

"Are you?"

In response, Ramin took Noah's erection and held it upright. He shifted up, angling his hips. Brought Noah up to his waiting hole and began to sink.

"Oh," Noah gasped as he breached Ramin's entrance.

Heat. Pressure.

Bliss.

He held Ramin up, flexed involuntarily, felt the tight ring of Ramin's muscle contract around him. Ramin grimaced and held on to Noah's chest. Noah brought his hands up to hold Ramin's butt, kneading the cheeks, pulling them apart, waiting for Ramin to breathe and keep going down.

"Fuck, Noah," Ramin groaned as he began to settle.

Noah forced himself to keep still, because every muscle wanted to contract, thrust up, end the beautiful agony of Ramin's torturous slide down his length. Ramin's eyes were closed, his brow furrowed, as he paused and clenched all around Noah, the sensation driving the breath from Noah's lungs.

"You okay?" he whispered. He was halfway in, but he'd felt himself hit some sort of barrier, a tightening that had Ramin wincing.

Ramin nodded, but he didn't look okay. He was sweating. His eyes weren't just closed, they were squeezed shut.

"I'm hurting you."

"I'm fine," Ramin grunted, but just then his hole spasmed around Noah. "How much is left?"

"Hey. Stop."

Ramin shook his head, breathed deep, tried to go down again, but Noah held him up.

"Ramin. Baby. I'm hurting you."

"I can handle it."

"I can't." Noah felt his erection flagging.

"Fuck." Ramin sighed and let Noah help him off. Noah's penis fell heavy between his legs as Ramin settled back onto Noah's stomach.

"I'm sorry," he said. "I thought I could take it. I *want* to take it."

"It's okay, baby." Noah pulled Ramin down so they were chest to chest, wrapped him up in a hug. "I love you."

"I love you," Ramin said. "Damn it. Just give me a second. I'll try again."

"You don't have to." Noah wasn't sure he could get hard enough to try again. At least not in that position. He couldn't stand seeing Ramin in pain. "I know it's big. We can do other things."

"No. I need you to fuck me." Ramin leveraged himself back up. He reached behind him, grabbed Noah's length and started stroking him back to hardness, but he looked like he was getting ready to go off to war.

"Wait." If they were going to do this, they had to do it a different way. "Let's try something else. Here, get up. Get on your back."

Noah didn't have a lot of experience with guys—or with the back door—but he did, in fact, have experience. Enough to know how to help a partner open up their hips. Enough to know how to work his angles to bring them pleasure.

And yeah, maybe he'd also once seen a YouTube video with a unicorn that pooped rainbow sherbet when its hips and legs got in a better alignment.

So Noah stood at the foot of the bed. Ramin lay below him, breathing hard, a vision of beauty, and Noah might've sketched the scene, but Ramin was his and his alone. No one else got to see him like this.

Only Noah.

Noah grabbed Ramin's feet and pulled him closer, hooked his arms under Ramin's knees and spread them outward and forward, toward Ramin's chest.

To his surprise, Ramin's legs kept going and going until he was nearly in a split.

"Wow," he breathed.

Ramin shrugged. "I do a lot of yoga."

Noah took in the planes of Ramin's body spread out beneath him. The secret part of him, pulsing, waiting.

"You are perfect."

Ramin flushed with pleasure.

"Ready to try again?"

Ramin nodded.

Noah pressed forward, breaching Ramin's entrance, studying Ramin's face for any sign of pain, but with his hips elevated and his legs splayed, he let Noah in more smoothly.

More deeply.

Noah savored the heat, the squeeze, as he pressed slowly, inexorably into Ramin's core, but Ramin never flinched. If anything, he looked surprised, his eyes wide, his mouth hanging open, as Noah sank into him.

Noah felt that internal barrier again, but this time it yielded. Ramin let out a long, high note, a keening cry of pleasure so pure, so sexy, it had Noah clamping down on his urge to climax.

And then he was in, all the way to the hilt, his balls resting against the base of Ramin's spine. Ramin was hot all around him, clenching rhythmically, not in pain as far as Noah could tell, but in pleasure. In desire.

"Oh, fuck, Noah," he sighed.

"I'm all the way in you, baby." Noah flexed himself, felt Ramin's internal muscles flutter all around him. He pressed a hand into Ramin's lower stomach. "Can you feel it?"

"I can feel it," Ramin gasped. "God, can you feel yourself?"

Noah couldn't, not really. He was pretty sure that was a myth.

Still, he flexed again, pressed down harder.

"Fuck, Noah." Ramin's head rolled back.

Noah backed off a bit, pushed in again slowly, experimenting with his angle, trying to find Ramin's prostate. He leaned over to kiss Ramin's knee, the closest bit of skin he could reach. "You're perfect."

"So full," Ramin muttered. "God, Noah."

"You ready for me?"

"I'm ready." Ramin met his eyes. Desire and determination made them sharp as emeralds. "Now fuck me."

forty-three

Ramin

This was not how Ramin expected his day to go.

He hoped he'd get to talk to Noah. Dared to dream Noah loved him back. But this?

God, this was beyond dreaming.

He'd prepped this morning, prepped long and thorough, spurred by what Arya liked to call the Dixth Sense—that feeling that maybe, just maybe, if all the stars aligned into a perfect phallic constellation, you might get fucked. But he hadn't believed it would really happen.

And now here he was, on his back, impaled on Noah's cock.

The first time Ramin saw it, he hadn't thought it was an asswrecker. He'd managed it in his throat just fine, after all. Three times now. But after feeling it spread him open, he was forced to conclude he might have miscalculated.

Was he too old to take up poppers? Were poppers even legal in the EU?

Anxiety and anticipation had warred in him as he'd rolled the XXL condom down Noah's cock. What if Noah didn't actually know how to use it?

He needn't have worried, though. Noah was gentle and patient, more than Ramin had been. Usually riding worked for him, even with bigger dicks, but he'd clenched up as soon as Noah breached him.

But now? This? His legs splayed, his hips raised, Noah standing over him with an ecstatic light in his eyes?

This was good. This was better than good.

This was heaven.

Noah had slid right in with barely any pain, brushing past his prostate, right through his second sphincter with barely a hitch.

Ramin had never been so full in his life.

He couldn't stop the sighs of pleasure leaking from his open mouth as Noah began a steady rhythm. He hitched Ramin's legs first lower, then higher, each time adjusting his angle of attack, and Ramin's eyes nearly burst from his skull when the blunt head of Noah's cock bumped right against his prostate.

"Fuck!" he cried.

Noah paused, but Ramin grunted.

"Green light!"

It was so good. *So good.* Noah's chest gleamed with a light coating of sweat. His arms flexed as he thrust.

"I love you," he grunted, and Ramin felt it in his core.

Noah added a roll to his hips, lighting up Ramin's insides with even more pleasure, and took a long, slow thrust all the way in. He held his cock as deep as it would go inside Ramin, grinding his hips in a circle, leaving Ramin gasping for air.

But it wasn't enough. Ramin needed more. He needed to feel all of Noah. Feel his warm skin. Feel the veins in his cock. Feel the load Ramin was going to fuck out of him.

"Take it off."

Noah slowed. He tilted his head. "What?"

"The condom. You can take it off. If you like."

Ramin felt the throb in Noah's dick. He squeezed his walls, which earned a wince of pleasure from Noah.

He stared down at Ramin, slack-jawed.

Did Noah not want to? Was he worried about disease? Or shit-dick? The former wasn't a worry, Ramin was negative across the board, but the latter...well, even with the Dixth Sense, bodies were weird sometimes. You could never be a hundred percent sure.

"Sorry. Forget it."

But Noah kept staring at him.

"You're sure? You really want me to?"

Ramin had never wanted anything so much in his life.

"I don't want you to think you have to. Safety is sexy." Noah dropped a kiss on Ramin's leg. "I love taking care of you, baby. Always."

Sweet Noah, always looking out for other people.

In response, Ramin clenched his Kegel muscles, savoring the way Noah's shoulders hitched all the way up to his ears.

He looked Noah in the eyes. "I need it."

Noah swallowed.

"Take it off."

Noah slid out, and Ramin ached at the emptiness. Noah peeled off the condom and reached for the lube.

"Use extra," Ramin said. His ass was already getting chapped. "More than you think you need."

"Okay." Noah lubed himself up, picked Ramin's leg back up with a wet, slippery hand. "You ready?"

Ramin nodded.

Noah pressed against his entrance, and Ramin shuddered at the feel of hot skin, the press of Noah's wet, leaking cock against his yielding hole.

"Ahhh," he sighed in a high register he didn't know he could hit as Noah's cock grazed his prostate again. Cold shot up his spine, his nervous system overwhelmed by the pleasure. He tried to keep his eyes open, but he couldn't. They rolled up as he breathed in ecstasy.

"You feel amazing, baby," Noah said. "You take this cock so well."

Ramin clenched his sphincter to fight off the wave of pleasure that nearly had him coming. He loved when Noah talked all filthy.

"I'm yours." Ramin groaned as Noah pulled out achingly slow and then thrust in fast. "All yours."

Noah began fucking him in earnest, finding a solid rhythm, throwing in a little hip twist now and then, bending his knees to scrape against Ramin's prostate, thrusting deep and holding it while he flexed his cock.

Noah rammed into him hard. Ramin's back arched, eyes popping open in surprise.

"Oh my God," he wailed. "Fuck me like you mean it."

"I mean it, baby." Noah's pace picked up. "I've wanted this for so long."

"Me too," Ramin whined. "I've wanted it for twenty years."

"Yeah?" Noah's smile turned cocky.

"I wanted your big strong wrestler cock."

"That's right, you did. Everyone thought you were a nerd, but I always knew you were a little slut." Noah gave a hard thrust that made Ramin cry out again, a high keening that surprised even him.

It was so loud, so pure, so unexpected that Noah paused, a question in his eyes.

"Green light!" Ramin ground his ass back against Noah. "Use me."

Noah's fingers dug into Ramin's legs.

"Then take this cock," Noah growled. "Make me nut."

Noah fucked him harder, pulling nearly all the way out before slamming back in. Cold fire burned deep within Ramin. His dick was aching, leaking a river of precum into his navel, trailing down his stretch marks to the towel below. His core was clenching up.

He reached for his dick. "I'm close."

Noah smacked his hand away.

"You don't come until I say you can."

Warmth flared along Ramin's entire body as he obeyed, as Noah kept working him, as his entire world contracted to the point where their bodies met.

"Oh God, Noah," Ramin whined. "Your cock."

He got that shimmery feeling between his legs as Noah's dickhead grazed his prostate again. Ramin hadn't come hands-free in years— he'd been beyond astonished when Noah had—but he recognized the signs. His chest tightened. His ass muscles fluttered uncontrollably.

He didn't know if he could obey Noah, not at this pace.

"Breed me," Ramin groaned, hoping Noah liked dirty talk as much as he did, bearing down as hard as he could. "Get your nut."

"Fuck," Noah whispered, pleasure lighting his face from within as he slammed into Ramin and held it in, so deep. Ramin could feel the pulsing of his cock, the warm wetness deep inside as Noah came. Ramin's head fell back to the bed, eyes closed as he savored the feeling.

Noah kept pumping, kept grinding his hips against Ramin, though his rhythm slowed a bit. "Good boy."

Ramin gasped. "Fuck, Noah."

Noah grinned and picked his pace back up, slicked up by his own cum. That shimmering feeling built inside Ramin again.

"Oh fuck," Ramin grunted.

"Yeah, baby," he said. "You gonna come for me?"

"Uh-huh."

Noah shifted his angle, and Ramin saw stars.

The prostate orgasm didn't slam into him. Instead it built and built and built, sparking along his nervous system, until all his senses were honed to a single point deep inside where Noah's cock kept slamming into him.

And then he crested, like a cup overflowing with water, like a wave rolling onto shore, and the pleasure consumed him, and the contractions started deep inside, and he spilled out onto his belly as Noah looked down at him, a light in his eyes like he'd just seen God.

And maybe he had.

Maybe they both had.

A whine of pleasure burst from deep in Ramin's lungs as the pleasure carried him away.

Finally, finally, Ramin came back to earth, to find Noah still fucking him, though his pace was flagging.

They both breathed hard as Noah slowed and then stilled. He trailed kisses along Ramin's legs, massaged his thumbs into Ramin's aching hamstrings and finally released them.

Noah's cock slipped out. Ramin clamped down as hard as he could to keep everything inside. Fuck, was he gaped? He couldn't move. Didn't even want to.

Thank God for sex towels, at least.

Slowly, starting at his soles, Noah kissed up his body. He was sweaty, hair messed up, face red, as he teased and tasted and tantalized Ramin, even pausing to sample Ramin's load where it pooled in his belly button.

How was this even real?

A sudden aftershock had Ramin shuddering. His body was still sparkling. He could've floated off the bed without Noah holding him down.

Noah. Who loved him.

And Ramin loved Noah back.

It's a tough life.

Finally Noah made his way up to Ramin's face, hovering over him in a push-up. He brought a hand up, tacky with lube, but Ramin didn't even care as he traced Ramin's neck, his jaw, that soft spot behind his ear that made him melt.

"I love you, baby." Noah leaned down to kiss him.

"I love you." Ramin kissed Noah back, slow and tender, tasting himself on Noah's tongue. Fuck that was hot. He sucked Noah's tongue hard.

Noah let out a little giggle. Ramin's favorite. He couldn't stop from smiling, but the smile let Noah's tongue escape.

Noah broke the kiss and nuzzled his nose against Ramin's throat.

"You're perfect." Noah relaxed, collapsing and pinning him against the bed. Ramin relished the contact. Relished being trapped.

He never wanted free of Noah.

Satisfaction settled over him like a warm blanket. His body was buzzing. Every fiber of him sparked with the knowledge that he was right where he belonged. With the man he belonged with.

He wanted to stay here forever, safe in Noah's arms, cuddled and cradled and protected and thoroughly fucked. Together.

An annoying voice in the back of Ramin's head reminded him that this was temporary. That this wasn't real life. That Noah had to go home. That neither of them lived here. That they had so many questions to sort out.

But fuck it. That was a problem for later.

For now?

For now...

Fuckety-fuck.

"Get up," Ramin whispered.

"Huh?"

"I need to get up." He felt it. He couldn't hold it any longer. "I need the bathroom."

Otherwise this beautiful, romantic, sexy moment was about to be interrupted by a wet, juicy fart.

"Dov'è il bagno?" Noah murmured into Ramin's ear. He let Ramin up, but not without one last kiss. "Love you."

forty-four

Ramin

They took turns cleaning up in Ramin's shower. Ramin went first, since he was the messiest. He prayed Noah didn't hear the aftermath of their lovemaking. He'd probably hear it sooner or later, though. It was inevitable, if they kept this up, and if Noah minded, well, he shouldn't have had such a big dick.

Noah went after. Ramin heard a few muttered complaints as Noah banged his elbows in the too-small shower.

No shower sex here, that was for sure.

Ramin was tempted to go back to bed, both of them naked, and cuddle until they were recharged and could go again, but the truth was, Ramin didn't think he *could* repeat today. He was sore. He'd need to recover.

He couldn't wait to recover.

Besides. They still had things to talk about. They were mature, responsible adults, who communicated about their wants and needs.

Right?

"I really am sorry," Noah said, once they had cozied up on the stiff red couch. Both of them held glasses of Grignolino. "For leaving you."

Ramin swirled his wine and met Noah's eyes.

"There's nothing to forgive. You panicked. I've made plenty of poor choices when I was panicked. But if it makes you feel better, I accept. Okay?"

"Okay." Noah swirled his own wine and tasted. "This is good."

"Right? And it was only six euros."

Noah nodded, impressed. "Nice."

"So what's going on with Jake? I meant to ask, but..."

"But you got distracted with our lovemaking?"

Ramin laughed. Now that they were out of fucking mode, Noah was back to euphemisms. Ramin didn't mind, though. He liked that Noah was careful with his words. He knew that Noah would be careful with his heart, too.

"So..."

"So, Jake's going to be fine. He'll need to recover for a few days, which will put a damper on Angela's sightseeing itinerary, but Nonno and Nonna are around to help. And me too, obviously."

"And me. Actually, I got something for him."

Ramin ran to the closet and came back holding a large, loud box. When Noah saw it he giggled.

"You didn't."

Ramin handed over the Lego Spider-Man set. It was nearly a thousand pieces and had twenty-some minifigures. He'd grabbed it this morning, just in case... actually, not in case of anything. Just because he wanted to. Because he cared about Jake.

Noah set down the box and picked his wine back up. "Jake might ask you to adopt him."

Ramin chuckled. "He can get in line. I still want Nonna to adopt me."

Still, he wouldn't mind being a trusted adult in Jake's life. He liked that idea. Maybe even a stepfather, someday.

Maybe.

"And another thing." Noah's eyes seemed to dance.

"Yeah?"

"Jake wants to stay. With me. In America. He's not moving here."

Noah's joy was something palpable, radiating outward, warm and soft and holy. Ramin basked in it. He leaned in and planted a soft kiss on Noah's wine-stained lips.

"I'm happy for you."

"Thanks. I'm...well. Still feeling a lot of things about it. Including some guilt."

"Noah—"

"I know. It's something I'm going to work on with my therapist. But at the end of the day, I'm happy. And relieved. And...excited?"

"Yeah?"

"Yeah." Noah bit his lip. "I, uh, hope all three of us can spend time together when we get back? Jake really does like you, you know. Even if you don't give him way-too-nice Lego sets."

"I like him, too," Ramin said. "Otherwise I wouldn't get him the way-too-nice Lego sets."

"You are ridiculous." Noah sighed. "I love you, you know."

"I know." Ramin sipped his own wine. "So what's next?"

"Next?" Noah considered. "Well, we're here another week, which works out because then Jake will be well enough to fly back home."

Ramin's heart clenched. He forgot Noah was going back so soon. He still had six more weeks booked.

He tried to keep his face neutral. Should he cancel the rest of his trip? Go back? Or beg Noah to stay? *Could* he?

"What?" Noah asked.

"Nothing." It would be selfish to even ask.

So naturally, Ramin blurted out, "I wish you'd stay."

As soon as he said it, he snapped his mouth shut. So much for post-nut clarity. This was more like post-nut verbal diarrhea.

"Sorry. That's...I mean, you have Jake and all, and I don't want you to feel pressured."

But Noah gave him a shy smile.

"I was kind of hoping you'd ask."

Ramin blinked. "You were?"

"Yeah." Noah swallowed. Ramin shivered at the memory of his lips on Noah's neck.

God, he was like a horny teenager.

He liked feeling like a horny teenager.

"I don't want to cramp your style, but if you'd have me . . . I'd love to stay with you."

"Really? What about Jake?"

"I need to show Jake that love is worth chasing. That it's worth fighting for. Worth sacrificing for."

Ramin reached for Noah's hand, twined their fingers together. Every time he thought he knew Noah to his depths, he found new layers.

Noah was a revelation.

"I can't stay as long as you," Noah continued. "Not with my job, not with Jake's school, not with all the changes about to happen. But I *do* have more vacation days I can use. If you like . . . if you'll have me . . . I could stay until the end of the month? And then I can go back to help get ready for Angie's move."

"Then *we* can go back."

Noah was right. Love *was* worth sacrificing for. But Noah couldn't be the only one making sacrifices.

"I'm not going to stay without you."

"You don't have to do that," Noah said.

"I know. But being with you made me realize something."

"Oh yeah?"

"I'm okay. Just the way I am. I'm not boring, and I don't need to reinvent myself. I'm happy with who I am, and I'm happy when I'm with you. I want to be where you are. So if we go back, we go back. Simple as that."

"Simple as that? What about this place?" Noah gestured around the apartment.

"Francesca and Paola won't mind. They're rooting for us."

Noah laughed. "Are those your—"

"My lesbian landlords, yeah." Ramin squeezed Noah's hand. Just like that, they'd figured things out. Made a plan. Together.

It felt fake. It felt like a movie. It felt like a dream, one he was destined to wake up from.

"Hey. What're you thinking?" Noah scooted closer, rested his hand on Ramin's thigh.

Ramin couldn't believe there was a time when he was afraid to let Noah touch him.

"I don't know. It's like...I don't know how to explain it. But it's like, it all feels too easy."

Noah's eyes were so kind, Ramin wanted to drown in them.

"Life's hard sometimes," Noah said. "Yours more than most. Is it so wrong to enjoy something being easy for once?"

Was it? Ramin wasn't sure.

But he'd told Noah, once, that he was living for his parents, too. For their dreams. And for the dreams of his queer elders, too.

"I guess not."

"Good. It's a tough life." Noah raised his glass.

Ramin smiled and toasted. "It's a tough life."

Noah drank, then leaned in for a loud, obnoxious smooch. He sat back with a smirk. "For what it's worth, Jake's teenage years are still ahead of him, so if you're worried about things being too easy, don't worry. They won't be for long."

Ramin laughed. He tried to imagine it. Jake growing up, going to high school, living with Noah and maybe with him, too. Maybe they'd all move in together somewhere, or maybe Noah and Jake would move into Ramin's house, since he had plenty of room.

Maybe that was their future.

Or maybe not. There were a million, million possibilities.

What mattered was, they'd figure it out as they went.

Together.

forty-five

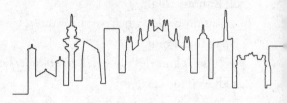

Noah

One Week Later

"Are you sure I can't take it in my carry-on?" Jake asked.

"I'm sure," Noah said, zipping Jake's suitcase closed with the enormous Lego set squashed between his clothes. "Minifigures only. You promised, remember?"

Jake sighed and flopped backward on Noah's bed. "I remember." He held a Scarlet Spider minifigure in his right hand, walking it along Noah's duvet.

Jake really had promised. And Noah trusted his son to keep it.

Just like Jake trusted Noah to keep his promises. And understood that not everything was a promise. Sometimes, it was just a hope.

Noah stood, ignoring the little pop in his left knee, and hauled Jake's suitcase upright. Jake's carry-on was packed, too, and ready to go. Noah's own suitcase was still open on the bed, filled with laundry he'd do at Ramin's once he moved in.

He'd moved his more adult items to Ramin's beforehand. He hadn't actually looked at the care instructions for his singlet. Apparently it had to air dry, and he couldn't exactly leave it hanging around in his bathroom at the hotel.

He imagined it on Ramin's folding laundry rack instead, blue spandex amidst all Ramin's clothes. He wondered if Ramin ever sniffed it.

And then he felt himself getting hard and tried not to think about it.

He had another ten days with Ramin, ten days to explore Italy—not to mention each other's bodies—and this thing between them. This beautiful, new, familiar thing.

Love.

"Dad?"

"Yeah, buddy?"

"When you get home, is Ramin gonna be my new stepdad?"

Noah nearly tripped. "What?"

"When Lyla's mom got remarried, she got a stepdad." Lyla was one of Jake's classmates. "He wanted her to call him Dad, but she calls him Steve."

"I don't know, Jakey. We're still figuring it out. I promise we won't make any big decisions like that without talking them over with you, too." He mussed Jake's hair. "And don't worry. You won't have to call Ramin Steve."

Jake giggled. The sound soothed Noah's soul.

Jake's energy was still a little low in the afternoons and evenings, but he'd bounced back from surgery quickly. He was already trying to get gelato every meal again. And in between meals.

Basically every chance he could get.

An empty paper cup sat in the trash can from this morning. Noah and Angela really needed to get back in the practice of saying no to Jake sometimes. But Noah wasn't the only one shaken up. Angela admitted she'd been too permissive with him lately, too, but she assured Noah things would go back to normal once they got back to the States.

Angela poked her head through the open door connecting their rooms. "What're you two goofing off about?"

"Nothing," Noah said. "Just teasing Jake."

"Steve," Jake said in a deep voice and cracked up again.

Noah met Angela's eyes and shrugged. She pretended to roll her eyes at their antics, but she pressed her lips together, too, a sure sign she was holding in a laugh.

"Nonno's almost here. You all packed up?"

"Jake is. I've got a bit to finish. I can check us all out when I'm done."

"Okay. Mind helping me with the luggage?"

"Come back and visit us soon," Nonna said, pulling Jake into a tight hug, kissing his cheeks over and over.

"I'm coming for summer break!" Jake said.

Noah and Angela and Jake had already talked it over. Jake would stay with Noah for the school year, Angela would visit over Christmas, and Jake would visit her over the summer.

Noah might visit, too—not for the whole summer, but for a little while.

Ramin might come along, too.

"I can't wait!" Nonno said, taking his turn to hug Jake. "Bring your fishing rod, okay?"

"Okay. I'll try." Jake's face turned serious. "It's okay if we don't have time to go fishing, though. I'll still love you."

Noah grinned. That was progress. Right?

As he loaded the suitcases in Nonno's car, he spotted a familiar striped tank top out of the corner of his eye. Ramin glanced both ways before jogging across the street, ignoring the crosswalk completely.

"Hey."

Noah pulled him in for a kiss. "Hey."

Ramin took his time hugging Angela and Nonno. He gave Nonna an extra-long hug and said something that Noah couldn't catch but that had Nonna blushing. Then he knelt down next to Jake.

"See you soon, okay?"

"Okay."

"We can play with your new set when I get back, if you like."

"Really?" Jake asked.

"Really. If you don't mind."

"That sounds cool."

"Good." Ramin glanced Noah's way, then looked back at Jake. "Thanks for letting your dad stay with me. We'll be back home soon."

"Okay," Jake said. "Don't worry. I won't call you Steve."

Ramin looked back at Noah, bewildered.

Noah could only laugh as Jake threw his arms around Ramin's neck. Ramin hugged him back, tight.

Noah's chest lightened. He looked at all his favorite people, standing in the Italian sun, smiling and laughing, even though they were saying goodbye.

No, not goodbye. Just see you later.

"I love you, buddy. More than anything," Noah said when it was his turn to see Jake off.

"Love you too, Dad." Jake hugged him tight.

Noah brushed the hair off his forehead and kissed it.

"I'll see you soon, yeah? Try not to burst anymore appendixes."

Jake cheesed and got into Nonno's car.

Noah wrapped his arm around Ramin's waist as they watched his family drive away.

He waited for the anxiety to hit. Or the guilt. He was letting his family go home without him. He was being selfish, staying in Italy for another ten days, just him and Ramin.

But it was okay.

They were all okay.

"So," Ramin said, leaning his head against Noah's shoulder. "What now?"

"Now I still have to finish packing," Noah said. "And checking out."

"I can help."

"Thanks, baby."

Noah would never turn down Ramin's help.

"What about after?"

Ramin fiddled with one of his studs. Noah reached up and twisted the other, which got a shy smile out of Ramin.

"There's lots of cities we could visit." His smile turned devilish. "And lots of bathrooms I could blow you in, too."

Noah giggled, though his penis twitched in his jeans.

Both things sounded...well. They sounded like heaven.

"Why wait for a bathroom?" Noah asked. "I don't have to check out until noon."

Ramin sighed. "I love you, you know."

"I love you too."

And then he dragged Ramin toward the elevator.

They had the room for another three hours, and Noah intended to make the most of them.

epilogue

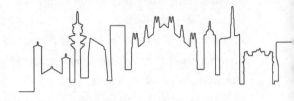

Ramin

One Year Later

They took the lifts up to the terraces of the Duomo—no stairs, not on a day like today. Ramin had no intention of getting all sweaty.

Not until they were back in bed, at least.

Tourists packed into the elevator. Noah pressed Ramin into the corner as they ascended. He linked his pinky with Ramin's. Excitement danced in his eyes.

Despite the extra time last year, they'd never actually made it back to the Duomo. They'd met up with Maria and Tomaso in Verona. They'd ventured farther south to see the museums in Florence. They'd explored Milan's nooks and crannies. They'd lived, laughed, and made love every day until it was time to go home. Together.

And they'd been together ever since.

The past year hadn't been perfect. They'd had fights. They'd learned how to annoy each other, but they'd also learned how to apologize to each other. They were growing, learning how to be, how to smooth out each other's rough edges, how to support each other, how to listen.

How to have make-up sex.

Six months ago, after a lot of discussion—not just with Noah but with Jake and Angela, too—Noah and Jake had moved into Ramin's house. He had the space, Noah's lease was up, and though Jake was sad to move schools, he was excited to have a backyard again. Not to mention a finished basement he'd swiftly taken over with a veritable Lego fortress. Ramin had to wear slippers when he went downstairs to do laundry, lest he step on a stray brick.

Still, he was glad to put up with a few stabs to the plantar fascia in exchange for the laughter and shouts of joy that carried upstairs from Jake and his friends.

They'd even started talking about getting a dog.

Ramin had never had a dog before.

He couldn't wait.

And now here they were, back in Milan, a year after they'd found each other again. Jake had spent the summer in Como with Angela and Nonno and Nonna. Noah and Ramin were headed there in a few days to visit, and then the three of them would fly home together.

For now, though, it was just Ramin and Noah.

Remembering where they found each other again.

Where they fell in love.

What could be more perfect?

Well, one thing, and Ramin's stomach was in his throat at the thought of it. Last time he'd tried this, it hadn't gone well. But that was then. This was now. Ramin wasn't Elle Woods, Noah wasn't Warner, and they weren't at a swanky restaurant.

They were Ramin and Noah, just like they'd always been.

Still, Ramin checked his pocket for the twentieth time. Just to be sure.

The elevator opened onto the lower part of the terraces: a narrow marble walkway, with carved rails and columns to the right, and the sloping slabs of rooftop to the left. The setting sun turned everything a soft, pinkish gold that matched the flush of excitement in Noah's skin.

"Oh, wow," Noah whispered. They didn't have time to stop yet, not with another lift full of people already on the way. They followed the edge of the transept and turned left at the corner, past a little guard booth, then right again to follow the northern edge of the nave. In the Galleria across the way, tourists drank their Aperol spritzes seated on patios beneath orange umbrellas. Far below, folks mingled with the pigeons in the piazza.

Noah and Ramin passed beneath buttress after buttress, each decorated with several sizes of statue, and topped by spires capped with even more statues.

"It's incredible," Noah said. "Can you imagine? All the work that went into this?"

While Noah admired the architecture, Ramin admired Noah.

Every day he loved Noah more.

When they'd first gotten back to Kansas City, Noah's attention was divided between work, helping Angela get ready for the move, and getting Jake settled full-time at his apartment. But they'd carved out time to be together, too, and as Ramin had started helping more and more with Jake, Noah had actually found time to do the things he enjoyed, beyond his daily gym routine.

He'd started taking drawing classes at night. Ramin's house was littered with sketchbooks, all in different sizes, all in different stages of being filled. And Noah was making more friends, too, at church, at the gym, in class. He was blossoming, and Ramin loved to see it.

Noah had become a staple at Shiraz Bistro, too, sharing Thursday night dinners with Farzan and David and Arya, who grumbled good-naturedly about being the fifth wheel.

Ramin knew Arya was happy for him, though, because Arya told him all the time.

And sometimes, when Noah had the day off, and Ramin had a day full of video conferences, Noah would stand out of view of the camera, in nothing but one of his singlets, teasing Ramin as his bulge grew, trying to draw him into a little afternoon delight…

Ramin shook himself. Was it blasphemous to get an erection on top of a cathedral? He wasn't going to risk it.

They reached the western end of the nave, where a set of stairs led upward to another level of terraces. The steps were narrow and steep, some of them scooped hollow from millions of footsteps over the years.

Finally they reached the upper level, which ran directly over the center of the nave. A slight ridge down the middle formed two gentle opposing slopes.

Milan's cathedral didn't have a dome. Instead, the edifice climbed higher, with flying buttresses and statues everywhere, until it was capped by a gleaming gold statue of the Virgin Mary.

The terraces were crowded with people standing on the center ridge to take selfies or group photos, but along the sides, at the end of the sloping slabs of roof, walkways led to arched windows looking out over the city. Ramin followed Noah as he gazed at the skyline stretching out beyond them, pointing to landmarks they recognized or statues that were particularly beautiful.

Loudspeakers made an announcement in Italian. Ramin and Noah (and Jake) had been practicing all year, and he could pick up most of it now: No picnics (who was bringing picnic baskets up to the Duomo?), no smoking (why did so many Italians still smoke?), no lying down (weird), no professional photos (that one, at least, made sense).

Ramin swallowed away the sand in his throat. There was no prohibition against what he was planning. But this *was* a functioning cathedral. It wouldn't hurt if they were a little farther away from the stairs, where a bored-looking guard gazed out from another tiny booth.

Once they reached the corner, Noah pulled Ramin in close for a few selfies. Ramin tried to make sure he didn't brush the contents of his pocket against Noah's hip.

Noah showed Ramin the photos. Milan lay golden and gleaming in the sunset behind them, but Noah's eyes were brighter still.

"Perfect," he muttered.

It *was* perfect. Ramin's heart hammered.

This was it.

He was done waiting.

While Noah was distracted admiring the Museo Novecento across the way, its huge arched windows sparkling in the light, Ramin pulled out the box from his pocket.

"Noah?"

"Huh? Yeah?" Noah turned, looked at Ramin, saw what he was holding—and froze.

Ramin broke into a sweat, despite the pleasant breeze across the terraces.

"Noah Bartlett," Ramin said. "This last year has been the best of my life. You've filled my days with love and laughter and joy, and I want to spend every single one with you, from now until the day I die."

He got down on one knee.

Fuckety-fuck, please-please-please let Noah say yes.

"Will you marry me?"

Ramin held his breath. The murmur of the crowd died away. Time slowed. Pigeons paused in their flight. All while Ramin waited.

He'd seen so many beautiful things in Italy.

The waters of the Ligurian Sea. Michelangelo's *David*. The sun setting over fair Verona.

But the smile that dawned on Noah's face put them all to shame.

"Yes." Noah took Ramin's hands with a joyful laugh and helped him back up. "Nothing would make me happier."

He pulled Ramin into a kiss—a quick, chaste one, given they were not only in public but also on holy ground—then stood back as Ramin pulled the pair of rings out of their box. They were matching black tungsten bands, each set with a single pale green emerald.

Noah's favorite color.

Ramin slid on Noah's, then let Noah slide on his.

Noah let out Ramin's favorite giggle. "We're going to get married!"

"Assuming we don't get smote for getting gay-engaged at a church."

"God is love," Noah said. "I'm not worried."

Ramin pulled out his phone. He grabbed a selfie of his own, took a quick picture of their hands together with their new rings. Then he started a FaceTime call.

"Now? Here? Really?" Noah asked, incredulous. He'd never complained out loud, but he lived with Ramin, which meant he was constantly in the background of Ramin FaceTiming Farzan and Arya.

This was different, though.

"I promised."

Jake's face appeared. Once the light adjusted, Ramin recognized the back room of Enoteca Russo, cases of wine stacked to the ceiling.

"Did he say yes?" Jake asked without preamble, his eyes wide and hopeful.

Noah laughed and squeezed his face into frame. "I did."

"I told you he would!"

"You did," Ramin agreed. "Thanks for letting your dad marry me."

Jake grinned so wide, his face nearly split in two. He'd lost an upper canine the day before he left for Italy, an unfortunate incident involving a game of basketball in one of the neighbor's driveways, but his new tooth was almost all the way grown in.

Jake was growing up too fast, and Ramin had only known him for a year. How could Noah stand it?

"Now you'll both be my dads. For real."

"Congrats, you two!" Angela squeezed in next to Jake, a radiant smile on her face. Life in Italy suited her. She seemed more relaxed, more happy, more at home than Ramin remembered her last year. Noah had mentioned the change, too. How glad he was for her.

The transition had been difficult, but all of them were happier now.

"Thanks, Angela."

"Tanti tanti auguri!" Maria chanted as Jake swiveled the phone to her and Tomaso. "It's a tough life."

"It's a tough life!" Ramin agreed.

"Don't forget, you promised I could be your ring bearer!" Jake pointed out.

"I remember," Ramin said. "Okay. We better let you go. People are staring."

"Okay, love you, bye!" Jake hung up without even letting them say bye in return.

Noah chuckled, but then his face turned serious. "You asked Jake if I could marry you?"

Ramin shrugged, tucking his phone back into his pocket.

"Iranians think of marriage as a joining of families. And I thought, well, what could be more important than making sure he agrees to us joining?"

Noah pulled Ramin's hand up and kissed him right on the ring finger. It was a strange sensation, that simple band of metal, already warming from his body temperature.

Strange and wonderful.

Ramin was never taking it off.

He tugged Noah's hand up so he could return the gesture. Noah's finger looked good with an engagement ring on it.

Ramin sighed, gazing out at the city beyond, but he sensed Noah was still looking at him and turned back.

"What? Do I have pit stains?" His flop sweat had been truly heinous.

Noah just laughed. "No."

"Then what?"

Noah looked at him, wonder written in his smile. His eyes sparkled as he pulled Ramin in close.

"You, Ramin Yazdani, are full of surprises."

For Farzan and David's swoony,
spicy romance, be sure to read:

And don't miss Arya's turn for love, coming in Fall 2026!

Acknowledgments

Writing a book is not unlike making wine—it takes time, attention, patience, and a team of folks dedicated to finding the fullest expression of their craft. I've been lucky to be part of such a team.

Thanks to Molly O'Neill for always pushing me to be the best writer I can be, and for the grandest of Italian adventures. Thanks to the entire Root Literary team—Holly Root, Taylor Haggerty, Kurestin Armada, Jasmine Brown, Samantha Fabien, Melanie Figueroa, Gabrielle Greenstein, Stacy Jenson, Alyssa Maltese, Kat Miller, and Jessica Saint Jean—for championing me and my work, to Heather Baror-Shapiro for sharing my books around the globe, and to Debbie Deuble Hill at APA for all that you do.

Thanks to Sam Brody, editor extraordinaire, and the entire team at Forever: Leah Hultenschmidt, Estelle Hallick, Dana Cuadrado, Caroline Green, Carolina Martin, Daniela Medina, Anjuli Johnson, Rebecca Holland, Taylor Navis, Xian Lee, Maisa Nammari, Laura Essex, Susan Moon, and Nathan Lincoln.

Thanks to Forouzan Safari for another stunning cover. I can't look at it without smiling.

Thanks to Tyler Estabrook and Margaret Lumetta for the adventure in Verona (still can't believe we got a free Toto concert out of it); to Suzanne and Jesse Young for the picture-perfect writing retreat in the hills of Tuscany; and to the smoky-voiced bartender at Le Volpi e l'Uva in Florence who told me, when we ran out of Nebbiolo and had to switch to Barolo, "It's a tough life," thereby inspiring this book's motto—and my own as well.

Thanks to Sierra Simone for being my Romance Gandalf; to Julian Winters for reading (too many) versions of this story to help me get it right; to Natalie C. Parker, Tessa Gratton, Tara Hudson, and Lana Wood Johnson for always being my sounding boards; to all my writer friends (I'm both blessed and alarmed to find the list has gotten too long to mention everyone); and to every romance author who has welcomed me into this community with open arms.

Thanks to Barry Tunnell and the team at Tannin for being my Cheers, the place where everybody knows my name, and for expanding my wine horizons; and to Carley Morton, Jess Johnson, and the entire Under the Cover crew for your dedication to excellence in smut peddling.

Thanks as always to my family for their endless love and support, even when I write about boning.

Thanks to every librarian, bookseller, influencer, booklover, and reader who has picked up one of my books over the years. I hope you always find a home in my pages.

YOUR BOOK CLUB RESOURCE

Visit **GCPClubCar.com** to sign up for the GCP Club Car newsletter, featuring exclusive promotions, info on other Club Car titles, and more.

Find us on social media: **@ReadForeverPub**

Reading Group Guide

Questions for Discussion

1. Ramin (drunkenly) decides that he needs to reinvent himself and chooses to do so alone in Italy. Have you ever decided to reinvent yourself? How did you do so? Did you feel you had to be alone, away from your friends, to accomplish it?

2. Noah's fraught relationship with his parents is always in the back of his mind, impacting his relationships with his son and his ex-wife and his blossoming new romance with Ramin. How does your relationship with your parents impact your other relationships?

3. Like many folks who find themselves dating in their thirties (and beyond), Noah has a young child. How well does he balance being a dad with being in a new relationship? Does he introduce Jake and Ramin to each other at the right pace?

4. While *It Had to Be Him* is far from a retelling of the 2001 classic *Legally Blonde*, it features several winks and nods to the film, most notably the restaurant breakup between Ramin and Todd. What other parallels did you find?

5. Ramin's friendship with Farzan and Arya is a huge component of his identity—and though they are not with him in Italy, they are never far from his mind, whether he's talking to them or simply imagining them giving him advice. What are the life-defining friendships in your life? How have you handled time apart?

6. Noah and Angela remain friends and co-parents after their marriage ends, though their dynamic changes across the course of the story. Would you call their relationship healthy? Have you ever maintained a positive relationship with an ex?

7. When Noah and Ramin dip their toes into the world of kink, Ramin is more familiar with it than Noah, but neither are experienced. Noah turns to research to understand things like dom/sub dynamics. How else do both men handle this new experience? What do they learn about themselves and each other?

8. The city of Milan and Italy as a country take center stage in the book. In many books, setting itself becomes a kind of character. Did Milan come to life on the page? Did being in Italy have an impact on Ramin's and Noah's journeys?

9. Ramin and Noah have known each other since high school—and have been attracted to each other (at least subconsciously) ever since. Do the flashbacks to high school change your understanding of their attraction and relationship? Do the scenes capture the feelings of being a teenager with an unrequited or not-yet-understood crush?

10. Though Noah and Ramin weren't together romantically in the past, they both acknowledge their attraction in retrospect. Does this qualify their love story as a second chance? Why or why not?

11. Ramin and Noah fall in love in ten days—and even comment on how strange it is that such a thing is possible. Have you ever fallen in love, or experienced any sort of intense relationship, in such a short time frame? Did it last?

12. Ramin and Noah connect both romantically and sexually after needing to share only one bed—a classic trope (and one of the author's favorites). What other tropes were present in the book? Were they used traditionally or subverted? What are some of your favorite tropes?

About the Author

ADIB KHORRAM is the queer Iranian author of *I'll Have What He's Having*, which was an instant *USA Today* bestseller. He is also the author of the young adult novel *Darius the Great Is Not Okay*, which earned the William C. Morris Debut Award, the Asian/Pacific American Award for Young Adult Literature, and a Boston Globe–Horn Book Honor, and was named one of *Time* magazine's 100 Best YA Novels of All Time; his other young adult novels, *Darius the Great Deserves Better*, *Kiss & Tell*, and *The Breakup Lists*, as well as the picture books *Seven Special Somethings: A Nowruz Story* and *Bijan Always Wins*, have garnered critical acclaim, starred reviews, and bestsellers.

He grew up in Kansas City—the Milan of the Midwest—but he'd rather be in the real Milan, sitting on a patio, enjoying a limoncello spritz.

You can learn more at:

AdibKhorram.com
Instagram @AdibKhorram
Bluesky @AdibKhorram
Tumblr @AdibKhorram

YOUR
BOOK
CLUB
RESOURCE

**READING
GROUP**

Visit **GCPClubCar.com**
to sign up for the **GCP Club Car** newsletter,
featuring exclusive promotions, info on other
Club Car titles, and more.

GRAND
CENTRAL

FOREVER

balance

LEGACY
LIT

DA CAPO

CARDINAL